Ma... ...even
befo... ...She
still ... ...her
name on, not just any book, but on her favourite books.
Maisey lives with her supportive, handsome, wonderful,
diaper-changing husband and three small children,
across the street from her parents and the home she grew
up in, in the wilds of southern Oregon.

Lynn Raye Harris read her first Mills & Boon romance
when her grandmother carted home a box from a yard
sale. These days Lynn lives in North Alabama with
her handsome husband and two crazy cats. Lynn was
a finalist in the 2008 Romance Writers of America's
Golden Heart® contest, and she is the winner of the
Harlequin® Presents Instant Seduction contest. You
can visit her at www.lynnrayeharris.com

Originally from England, **Carol Marinelli** now lives in
Melbourne, Australia. She adores going back to the UK
for a visit – actually, she adores going anywhere for a
visit – and constantly (expensively) strives to overcome
her fear of flying. She loves the fast paced, busy setting
of a modern hospital, but, every now and then admits
it's bliss to escape to the glamorous, alluring world of
her Mills & Boon heroes and heroines. A bit like her
real life actually!

Scandals
COLLECTION

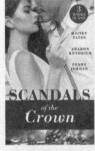

June 2018

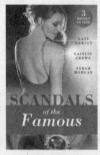

July 2018

August 2018

September 2018

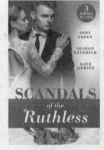

October 2018

November 2018

Scandals of the Royals

MAISEY YATES

LYNN RAYE HARRIS

CAROL MARINELLI

MILLS & BOON

Published in Great Britain 2018
by Mills & Boon, an imprint of HarperCollins*Publishers*
1 London Bridge Street, London, SE1 9GF

Scandals of the Royals © 2018 Harlequin Books S.A.

Princess From The Shadows © 2012 Harlequin Books S.A
Special thanks and acknowledgement are given to Maisey Yates for her contribution to *The Santina Crown* series.

The Girl Nobody Wanted © 2012 Harlequin Books S.A
Special thanks and acknowledgement are given to Lynn Raye Harris for her contribution to *The Santina Crown* series.

Playing The Royal Game © 2012 Harlequin Books S.A
Special thanks and acknowledgement are given to Carol Marinelli for her contribution to *The Santina Crown* series.

ISBN: 978-0-263-26722-8

08-2018

Printed and bound in Spain
by CPI, Barcelona

PRINCESS FROM
THE SHADOWS

MAISEY YATES

For my kids, Aidric, Kian and Alani. You provided a lot of inspiration for this book. Thanks for always keeping me on my toes, and for teaching me about love every single day.

CHAPTER ONE

"WHAT do you mean she's gone?" Prince Rodriguez Anguiano looked down at Eduardo Santina, King of Santina, and his future father-in-law, and swore he saw sweat beading on the older man's brow.

The king was known for being formidable, tough and un-bending. Watching him sweat was unexpected. And more than a little bit interesting.

King Eduardo cleared his throat. "Just that. Sophia is gone. She left with a maharaja."

Rodriguez felt a smile tug at the corner of his mouth. "A maharaja? Is marrying a prince not enough for some women? They feel the need to pursue a more…exotic title?"

King Eduardo's face darkened, color creeping into his cheeks. "She has done so without my permission."

"I'm assuming, since my intended fiancée has run away with a maharaja, the wedding is off?" The king only looked at him and Rodriguez felt a vague sense of relief wash through him. He had been prepared to do the marriage thing, but truly, he hadn't been looking forward to it. In his estimation it was a ball and chain situation, and he didn't know anyone who would willingly shackle themselves in that manner. Yet people did seem to get married. It was the heir factor, one he couldn't ignore forever, but for a while longer, maybe.

Sophia had been pretty enough, a beautiful brunette with a

real classic beauty. But even that would get old after a while. Now he could go back to Santa Christobel and celebrate with a blonde. Maybe a redhead. Maybe both. Not that he usually went in for that sort of thing but he'd had six long, unheard-of months of celibacy so that he could present his future bride with medical proof of his good health. And now that there would be no wedding, it had just been six months of physical torture.

"Father?"

Rodriguez turned, his ears always tuned in to sultry, feminine tones. But in this instance, the tone did not match the looks. One of Eduardo's other daughters was standing in the entryway, sleek brown hair hanging just beneath her chin. All no-nonsense and practical, as was the rest of her attire.

Wide-leg beige slacks, a white button-up top and metallic ballet slipper-style shoes. She looked like she'd stepped out of the pages of a business-casual catalog. She was tall, slim, only a couple of inches shorter than he was, and her face was pleasant enough, but with none of the flash and paint he was accustomed to seeing on a woman.

"Sorry," she said, inclining her head. "I didn't realize that you were busy." She turned to go, and for some reason, he was sorry to see it.

"Carlotta."

She paused and turned back again. This time he noticed how green her eyes were. "Yes, Father?"

"Stay for a moment."

Carlotta gave him a brief icy look before turning her focus back to her father.

"This is Prince Rodriguez Anguiano. Your sister Sophia's fiancé."

She looked at him again, her expression blank. She was strange, contained, demure almost, and yet he could sense something beneath it. Something she seemed determined not to reveal.

"Charmed," he said, flashing her a grin. "Though I don't know that I'm Sophia's fiancé any longer. As she's run off with the maharaja."

Carlotta blinked owlish green eyes at him before shooting her father a worried look. That's where her emotion was, reserved for the old man. She seemed to fear him, or at least feel nervous around him. Rodriguez couldn't even find the slightest bit of fear in himself. The king posed no threat to him. A lion who was all roar and no maul. He knew the other kind, the kind who wouldn't hesitate to tear out your throat. It made it very hard to take a man like Eduardo Santina seriously.

His daughter, on the other hand, seemed to feel differently.

"She did not 'run off' with the mahar—with Ashok," Eduardo said.

"I don't care if she walked, ran or flew in his private jet. The bottom line is the same. I am out a fiancée, and we seem to have no more marriage bargain," Rodriguez countered.

Carlotta shifted on her sensible shoes. "Can I go?"

"No," her father said.

"I don't really care what you do," Rodriguez threw in, mildly amused by the whole situation. What adult woman asked her father for permission to do anything? Obviously not his ex–intended bride, Sophia Santina. But apparently Carlotta Santina was another matter.

Carlotta's eyes narrowed slightly in his direction, before flickering back to her father. "I need to call Luca before…"

"It can wait, Carlotta. Do me this one favor," Eduardo bit out roughly, the strain of the situation not well hidden.

Carlotta seemed to shrink and Rodriguez felt his stomach turn sour. *Dios*, but he hated men like that. Men who used their strength, their power, over others like that. Over their own children.

"I'm done here, actually," Rodriguez said. "If you have no bride for me, I have no reason to stay." *Unless one of the maids is looking to get lucky.*

"Tell me, Rodriguez, did you have feelings for Sophia?" Eduardo asked.

"You know I didn't. I didn't even know her. I won't insult either of us by pretending otherwise."

"Then it was her name you needed? Not her?"

He couldn't care less who he married so long as she could produce heirs and do a nice royal wave from a balcony. "You know that to be true."

"Then I do have a bride for you." Eduardo turned his dark eyes on Carlotta. "You can have Carlotta."

Carlotta blinked hard and looked from Rodriguez back to her father. She was certain her ears couldn't be working right, because she had thought she'd heard her father give her away. Like she was a thing. A parting gift for the visiting prince.

Are you shocked? He already believes you gave yourself away.

She shook the thought off and continued to stare at her father, letting the silence fill the room until it became oppressive.

Finally, Rodriguez laughed, a short, harsh sound. "A trade?"

"A way to keep our bargain, Prince Rodriguez."

Carlotta shook her head, and she knew her eyes were probably comically large in her head. She closed her mouth. She hadn't realized it had dropped open.

She'd been completely floored by her sister, sweet Sophia, running away from her arranged marriage to Rodriguez, especially as it was so important for Santina and Santa Christobel to forge an alliance. She'd been the first to warn her sister about the unflattering headlines. *Princess Sophia Joins Mile-High Club.*

But she hadn't realized that she would get dragged into the whole debacle. And certainly not to this degree.

Rodriguez flicked her a dismissive glance. "I have no interest in taking a wife who nearly faints at the thought of becoming my bride. I'm certain I can find someone my mere presence does not offend. We have no deal, Eduardo."

He turned and walked out of the room, leaving Carlotta alone with her father. It was a new kind of silence that filled the room now. One bursting with rage, combined with a kind of leaden disappointment that she could feel down in her soul, weighting her, climbing in her throat, threatening to strangle her.

She knew this feeling. Had felt it before. In this very room. In this very spot.

Nearly six years ago she'd been here. In her father's office. Her knees locked, her feet glued to the carpet, hands clasped tightly in front of her. Her entire body shaking, a cold sweat covering her back, her neck.

I'm pregnant.

They had been the two most terrifying words she'd ever spoken in her life. And directly after them had come the most sickening minute of silence she'd ever endured.

Until now.

"Father, I…"

"Carlotta, after all I have done for you," he said, his voice thick with disappointment, "you cannot do this for me? For your country? You brought so much shame upon us, all of us. The people of Santina, your family."

"I…I only came in to tell you that I have to return tonight." She couldn't deal with her father's words. They hurt too badly. They rang too true. "Luca needs me and…and then you throw a prince at me! A marriage proposal. I don't…"

She swallowed, trying to suppress the panic that was starting to rise in her. "What do you expect of me?"

Her father looked down at his hands, folded in front of him on his neat, expansive desk. "I had hoped that you would understand how important this was. I had hoped you would understand your duty. After all our family has endured recently in the press, thanks to your brother. After the way they publicized your shame."

Carlotta felt her face grow tense, needles of icy cold rage dotting her cheeks. Luca wasn't her shame. And he never could be. Even if the press had been determined to make him so.

The Sole Santina Bastard. A favored headline at the time of Luca's birth. She could only thank God they didn't know the whole story. That they didn't know the half of the sins she was capable of committing when she let the hold on her control loosen.

And Father is the only reason they don't.

That brought the guilt. Right on time.

"I have always believed that you would do great things, Carlotta," he said, his voice softer now. "This is your chance to prove me right." He looked up at her, his dark eyes shining, and she felt her stomach tighten. "You are my most beloved daughter. I did everything in my power to protect you, to keep the press from finding out the details surrounding Luca's birth. Is it so much to ask for this?"

She felt like she was choking, as if her throat was getting tighter with each word her father spoke. Yet another reason she avoided Santina. Her family. The obligations of being a princess. The horrible, crushing guilt.

Not for the first time, she felt like coming home had been a mistake. She didn't know where she fit anymore. She'd been on the fringes of the glamorous engagement party, not entirely able to join in with her family. Not able to join in with her brother Alessandro's new in-laws, the Jacksons, and their carefree, crass style of behavior. In a way she almost envied the Jacksons. They didn't have to worry about how they were perceived. They didn't seem to worry about anything.

Yes, but you do.

It was easier when she was in her home on the Amalfi Coast. When she was just Carlotta, Luca's mum.

But that was a dream. A dream she'd escaped to when she'd been pregnant, alone and scared. Heartbroken. Hounded by the press.

She'd been weak then. But she could never have come out of it remaining weak. It was either grow a spine or melt into a puddle and die. And for Luca's sake, melting had never been a viable option. She'd had to find inner strength, and she'd found it quickly.

Still, facing down her father brought back the girl she'd been. The one who had wanted to please him so badly. Who had only wanted to do right. With everything that was going on, Sophia's very public fall from grace, Alex's marriage... maybe it was her chance to grab a little redemption. To be the daughter her father seemed to believe she still could be.

"What is the precise nature of your agreement with...with Prince Rodriguez?" she asked, licking her suddenly dry lips.

"Anguiano needs an heir," said Eduardo. "His father is dying. As good as dead. Incapacitated and in hospital. It's time for Rodriguez to take the throne of Santa Christobel, and that means he needs a wife."

"And what's in it for us? For Santina. I mean, I understand it in a general sense. But if I'm actually going to... marry Prince Rodriguez, then I need to know exactly what we stand to gain."

"Can you imagine it, Carlotta? What such an alliance could bring? Ease for educational programs between the nations. Trade. A valuable ally to stand with should conflict ever arise. All cemented by marriage. Children. It is unfathomable in its value."

"Gems," she said softly, a realization washing over her. "They have diamonds. Ruby mines too. A host of other natural resources."

"It cannot be overlooked. They are a wealthy nation. And that makes them even more valuable. Sophia knew her duty. She has abandoned it. But I trust you, Carlotta. I trust that you will do what is right."

What *was* right? She had tried to do what was right for most of her life. Barring one giant mistake, she always had. It had always been her goal. To be the kind of daughter her parents deserved and desired. She didn't know if she could take it this far though.

She closed her eyes for a moment, pictured her house on the beach. The quiet. Her son running through the halls with his arms full of stuffed animals that had most definitely seen better days. Things were simpler there. She didn't have to work so hard to be the Carlotta that she was expected to be. The one she feared deep inside she never truly could be.

But while she had left palace life behind, she hadn't left her title. She hadn't truly shed her duty.

That was bred into her. A part of her. Even if she tried to ignore it.

And then, there was her father. Who had never given up on her. Not even when she'd let him down, dragged the Santina name through the mud. Put them on par with the kind of tabloid fodder he despised.

For all the cruel words her family had bandied around about her older brother Alessandro's future in-laws, the very same could be said about her. It *had* been said about her, in bold print, on newsstands all around Santina.

Scandalous. Immoral.

Her family, her father, had never thrown those words at

her, but she knew it had been thought. How could they not think it? She had. Worse, she knew it was true. A lifetime of keeping her passionate, exuberant nature on a tight leash, and in one great fall from grace, all her efforts had been reduced to nothing. She had tainted her family name, had brought them ridicule, the disgust of a nation who saw her as a clear sign of the degeneration of the royal family.

The question was, how badly did she want redemption? Enough to marry a total stranger? The prince of a country she'd never been to? The man her sister had been engaged to, until she'd broken it by hooking up with Ash on his private plane.

She looked at her father. He had aged in the past few years. She hadn't been around to see it. She wondered how much of it was her fault. How many lines on his face were from dealing with her transgressions.

It made her sick to think of it.

But she could be the one to fix things here. The one to save the day. To be the daughter her parents had imagined she would be. It was almost embarrassing that she wanted it so badly. That she cared so much. But she did. She needed to look at her father and see something other than disappointment in his eyes.

"What do you need me to do?" she asked.

Rodriguez reclined on the bed, his shoes consigned to the floor, along with his tie. His plane would be ready soon, and then he would be leaving Santina, and with it, the little melodrama that the Santinas seemed to be living.

He didn't waste his time on this sort of thing. He lived. He didn't regret. He didn't worry. He didn't think more than he had to. Not about anything beyond the here and now anyway.

There was a soft knock at the door and he wondered if it was a maid, then chuckled at where the thought took him. It

really had been too long since he'd had sex. He'd been expecting to pick up a fiancée so he'd imagined his celibacy
wouldn't have lasted beyond tonight.

"*Sì?*"

The door opened, and it wasn't a maid. It was Princess
Carlotta Santina, still in her drab outfit, her lips pursed tight.
She didn't look like she was here to alleviate him of his celi-
bacy either.

"I thought we might have a talk." No, definitely not.

"Did you?"

She nodded, the setting sun filtering through the window
shimmering over her straight, glossy bob. "I thought, since
my father just tried to...use me as a stand-in for my sister,
we might..."

"I'm actually done with that now." He really wasn't in
the mood for whatever kind of rant she'd come to throw at
him. Or was she here to apologize? The way she'd looked
at her father, the way her shoulders had folded in, her hands
clasped tight in front of her, almost like a shield. Like she
feared him...she would come and apologize.

"I'm not," she said, the slight steel in her tone surprising him.

"Is that so?"

"Yes. My father explained the situation to me more fully.
I...I knew that you and Sophia were engaged, in a sense, but
I did not know the specifics. I don't live in Santina so I'm not
really in on everything that goes on here and Sophia didn't...
she didn't really say much of anything about you. I only got
wind of how big of a deal it was when the story broke about
Sophia being caught with Ash on the plane."

"That's because I've barely met the girl. No reason for
her to talk about me."

Carlotta cleared her throat. "Yes, well...*the girl*, is gone."

"With the maharaja."

He saw the corner of her mouth twitch. "Right. With Ash. Alex's friend. And you still need a wife."

"Need is a strong word."

"Do you or don't you?" she asked.

"Eventually."

"How soon is this *eventually* you speak of?"

"Truthfully? The sooner, the better. This will be a time of transition for my people." He thought of the responsibility, the weight of the crown. It was heavy on his shoulders. Already he'd moved back into the palace in Santa Christobel. He felt like it would choke him, being inside those four walls again. "Anything that can be done to ease their fears at this time would be welcome. Marriage, my marriage, would help with that."

They wouldn't be mourning his father, that was for sure. Carlos Anguiano was not much loved. And while Rodriguez had essentially been running Santa Christobel for the past several years, his father had remained the figurehead.

"It would mean a new start for my people. A fresh beginning," he said.

"Well then, I guess I have good news for you."

"What is that?"

"I haven't run off with a maharaja, so…I happen to be available to marry you. At your earliest convenience."

It was a rare moment that found Rodriguez Anguiano speechless.

"Excuse me?" he asked.

"I'll marry you."

"What happened to the emphatic no from earlier?"

"I was shocked. In shock. I wasn't prepared for something like that."

"To be offered up as a replacement wife in your sister's absence?" He sat up and swung his legs over the side of the bed, standing quickly.

"I wasn't…exactly expecting that, no. I thought I'd come to the party, have a couple of drinks and go home. Wasn't really anticipating acquiring a husband."

"And yet you have changed your mind?" he asked, pacing in front of her, adrenaline surging through him, joining the unrest he'd already felt being contained in the walls of the castle in Santina. That he'd been feeling since he'd boarded his private plane, on his way to collect what could only be described as a ball and chain.

"We need this, don't we? The marriage I…" He watched her throat convulse as she swallowed. "I have always known that I would face an arranged marriage of some kind."

She spoke the truth. From the cradle they'd all known their marriages would likely be arranged by their parents. Because duty came first, the allegiance to the family name. To Santina. Alex had long been promised to Anna, a woman more than suitable to be the future queen of Santina. But that was before he'd gone rogue and set his sights on Allegra Jackson. And of course Sophia had been promised to Rodriguez. Natalia's engagement was in the process of being arranged. She didn't know about Matteo, but it was less urgent now that Alex was formally betrothed.

Before Carlotta had… Well, if not for Luca her father would have likely arranged a marriage for her years ago. As it was, she had been sort of taken out of the "dynastic union" running when she'd had her son.

Well, apparently not really out of the running. She was good enough to play second string. Good enough to marry the renowned rebel prince of Santa Christobel. A man who lived dangerously and loved often. Well, not *loved*. He made love often, according to the tabloids. A new woman on his arm every weekend to accompany him to Europe's most exclusive parties. Fast cars, fast dates.

The kind of man who represented recklessness, lawlessness, total disregard for honor. A man who served his own passions. The kind of man she hated. The kind of man she was so easily drawn to.

"As have I," Rodriguez said, his dark eyes unreadable, the little curve of his mouth still present, like it had been earlier. It was a kind of ever-present near-smile that made it look like he was mocking her. It made her stomach feel like it was being squeezed tight by an invisible fist.

She cleared her throat. "So, while I hadn't really penciled a wedding into my day planner, it's not a…it's not a total surprise."

What was her other option anyway?

Well, there was staying in Italy. That was a good thought. Hiding. But she didn't know if it served any real purpose. The only person it really helped was her. It allowed her to lick her wounds in private. It allowed her to hide Luca from royal life. Something part of her wanted to do, but something she also knew wasn't fair. He was a Santina. He was a royal. It was a part of him, and it didn't do him any good to force him to deny that part of himself. No matter how much simpler it would be to just raise him as an ordinary little boy. Who wasn't tabloid fodder. It wasn't reality.

"I don't suppose you really had other life plans either," she said.

"I don't plan. I live."

"Well…I suppose that means you don't have a woman back home you're dying to see. Someone you'd prefer to marry."

"I'll be honest with you, Carlotta, I prefer not to marry. But I need an heir. One that isn't a bastard."

She flinched when he spoke the word. She hated that word. One used to label an innocent child, to make them suffer for the perceived sins of his parents. Did Rodriguez know about Luca? He had to know. So, he'd chosen the words to wound her.

"Why?" she said. "Do you have many? Children, I mean."

"Me? No. I always use protection." Such a throwaway statement. Spoken like a man who never thought about anyone but himself.

She gritted her teeth. "It doesn't always work."

"True. But in the event that a pregnancy had resulted, you can bet the woman involved would have told me. I'm rich. Titled. She would have wanted her piece."

"You would have owed her a piece," she said. "At minimum."

"I'm not arguing that. My point is that, whether I want marriage or not, I need it."

"Preferably to me."

He looked at her, his dark gaze dismissive. "Because of connection to this family."

"I didn't seek to imply otherwise. It's the only reason I would marry you."

"Because your father told you to. That's the reason."

She felt her cheeks heat. "He has good reasons."

"Fine. But you're still doing it because he asked you to."

"And your father has nothing to do with any of this?"

A muscle in his jaw ticked, the light in his eyes turning black, deadly. "My father can hardly lift his hand anymore. He is weak. What I do, I do for my country."

"Same goes for me. But my family *is* Santina."

"Thank goodness mine is not Santa Christobel. Santa Christobel is better than the Anguiano legacy has been thus far. But I intend to do better."

"And I intend to…be a part of it." It was strange, lobbying for something she wasn't certain she wanted. But she needed it. Everything else aside, her father was right. She had made mistakes that had cost the family. And he had covered for her. Had done everything in his power to keep her from being utterly humiliated and exposed.

In the scope of things, this wasn't so very much to ask.

"Does it get boring?"

"What?" she asked, trying to ignore the glint of humor in his dark eyes. It made him seem…attractive. Well, he was attractive, glint or no, with his golden skin and dark hair that was much too long to be considered respectable for a man of his station. Chiseled jaw, a body that looked as though it would be hard like iron. It wouldn't be impersonal or cold like metal, though. No, he would be hot.…

She blinked, trying to reroute her thoughts. She didn't do the man thing. Not anymore. Just acknowledging the speed and ease with which he aroused her was…horrifying. Even more horrifying was the strength of it. Why was it so hard to be good? To be the woman she was supposed to be?

"Being this noble, does it get boring?"

"Yes. It does. Which is why I practice it in small doses." And throw it off altogether sometimes…

"Good to know that not even you are always respectable."

"Not even close." But she tried. She'd tried all her life. To ignore the fire that seemed to burn so close to the surface of her skin. To be the demure princess she was expected to be. It had been a battle all her life. One she'd lost completely when she'd met Luca's father. A lifetime of practiced restraint reduced to nothing in just a few short weeks.

He inclined his head. "All right then, Princess Carlotta, you have yourself a marriage bargain. My plane leaves Santina late tonight and I intend to take my future wife with me."

"I…I can't leave from here. I can't leave tonight." Luca was still in Italy, with his nanny. So were all of her things. Her real things, not her princess trappings.

"Why is that?"

"Because I don't live here at the palace. I don't even live on the island. I live in Italy. My home is there, my…everything." She didn't know what stopped her from saying something about Luca. Maybe because he hadn't mentioned him. The whole thing seemed so mercenary. So cold. Adding him to it…it just seemed wrong.

"Fine. We'll stop in Italy on our way to Santa Christobel."

Oh, yes, and pick up her five-year-old with Mr. Tall, Dark, Sexy and Imposing standing in the doorway with that mocking grin of his. No thank you.

"I can make my own way to Santa Christobel," she said archly. "I need time to prepare."

"Have a lover you need to cast off before we get married?"

She nearly snorted. She'd lived the past few years completely abstinent after only one, near emotionally fatal affair. "Oh, yes, a stable of them. You?"

"I don't intend to cast anyone off."

"Excuse me?"

He shrugged. "I don't intend to cast off any lovers just because I'm getting married."

Her stomach twisted. Men. They really were all the same. Cheating, lying jerks who only cared about pleasing their sex drives. "I hope you don't think you'll be in my bed then. I don't share."

A slow smile spread over his handsome face, teeth bright white against his tan skin. "I do."

"What does that mean?"

"It means I don't ask for what I don't give."

"Fidelity?"

"Exactly."

"Well, I ask for fidelity." *I've never gotten it, but I'd like it.* "And if you're going to be in my bed, you won't be in anyone else's." She couldn't believe she was even talking about beds and sex with a man she'd only just meant.

It was making her face hot, and not, she suspected, from embarrassment. From that nearly six years of celibacy maybe. From the thought of a man's hands, *his* hands, on her skin again. Kissing. Caressing.

She shifted and tried to ease the knot in her stomach with a deep breath. That was one part of marriage that wouldn't be so bad.

Unless he's actively sleeping with other women the whole time.

Yeah, that was a definite no-go for her. And anyway, contemplating sleeping with him was…he was a stranger and it was bad with a capital *B*.

"We will discuss this no more. Not now."

She raised her brow. "Excuse me?"

"It is immaterial. Fine details you and I will work out later. For now, the real question is, will you marry me?"

He didn't get down on one knee or anything, thank goodness, because that would have been just too much. He stood in front of her, arms crossed over his broad chest, a knowing smile curving his lips. He exuded confidence. Charm. That kind of cocky, arrogant sexiness that said he knew just what he could make a woman feel.

He wasn't the first man she'd met who exuded those things.

He took a step toward her, his dark eyes trained on hers, and for a moment, it felt like the world had closed in on them. So that it was just the two of them.

Rodriguez didn't touch her, he didn't even make a move to touch her, and yet she felt like he had. Could feel the warmth coming from his hard body and she wasn't afraid of him putting his hands on her, she was wishing he would. Aching for it.

"A simple question, a simple answer," he said. "Yes or no?"

She met his dark gaze, her heart hopping in her chest

like a caged bird making a bid for freedom. She opened her mouth to speak but her throat was dry. She swallowed, trying to find her balance, her confidence.

Trying to find the woman that knew all about men like him, who knew that charm was nothing more than smoke and mirrors; that sex, no matter how fulfilling or meaningful she might find it, was nothing more than a little bit of amusement for men like him, and that they would leave the woman to pick up the check. A week's worth of fun for them, could mean a lifetime of payment for the woman involved.

It had for her.

And she would never be that stupid again. She would never again buy into the kind of sweet lies that could be issued from wicked, sexy mouths like his. Not even if she was married to the charmer.

Married. Was she really going to marry him? Could she really go back to her father and tell him she'd decided not to?

"Yes," she said, the word weak, breathless. She cleared her throat. She didn't do weak and breathless. Not anymore. She'd made the decision, she would stand strong in it. "Yes, I will marry you."

CHAPTER TWO

HE WAS a small boy. He barely came to the top of Carlotta's hip. Dark hair, the same green eyes as his mother.

His mother. Carlotta.

Dios.

He knew it, the moment he saw her bend and help the little boy from the back of the limo when they'd pulled up to the palace, knew from the moment he saw the boy's face. That same sullen expression, the stubborn chin, he was hers.

He had inherited a child, along with a fiancée.

Part of him knew it shouldn't matter. That it didn't truly change anything. He and Carlotta had been planning on having children. He needed an heir after all. That he would be a father one day was, and had always been, a given.

Another part of him felt a kind of bone-deep terror that had been absent from him since he was a boy himself. He remembered that day, the day when his emotions had finally given beneath the strain of living a life beneath his father's iron fist. The day his emotions had deserted him entirely.

Well, that fear he'd thought long gone was here now. Because of the boy. Reflected in the boy. He was afraid, his eyes wide on the castle in front of him. It couldn't be his first time seeing a palace. His grandmother and grandfather were the rulers of Santina. He *was* a Santina.

Carlotta looked at him, her green eyes hard. "Hello."

"Hola," he said.

"Hi." This from the boy.

Rodriguez looked down at him, swallowing, trying to bring some moisture to his suddenly dry throat. It seemed like the right thing to introduce himself to the boy. Did you introduce yourself formally to a child?

Annoyance mixed with uncertainty. Carlotta had managed to catch him off guard twice now. They were the only two times it had happened in his recent memory. This wasn't a trend he liked.

He would just approach the chiild as he would an adult. "I am Prince Rodriguez Anguiano. What is your name?" That earned him little more than a wide-eyed stare from those green eyes.

"Luca," said Carlotta. "His name is Luca."

That she answered annoyed him, like she didn't want her son speaking to him. It also made him feel a small measure of relief. Because it spared him from having to talk directly to Luca.

"Come with me," he said, turning and heading to the palace.

He nearly laughed. He had been pretending that marrying Carlotta rather than Sophia changed nothing. And had been managing quite well. But now there was this…complication.

This was a difference that would be hard to ignore.

The massive doors to the palace opened and he ushered them in to the cavernous entryway. All glossy marble with a domed ceiling depicting intricate scenes of men and angels. Not to his taste at all. He'd never felt at home here. There was a reason he'd spent his young adult years in France and Spain, a reason he had his own penthouse in Barcelona still, even though his time avoiding Santa Christobel was over.

But now that his father was in the hospital, now that running the country was up to him, he'd had no choice but to come back. Even though it made him feel like he'd crawled into someone else's skin. Ill-fitting. Uncomfortable. Nearly unbearable.

Now, another role he wasn't made for. Husband. Father.

"There is no…no room prepared for Luca," he said, careful not to look down at the top of the boy's dark head.

"What?" she asked, finely arched brows locking together.

He gritted his teeth against rising annoyance. "Had you told me there would be a need…"

"You didn't know?" She shot a look to Luca, then back to him, her eyes round with shock. "How did you not know?"

Luca was watching both of them, confusion in his eyes. That was something he remembered well about being a child. That lack of control. Knowing that your fate was in the hands of the adults around you. How little sense it made sometimes.

His stomach tightened, and he looked down at the boy again. "Luca, perhaps you would like to come out to the garden?"

The garden. Such as it was. It was a massive, sprawling green field in comparison to most lawns. But it was likely to keep a child busy. At least, he thought it would.

Luca nodded. "I like to play outside. Do you have a slide?"

Rodriguez looked at Carlotta, then back at Luca, a strange sensation—nerves?—making it hard to breathe. "No. No slides. But we could put one in." Put one in? Like they were staying?

Of course they were staying. He'd signed a new marriage contract with King Eduardo before leaving Santina. But he hadn't known about the child. About Luca. He'd known that he and Carlotta would have an heir…but an heir was… It sounded very detached. Unreal. The little boy with serious green eyes was real.

Too real.

"You don't have to put a slide in," said Carlotta. "Well, not

today. Eventually I guess it might… Luca, let's go outside."
She held out her hand and Luca wrapped his small fingers
around hers. She looked at Rodriguez and he nodded, leading her through the entryway and down the main corridor
that led out to the back terrace.

They stepped outside into the warm evening, the heat
of the day long past, the setting sun casting electric orange
stripes over the vivid green lawn.

"There isn't a pond or anything is there?" she asked, eye-
ing the fenced-in area.

"No. It's safe for him. This part here is just grass."

"Go, run," she said.

Luca smiled at Carlotta and trotted off the terrace, and
Carlotta watched him, a soft expression on her face.

"The plane ride was long," she said. "He really needed to
get out and move."

"I can imagine." He'd learned not to fidget from a very
early age. It had stayed with him into adulthood. Sometimes,
even now, if he was in a meeting and he found himself fidgeting, he could still imagine that the sharp crack of a ruler
on his shins might come next.

"How did you not know?" she asked.

"About Luca? How was I supposed to know?"

"It was… The press, they… He's the only illegitimate
Santina. The headlines were not kind."

"I don't read tabloids."

"You don't?"

"No."

"Not even when they're talking about you?"

"Especially not then," he said.

"How do you…I mean, how can you not? I had to…I had
to know what they were saying." She looked away from him,
her eyes on Luca, who was now turning circles in the middle
of the large expanse of grass. "I suppose, looking back, it

wasn't the healthiest thing for a hormonal, pregnant woman to do. But I just felt like I needed to know."

"I don't care what they're saying. Anyway, what they write about me is simply a rundown of my weekend's events. If I want a recap, I'll look at the pictures I took."

She turned her head sharply, her eyes wide. "Pictures?"

"Oh, so you've read about me then," he said.

"I said I read tabloids. Anyway, who hasn't read about you?"

"Probably a few priests who are trying to deny the existence of evil in the world, but we aren't supposed to be talking about me right now. I didn't know you had a son."

"Does it change anything?"

Did it? He'd never planned on being very involved with his wife and children. He just…he couldn't think of a single thing he could add to their lives. They would serve their purpose, likely better without his interference. He knew nothing about family. The only thing he knew about children was what not to do with them.

That was something, he supposed.

"I don't know that it does," he said. "Is his father in the picture?"

"Luca doesn't have a father." Carlotta felt her cheeks get hot as Rodriguez fixed her with a hard stare. "Well…obviously he has a father," she said. "But he doesn't have an involved father."

"Messy breakup?" he asked.

It suddenly seemed a bit harder to breathe. "You could say that." It would be an understatement, but she wasn't in the mood to elaborate.

"So I'm not going to get tangled up in any sort of custody thing?"

"Absolutely not. Is that your only concern?"

"I don't see anything else that should concern me."

"You don't see how having a son concerns you?"

His eyebrows locked together. "He's not my son."

Carlotta's heart twisted tight. It was a fair enough statement. Luca wasn't Rodriguez's son. And they'd been at his home for all of fifteen minutes. He wasn't being cruel. Still, it felt a little cruel. "No, I know. But he is a child, and if you're going to be my husband he will be your stepson, and that means some of the responsibility…"

"He has a nanny?"

"Yes. She had to stay behind for a couple of days but…"

"In that case, I see my responsibility will be limited."

Anger burned in her, threatening to swallow her whole. "And will it be the same for *your* children? Because if not, you and I have no more to say to each other. Luca is my son. He's my world and if you—"

"Yes. It will be the same for our *child*. I don't intend to have any more than is required."

"If we have a girl?"

"Then we will have to have more, I suppose."

"I don't…I don't even know how to have this discussion with you," she said, panic clawing at her stomach. How could she stand here talking children with this stranger? Was she really going to marry this man?

Yes. Because the other option was going back to her father, standing in that spot in his office and telling him, yet again, how badly she'd failed the Santina family. She couldn't do it. The guilt would consume her. She lived with enough guilt. No sense in adding to it.

But one thing she had to be sure of. For Luca. And if Rodriguez couldn't handle it, she would walk away, no matter how disappointed her father was. No matter how much compound interest in guilt it earned her.

"Will you adopt him?"

Rodriguez stiffened, his posture totally rigid. "What?"

"Will you adopt Luca? Give him your name. The same

name I will have. The same name his half-brother or -sister will have. Will you make him a part of this family? Because if not, I'll walk away now."

A muscle in Rodriguez's jaw twitched. "I cannot name him as my heir."

"I don't expect you to. But I cannot have him be alone in that way." Just the thought of it made her throat ache, made it get unbearably tight. "I need him to know that he has a father. That he isn't the only one who isn't a part of a family."

"Having a father can be vastly overrated," Rodriguez said, his voice rough.

"Give him your name. Your protection. And I will marry you. Be your wife in every sense. But you have to make my son yours, as much as your other children."

She watched as his Adam's apple bobbed, his eyes fixed on Luca. "Then I will adopt him after the marriage. All of this can be simple enough. We marry, we produce an heir. We lead separate lives."

"Why?"

He looked past her, at Luca, who was now lying on his back looking at the sky. Then he looked back at her. "Because I'm not after a perfect, happy family. I want to do what is right by my country. What is necessary."

"The way that disrupts your life the least?"

"And yours, Carlotta. You can keep living as you please here. You'll have very little obligation to me. This marriage will be like a job you can clock in and out of. On for public appearances, off when it's done."

"So, I get lovers too, then?"

He shrugged. "What's good for the goose."

"Just not while we're—"

"Mommy!"

She turned sharply and saw Luca, standing right at the edge of the terrace. He had a way of darting from place to place with no warning, her son. It had never really been a problem before.

"Yes, Luca?"

"I'm bored."

"And tired I'll bet," she said.

"No." He shook his head for emphasis, the serious expression on his face reminding her of her brother Alessandro. She was so thankful that he seemed to have none of his father in him.

"Yeah, I don't believe that, *figlio mio*, but nice try," she said, running her fingers through his dark hair, ruffling it.

"There is a room next to yours," Rodriguez said, his manner suddenly awkward. Luca did seem to make him nervous and she wasn't really sure why. "He can stay in there."

"Good. If we could have his things brought in, that would be great."

Rodriguez nodded curtly. "After he's in bed, perhaps you and I can have dinner."

Carlotta wasn't sure how she felt about that. She liked having Luca as a buffer. It was much more comfortable.

Ironic that you feel the need for a buffer since you're planning on having a baby with the man. No buffers then.

That thought had her hot all over. Well, not so much the pregnancy and childbirth aspect of it. She'd hated being pregnant. Every moment of it. It had all been sickness and sadness. A little bit of denial. Only when Luca was placed in her arms had everything truly come together. And from that moment, she'd been lost. Everything that had come before it—the pain, physical and emotional—had paled in comparison to the love that had flooded through her when she'd seen her son for the first time.

She'd already done it once without a man in the picture.

"Great. We can talk more then," she said, wondering if any amount of talking would ever make the situation seem normal.

* * *

After spending a couple of hours getting Luca settled and conked out in his new room, Carlotta went back to her room and selected a nice dress from her collection of, admittedly, out-of-date clothing.

Clothes just didn't matter when you hardly ever went anywhere and certainly never went on dates. As Queen of Santa Christobel she would need new clothing....

Oh. *Madre di dio*. She was going to be the Queen of Santa Christobel. She had sort of been stuck on being Rodriguez's wife. On what it would mean to marry him and share his bed, and have his baby, and uproot her son from his home in Italy. She hadn't even gotten to the queen bit.

She tugged the dress off the hanger and sat on the bed in nothing but her bra and panties, the plush, silken comforter billowing around her, enveloping her. She clutched the rust-colored dress to her chest and breathed in deeply, trying to stop the room from spinning.

This was not her life.

And what is? Self-imposed exile in Italy? Living it up, aren't you, Carlotta?

She had known she'd have to get back into the swing of things eventually. Start living life beyond the four walls of her home. She hadn't really intended on doing it in such a grand way.

Life had seemed...still, for the past five years. No, not still. Because Luca always changed. Every day there was something new and exciting for him, and she lived it, loved it. Loved him. But for her...there had been nothing. It had been like being wrapped in a cocoon. Now she was torn from it, and she doubted she'd had any grand transformation.

She didn't know if she was ready for this. And she didn't really have anyone to talk to. Normally she would call Sophia but since she was currently shacked up with Ash in India and Carlotta was now engaged to the man she'd been intended to marry...

Well, she deserved to be dragged into it, all things considered.

Carlotta took her phone out of her purse and tapped the icon on the screen for text messaging. She'd sent Sophia a blistering message when she'd found out she'd run off with Ash. Now, well, she couldn't really blame her younger sister. This was…it was overwhelming. Maybe if Ash had been standing by with a private plane she would have run off with him too. Though she wouldn't have hopped into bed with him.

Hope you're having a blast in India. BTW, I'm marrying the fiancé you ditched. Good choice, he's an ass.

She hit Send on the message, then tapped the screen again, a smile curving her lips. She hit the New Message icon.

He's also a total stud. So that's some consolation.

This time when she hit Send, her smile was smug. She hoped Sophia was happy, whatever she was doing. Well, she had a fair idea of what her sister was doing, since she'd been caught in Ash's bed on his private plane.

Sophia was the one person who didn't seem completely ashamed of her and Luca. But while she wished her sister a lifetime of happiness, and if that included a torrid affair with Ash, fine with her, she deserved a *little* goading, all things considered.

Her phone pinged and she picked it back up. New message from Sophia.

At least our father will be pleased to have both of us marrying fellow royals.

Married? She'd just thought Sophia was sleeping with him. Well, then things really had worked out in her father's favor. One daughter to a maharaja, the other, the one who'd been mired in total disgrace, married off to a prince.

She typed in another quick message. Congrats, Soph. Love ya.

She snorted and tossed the phone onto the bed. Yes, this was all working out great for Eduardo Santina. Hopefully it would work out even half as well for her.

There was a sharp knock on her door and she scrambled from the bed, stepping into the dress and contorting her arm so that she could tug the zipper up. "Just a second."

She got it midway up, then reached over her shoulder and grabbed it from above, tugging it up the rest of the way. She looked in the mirror and pulled on the neckline, trying to make sure everything was in its proper place. Her figure was a bit fuller since her pregnancy and sometimes she wasn't quite sure what to make of her new curves.

Not that they were pin-up worthy or anything. But at least she could fill out the top of her dress now, with a little cleavage.

She wondered what Rodriguez would think. If he would check her out. That made her cheeks feel hot. She tried to find some hold on her control, tried to keep in command of her body's reaction.

This is what happens when you give in. When you're weak.

That was what her father had shouted at her the day she'd told him she was pregnant. The day she'd told him who the father of her baby was through heartbroken sobs. It was so easy to feel the shame, the sick, crawling feeling of dirt on her skin, as she confessed the truth about Gabriel.

She was determined never to be weak again.

"Ready," she said, turning away from her reflection, redirecting her thoughts.

The door swung open and Rodriguez was there, leaning against the frame. *He* didn't look last season, not even close.

His crisp, white shirt was unbuttoned at the collar, revealing a wedge of golden brown skin and just a little bit of dark chest hair. His dark hair was disheveled. He looked like a man who'd just come from his lover's bed.

She wrinkled her nose. She'd been upstairs for a couple of hours, it was entirely possible that he'd...

"So, how was your evening?" she asked, stepping past him, out into the corridor.

"Fine. I had some work to see to."

"Great."

"You?"

"Luca seems settled in. I don't know if he really understands that we're staying here. But then, I guess that makes two of us."

"Three," he said, walking ahead of her, taking the stairs two at a time. She followed as quickly as her kitten heels would allow.

"You don't feel at home here?"

He stopped at the bottom of the stairs and looked up at the painted ceiling. "I never have."

"You could...redecorate."

A short laugh escaped his lips and he stuffed his hands into the pockets of his dark slacks. "That's almost like suggesting I paint over the Sistine Chapel's ceiling. I mean, not quite, but as far as Santa Christobel and our history is concerned, it is."

"Well, that would be a bad idea then."

"Very likely."

He paused and turned to her, placing his hand on her lower back. She felt the heat of his touch blaze through her, like fire had ignited in her bloodstream, moving through her like a reckless spark on dry tinder.

Was she so desperate for a man's touch that such a simple thing could turn her on so quickly? Well, clearly she was. A man she didn't even know, a man she wasn't sure she liked. She truly was no better now than she'd been six years ago. It was still there, that reckless passion. The one she'd worked so hard to shove down deep, to lock away forever. It was a sobering, gutting realization.

"This way," he said, unaware of the turmoil his hand on her back had caused.

She kept her shoulders straight, tried to keep it so his hand only touched the fabric of her dress and didn't press it down so that it came into contact with her back again. Because that had been far too disturbing.

The dining room was as opulent and formal as the rest of the house, the sprawling ceiling mural continuing through, with scenes of a massive feast painted just above the long, expansive table.

"Cozy," she said.

That earned a laugh from Rodriguez. "Isn't it? Perfect for an intimate dinner for two. Plus twenty."

"The palace in Santina is a bit like that. It's daunting. Luca…he's not used to this."

"Why did you take him away from Santina?"

"The press," she said, her voice soft.

He pulled a chair out for her and she sat, touching the golden fork that was set beside an ornate dinner plate.

"It was bad for you?" Rodriguez took his seat opposite her.

She looked nice tonight, pretty even. She dressed too plainly for his taste, her hair too well ordered and smooth for his liking. But she was attractive, more than he'd given her credit for the first time he'd seen her.

She looked up, her green eyes hard. "I have the only illegitimate child in the entire Santina family. Going back generations."

An incredulous laugh escaped him. "That anyone has ever

owned up to. Do you honestly think there haven't been others?"

"My father said..."

"I'm sure there are descendants of Santina bastards all over Europe. It's the nature of things."

She gritted her teeth, her eyes suddenly bright with rage. "My son is not a bastard."

"That isn't what I meant."

"Pick your words a bit more carefully then."

She had teeth. And claws. Neither of which he'd seen in the interaction with her father. However, when it came to the boy, she was fierce. Good. It would make her a good mother for his heir. Protective. Strong. Something that had certainly been lacking in his life.

She would be a good queen too. While he found her a bit plain, it would suit her position. She had that regal quality to her. He preferred a sex-on-legs quality when it came to his bed partners, but a wife needed something else entirely. And Carlotta had that something else.

He hadn't fully appreciated it until that moment.

"Noted, *princesa*."

"Anyway," she said, looking back down at her empty plate. "That's why I've been in Italy. It's simpler there. I came back for the engagement party. A chance to see someone else mess up."

"You think your brother is making a mistake?"

"In my father's eyes he is. It's petty. But...I don't like being the bad one."

"I've never minded bad girls." He watched her eyes round with shock, and he also saw a spark of interest flash in those green depths. Perhaps his bride-to-be wasn't quite as plain as he had imagined.

Maybe there was more beneath that prim and proper exterior.

It was certainly a fascinating thought. One that caused a flash fire of arousal to roar through his blood. Six months without sex. *Dios*, that was a long time. The longest he'd gone since he was sixteen and he'd found out that life came with some very lush and interesting perks.

Women were just another of the many reasons he didn't mourn the loss of his childhood. Giving women pleasure, taking his pleasure with them, had provided him with moments of total release. Oblivion. He had always treasured those moments.

"No, you haven't, according to your tabloid reputation," she said. "Which reminds me, and I'm sorry to bring it up just before dinner, do you have a clean bill of health? I mean, have you had a recent physical? Because from what I've read, you've been around."

"Not wrong of you to bring it up," he said, ignoring the unfamiliar prickle of shame. "Being safe is important. And I always am. And it so happens, I have a doctor's report for you."

"I... That's more than I expected."

"It's reality. I've never denied living a certain lifestyle, but I'm careful, and I make sure to protect my lovers. As I will make sure to protect you."

Carlotta felt her body getting hot again. She felt the need to remind herself that she'd done the swept-off-her-feet-and-into-bed-with-a-stranger thing before. And while it had been a glowing, heady few weeks, it had been a cold and stark reality when she'd woken up to the truth about the man she'd given her virginity to. The man who'd left her pregnant and alone.

Well, whether he'd left or not, she would have kicked him to the curb once she learned the truth. He'd just saved her the trouble. And the truth had kept her from tracking him down.

A little sliver of flame wound its way through her body as she studied Rodriguez. She took a deep breath, hoping that might help extinguish it. That she would be able to maintain control over herself.

It was proving to be more difficult than it should.

"And how will you be certain of your health if you're…if you're taking other lovers?" She swallowed. "Don't make a fool of me. If you sleep around, I want to know. Don't ever lie to me."

She supposed in a way, she would deserve a cheating husband. Poetic justice in many ways. She would be the one at home with the children, wondering how her husband's business trip was going while he was really wining, dining and bedding another woman.

She nearly gagged.

"Just don't lie," she said again. That was the part she couldn't stand. The lies. Being manipulated into believing a man was someone he wasn't. Falling in love with the facade.

He looked at her, his dark eyes unreadable. "You want to know about the other women?"

"I will not be treated like I'm stupid." Even if she was. Even if she had been terminally stupid in the man department at one time. She never would be again.

"I will give you my honesty. What you choose to do with it is up to you, but I will never lie to you. If you want the truth, you can have it."

It would probably be easier to just take her charming husband into her bed when he was home, and ignore him when he wasn't. But she wouldn't live that way. She wouldn't be that woman.

"I do."

"I will have the same, *princesa*."

"Of course. And fidelity while we are trying to conceive is non-negotiable. You are not having me and a harem at the same time."

"You are not quite what I expected." He leaned back in

his chair and appraised her, his gaze open, honest as he said he'd be. He didn't bother disguising the fact that he was assessing her. Didn't bother to hide it when his eyes dropped to her breasts.

And she couldn't suppress the mild bit of satisfaction she took in him checking her out.

"Well, of course I'm not," she said, trying to ignore the little of prickle of heat that was starting at her scalp and migrating down. "You were expecting to marry my sister. We're not even remotely similar. She's shorter for one thing."

"And quieter, if I remember right. Though I don't know that I ever engaged her in conversation."

"You're hardly marrying for the conversation though, are you?"

"You're more engaging than I imagined you to be, it might actually have just moved up on my list of desirable qualities in a wife."

"Good thing, because you appear to be stuck with me."

"And you like making…conversation?"

"I'm a little bit out of practice making any kind of conversation that doesn't involve the physical ailments of stuffed animals, or require me to refer to myself as Mama."

She noticed a little bit of tension in his brow, the lines of his handsome face tightening. For all his carefree manner, there was more to Rodriguez than he showed the world. Although she wasn't sure if it was better than what he did show.

"So," she said, clearing her throat and tapping the dinner plate with her fork. "Are we…eating?"

As if on cue a man came in carrying a tray with two plates on it, which he set on top of the fine china in front of Rodriguez and in front of her.

"Paella del mar," he said. "I hope you like shellfish."

"It would be sacrilege if I didn't. Santina is a part of the sea. It's the life force of the country."

"As it is here in Santa Christobel. That, at least, should be similar to your home."

She looked down at the rice and pushed the shell of a muscle with the tip of her fork. "Santina hasn't been my home for a long time. How will your people feel about this?"

"About what?"

"You marrying a woman who has a child. Clearly, I'm not your standard-issue virgin princess."

"I doubt my people are under the illusion I have any desire for a virgin princess. I'm certainly not a virgin, neither do I pretend to be one."

For some reason, his immediate dismissal of the idea gave her a strange rush of pleasure. She shouldn't care whether he approved of her or not, and yet, for some reason, it satisfied her to know that he hadn't really expected, or cared, if his bride were pure as the driven snow.

"What you desire, and what's expected, are two very different things."

"I assume you're an expert?"

"I can claim a bit of experience in the area, yes," she said. She really didn't want the conversation to go in that direction. Someday, maybe. But not now. She was fairly certain her brothers didn't even know the circumstances surrounding Luca's birth. She wasn't really eager to spread it around. "I'm just not certain what your people will make of you taking a single mother as your bride."

"I didn't ask them," he said simply, taking a bite of paella.

"That simple?"

"I am to be their king."

"But there are appearances to worry about and…appearances." Appearance was of the upmost importance to her father. Her mother and father conducted themselves with an old-world grace. They maintained an aristocratic distance from their people, and from the press, that was rare in the modern era. At least, they had. Until she had shattered some of that respectability with a very high-profile, undeniable mistake.

She knew her father might have forgiven her for her mistakes, but he'd never forgotten them. *She'd* never forgiven herself for it. And here Rodriguez was talking as though appearances didn't matter?

"Do you honestly think I care about the way the media sees me? The way the people see me? I have done well for them, and while my father has been fading from this world I have already been seeing to the duties of the king. I will continue to do well for them, to make the country prosper. I will marry and I will continue the line. No more can be asked of me."

"Just because you...said so?"

"Yes, just because I said so."

"And you'll adopt Luca."

"I will give him my name, as I said I would. I keep my word, *princesa.*"

"I don't have a great track record with men and their word," she said, regretting the words as soon as she spoke them.

"On this you can trust me, Carlotta," he said, his voice low, sincere, the mocking edge to his lips gone. "I don't play with people. Power is one of those things that can make a man feel invincible. It can make him feel as though he's entitled to harm those he sees as beneath him. I am everything that the press says I am. The stories are all true. So yes, I have some sins to my credit. But I don't hurt people. I don't lie."

Carlotta looked at him, at his dark eyes, and she felt her heart rate speed up. "I believe you."

CHAPTER THREE

"My jeweler will be arriving later."

Carlotta looked up from the drawing Luca had just handed her and nearly choked as she watched Rodriguez walk into the playroom. The staff had spent the afternoon furnishing and arranging everything. Now Luca was fully equipped with a new bed for his room, a small table and chairs, where he was currently sitting, coloring, and a matching, hand-carved toy box for his most prized possessions. Although his favorite stuffed owls held pride of place on a shelf by his bed.

"What jeweler? What for?" she asked, the answer landing about the time the words left her mouth.

"For your ring."

She looked back down at the paper. "Right."

Luca turned in his chair. "Hi."

Rodriguez attempted a smile, his jaw tightening. "Hi, Luca."

"Why do I need to see the jeweler?"

He lifted one dark brow, his focus shifting back to her. "So you can choose the ring."

"Well, I don't see why I really need to choose it."

"Do you have a crown?" Luca asked, his green eyes still fixed on Rodriguez.

Rodriguez looked back at Luca, a flash of discomfort crossing his handsome face. "There is a crown. One that has been in the Anguiano family for a long time. But I don't wear it."

"I would," Luca said, turning back to his drawing.

Rodriguez's brows locked together. "What were you saying?" he asked, his dark eyes not leaving Luca.

"I don't see why I need to choose the ring." Carlotta bent and set the picture down on the table, then straightened. "I mean, it's a ring."

"Your engagement and wedding ring."

"Yes, but it isn't as though…" She looked down at Luca and frowned. "Luca, I'm going to go talk to Rodriguez for a moment."

Luca looked up. "But I'm going to color."

"That's fine, just stay at the table. Color on the paper only. Out here." She stepped out into the corridor and Rodriguez followed, pulling the door mostly closed behind him.

"You don't seem to be distracted by Luca's interjections," he said.

"He's a kid. He does that."

"I would not have been permitted to do that."

She crossed her arms beneath her breasts. "And you don't think he should be allowed to?"

"There is very little from my childhood I would use as a model when raising a son. I don't mind his comments. I'm just not used to it."

"Oh." She relaxed her stance. "I was saying it's not like our marriage has a whole lot of significance. You intend to do as you please. It isn't as though the ring will have any real value to me."

"You'll want it to match your style, *si*?" he asked.

"I suppose but…"

He frowned, his forehead creasing. "Why aren't you pleased?"

"Pleased?"

"You get to look at diamonds and pick your favorite. Women like that."

She shrugged. "I've had a lot of diamonds." Jewelry didn't mean anything. It was money, money could buy a lot of things. Jewels sent to her at birthdays and holidays while her family stayed hundreds of miles away, that didn't do a lot to offer comfort.

"And you do not want…more?"

"Does it bother you?" she asked.

"I thought this would please you," he said, his tone exasperated.

"I didn't say I was displeased, Rodriguez. I just…I didn't know you were going to the trouble of having a jeweler come with a display for me to peruse. I wasn't expecting it. Neither do I require it."

"Let me give you something," he said. The tone in his voice changed, there was something different there, something dark. She didn't truly understand it, but in some ways, she doubted if he did either.

"I'll choose a ring. But you are already giving me something. You're giving Luca your name. It…it means a lot to me. The Santina name has been nothing more than a curse to him in so many ways. Because him bearing my last name marks him. No matter how much I wish it didn't," she whispered the last words, the pain strangling her. Whenever she thought of what she'd done to her son, to his life, with her bad decisions, it made her feel like she was bathing in the shame of it all over again. In the agony.

He deserved a mother who made better choices. Her mother and father deserved a daughter who made better choices. At least in this marriage to Rodriguez, she had a small shot at redemption.

Not just for herself. For Luca. For him, bearing the Anguiano name would erase so much stigma from his life.

In time, people might forget. He might stop being punished for *her* sins.

That alone made the marriage worth it.

"I don't know if my family name will serve him any better," Rodriguez said.

"It will."

Their eyes met and Carlotta felt the impact like a punch to her stomach, making her breath shallow, her entire body tense. There was something about him, something beyond the masculine beauty of his face, the perfectly square jaw, the dark, compelling eyes. He possessed a kind of sexual magnetism. The sort of charm that could make a woman lose her mind, and her clothes, in less time than it would take for him to properly execute a pickup line.

She could feel her body changing. Her breasts getting heavy, her limbs trembling, her stomach tightening, an ache building in her core. All it took was a look. He didn't have to speak, didn't have to move, and her body was ready for him. For his touch.

How did he do it? How did he peel her control away, strip by strip, like a flimsy silk covering? Not even Gabriel had been able to do that. She'd made the decision to cast off propriety and have an affair with him. With Rodriguez…she was trying to ignore it. Trying to hang on, and yet she couldn't.

She backed away, gripping the knob on the playroom door, counting on the reminder that her son was right there to be her lifeline, to be her link to sanity.

"I'd better go check on Luca."

He nodded sharply, his eyes never leaving hers. "I'll send one of my staff up to sit with him in a couple of hours when the jeweler arrives. Is that all right with you?"

She nodded, not trusting her voice. It might come out all breathy and shivery. She certainly felt shivery. She backed into the playroom and closed the door behind her, trying to ignore the steady pounding of her heart.

She knew about men like him. Men with charm. Men who made promises with their eyes. Promises of pleasure that young, naive women might mistake for a promise of love.

But the only real promise in men like him was the promise of heartbreak. She knew that. She had the battle scars on her heart, on her life, to serve as reminders.

Rodriguez was a danger, not simply to her heart, but to her control. She had to keep her control. She couldn't afford to let it go. She would give him an heir, and after the wedding, she would give him her body. But it would only be for that purpose.

It could never be anything more.

"Good night, *figlio mio*." Carlotta leaned forward, the cinched waist of her dress digging into her less than toned stomach, and kissed Luca on the forehead.

"Are you going to sleep too?" he asked, his eyes trained on hers. Luca was always so tuned in to her. She imagined it was because it was just the two of them. She poured everything into him. All of her love, all of her energy. It was the most exhausting, rewarding thing she'd ever done with her life.

And now it was changing. Her sweet, peaceful, somewhat boring life. She didn't want it to change. For a moment she just wanted to freeze time. Keep it here, with Luca. With him so small and trusting that his mother had everything under control. His trust in her helped her believe in herself.

But she couldn't stop time. And her control was slipping fast.

"No," she said, trying to force a smile. "I'm meeting with the prince."

"He has a funny name," Luca said.

"Luca! No, he doesn't." Hard for a five-year-old to say though.

"Is he your boyfriend? Elia from school said her mama has a boyfriend."

"Do you even know what a boyfriend is?" she asked, hoping to put off answering the question, since she wasn't really sure what to say about all of this. Rodriguez was…he was nothing to her and her fiancé at the same time, and there was really no clean way to explain that to a child. *She* didn't really understand it.

"No."

"I told you we were going to be living here. And it's because Rodriguez and I are getting married." She sucked in a sharp breath and cursed the tiny zipper of her dress as it dug into her rib cage. "That means he'll be my husband."

"Will he be my dad?"

The thousand-euro question. And she had no clue how to answer it. It also betrayed that Luca did realize it was just them. And that there should be more. That he should have a father. But his father already had a family, and didn't leave any room for them.

Her heart tightened. "Yes, Luca. If I'm married to him, he'll be your dad."

He was adopting Luca, and no matter how involved he was, legally, he would be Luca's father. And she would not let him hurt her son. There was no amount of atonement worth that.

"Good. Where's Sherbet?"

"Here." She reached up to the shelf above his bed and retrieved one of his ratty stuffed owls, much loved and often washed so that his synthetic fuzz was clumped together. "Now, good night, Luca."

"Night," he mumbled, already drifting off to sleep.

She crept from the room and flicked the light off, and

nearly ran into the solid figure of Rodriguez when she stepped out into the corridor.

"Madre di dio!" she hissed, her hand on her chest over her raging heart. She would pretend, for now, that her physical reaction was due to him startling her and that it had nothing to do with the fact that he was dressed in a perfectly tailored dark suit that clung to every hard muscle on his lean body. Nothing at all to do with those dark, glittering eyes, the chiseled jaw, the wicked mouth, always curved up as though he was laughing at her expense.

Nope. It was because he'd snuck up on her.

"I have a funny name?" he asked, one dark brow raised.

"You were eavesdropping?"

He shrugged, not even a hint of conscience showing. "Funny kid. He's smart."

She felt a smile tug at the corners of her lips. "He is."

"Lorenzo is here with the rings. Come with me." He looped his arm through hers, a polite gesture. One a visiting dignitary might bestow upon her, back at the palace in Santina. But this was different.

Because every time Rodriguez touched her, it was like throwing a match into a can of petrol. It made her want to escape her own body. To climb out of her skin so she could get away from the heat, and the fire. The desire that made her want to turn to him and put her hands on his chest, to feel if it was just as hard and muscular as it looked.

How did he do this? How did he demolish all of her hard-earned control with just a look?

She hadn't been alone with a man who wasn't a relative since before Luca was born. It was making her hormones a touch unpredictable. And a lot overenthusiastic.

That was why. That was her story and she was sticking to it.

She clenched her jaw tight and followed him down the

long, marble-tiled corridor and through double, oak wood doors into a large study. This had a bit of Rodriguez in it. At least, as she imagined him. Large windows that overlooked the turquoise sea and white sand beaches of Santa Christobel. A pale wood desk that had no papers on it, a bright red rug that added punch to the pale color palette.

The desk had a tray on it, lined in black velvet, with at least fifty brilliant rings on display.

"Lorenzo thought we might like some privacy," Rodriguez said, not moving from his position by the doorway. "Go. Look."

Carlotta swallowed and made her way over to the desk. There was a mix of old and new designs, antique mixed with modern. Diamonds in every color, sapphires, rubies.

Carlotta was familiar with fine jewelry. She'd been given her first pair of diamond earrings when she was three. But this…this was different. There was a time when she'd dreamed of a wedding proposal. First from an imaginary suitor, handsome and dashing. And then she'd met the man.

Gabriel. A fitting name. Pale golden hair, beautiful blue eyes. He'd looked like an angel to her. So perfect. He'd made her heart race and her pulse pound, had made her tremble with the desire for things she'd never really wanted before.

When she'd met Gabriel she'd rushed to throw off the restraints she'd let hold her all of her life. Because he had become the one she'd fantasized about getting a ring from.

Until she'd found out another woman already wore his ring. That thought always brought a kind of sharp, rolling nausea that made her shake, made her body prickle with cold sweat. With disgust. Disgust aimed at herself, for all of the sins her passions had encouraged her to commit.

She closed her eyes, curling her hand into a fist for a moment, fighting old memories. She swallowed hard and forced herself to look back down at the rings. This was different, this, at least, was honest. It wasn't love, but she'd never really had love. She'd been used. She'd been discarded. She'd been tricked.

Even still, she wasn't innocent of every wrong that had taken place in that relationship.

At least now she was going in with her eyes wide-open. At least now her heart wasn't at risk.

"I don't even know where to start," she said. The gems blurred together as unexpected tears filled her eyes. Why was she being emotional? Because she was thinking about Gabriel? Thinking of him rarely made her cry anymore. It just made her feel sick.

"Start with what you like best." Rodriguez's voice came from right behind her, close enough that she could feel the heat from his body at her back.

She licked her suddenly dry lips and tried to ignore her racing heart. "Help me choose."

"It's not for me, it's for you."

"I know but…" She extended her hand and touched a ring with a white, square-cut diamond at the center. "I don't know."

"Then we'll have to see which one feels right." He reached from behind her, his arm brushing her waist as he picked up the ring she'd just touched. He took her left hand in his and turned her gently, like a dancer might twirl his partner.

She was face-to-face with him, so close now. He held the ring up and handed it to her. She was grateful he wasn't going to put it on for her. She didn't know what she would do if he kept touching her hand. Melt, probably.

Rodriguez watched Carlotta slide the ring onto her finger, her motions smooth and graceful. She was like that. Always. Smooth and dignified. It was hard to imagine her ruffled, even though he'd seen it. Carlotta had a sanguine surface, but when she was cornered, her inner wildcat came out.

He liked it. Even if he couldn't explain why. He tended to like simple women. Not stupid women, but women who had no baggage. Women who just wanted sex and fun. Parties, a night in his bed. And then he always had a gift sent to them later. Something to remember a good time by. It was uncomplicated.

It was enough, because it had to be.

But nothing about marriage was uncomplicated. Even less so when a child was involved. And much less so still when the woman was Carlotta. She had secrets. She had hidden depths. Passion that simmered just beneath the smooth, controlled surface. A passion she seemed to want to deny.

Normally, he wouldn't care about anything hidden. Give him surface. He could enjoy surface forever. But he would be living with Carlotta. Having children with her. Already there was Luca.

It made him want to know.

Her throat convulsed as she looked down at her hand, at the glittering diamond there. "Not this one."

He shook his head. "No, not that one. It's too…expected."

She laughed. "Well, maybe it is perfect. Because generally speaking, I'm expected."

"Why do you say that?" he asked, scanning the tray, his eyes fixing on a gold, ornate band with a pear-cut emerald set in the center.

"I'm here, aren't I? Marrying you, because my father asked me to. Because it was the right thing to do."

"I find that very unexpected," he said, taking the ring between his thumb and forefinger and pulling it from its satin nest.

"Do you?" she asked, green eyes, so close to the color of the gem, locked with his.

"Yes. I don't know very many people who would drop everything in their life to do what was asked of them. Granted,

I know several people who would drop everything to marry a prince, but I don't get the feeling my title colored your motives."

"I'm already a princess."

"And you don't live at the palace."

She bit her lip. "No."

"See? Unexpected." He offered her the ring and she took it gingerly, sliding it onto her ring finger.

She held her hand out, her focus on the ring now. "Very unexpected."

When she moved, he caught the scent of her. She smelled like clean skin and soap, a smell he wasn't sure he'd ever noticed on a woman before. Either because it was covered by perfume, or because he'd just never taken the time to notice, he wasn't sure.

He captured her hand, her skin soft and smooth. It was impossible for him not to wonder how it would feel for those delicate, feminine fingers to trail over his bare skin. Impossible not to wonder if her lips would be just as soft. On his lips, his body.

Six months. It had been six months, and his libido was really starting to rebel.

But she wasn't just a woman at a club. Someone to have a night of fun with. She was supposed to be his wife. The Queen of Santa Christobel. Clearing his desk so he could press her back onto the hard surface and have his way with her wasn't the kind of treatment she would be expecting. And anyway, it would scatter the jewelry.

Who cares? You'll be a terrible husband and father, but you could give her this.

Sex. He was good at sex. At making women feel good about themselves. And in the process, it made him feel good.

"I like this one," he said, shutting the images out of his mind.

Her eyes clashed with his. "You do?"

"Do you?"

She nodded. "Yes."

"Then you should have it," he said. "And it only seems fitting that I ask you again. Will you marry me?"

"I…"

He moved his thumb over the back of her hand, relishing the silken quality of her skin. He bent his head and pressed his lips to her knuckles, his eyes never leaving hers. He saw her pupils expand, a strange mix of curiosity and desire mingling in there.

"Say yes," he said, his lips brushing against her skin.

"Yes," she whispered.

He lifted his head, his eyes meeting hers. He saw a sheen of tears there. It made his chest feel tight. Had he made her cry? Was he already a source of unhappiness for her?

"Good." He managed to force the word out.

"Rodriguez…" She took a step toward him, her hand outstretched. And he wanted to draw her to him. To offer her some kind of comfort. To tell her things would be okay.

He took a step back, denying the impulse. This was why he was so intent on them leading separate lives. He couldn't fulfill her needs, not the emotional ones. And why he cared, he didn't know.

He didn't understand this, the tightness in his chest mixed with a strange attraction that had been growing in him from the moment he'd seen her. Slow and steady, not hot and instant. But it was there. Smoldering. Constant. And what he was feeling now, it wasn't easy. It wasn't casual. Maybe that was what happened when you asked a woman to marry you.

"See you in the morning."

He turned and walked from the room, ignoring the hurt he'd seen on her face. He'd done the wrong thing. But it wouldn't be the last time. It was better they both get used to it.

CHAPTER FOUR

"THERE will be a formal announcement of our engagement today." Rodriguez walked into the dining area, where she and Luca were having breakfast, looking respectable in his tailored suit, yet somehow managing to look disreputable at the same time.

Or maybe that was just Carlotta's mind, objectifying him. She'd certainly been doing a fair amount of it lately. She'd been absent any sort of sexual thrills for quite a while, and one thing Rodriguez provided, just by walking into a room, was sexual thrill. So, it wasn't entirely her fault.

Anyway, there were scores of tabloid tales, provided by exes, talking about all his prowess. Prowess she would be experiencing soon.

Her face got hot and prickly.

"How formal? Are you sending an aide or…"

"We're having a press conference."

Carlotta set her coffee cup down on its saucer. "A press-conference press conference? With a room full of reporters and flashbulbs and hideously invasive personal questions? That kind of press conference?"

"If there's any other kind I haven't yet been to it."

Luca took another bite of churro and Carlotta winced as he set it down on the white tablecloth, then planted his sticky, sugar-coated hands on the formerly pristine surface. Rodriguez didn't seem to notice. "What's that mean?"

She waited to see if Rodriguez might answer, but he seemed as oblivious to the question as he'd been to the sugary handprints. Or at least he was pretending to be.

"There will be reporters, people who work for the television news and the paper, and they're going to come and ask Rodriguez and me questions. Take our picture."

"Me too?" Luca asked.

Carlotta shook her head. "No. You would be bored. You'd have to sit still."

Luca frowned. "I'll stay and play with Angelina. She said she had movies." His nanny had arrived late the night before and Luca was thrilled to see her.

Angelina hadn't been full-time when they'd lived in Italy, but she'd agreed to drop her other charges and come to Santa Christobel to live in the palace. Because now life was different. Carlotta had responsibilities outside of her son. It was sort of jarring and depressing.

"Good," she said, her response halfhearted now.

"We only have a couple of hours to prepare," Rodriguez said.

"And why didn't you tell me this last night?" she asked.

"It didn't seem…important." The way he said that, the way his tongue caressed the words, his deep voice almost like a physical embrace, it reminded her of everything that had happened last night. And everything that hadn't. Everything she'd wanted to feel, and then been ashamed for later.

She'd wanted him to do more than kiss her hand. Had wanted to feel the slow glide of his tongue sliding over her skin as he made the contact more intimate. Had wanted to feel the hot press of his mouth on her neck, her lips, down again to her breasts…

It was as though part of her, a part she'd ignored and forced down deep inside herself, had reawakened. She really, really didn't want that part to wake up. She'd given in to that wild, reckless bit of herself before. The one that had always wondered what it would be like the slide down banisters and run barefoot on the palace lawn when she was a child. The one who wanted to find out what it was like to have a wild, passionate affair as an adult. Oh, yes, she'd given in to that part of herself once. Only once.

And she'd paid for it. Endlessly.

She loved Luca more than her own life, which made it hard to regret everything. But shaming her family like she had, bringing the paparazzi down on her head. The fact that, whether the other woman knew it or not, Carlotta had taken someone's husband into her bed. And her final moments with the man…the ones she could never erase…she regretted all of that bitterly.

It galled still. Made her feel dirty every time she thought of it, as though there was a permanent film covering her skin. One that never washed clean, no matter how many times she showered. No matter how many times she chose the sensible option instead of the risky one. It was always there. Waiting to betray her.

And now that she was experiencing this uncontrollable… thing around Rodriguez, it was coming back stronger than it had been in years. Along with the reminder of what happened when you chose impulse over propriety.

"Well, it is important. I have to get ready."

His lips twitched. "You look fine."

She put her hand to the back of her head to see if the high, spiky ponytail she'd managed early that morning was still there. "No. I don't," she said, after confirming that she was still, in fact, a disaster.

"All right, maybe you should get ready."

She stood, trying to remember all of the grace and poise

she'd learned living in the palace in Santina. It was sort of laughable when one had the crazy ponytail and gray sweatpants. Even if they were cute gray sweatpants.

She was going to have to get into the mindset of being on show again. All the time. All day, every day. That was royal life, and even though she'd let herself forget it these past five years, it was still there in her.

Along with a few other things she thought she'd left behind.

She looked down at Luca, who had a ring of sugar around his mouth and half a churro and cup of hot chocolate left to eat. "Can you stay with him while I get myself sorted?" she asked.

Rodriguez looked down at Luca, trying to keep his face blank of emotion. A tough thing to do since his chest was tightening with a strange feeling he was reluctant to identify. Fear. He was afraid of a five-year-old boy. Wasn't that a joke.

"Fine," he said, taking a seat a few chairs away from Luca.

"I'll be back in a bit. I'm good at getting ready fast."

Carlotta walked out of the room, and he felt compelled to watch. The way the loose, gray pants hugged her pert butt when she walked was the biggest tease he'd come across in a while. Because she should have looked plain. Boring. And yet, something about her face scrubbed free of makeup, and her hair so obviously unstyled was…eye-catching. He had to look twice. A third time.

And he'd had to watch her walk—sashay, really—from the room like she was in her finest dress and heels, when she was wearing slippers and sweats. Shockingly, he'd found a lot to look at.

"I like these."

Rodriguez turned his head, Luca's little voice as effective as a bucket of cold water in his lap. The arousal that had tightened his gut eased and the tightness in his throat returned.

"Do you?" he asked, assuming Luca meant the churro he was holding up in his little hand.

He nodded. "I like this table too. It's big. I bet you could fit a really big cake on it."

Rodriguez looked at Luca, not sure of what he was supposed to say to that. The boy just kind of…chattered. About cakes and crowns and whatever came to his mind. It didn't make him angry. That kind of thing would have made his father angry. As a result, he hadn't chattered much, and he'd never been around children who did.

He'd never really been around children at all, not even when he was one.

Dios. He was actually sweating. Small beads of cold moisture forming on his brow, his back. Being near Luca made it so easy to remember…

"I like chocolate cake. With sprinkles. It's what I had for my last birthday. And I got Sherbie and Sherbet."

Rodriguez sucked in a breath. "And they are?"

"My owls. They aren't real. They're toys."

"And he thinks *I* have a funny name," he muttered.

"What?"

"Are you going to school this year?" he asked. That seemed safe. And normal. Not something random about stuffed animals.

"I don't know. I was going to, but Mama said that now I might not. I might have school here. Because it's different to live in a castle."

Images of his own childhood, lonely, with no one but adults around him. On a good day, a stern nanny or teacher. And then there were days when there was only his father.

"It can be," he said slowly, his eyes meeting Luca's. "But it can be fun." He wasn't sure if that was true. All of his fun had been away from the castle. Well, that wasn't entirely true.

He'd discovered women here, at a much too early age. They had been a revelation. A way to feel happy.

He frowned. He knew already he didn't want that for Luca. Growing up fast had been a must for him, but the thought of this boy behaving like he had in just ten short years…that didn't settle well with him.

He tried again. "If you want to go to school away from the palace, we can arrange it." Luca nodded and Rodriguez wasn't at all sure he'd understood what he was saying. "I mean, you can stay here for school if you want." He looked over his shoulder and at the door Carlotta had walked out of only a few short moments ago. "Or you could go to a class with friends."

"I think it would be more fun with friends."

"I'm sure it would be." Rodriguez couldn't comment on that for sure either. "We'll talk to Car—your mama."

Luca's nanny, a petite redhead with pale skin and freckles, walked in, a smile on her face. "Good morning, Your Highness," she said, her focus on him, her smile bright. "And good morning to you too, Luca."

Rodriguez stood, hoping the swiftness of the motion didn't betray just how eager he was to get out of the room. "*Buenos dias.* You must be Angelina."

"I am," she said, clasping her hands behind her back. She was cute. In a flashier way than Carlotta, thanks to her fiery red hair and glittering golden eyes. Not so long ago, a week ago, he would have been tempted to make a pass at her.

But now he thought she didn't quite measure up to Carlotta's quiet sophistication. Carlotta was…sleek. Her hair always so neat, except for this morning, her appearance always perfectly pressed. Again, except for this morning. And that added dimension had only made her more interesting. She had layers. He couldn't remember ever caring if a woman had layers before.

Strange.

"Nice to meet you. I have…"

"The press conference," she said, moving to the table and sitting right next to Luca. He should have done that. Not sat with three chairs between them as though the boy were a leper.

"Yes. The press conference." He took one last look at Luca, who had his serious green eyes trained on him. "I'll… I'll see you later, Luca."

Luca brightened, a smile curving his small mouth. "Bye."

Rodriguez turned and walked out of the room, trying to ignore the uncomfortably tight feeling in his chest.

For Carlotta, the press held about as much appeal as a food-borne illness and all the charming symptoms that came with it. They were, in her estimation, beneath contempt. People who preyed on the mistakes and tragedies of others, weaving them into salacious stories for the consumption of a scandal-hungry public.

Walking into a room full of the vultures was about the lowest thing on her to-do list. Still, she was doing it. In style too. With the kind of heels normally reserved for…well, never. She'd gotten out of the habit of wearing high shoes when pregnant with Luca. Then after he was born, carrying him in heels was about as practical as waddling around in heels with a big pregnant belly.

So, her fabulous, sky-high black stilettos had been on hold in the back of her closet for years, and now, paired with a se-date, but cheery, yellow sheath dress, she was looking quite… well, almost sexy, in an understated way. It was a welcome break from her typically sedate appearance. At least, that's what she was telling herself.

She took a deep breath and started down the long corri-dor that led to the room they were holding the conference in.

She was confident. Strong. Sexy—at least, she had been in another life, and was trying it out again. She could do this.

She lengthened her strides and tipped her chin up, the razor-blunt edges of her hair skimming her shoulders. Yes, she could do this. She was strong, sexy and in control.

She rounded the corner and ran into Rodriguez's broad frame, her breasts and tipped-up chin hitting the hard wall of his chest and his neck, respectively.

"Oh, I'm sorry! This is… I'm sorry," she said, fighting the urge to ramble. When had she become so…not a princess? Just clumsy and coming to breakfast in her sweats and… and she couldn't do that now. She was in a palace. She was marrying Rodriguez.

She had to change. Again. Just when things had been getting really comfortable it was all changing again.

Oh, no. Not this, not now. Tears were stinging her eyes, her throat tight and aching. This was not the time for an emotional breakdown.

He put his hands on her shoulders, his dark brown eyes meeting hers, sending a little zing of electricity through her. "It's fine."

She swallowed hard. "I don't…I don't really want to do this."

His brows locked together. "Are you okay?"

"It's just…" She blew out a breath and waved her hand. "Me. And the media. I don't like to be in the news."

He frowned. "Because of Luca?"

"Because of what they did to me when they found out I was pregnant with Luca. Do you have any idea…?" She blinked and looked away. "It was horrible. They followed me everywhere. Crowding me while I ate. I was sick all the time anyway and to have a camera shoved in my face while I was just trying to have a relaxing meal…and there were pictures of me walking with my belly circled, drawing attention to it, along with the flattering headline *Who's the Father?* And when they realized we weren't telling them, they switched to things like *Has Princess Carlotta Put on Too Much Baby Weight?*"

His thumbs moved up and down, from her satin-covered shoulders down to the bare skin of her arms. "I know. It's a necessary evil though. The way I can communicate with my people. They've written…I don't even know what all they've written about me. Things about my exploits. Most probably true, but not something I want to read in black and white. Not something I'd want my maiden aunt to read."

"Do you have a maiden aunt?"

"That was for illustrative purposes. The point is, the press is a part of royal life, of our lives. I employ a 'keeping my enemies closer' strategy with the media."

"And does it work?"

He smiled, that wicked half-smile of his. "I have no idea, I don't read that sort of thing, remember?"

"You mentioned."

He slid one hand down her arm, warm fingertips trailing over her skin before he took her hand in his. "Now, let's go have a press conference."

Her heart started moving to its own rhythm, too fast, too hard, to be normal. Why did he have to be charming? Or, the bigger question, why did it work on her? Why did it make her stomach tighten, her nerve endings sizzle, when she knew how easy this kind of charm came to men like him?

She didn't know why. She only knew it did.

"Okay, I'm ready."

His smile widened, and as it did, she felt something in her chest expand. "Good. Now, try not to run into me on your way in."

CHAPTER FIVE

"Where did he propose?"

This question came from one of the reporters in the front, directed at Carlotta, who seemed stiffer than usual at his side. He'd gotten a glimpse of the depth of her discomfort in the hallway. Visible cracks in that smooth veneer of hers.

"He… In his office," she said.

It was true, even if it was a very unromantic picture to paint for the press. Not that he really cared. The press would take what they said and do whatever they pleased with it. That was how it worked. They didn't get a vote on how they were portrayed in the media. He'd given up caring years ago.

But Carlotta cared. He could see it, in her stance, in the tenseness in her body. She cared a lot.

"You make it sound dull, Carlotta, when we both know it wasn't." He turned to her and brushed his thumb over her cheek gently, fascinated by the stain of pink that spread over her cheeks, beneath her smooth golden skin.

"Of course it wasn't," she said, her voice stronger now. "But I didn't want to give away the entire story. You were so sweet and romantic."

Her comment made his breath rush out on an involuntary chuckle. "All right. Then we won't tell them about the doves." He tossed the crowd of reporters a look. "Boring story. Next question?" With any luck, their little display would have the reporters writing about secret glances and shared jokes.

"Prince Rodriguez, you're the first ruler in the Anguiano family to marry a woman who already has a child. What does that mean for the country? Are you concerned about watering down the line?"

He heard Carlotta suck in a sharp breath and a strong surge of some unidentifiable emotion rose in his chest. It burned. He felt like there was a pool of fire in his chest, and if he gave it free rein it would take over. And if it did…he did not know what he would do.

Teeth clenched, he forced words forward. "Luca is a child, not an incidental. He is off-limits. Next question, and if you cannot keep it on a topic I approve of, we can be finished here."

More questions followed, about the wedding date, how they met. All of which he glossed over with practiced ease.

"I think that's enough for one morning," he said.

"Pictures?" A photographer stood up in back.

Rodriguez nodded his head once in affirmation and drew Carlotta to his side, his arm wrapped around her waist. She felt cold. The fire in his chest kindled again. He leaned in, his lips touching her ear. "Try to smile."

She turned to him, her mouth only a whisper from his, her full lips looking soft and more tempting than he could remember lips ever looking. He wanted to kiss her. And his mind was going no further than that. The need for a simple kiss…he couldn't remember ever wanting that.

But this wasn't the time.

He turned to the photographers and offered a smile. Carlotta did the same, her head angled just perfectly toward him, almost as though she were deferring to him. They made quite a picture. A royal couple who looked better than his parents ever had, for the short amount of time they'd been a couple.

At least in pictures they looked like all Santa Christobel would expect of a ruler and his queen. Maybe these images would blot out the ones they'd looked at for years. Pictures of him with leggy blondes in tight skirts, driving fast cars, leaving notorious nightclubs. And then, one of their favorite sequences, he and a date entering a luxury hotel in the early-morning hours, him leaving a couple of hours later, and his date, dashing out in the daylight hours, wearing the same thing she'd worn the night before.

They loved that one. A look at the scandalous prince. After a while, reading his own exploits had bored him. And sometimes it made him…

He shut his mind on the thoughts. This wasn't the time to reflect on all of that. Standing in the formal reception hall, the state seal behind him, his fiancée at his side, it made it seem like another life.

"Thank you," he said, nodding again and dropping his arm from Carlotta's waist. He moved to exit and she stayed with him, walking closely beside him.

She really was the perfect royal wife. At least in public. That was all that mattered.

As soon as they were outside the room, Carlotta seemed to deflate as she released the breath she'd been holding. "That was…"

"I know. I'm sorry that man mentioned Luca. It was out of line. I won't tolerate it."

"Thank you," she said, her voice muted. "Thank you for standing up for him. I know that you aren't… I know you don't really like kids."

"What? Who said I didn't like kids?"

"He makes you uncomfortable. I can tell."

Rodriguez shifted, a vague feeling of…embarrassment,

something he wasn't sure he could ever remember experiencing, washing through him. "That doesn't mean I don't like children. I have no experience with them."

"You've never dated a woman who had a child?"

Vaguely, he remembered that there had been a woman who'd left the hotel before him once. He was almost certain she said something about needing to get back so her baby-sitter could go home. "I… Not one that ever introduced me to her children."

Carlotta began to walk down the corridor, back to the private palace quarters. He followed, his eyes drifting to the rounded curve of her backside. His body most definitely approved of the view.

"I didn't have any experience with children either. I don't remember if I'd ever held a baby until I held my own. And then, he was so tiny and perfect…I loved him right then. And I knew I didn't need any experience. I just needed to love him." She tossed him a glance over her shoulder. "Of course, I now go through intermittent, crippling bouts of wondering whether or not I'm doing the right thing for him, but, essentially, I trust that just…loving him is enough."

He stopped walking for a moment. "Do you think all mothers feel that when they hold their babies?"

She stopped too, turning to face him. "I…I don't know. It was so strong for me. I know my own mother…she loves us, but she's…she's distant."

"Not as distant as mine, I bet," he said. "I haven't seen her since I was younger than Luca."

"That's… I'm sorry."

He shrugged. "I'm not. I don't do regret."

Carlotta looked at Rodriguez's face. The teasing smile was gone from his lips, but there was no regret in his expression. No longing or sadness. Just blank acceptance. The absence of emotion there was nearly frightening, like she was seeing past the veil, just for a moment, and into the man. That beyond his humor and easy manner there was a deep, dark void, one barely covered by a thin veneer that was in danger of being stripped away at any moment.

It was an insight she wanted to turn away from. An insight she longed to ignore, pretend she'd never seen. But she wasn't sure she could.

"Well, I am," she said. "Even though my mother and father can be difficult sometimes, I do love them."

"Your father basically sold you into marriage, and you call that love?" he asked, a hard note lacing his voice, stripping the velvet off his normally enticing tone.

"Because he needed me. I'm royalty, a different set of responsibilities comes with that. You ought to know all about it."

"And you're doing your penance, right?" He seemed determined to make her angry, and it was working. It was working really, really well. It was easy to forget he'd just stood up for Luca. Easy now to just let all of the goodwill she'd allowed to build up between them slip right through her fingers, while clinging tightly to everything she'd tried so hard to ignore.

The helplessness, the sick, awful feeling that came with being used. The sense that she was little more to anyone than a pawn to be moved around on a chessboard.

And the anger. That was the easiest to latch on to.

"I'm doing the right thing," she hissed. "Maybe I haven't always. But I'm doing it now. Even though it means a lifetime of this." She waved her arm, indicating the palace itself. Including Rodriguez in the sweep. "Because there's more to life than just being happy, or satisfying base urges, or following your passions, whatever they might be at any given time. It's about responsibility."

"Perhaps. Why do you think I'm here? Why do you think I'm even in Santa Christobel and not in my apartment in

Barcelona with a redhead? Responsibility. Don't assume I don't understand. But my sense of duty is not driven by guilt."

"Well, it's easy for you, isn't it? Don't you plan on just going along like Luca and I never happened to you?"

He paused for a moment, a muscle in his jaw jumping. "I did. But you seem pretty determined to make that an impossibility." He advanced on her, his eyes locked with hers. She held her ground, mostly because she didn't want to escape him. Whatever he had in mind, it didn't scare her. It made her body feel tight, even while her muscles seemed to melt into pudding.

"What exactly does that mean? And do you expect an apology?" she asked, crossing her arms beneath her breasts, hoping that bracing herself like that might keep her body from trembling.

"No, princess, not an apology." He stopped, just inches away from her, then he leaned forward, his palm flat on the wall behind her. She expected him to kiss her, to grab her, for his mouth to crash down on hers.

Her heart was trying to climb up her throat and escape, her pulse pounding so hard she felt dizzy, expectation and a huge helping of longing overtaking her senses. But there was no taking. No crashing.

He extended his hand, drew his finger along the line of her jaw, from her chin to just beneath her ear, the move slow and sensual, intoxicating. Then he brought his other fingers into play, sliding down her neck, his touch featherlight as it skimmed her sensitive skin. His hand drifted down, playing over the line of her collarbone, stopping right at the swell of her breast.

Her eyes clashed with his, the dark intensity she saw there drawing the knot of arousal that was building in her to even more extreme levels. Her body felt heavy, a sharp pain building and spreading at the apex of her thighs. What she wanted, and how quickly she had gotten to the point of wanting it, shocked her.

She'd never been a hot and fast girl. She needed time. But those few brushes of his fingers had been equivalent to thirty minutes of good foreplay. She had to make the decision that it was what she wanted. There was no way for her to make a decision now. She was helpless. Completely swept up in the desire she felt for him.

She just wanted him to close the distance between them. To push her roughly against the wall and let her feel the hardness of his body against hers...in hers.

Ultimately, she was the one that moved, the one who angled her head so that her lips could touch his. Heat exploded in her as soon as their mouths met, a hot, reckless urgency overtaking her.

His kiss was hungry, but hers was starving. She needed it like air, with a desperation she hadn't known lived in her. She planted her hands firmly on the back of his neck, fingers lacing through his thick dark hair as she held him captive against her.

He kept one hand flat on the wall, the other on her lower back, his large hand splayed over her, his heat so perfect and wonderful and not enough.

When they parted, it was with a moan of disappointment from her. His breath was coming in short, sharp bursts, and she was really glad to see it. To know he'd been affected too.

"That," he said, his voice rough, "that is what makes you hard to ignore."

Her stomach tightened, this time not with pleasure. She hated this. That he was able to demolish all of her barriers like this. That he brought up the hot, fiery passion in her that she'd fought for so long to ignore.

Hadn't she learned anything? Rodriguez was going to marry her, but he would be just as faithful of a husband as

Gabriel had been to his wife. The only difference was that instead of being the bit on the side, she'd be the one raising his children, keeping the household and family going while he was off pleasing himself.

Was that why Gabriel's wife had stayed? Because Gabriel had her, body and soul, while she had nothing of him but his passing, occasional sexual interest?

And was that what Rodriguez would do to her?

No. It wouldn't happen. She wouldn't let it.

But she feared that with Rodriguez, the choice might not be hers. Because he didn't simply test her willpower. He smashed it into a million pieces. Pieces that were so tiny she feared she might never be able to assemble it again.

"I'll bet you say that to all the girls," she said tightly, turning from him and walking down the corridor. Away from him. Away from the temptation he represented.

And she tried to fight the depression that was creeping over her like fog, drowning out the lingering arousal and leaving in its place the stark realization that time and experience hadn't changed her. She hadn't truly mastered that wild, passionate part of herself. She'd simply managed to hide it for a while. She wasn't in control, and Rodriguez seemed to be out to prove it.

Madre di dio. Things could not get any worse.

"Are you serious? A birthday party?" Carlotta looked at Rodriguez and tried to ignore the slight fluttering that seemed to be taking place everywhere in her body.

She'd managed to steer clear of Rodriguez since the press conference, and since the kiss in the hall. She'd seen him, talked to him, but mostly she'd filled the two weeks since by acclimating Luca to his new home, visiting the local school, making a plan for him to attend in September.

But that didn't stop her from wanting him. From staring

at him every time they happened to have a meal with him. From fantasizing about him in her bed every night. In the shower the next morning.

She blinked and tried to concentrate on what he was saying.

"It's for one of the heads of state, and it's one of the really fun things we get to do as rulers of Santa Christobel. You know, go stand on hard marble floors eating soggy appetizers until our backs hurt."

Carlotta wanted to melt into the settee she was perched on. She already felt spent. Rodriguez had been at the palace all day and avoiding him was starting to feel like a full-time job. She'd taken Luca to the cinema in the morning and then she and Angelina had taken Luca out to the beach for the afternoon. She currently felt grubby, exhausted and more than a little bit grumpy.

"On such short notice?"

He acted so calm around her. It was irritating. After the stupid fight, the passion explosion, the continued fighting.

She closed that line of thought down. She wasn't going to remember that. It had been two weeks. No. She didn't recall any of it. And her lips did not still tingle. Neither did any other part of her.

"Sorry, I only just got the invitation passed to me, but it really is too important to miss."

It was infuriating, and it shouldn't be, that he seemed entirely unaffected by the kiss-she-did-not-remember. Because he should look tense. Or unsatisfied. Or angry. Just…something. Rather than his typical, easy-breezy self. The mocking curve of his lips had returned.

She blew out a breath. "I know this is what it's like. Public appearance after public appearance. And then, after, you go home and go to your separate bedrooms, then get up the next day and start over. It's what my parents have always done. They're professionals at this."

"So you can do it too. I'm certain of that."

"I'm certain I can…I never wanted to. For a while I thought…" She shook her head. "Sorry, I'm sharing…I don't know what got into me."

He sat in the chair across from her. "I have nowhere to be until 8:00 p.m. Share away."

"Why?" she asked, narrowing her eyes.

"Shouldn't I know? I'm going to be your husband."

"It's boring. But fine. I used to think I would get married for love. That my husband and I would have this grand passion that could not possibly be satisfied by separate bedrooms. I used to want…more than the sterile palace life I was raised in."

"And now you've lost that dream?"

She snorted a laugh. "I lost that dream six years ago."

"Because you got pregnant?"

"Because of the man who got me pregnant. I don't like to call him Luca's father. He's never met him, so how can he be a father? But he…I thought he was the one, you know? I was stupid. I know better now. That's just a bunch of romantic nonsense, it's not reality. This, what we're doing, is so much more meaningful."

"Even though you hate it?"

She sighed. "At least there's a reason. There's something more firm than…love. Whatever that's supposed to be."

"I don't know that I've ever met a woman as cynical on the subject of love as I am."

"Well, now you have. We got distracted in the hall earlier," she said, averting her gaze, "but the real reason I'm doing this isn't about penance. It's about doing something that matters. I can't matter while I'm hiding in exile in Italy. I certainly didn't contribute to the greater good when I started a relationship with *him*. There's more to life than passion. Duty, that's real. Marrying to better my country? Your country? There are benefits to that that no one can take away. It's all so much more permanent than some ephemeral notion of love."

"And lust? What are your feelings on lust?" The teasing light in his eyes was gone again, replaced by something dangerous, that intense darkness she'd sensed in him earlier.

"Lust is unnecessary, certainly nothing to overturn one's life for."

"Lust keeps things interesting," he said.

"And what's the point of lusting after a husband who intends on taking other women to his bed?" she asked, her words clipped.

"That's only sex. Sex is cheap, Carlotta."

She laughed. "Sex has always been very expensive for me. But then, I suppose that's how it is for women."

"I suppose so. Are your brothers virgins?"

"What? I would never, not for any amount of money, ask them, but I can give you a very confident no."

"Your other sisters?"

"I don't…I don't think so…well, Sophia's married now and Natalia…the press wrote about one of her affairs, but it all blew over quickly enough." Carlotta's twin had always been the audacious one. The one who did what she pleased. She laughed off her indiscretions, and the world laughed them off with her. Her parents simply ignored her antics.

And Carlotta had been the good one. The one who'd never done anything without the express permission of her parents. She'd envied Natalia. So much it burned sometimes. She felt like she was on the outside of this glowing sphere her twin lived in. One where she could do whatever she wanted and nothing could touch her, while Carlotta ached to break the chains that held her in place, and couldn't.

Then she'd met Gabriel. And she'd followed her lust, purposefully decided not to care what her parents might think. To embrace the rush for the first time instead of just turning away from it.

And the fallout of that decision made Natalia's behavior pale in comparison. The Sole Santina Bastard. That was her claim to fame.

"So no one in your family is a saint. Why is it you're the bad one? Because you got knocked up?"

His words were stark. But honest. She swallowed. "Wow. Charming."

"Honestly, why are you worse than they are? Is it just that no one has physical evidence of their sexual history? The public has plenty of evidence of mine—they think I'm suave, if a bit feckless, but they like me. No one calls me names or degrades me. And I'd bet none of them do it to your brothers."

"You don't understand…"

"It's hypocrisy. Plain and simple. That's why, in our marriage, if I'm not going to be faithful I certainly don't plan on holding you to our vows."

He was missing the real issue. Sure, some of her being "worse" had to do with her carrying visible consequences of something other people did behind closed doors without anyone else being any the wiser. But the biggest part had to do with the fact that Gabriel had been a married man, with a wife. Children. But admitting that was too…it was too hard. To look Rodriguez in the eye and confess that she'd been seduced by a married man? That she'd been so stupid she'd missed the signs? She'd already had to admit it to her father. He was the only one she'd had to explain anything to. And that was enough.

"So you think women have just as many rights as men when it comes to sex?" she asked.

"I think it's a ridiculous double standard. Men want to

have sex with whoever they want while they limit women. Then who are the men going to sleep with?"

"A philosopher," she said dryly.

"Just all for equal rights."

"Wow. Well." She stood from the couch, her insides feeling oddly jittery. "I'm going to go and see if I can find something suitable for tonight."

"It's been taken care of. Come on, I'll show you."

She wished he wouldn't, because she kind of needed a Rodriguez reprieve, but she wasn't about to admit that to him.

"All right, lead on."

She followed him back to her room, her mind going over the conversation they'd had in the study. He didn't look at her any differently for having a child out of wedlock. Her family was so traditional, that she was the only Santina to ever give birth to a bastard had been major news. It had made her mother hardly able to meet her eyes. Had made her father look at her as though she were dirty, something almost beneath contempt at times.

To have someone simply not see that dark mark on her record…that was something she hadn't thought possible.

It had altered her own parents' perception of her so profoundly she'd assumed everyone must look at her and see a big scarlet *A* branded across her chest, even without knowing the full story.

He pushed open the door to her room and stood there, allowing her to enter first. Rodriguez had that smooth, surface chivalry down to a science. It probably made women melt at his feet. If his dark good looks, hot body and wicked grin hadn't already done the job.

"I went out today and I was driving through downtown when I saw this." He took a garment bag out of her closet. "And it made me think of you."

"Did you go through my things?"

"No, I asked one of the household staff to put it in the closet."

"Oh."

"You don't like it when people go through your belongings?"

"Would you?"

"I don't know. I live alone so I don't have that problem." His eyes locked with hers. "I did live alone anyway."

"Now you have us."

"And servants. You can never be truly alone in a castle. Even if all of the staff left there would still be ghosts wandering the old dungeon."

"You have a dungeon here?"

He smiled. "You interested?"

A reluctant laugh pulled up from her stomach. "Not really my thing." She took the garment bag from his hand. "You should be used to staff. You lived here when you were a boy."

"Until I was old enough to go to school. When I was eight I went to boarding school."

"That's so young! I could never send Luca away. Not in three years' time. I don't think I ever could."

He looked at her, his eyes blank, that darkness that lay beneath the surface a palpable force. "I liked school."

"Good." She unzipped the back and her mouth dropped when she saw the black lace dress that was nestled inside. "This is…there's not much to it."

"It will look perfect on you."

"I don't flaunt. I'm a mother."

"You are a woman," he said, his voice firm, insistent. "Don't forget that. Whether you're Luca's mother, my wife or the Queen of Santa Christobel, you are a woman and there's no crime in remembering that."

"I…I know that. I remember. How could I forget?" Of course, for her, being a woman was basically a crime. She didn't know what to do with that part of herself. The part that wanted occasions to dress for. The part that wanted a man in her bed. It was easier to simply be Luca's mother and ignore everything else.

"You dress nicely," Rodriguez said. "But not sexy."

She frowned. "I thought my press conference dress was sexy."

"No, *you* were sexy in it. It would only be considered sexy at a tea party."

She looked him over, at his black pants and shirt, so lovingly fitted to his body, making him look dangerous and attractive. "Well, you dress like you're on the prowl."

"I generally am," he said, offering her a crooked smile. "Now go try the dress on."

She shot him a deadly glare and folded the bag over her arm, heading for the dressing room that was just off the main portion of the bedroom. She got out of her beach clothes and tugged the flimsy dress up over her curves.

She contorted her arm and tugged the zipper midway up her back, unable to finesse it all the way up. She swallowed, her throat suddenly dry. So, she'd ask him for help. He was going to see her naked after the wedding anyway. And this wasn't even naked, this was just a partially exposed back. A bathing suit, even a modest one, would show much more than the dress put on display.

But it wasn't so much about the amount of skin as it was about what Rodriguez made her feel.

Well, she wasn't giving him that power. She owned her body, and she wasn't a slave to errant desires.

She opened the door and poked her head out. "Can you zip me?"

The teasing light in his eyes vanished again, like a candle thrust into the wind. He frightened her when he looked like that. Because he lost that easy manner completely and he became someone—something—else entirely. Dangerous. A predator. And she had the feeling she was the prey.

"Sure," he said, walking to the dressing room door. Her heart pounded in rhythm with his steps and she did her best to ignore it. To ignore the languid heat that seemed to be inside her bones, spreading through her, making her feel weak and shaky.

She turned and braced her hand on the door, anything to disguise the slight trembling in her fingers.

He didn't bother to pretend, even for a moment, that the brush of his skin on hers was accidental, didn't pretend he was simply helping with the last bit of the zipper. His finger trailed up the line of her back, hot and exciting.

She tensed, drawing her shoulders up.

"Relax, *querida*," he said softly, his knuckle brushing against her shoulder.

"Then you're going to have to stop touching me."

She felt his fingers toying with the zip tab, his other hand moving to her waist, his touch light but so…present. She felt it all the way down to her toes and every interesting point in between.

"Not possible if you want me to help you with your dress."

"You're taking liberties," she said, her voice stiff.

"Don't you sound like the maiden in a Regency drama? I quite like it."

"Next you're going to tie me to the railroad tracks…"

"You're mixing your time periods."

She rolled her eyes, then realized he couldn't see her face. "That's beside the point."

"Sorry, but I find it counterintuitive, covering up a woman's skin, I mean."

"You are shameless, Rodriguez."

He put his hands on her arms and turned her, and she

sucked in a sharp breath when she stopped, her face inches from his. "I can be," he said.

"Well, I wish you wouldn't. Be...so shameless."

She looked into his eyes, past the glimmer of humor, to the predator. Her body responded. And it wasn't the flight response she should be having. Maybe she wasn't the prey. Maybe she was a predator too. Maybe her body was on the prowl too. Looking for a mate. She looked down, breaking the visual hold he had on her.

"If you really wish, Carlotta." He moved his hands, reaching behind her and tugging her zipper into place. "I think the dress looks perfect." He took a step back, as though they hadn't just been caught in the most sexually tense moment in the history of sexual tension.

She swallowed hard and turned to face into the dressing room so that she could see herself in the full-length mirror. The dress wasn't really as indecent as she'd imagined—the black lace gave hints of skin, but, thanks to the lining beneath, covered anything that really mattered. It was long, a mermaid-style skirt that flared out past her knees, swishing as she walked.

"It's beautiful," she said, hating to admit he was right. Not enough to give up the dress, but enough.

"I knew it would be."

"A man with much confidence," she said.

"No. How could it be anything but stunning on you?"

She looked at his reflection in the mirror, her eyes meeting his indirectly that way. "Rodriguez, I...I don't need the whole playboy act, okay? I'm marrying you. It's done. You don't need to do this."

She knew, the moment she said the words, that she'd said the wrong thing. His eyes flattened, his mouth thinning into a line.

"If that's what you want," he said, his voice sharp.

"I just... Thank you for the dress."

He nodded and turned, walking out of the dressing room and, judging by the click of the door, her room.

This was why she didn't date. Too messy. And good job, Carlotta, she'd insulted her date right before they were meant to go out. And after he'd given her a beautiful gown.

She wanted to growl in frustration. Instead, she picked up a tube of red lipstick and leaned in closer to the mirror. She was going to chase the sexy look tonight. And maybe, just maybe, she and Rodriguez would manage not to have another fight.

CHAPTER SIX

SEXY didn't begin to describe Carlotta in that black lace gown. It should be illegal. Or they should be alone in one of the expansive bedrooms of the palace, with nothing but free time and an enormous bed at their disposal.

Instead, they were in a crowded ballroom, people everywhere. Normally he enjoyed parties. They were fun, shallow diversions that allowed him to block everything out and focus on nothing but easy, happy things.

Now it was grating his nerves. Because too many people meant he had to behave himself. He wasn't just the rebel prince anymore, he was the future king. He always had been, he knew, but it had all been distant and murky, and he'd been in no hurry to move back into the palace. Back to the source of his darkest moments.

Well, the reprieve was over. Which was how he found himself here, at a party for an octogenarian he'd never met, keeping his hands off of his ultra-desirable fiancée.

"I used to hate these things." Carlotta leaned in, ruby lips brushing his earlobe as she whispered to him. "What's the deal with putting all the food on toothpicks? And honestly, room-temperature shrimp sitting on a tray for five hours?"

He choked a laugh out through his tightened throat. "I can't argue with that."

"I used to hate them," she said. "But now it's been so long since I've been out, I'm finding it really enjoyable."

"What about your brother's engagement party?"

She blinked. "That was…interesting. And stressful. I can kind of see why it made Sophia run off, no offense."

Oh, yes, Sophia. His original intended bride. She never even crossed his mind. It didn't seem right, the thought of another woman standing at his side now.

"None taken," he said, shaking his head when a passing server offered him a shrimp cocktail.

"It was sort of fun watching the Jacksons. They don't care what anyone thinks. It's kind of…refreshing."

"You think?"

She looked at him, green eyes glittering. "I care too much. I've spent so much of my life trying to be who I thought I should be. So yes, it's easy to envy people who clearly haven't got a care in the world about their image."

"Unlike the people here." He surveyed the room, filled with stuffed shirts and black, conservative gowns. "I wonder if any of them have secret lives?"

"Don't we all?" she asked.

"Well, *we* don't. Hard to keep secrets when the press follows you all the time."

"True. Anyway, I like the dress. I'm sorry I fought with you earlier."

"I like the dress too." He'd like it better pooled into a puddle of black lace on his floor, but he would take what he could get.

What was it about her that captivated him? Had he really thought her plain only a few days ago? He hadn't been paying attention, clearly. With her dark hair pulled back into sleek bun, her curves emphasized by the fitted dress, olive skin visible in teasing amounts through the lace and the perfect amount of makeup to highlight her features, she was nothing short of stunning.

"You look beautiful," he said, because that was the kind of thing he said to women. But... he meant it. He always meant it, but usually he was performing a seduction. Words, then touch, then bed. But at the moment, he simply felt it was important for Carlotta to know.

Carlotta didn't want to feel anything when he said that. She knew how men worked. She'd fallen prey to easy lines like that in the past. So she really shouldn't be feeling a rush of heat spreading through her. No flush of pleasure, no rapid heartbeat.

She did though. Because Rodriguez was charming. There was a reason women swooned straight into his bed when he smiled at them. He was hot. And she was celibate.

But she wasn't stupid.

"Thank you," she said tightly.

"You don't like compliments?" he asked.

"I don't like insincere compliments."

"I was sincere."

"I... That's not really what I meant."

A smiling woman whose face looked like it had been frozen into a permanently surprised expression approached them with her shorter, older husband on her arm. She spoke in rapid Spanish to Rodriguez, and Carlotta could only catch half of it.

"Your new fiancée?" she asked, flashing a smile that showed unnaturally white teeth.

"Sì," Carlotta said, accepting the other woman's double-cheek kiss.

"Muy bonita!" she said.

Rodriguez shot her a look. "I did tell you. Though perhaps you will take Señora Ramirez's word for it?"

Carlotta returned his look with a deadly one of her

own before turning her attention back to Señora Ramirez. *"Gracias."*

The *señora* kept talking and Rodriguez translated when Carlotta didn't understand.

"She wants to know when the wedding is," he said, a question in his tone, as if he were wondering the same thing.

"Tell her we're in no hurry." Carlotta looked beyond Rodriguez and felt her heart sink into her stomach.

"I'm in a hurry," he said, his voice hushed, his hand snaking around her waist, palm resting on her hip.

She cleared her throat. "Well, after my brother Alex gets married maybe…"

That set Señora Ramirez off into a flurry of excited chatter, about invitations and gowns and two royal weddings, how exciting! Her husband just stood next to her, his expression blank.

If Carlotta weren't so overwhelmed, she would probably be fighting back laughter over the poor man's plight. Her own parents were so suitably matched. Both so stoic and regal… well, stoic in public at least. She knew what it looked like when her father was angry. Angry beyond words.

Now she was wishing she'd taken the last passing server up on his offer of room-temperature champagne.…

"Ah, *bailar.*" Señor Ramirez spoke for the first time as strains of classical music filled the ballroom.

"I think I am needed now," Señora Ramirez said. "You should dance too." She turned to her husband and the look of pure, undisguised love that passed between them made Carlotta feel like she'd been hit in the chest with a rock.

The way they looked at each other…it told her what she didn't want to believe. That not everyone was cold in their marriage, like her parents. That not everyone lied, like Gabriel. That there was love and happiness.

It would just never belong to her.

You have Luca. That's real love. Permanent love.

"Care to dance, *princesa*?" Rodriguez turned a devastating grin her direction.

No. She really, really didn't. Because it brought back memories of another dance, on another night, and all of her weakness.

"Of course," she said, offering the Ramirezes a smile for good measure.

Rodriguez kept his arm around her waist and they followed the older couple out onto the area in front of the stage that had been kept clear for dancing.

When they were out in the center of it, he pulled her in, clasping her hand in his. "Try not to look so much like you want to chew me out," he said dryly, resting his cheek against hers.

She closed her eyes, sucking in a sharp breath, and just for one moment reveled in the feel of his hard body so close to hers. The light brush of stubble from his face. He was a man. So different from her. His body promised the kind of satisfaction that eluded her when she was by herself, more than a simple climax, but real, hot human touch. His scent would surround her, his heat.

She shivered as he moved in time to the music. Nothing sexy, nothing that should send tremors of arousal through her. It was just a dry, classical piece. But Rodriguez's touch made it seem like more. It made the strains of the cello warm, made the music wind through her body, wrapping around her, as though she were a part of it. One of the instruments. And he was playing her.

She couldn't even bring herself to care, she wanted to embrace it.

This wasn't safe. This wasn't controlled. And she didn't care.

Because tonight she felt like a woman. And he was right,

she had forgotten what that was like. She hadn't seen the point in remembering. It was so much safer to get lost in the world of dinners at home and imaginary games with cuddle toys.

There was nothing safe about being in Rodriguez's embrace. She'd discovered that earlier in the corridor when they'd kissed. When she'd all but attacked him, truth be told.

No, his embrace was danger. Delicious, dark, decadent, probably bad for her, but all the better for it. Part of her wondered what was wrong with her. The other part didn't care. Not now. He was stealing control out of her hands. And she was letting him.

"Feeling warm?" he asked, his voice a whisper, his lips pressed against her earlobe.

"How did you know?"

"Because I am."

"We might…step outside for a moment." *Bad idea, Carlotta. Very bad.*

"Sounds like a plan to me." A dark, glittering fire lit his eyes and she knew that it was the kind of bad idea that she'd had before, and yet, it felt different. She felt different. Not all glowy and wide-eyed, hoping for some kind of emotional revelation.

She just wanted him to touch her. Her only fear was that he wouldn't.

He kept his arm locked around her waist and she led the way through the crowd, to the back of the ballroom and out onto the vast terrace. It was warm outside, ocean mist hanging thick in the heated air.

"The beaches in Santa Christobel are famous. And I don't believe you've been yet," he said, sliding his hand over her waist and to her hand, lacing his fingers through hers.

"It's dark," she said dryly.

"This is where I say something pithy about the moon reflecting off the water. Or where I would say something to that effect if I were toying with you." He tightened his hold on her hand and halted his steps. Carlotta stopped and turned to him, studied his face, his dark eyes glittering in the dim light. "But I'm not. The simple truth is, I have wanted to have you to myself from the moment I saw you in that dress. I'm luring you away from the crowd so I can get you alone."

She sucked in a breath "Are you planning on having your wicked way with me?" She'd meant to tease, but unfortunately her question sounded completely sincere and a little bit breathless.

"Is that what you want?"

"Why don't we go down to the beach and…see the moon."

"Sounds like a line. I should know."

She shot him her deadliest glare, one that would have sent a lesser man running for cover. But there was nothing lesser about Rodriguez. And it was dark, so her look was probably completely wasted. "Rodriguez, this isn't easy for me, can we just walk?"

"And not talk?"

"That would probably be best." She didn't want to think. She wanted…she didn't want to think about what it was she wanted either, because there was nothing smart or good or self-controlled about what she wanted. It didn't really matter if Rodriguez was the man she was supposed to marry. She didn't have any of the feelings she should have for a future husband for him, she just…needed him.

The need was elemental. It wasn't a pursuit of rebellion, it was physical. As necessary as breathing. Terrifying and foreign in its intensity, but far too compelling to walk away from.

"Then follow me." He started walking again and she followed. He led her down a stone path that went from the house and disappeared into the thick, lush sand of the beach. "You might need to lose your shoes," he said, looking down at the glittering high heels she was wearing.

"Right."

He tightened his grip on her while she lifted one foot up and toed the first spiky shoe off, then the other. He picked them up off the sand, the feminine heels out of place in his large, square hands. "I don't want you to lose them," he said.

"Thanks." She didn't really care about the shoes. She couldn't. She felt somehow outside of herself and more connected to her body's physical needs than she'd ever been. Above and also deeply immersed in what was happening to her, to them. She just wanted to block everything out but the feelings that were moving through her. The desire and lust and things she'd ignored for so long. To embrace the heat in her blood instead of trying to suppress it.

For one moment, she just wanted to be a woman. To capture what had been ripped from her life, not just by Gabriel, but by her parents and their disapproval, the media and their cruelty.

She scanned the beach, looking for a place that might afford some privacy.

"This way," he said, drawing her forward, into a cove of palms that stood back from the water. There was a cabana there, linen curtains tied back on thick, wooden posts, blowing in the warm evening breeze.

A large, white mattress was placed in the middle on a wooden frame. It was clearly meant for two, and it was obviously meant for privacy. As private as one could get out in the open.

"Before you go and get angry, I've toured the property before. I haven't sneaked out of parties and brought dates here."

"Not here specifically."

"I never claimed to be a saint."

"Neither did I," she said, climbing the wooden steps that led into the secluded structure. "But I seem to have been trying to do an impression of one for most of my life."

She sat on the edge of the lounge and leaned back slightly, almost shocking herself with her boldness.

He approached the lounger and rested his knee on the thick, white padding, just between her thighs. He didn't touch her, but she could feel his heat, felt a hollow ache starting at her core and working its way into her stomach, making her feel needy and edgy. Nervous too.

He leaned in closer and she leaned back, the move reflexive. She could see a smile curve the corner of his wicked mouth in the dim lighting. He rested his hand next to her hip, brought his face closer to hers and she scooted back a fraction. He chuckled, resting his other palm on the other side of her so that he was over her, his lips so near her she would barely have to move to kiss him.

So she did it. She tilted her head up, bringing her mouth against his, her tongue teasing the seam. He tasted even better than she remembered. Until two weeks ago it had been so long since she'd been kissed, so long since she'd felt beautiful. So long since she'd wanted anything that was just for her.

He returned the kiss, his mouth hot and hungry, his tongue sliding against hers, the friction so sensual she thought it might kill her. She didn't think anything had ever felt so good. Her hands moved to his shoulders and she felt herself falling back slowly, her head resting against one of the throw pillows that had been placed on the lounger.

He put one hand on her leg and pushed the hem of her dress up, allowing her to part her thighs so he could settle between them, the hard ridge of his erection hot even through layers of lace and silk, teasing her sensitized body.

He rocked against her, teasing her with the slight pressure from his arousal, pleasure pouring through her like warm oil. She arched into him, wanting more, wanting him to keep kissing her. Wanting him to touch more of her. Wanting more in general.

"Touch me," she whispered against his lips, moving her hands from his shoulders to the front of his shirt, jerking the knot on his tie, loosening it and pulling it off so she could get to the buttons on his dress shirt.

She worked the buttons quickly, desperate to touch his skin. Desperate for more. She placed her palm flat on his chest, his flesh hot and hard, the hair prickly and masculine beneath her hands.

His chest vibrated with a low, masculine growl as he tore his lips from hers and pressed a line of kisses down her neck, sucking the tender skin where it met with her shoulder. She arched her back, a silent entreaty for him to touch her breasts.

And he knew just what she wanted. He moved his hand around to the back of her dress and with one deft motion he slid the zipper down, loosening the lacy garment so that he could tug the top down, baring her black strapless bra.

"Perfecto," he said, his palm grazing her rib cage, skimming over the tips of her breasts. Not even close to enough.

Her breath hitched, her entire body drawn so tight she thought she was going to explode. She'd never been so turned on, so fast, in her life. But she felt like she was ready to go over the edge at any moment.

He lowered his head, his tongue trailing just beneath the line of her bra, so close to what she wanted and still not enough. "Rodriguez. Please. I need more. I need you to touch me," she said, her words coming out halted, labored.

He reached his hand behind her again and undid the catch on her bra with a swift flick of his fingers. The night air was warm against her bare skin, and she couldn't feel embarrassed. Not even for a moment.

He swore, short and sharp, before lowering his head and drawing one of her nipples into his mouth. She gripped his head, lacing her fingers through his hair, holding him to her.

The heat spreading through Rodriguez was reckless. Dangerous. He enjoyed sex. Always. But it never took him over like this. Usually, the heat of desire was comparable to standing near a fireplace. Warm, something he looked forward to, but not something wild or dangerous. The feeling Carlotta gave him was more like a wildfire, burning hot, raging through him with nothing to contain it.

Her desire wasn't calm, it wasn't polite or restrained. She wanted him, and she wasn't shy about showing it. And he could give her no less. He had no ability to effect the persona of a smooth, experienced lover. Not now. He could only feel.

Her nipple hardened beneath his tongue and her obvious need for him sent a shot of pure, hard lust through him, making his erection jerk with the need to be inside her. His hands shook as he started to slide her dress down her hips. He couldn't remember trembling before sex since he was a sixteen-year-old virgin.

He felt her go stiff beneath him suddenly, her body tight when before she had been pliant in his arms. "Did you hear that?" she whispered, drawing away from him.

"No." His blood was roaring too loudly in his ears for him to hear anything.

"Madre di dio," she cursed, reaching down to the side of the lounger and retrieving her bra, quickly covering her lush breasts with the band of black fabric.

"What's wrong?"

"What's wrong?" she asked, her voice nearly hysterical as she tugged the top of her dress back into place and contorted her body into an odd shape as she reached for the zipper. "Anyone could have walked up here, that's what's wrong!" she hissed.

"Do you need help?" he asked, indicating her struggle with the zipper, his brain still moving slowly.

"Yes," she said, turning, her face angled down. "I thought I heard someone."

"I don't hear anyone."

"That isn't the point."

He tugged the zipper into place and she turned. "What is the point then?" he asked.

"That we could have been caught."

"So what? We're engaged."

"So?" she choked out, her words rising as she stood from the lounger. "So? You clearly have never been the center of a tabloid scandal. Oh, yes, you have, you just don't care! Well, I care!"

"Carlotta, there wasn't anyone out here. And anyway, we're engaged to be married, where's the scandal?"

"Where's the scandal? You can hardly find pictures of royals kissing each other politely, let alone…snogging…in a cabana!"

"We were a little bit past that point."

"Don't," she said, her voice trembling as she bent down and grabbed his tie, tossed it in his direction, "remind me."

"Why are you so angry? Nothing happened. There were no pictures."

"But there could have been!" she said. "And they would have been online and my…my son would have seen them. It's bad enough that Luca will be able to look his family up on the internet, see that they called him the Santina bastard. See the endless speculation about who his father is, the headlines intimating *I* might not know who it is. Should he also see pictures of me half naked on a lounge chair with a man?"

"No, I don't suppose he should but I am the man you're marrying."

"You keep saying that like it matters. It doesn't matter. What matters is that I... How can you understand? You just... can't."

"Try me, Carlotta. Do you think you have the monopoly on whatever it is you're feeling right now?"

"On this? Yes. I'm sure I do. At least when it comes to the two of us."

"I didn't think you were a saint. You're doing a great impression of someone who finds themself to be holier than thou."

"I *want* to be," she said sharply. "I want to be better than this. I need to be." Her voice broke on the last word, the desperation he heard there something he couldn't understand. Something he didn't think he wanted to understand.

"Better than what? People want sex, Carlotta. They need it. It's fundamental. A drive, like eating and sleeping. It's not wrong to want it."

"You say that because you have no idea what it means to face the consequences of it. It's not the same as eating and sleeping. You have to be careful. And I should be in control of myself...of my body. I should have control."

She turned and walked away, her arms crossed over her front like she was cold, holding on to herself tightly. He didn't follow her. She didn't want him to. He knew it. He wanted to. He wanted to find out what her problem was. To figure out why her rejection of him made his stomach feel tight, his body numb. It was more than unquenched desire. More than simple disappointment over not achieving a climax.

He wasn't sure what it was.

He watched her small figure until she made her way back up to the expansive home and slipped back into the ballroom. He hoped she didn't attract attention.

Not for his sake. For hers. Because she hated having her photo taken.

He couldn't remember the last time the needs of someone else seemed so much more important than his own.

CHAPTER SEVEN

CARLOTTA closed the door to Luca's room silently, her heart heavy. With responsibility. Anguish. Guilt. Nothing was ever simple.

She'd made a hasty retreat through the less populated portion of the mansion, and had managed not to run into anyone beyond a few members of staff. A trick she'd learned during her last idiotic affair.

That thought made her feel sick. Why was she still struggling like this? Why, when she knew the kind of pain it could cause, had she let her guard down?

The easy answer was that Rodriguez and her need for him had blindsided her. She liked sex, and yes, she'd missed it periodically over the past six years, but the need for completion had never, ever been like it had been tonight with Rodriguez.

This was just plain scary. Shocking in its intensity. It was taking her over.

She was tempted to go back in Luca's room and curl up with her sleeping son. Use him as a shield against everything Rodriguez had conjured up in her. Yes, he had reminded her that she was a woman, not simply a mother, a caregiver. But someone with needs of her own.

And she wished she hadn't been given that reminder.

She leaned back against Luca's bedroom doors and closed her eyes. And she gave in to the misery that was making her entire body feel too tight. She let one tear slide down her cheek, then another. A sharp, silent sob forced her to suck in a breath.

"*Dios*. Are you okay?"

She turned toward the sound of Rodriguez's voice, wiping away the moisture on her face, hoping he didn't notice that her hands were shaking. "F-fine, I'm fine."

"Luca?"

"Sleeping. I'm just…"

"I didn't hurt you, did I?" He took a step toward her, his dark brows locked together. "I thought…you seemed to want everything…"

"I did," she whispered.

"Did someone hurt you? Did Luca's father…"

She laughed, the sound hollow and watery. Pitiful. "Yes. Of course he did. We aren't together as one big happy family, are we? But he didn't…hurt me…not like you mean."

He looked over his shoulder, down the long corridor, vacant for now, but they both knew that staff were still milling around, even though it was past midnight.

"Come on," he said, touching her hand lightly. "Come talk to me."

She followed him, trying desperately to keep from dissolving into a dribbly mess. Because no one had really wanted to talk to her about what had happened. Not with any real depth or meaning.

Come talk to me.

The way he said it was like he really wanted to hear it. But she wasn't sure she could tell. Not when it seemed to live inside her, a dirty secret that roamed around in her belly like a hungry lion, consuming happiness, her joy in normal things. Reminding her, constantly, that she'd failed. That she could never be worthy of forgiveness.

He pushed open wide, double doors at the end of the corridor. His room, she knew. And yet, even though a couple of days ago she might have accused him of trying to seduce her, she didn't think that tonight.

Anyway, she'd practically led the seducing earlier.

The front section of his chamber was a sitting area, and that seemed neutral enough. She sat in one of the chairs, the one farthest from any of the other chairs, because if they were going to have this discussion, she was keeping her distance. Keeping her control.

Rodriguez didn't sit. He stood, leaning against the mantel, his posture relaxed, arms folded across his broad chest. He'd never put his tie back on and the top few buttons of his shirt were still open.

From her clawing at them like a deranged sex kitten.

Che cavolo.

"I'm sorry," she said tightly.

"Why?"

"The whole thing is…all of this. You were supposed to marry Sophia—"

"I was never particularly attracted to Sophia," he said, his voice rough.

"But Sophia wouldn't have… I guess it doesn't really matter."

"Carlotta, I get that you don't want to be the focus of tabloids and Luca does make things different. I know you're worried about him seeing things that have been written about you when he's old enough to look for them. Honestly, I had never given a thought to what any children of mine might think if they saw the stories written about me. I understand it now. But nothing happened tonight and…"

"Tonight," she said, choosing her words carefully, "proved that I haven't changed. I thought I had control over myself."

"So you said earlier, but I still don't get it. Chasing a little sexual pleasure, I don't see the harm in it."

"You wouldn't. But I know the other side of it, don't I? I know what happens when you let something have control over you." She drew in a shaky breath, her stomach tightening. "Everything seemed so perfect when I met him. I'd never met a man that I really wanted before. But everything he said sounded so nice, and everything he did felt so good. For a girl who had held on to her virginity for as long as I did, I think his seduction time was record breaking. For a few stolen weekends it was great. Gabriel was—is—a political ambassador that my family was working quite closely with at the time. Every time he came to the palace I would sneak out of my room to be with him."

"Carlotta, if you think you're the first girl to be seduced by the kind of man that makes promises but only wants sex, you're wrong. There are a lot of men gifted in saying just the right things, or the wrong things, to get a woman into bed. But that's his sin, not yours."

She laughed. "If that were the whole story, sure. I might believe you. I asked him one night, could we take things public. I was ready. Ready to marry him, or just live with him, whatever he would give me. But I wanted to spend the whole night with him, not sneak back to my room after he was finished with me. And that was when I found out about Kristen. She's Gabriel's wife of fifteen years. They have four children. And when he was away on important business trips, supposedly working, he was sleeping with me." Her voice broke.

"Carlotta…" he said, taking a step toward her.

"Don't. You have to hear the rest. I was…utterly heartbroken. Completely. And that was when I… This is what I can't forgive myself for, Rodriguez. I can't." For a moment, she couldn't speak, her voice buried beneath the pressure in her chest, the shame, the guilt. She was sick with it, heavy. She felt too tired to go on, and yet, she couldn't stop. She had to tell him. Had to let it out.

She swallowed hard. "He…he wanted me again. He wanted to still be with me." Her voice shook but she continued anyway. "He told me he loved me. And I believed him. And that night, I let myself forget about Kristen, just for a few moments. I let him have me one more time. Because I wasn't ready to let him go. Because for one, stupid moment, I believed him when he said we could find a way to make it work."

She choked on the admission, her skin crawling even as she confessed it out loud. "I can't scrub that night off my skin, Rodriguez. Not after six years." A sob assaulted her. "And tonight I proved that I haven't changed."

That was the part that no one knew. Something she'd never been able to speak out loud. The part that made it impossible to let it all go. She had been stupid enough, going into a clandestine, purely sexual affair with a man that she didn't really know. But trying to block out the full horror of reality when she'd heard it from his own lips? When she'd known, known his wife was at home, in their bed alone, and he was with Carlotta.

That was something she hated herself for. That she hadn't been able to stop loving him in that instant. That she had given in when she'd had a chance to turn back.

"The only real consolation of that is, by my dates, I was already pregnant. At least that last time…and it's hard to even talk about because the one thing, the only thing, I don't regret from that affair was Luca. But if I had gotten pregnant from that time, when I knew he was married…that would have been much harder to handle."

Rodriguez didn't speak, he only looked at her, his eyes unreadable, black bottomless pools, in the dim lamplight of the sitting area. He stood frozen and for one, horrible moment she was afraid he was just going to turn around and leave her there.

Then he moved to her, crouching down in front of her, clasping her hands in his.

"That man was a bastard. He took advantage of you, of the fact that you loved him. He cheated both you, and his wife. All of his children. He should carry the shame of this, and I'm willing to bet that he doesn't."

She forced a laugh. "I'm sure he doesn't. I'm sure he doesn't care enough about either of us."

He moved his thumb over the back of her hand. "What happened? After he told you, after the last time you were together?"

He kept holding on to her, offering her strength. She looked down at their hands, joined together in her lap. "I had to find my clothes. I gathered them up, and I went into the bathroom. Then I threw up."

It had been awful, her entire body shaking and then, with Gabriel watching from the bed, she'd had to stumble from the room, be sick right in bathroom, where he could hear. Where he would know just how much pain she was in.

"And then I got dressed, and I walked out. I avoided him the next day and prayed he wouldn't come back again. I started feeling sick soon after that and then I realized…and I had to tell my father. Everything. He made me tell Gabriel. And then he paid Gabriel a lot of money. To never come back. To keep quiet when the media discovered I was pregnant."

She breathed in deeply. "It wasn't like in movies where a woman finds out she's pregnant and it's somehow this wonderful moment. I was horrified. Numb. I had to go to the doctor and get tested for every STD under the sun because clearly our birth control efforts had failed, and there was no telling who else he'd been sleeping with. What he might have given me. And I just sort of existed for the next few months. I didn't want to feel the baby kick. It made it too real. But when Luca was born…that was like the movies. He was just so tiny and vulnerable. And he needed me. But I realized then how much I needed him too. He gave me purpose. He made me want to be better."

"And better is denying you have sexual desire?" he asked, his voice soft.

"That's what it's meant since Gabriel, yes. But it's not just that. It's everything. Things that feel good can be wrong. You have to trust in something more than feelings."

"He was a bastard."

"For cheating on his wife? Don't you plan on cheating on me?"

Rodriguez looked down at Carlotta, at her face, streaked with tears he wasn't even certain she'd noticed. The confession had cost her, and he could well understand why. And now, faced with her question, he felt like he'd been eviscerated by her words.

Yes. He had been planning on carrying on as he'd always done. But he had promised honesty. Surely that changed things? Now though, he didn't feel like it did.

"I promised you honesty," he said, his voice rough.

She nodded. "I know."

"I won't hurt you."

"Rodriguez..."

"I am not the same as he is." He said it to convince himself, and the sad part was, he didn't feel convinced. Not even remotely. He felt like he was deserving of every ounce of scorn he was ready to heap onto the man who had dared play with Carlotta in that way. Who had taken a young woman's fragile emotions and used them so he could find satisfaction in her body.

And for the first time he wondered how he was different than a man like that. Because he had always assumed his behavior was fine. He always parted with his partners on good terms. They had fun, in bed and out, he bought them gifts, he made them feel good about themselves. He'd never considered it wrong, not for a moment.

Now he wondered if he had ever left a woman feeling like that. If he'd truly only used his lovers.

No, he'd never been guilty of quite what Gabriel had. No children, no cheating.

But he had been planning on doing that. To Carlotta. To Luca. It would have been in the tabloids. Luca would be able to see it.

"I won't cheat," he said, the words falling from his lips before he had a chance to think them through.

"What?"

"I will stay faithful to you. If you will do the same for me."

"Forever?"

"Forever. I can't promise any deep, abiding emotion I…I can't." It was the honest truth, a limitation of his that he had accepted long ago. Embraced. "I just don't have that. But I can control my actions, and I never want to put you in the position of being hurt or humiliated again. I will never do to you what Gabriel did to his wife. And I don't want Luca seeing tabloid photos of me out with other women."

He had never believed he had it in him to be a good father. He still didn't. He knew nothing about it. The mere thought of his own father made him feel ill. But he wouldn't flaunt any kind of disrespect for Luca's mother. Wouldn't have Luca seeing evidence of infidelity in their marriage.

If Rodriguez had had a mother he could remember, he would have wanted the same.

And he didn't want to be anything like the man who was Luca's father in genes only.

She looked up at him, her green eyes rimmed in red from crying. "I promise to be faithful to you too."

He felt like they were taking vows now. Like everything spoken between them in this room would be binding.

"I need you to promise something else too," he said.

"What's that?" she asked, her voice a whisper.

"Gabriel's not invited into our bed."

She grimaced. "No problem."

"I don't mean literally, and I don't mean in the sense that I think you might fantasize about him or something. I mean any hang-ups he's left you with. The guilt. You loved him. It didn't just go away when he admitted he'd lied to you. I've never loved anyone, Carlotta. I know it makes people do things they wouldn't normally do. And I just want you."

She drew in a shaking breath. "I don't know if I can, Rodriguez. What I did was…I can't forgive myself for it."

"How long did your affair with him last?"

"Every weekend for about eight weeks."

"And you fell in love with him?"

"I was a twenty-three-year-old virgin. I thought I was in love with him the moment I went to bed with him, the night that I met him. I saw white dresses and diamond rings and forever."

"And if you had known he was married when you met, what would you have done?"

"I never would have let him touch me."

"He waited to tell you until he knew he had you wrapped around his finger. He's the one who should be ashamed. Deeply. He deceived you. He manipulated you."

"I still did the wrong thing," she insisted.

"And I am in no position to throw stones. I've made mistakes. That's another thing I'll never ask of you. I'll never ask you to be perfect, because I know I never will be."

"I think I can do that," she said, her voice trembling, a small laugh escaping.

"I know this isn't what either of us expected, but I think we can make it work." He moved his thumb over her smooth, creamy skin. His body responding to the silken texture, to her scent. Even now, he could remember how it had been to caress the even softer skin of her breasts. A tremor of lust rocked him.

"And you'll always tell the truth?"

"I will," he said.

"What are you thinking right now?"

He gritted his teeth. "I'm thinking about how much I want to continue what we started on the beach. How beautiful your breasts are. How much I want to taste them again."

Her cheeks flushed deep rose, her full lips curving up slightly. "Not exactly what I was expecting."

"But honest," he said.

"I want you too, but…"

"Forget everything right now. What do you want?"

"You," she said. "I want to make love with you. But…"

He leaned in and kissed her. Carlotta closed her eyes and let the touch of Rodriguez's mouth on her wash everything away. The guilt. The hurt. His kiss cleansed her, left her empty, wanting, then filled her again with desire, need.

She'd told him the truth and he still wanted her. Maybe she could do this after all. Want it. Want him.

She'd had her guilt tangled up in desire for so long. Had seen desire as her downfall. Not just sexual desire, but the wild part of herself she was afraid was always beneath the surface. She'd let a part of it out before, but Rodriguez, wanting him, made it flood her. She felt out of control, but in the very best way. What would happen if she gave in? Not on their wedding night, not when it was expected, but now. When it was her choice.

To follow her desire and prove to herself that she could have sex and pleasure, like a normal woman. To prove that she didn't have to spend her whole life being punished for one mistake.

She wanted to believe it. She wanted so much for Rodriguez's words to be true. She wanted to accept forgiveness. So badly she ached with the need of it.

"Yes, Rodriguez, please," she said against his lips. "Please make love with me." A rush of relief flooded her when she spoke the words. Like invisible bonds had broken and she was free. To feel, fully and completely, the need that he inspired in her. To want him as a woman wanted a man without the ghost of her past mistakes haunting her. Without inhibition. Without the cloying, crushing weight of expectation that had been on her all of her life.

She'd never felt anything like this before. She was immersed in sexual desire, in reckless need. There was no thought. No control.

His kiss deepened, intensified, and she returned it, her tongue delving deeply into his mouth, the feeling sending a thrill of pleasure through her, making her body ache for more.

He unzipped her dress quickly and she helped by unhooking her bra and letting it fall to the floor. She was eager to get back where they had been. To take what she'd denied herself earlier.

He didn't disappoint. Rodriguez lowered his head, tracing the valley between her breasts with the tip of his tongue. She shivered at the contact, her nipples tightening along with an answering clenching of the muscles low in her stomach.

His tongue edged nearer to her nipple and she held her breath, waiting for him to give her more. To give her what she wanted. He didn't. And it wasn't because he didn't know. His low, husky chuckle told her he knew exactly what he was doing to her. And that he was doing it on purpose.

"Rodriguez." She panted his name, not caring if she sounded like she was begging. Because she was.

She arched into him, and he honored the request, drawing one tightened bud deep into his mouth, the suction resonating within her, deep and low, making her internal muscles clench tight. He turned his attention to her other breast, and she let her head fall back, reveling in his attention, allowing herself to feel every sensation that was firing through her bloodstream.

He moved his head away and blew lightly on her damp skin, the shock of cold air tightening the bonds of arousal around her body, holding her captive to need.

She gripped the back of his head, her fingers wound tightly in his hair, every muscle in her body tensing, waiting to find out what he would do next. He kissed her, just beneath her breasts, then again lower, tracing a line to her belly button with the tip of his tongue before he gripped the bunched-up sides of her gown and tugged it down her legs.

"Still good, *querida*?" he asked, his voice rough.

"Yes," she breathed. "So good."

"It will only get better." He pulled her panties down her legs and parted them gently, his tongue gliding along her inner thigh.

Her entire body was trembling, nerves and arousal making her stomach churn. He traced the line of her delicate flesh, his tongue delving between her slick folds. A hoarse sound escaped her lips as she gripped his shoulders, trying to keep herself from jumping away from him. Making sure he didn't abandon her.

The sensations, the intensity of them, were almost too much. He continued to pleasure her with long strokes of his tongue and she felt like she was going to shatter and fall into a million pieces all around him.

When he pushed one finger inside her, she did. An explosion of pleasure roared through her, her core pulsing around him as he worked to draw her climax out to impossible heights, impossible lengths.

She felt weak after, spent, but far from finished.

He wrapped his arms around her and drew her down onto

the floor with him, then holding her tightly to his chest, he stood and began to walk into the bedroom area of his chamber. She'd never been carried by anyone, not since she was a child. He made her feel feminine. Cherished.

And it made warm and fuzzy feelings start growing in her. That was bad. She didn't want warm and fuzzy. She wanted hot and lusty. She managed to push past the post-orgasm languor and focus on how much she wanted him. All of him. In her. With her.

He set her on the edge of the bed and quickly stripped off his shirt and went to work on his pants, kicking off his shoes and socks, tugging his underwear down with the slacks and pushing them all to the side.

He was so much hotter than she'd even imagined. His muscles sharp, hard cut and deliciously defined, with just the right amount of dark hair over gorgeous olive skin. And when she looked down past his chest, and his impressive length, her whole body went liquid with desire.

She leaned forward to take her shoes off.

"No," he said. "Leave them."

She straightened and pushed herself backward so that her entire body was on the bed, and, never taking her eyes off his, she leaned back, her high-heel-clad feet flat on the bedspread, her entire body open and bare for him.

It was a little bit frightening, and also liberating, to offer herself to him, to see the stark desire in his handsome face.

"Remind me to drop the maharaja a thank-you note," he said, his words tight.

"Why?" she whispered.

"Because I'm very thankful he ran off with Sophia. If he hadn't, I wouldn't be in this moment. And I don't think I have ever wanted another woman the way I want you."

She shifted and rose up on her knees, coming back over to the edge of the bed. She gripped the hard length of his arousal and squeezed him, watching as his expression changed, as his control slipped.

She leaned in and circled the head of his erection with her tongue and a harsh sound escaped his lips. He pulled away from her, his chest rising and falling heavily. "Not yet," he said. "Not like that."

He leaned over and opened the drawer on his side table, pulling out a condom packet. She took it from his hand and tore it open, rolling it onto him surprisingly fast given how badly her hands were still shaking. From her semi-release, from her continued arousal, from nerves, excitement and just about every other feeling she could think of.

He joined her on the bed and she thought her heart was going to climb up her throat. He was sexy, and big, and amazing, and big, and she hoped everything still worked like it was supposed to.

"Relax," he said, drawing her to him, her naked breasts pressing tightly against his chest, the crisp hair there stimulating her nipples, making her stomach tighten, her internal muscles pulse.

He cupped her bottom with one large hand and lay back, bringing her with him, so that she was halfway on top of him. He kissed her, his touching helping to banish the sudden onslaught of nerves.

She shifted and brought the head of his erection up against the slick entrance of her body. He brought both of his hands to her hips, holding her tightly as she slid down onto his length. She couldn't hold back the sound of satisfaction as he filled her, stretched her.

"Oh, yes," she whispered, rising up again, then down, learning the right rhythm for both of them.

His grip tightened on her, one hand staying firm on her hip, the other moving over her breasts, teasing her nipples as she rode him.

When her orgasm hit, she leaned forward and braced her hand on his shoulder, holding herself still as wave after wave of pleasure washed over her, her breath coming in short, sharp bursts. He wrapped his arms around her and switched their positions, thrusting hard into her as he sought his own release. She moved against him, each one of his thrusts bringing her closer, impossibly, to another climax.

When she reached the edge this time, they went over together, his harsh growl of completion the final component that brought her to the brink.

They lay together, sweat-slicked limbs entwined, the only sound in the room their harsh breathing.

She'd had sex with Rodriguez. Because she'd wanted to. Because she'd wanted him. She had let go. Of everything. Of her control. She had let it all drop and she had simply been Carlotta. Not the woman she was supposed to be. Just the woman she was.

And the world hadn't crumbled. Quite the opposite. Things seemed right for the first time. She didn't feel like she was being suffocated in her own body, crushed beneath the weight, the expectation, that she would be able to be a perfect kind of superwoman.

With Rodriguez, she had simply been herself.

A tear slid down her cheek and landed on his chest. She felt free.

CHAPTER EIGHT

SEX was always good for Rodriguez. It was something he'd used, from a very early age, to escape from the world. To get lost in feelings that were purely good, so that he could block out a recent beating he'd received from his father's hand, or a verbal assault that had flayed him from the inside out.

But sex was never like this. It had never been about giving with no thought to what he might get back. Though Carlotta had given back more than he'd ever experienced before, it hadn't been his primary objective.

It hadn't even entered his mind.

Their bodies had simply worked together. The give and take so perfect and rewarding. He had been lost in her. In the touch of her hands, her taste, her scent. He could have lavished her with attention all night and not been satisfied. Not wholly.

That was another new and unique aspect. This sort of strange, bone-deep fulfillment that made him feel both sated and in need of more.

But not now. Now Carlotta was wrapped around him, her breath deep, warm and moist across his chest.

And he didn't feel trapped, or crowded, or anything he'd thought he might feel sleeping in the same bed with a woman.

He'd never, ever slept with a lover in the pure, literal sense of the word.

He was up and gone after sex. It was just the sort of liaison he conducted, the kind he was comfortable with. And he made sure he pursued women who wanted the same sort of arrangement.

He didn't want anyone in his life, only between the sheets. He'd managed to make it to twenty-nine without ever sharing a bed with a woman for the express purpose of what a bed had been built for.

He liked it. The warm weight of her on his chest, liked stroking his hand over her sleek, dark hair. And really enjoyed taking advantage of running his other hand over her bare curves, her skin silken beneath his fingertips.

Carlotta's body jerked and she pushed herself up partway. "Oh!"

"Are you okay?" he asked.

"Mmm," she whimpered, putting her hand over her face and scrubbing at it for a moment. "What time is it?"

He craned his neck behind them. "Six-thirty." And he hadn't slept at all. He'd simply lain there, dissecting the events of the night, enjoying being with her.

"Oh, no," she said, moving into a sitting position. "Luca will be up in a bit."

"Let Angelina get him."

"He comes in looking for me sometimes," she said, her voice thick from sleep. "I need to go back to my room."

A strange flash of something sharp and hot stabbed him in the gut. Was he jealous of a five-year-old? Impossible. And ridiculous.

Why was he arguing? He didn't need to sleep with her. They'd had sex. And that was what having a woman in his bed was all about. Yes, it had been nice to have her with him, but there was no reason for it to feel *essential* that she stay.

But he sat up with her, unwilling to lie back down if she was getting up. He stood and kicked his clothes, still bunched up by the bed, to the side. Carlotta's eyes were glued to him in the dim light.

"See something you like?" he asked, walking over to his dresser and digging until he produced a soft black T-shirt.

"A lot of something I like," she said softly.

He threw the shirt to her and she caught it. "So you don't have to walk back down the hall in an evening gown," he said.

"Is anyone up?"

"Possibly. But trust me, you in the hall in something you might have slept in is less of a scandal than you roaming around in the previous night's attire."

"Yeah, that's true." She didn't make a move to put it on, she just sat there, holding the soft cotton top over her breasts. He wished she wouldn't cover them up.

He wasn't used to this. This strange kind of tense emotion hanging in the air after sex. Sex was supposed to be a release but he felt…fuller somehow. Satisfied yet…yet in desperate need of more. As though he'd tapped into a hunger he didn't know he possessed, and now that he'd uncovered it, he was almost certain he would never be able to fill it.

He took a deep breath and tried to ease the tight sensation in his chest.

"Are you all right?" he asked, another thing he'd never been compelled to ask after being with a woman. It was all usually clean and focused. It was about the physical, for him and his partner, nothing more.

But Carlotta was going to be his wife. And there was nothing clean and simple about permanent. Or about what she'd told him. About the issues that she had.

Just thinking about that man, Gabriel, was enough to choke him. The bastard had taken something he had no right to. He had stolen Carlotta's love of herself.

"Yeah," she said, not quite meeting his gaze. "I'm good."

"You're beautiful," he said. Always when he said it to her, something he'd said easily to so many other women, it felt different. It felt real and essential. It felt like something he had to tell her. Something he had to make her understand.

"Thank you." She tugged the shirt on, and he watched, savoring every visible inch of her until she was covered.

"You don't really seem like you believe me."

"I'm not sure that it matters."

"Why not?"

"We're sort of stuck with each other, right?"

He frowned. "It matters because it's true. And because I don't feel stuck." That was true. He wasn't sure when that feeling had changed, and why it had changed after his promise to be faithful. If anything, the specter of a lifetime of sleeping with the same woman should be looming over him and taunting him with the hellish reality that such prolonged fidelity would bring.

But it wasn't. And he didn't feel any kind of dawning horror creeping over him. Right now, the only thing the thought of a lifetime of Carlotta in his bed brought was an intense, hard kick of lust.

"You don't?"

"I didn't promise to be faithful to you just to get you into bed. I promised it because I knew it was one I could keep, one I don't mind keeping."

"Hmm," she said, standing from the bed. "It's just a strange way of putting it."

"What do you want me to say? I'm trying to tell you, you're beautiful."

"I know, I just…Rodriguez I don't know what I'm doing. I… Thank you. Thank you for not wanting to cheat on me, and for thinking I'm beautiful."

"That makes it not sound very spectacular."

"It actually is. I wish you understood how much. Because I believe you."

His heart squeezed tight. "I think I understand."

She smiled. "Good. I'm going to go now and make sure Luca's all right."

Carlotta edged out of the bedroom and closed the door gently behind her, trying to ignore the dizzy feeling that was making her feel imbalanced and wobbly. She leaned against the wall and fought the urge to collapse. To cry. To scream, maybe.

She felt scared and excited. Hopeful in a way.

She felt like she had a piece of herself back. Or like she'd found herself for the first time. Like she'd punched a hole in the outer shell she'd built around herself from the time she was a child. Like she was ready to emerge from it fully, completely.

Now all she had to do was remember that the sex might feel good. Great. Amazing. But that didn't mean Rodriguez was going to confess his undying love for her. Just that right now it was good. And she believed him when he said he'd be faithful. To a point.

The one thing she believed, wholly and absolutely, was that he couldn't give love. It was that blank void she kept glimpsing, the bottomless pit of emptiness she could see in his eyes.

And when she thought of him, she needed to remember that, and not simply the way he'd looked at her when she'd told him her secret. With shock, and anger, not at her but directed at Gabriel, and with nothing but compassion and caring for her.

Even Natalia, her wilder half, had looked at her in open-mouthed shock when she'd started to tell her about Gabriel. About his double life. It was why she'd only *started* talking about him, and never finished the whole story.

Not until last night.

She was very glad she'd waited now. Because even if she and Rodriguez would never love each other, they understood each other.

And that was something rare. Nonexistent in her life. Sophia was the closest thing she had to a confidante anymore and, even then, she hadn't ever felt like she could really tell her everything.

But Rodriquez had stripped her bare. And she'd liked it.

A smile curved her lips even as a tear slid down her cheek. Now she just had to remember about the falling in love part and everything might go just fine.

She pushed off from the wall and headed to Luca's room, ignoring the small sliver of pain that lodged itself in her heart.

"Good morning."

Rodriguez walked into the dining room and was treated to a wide smile from a very perky Luca, who was dipping a churro in his hot chocolate, and a very shy smile from Carlotta, her cheeks glowing pink as she lifted her coffee cup to her lips.

"Morning," she said softly.

He wanted to kiss her, but he wasn't sure if he should. He'd never really worried about that. Not for a long time. He'd started flaunting his behavior the moment he'd outgrown his father. Just about daring the old man to try something with him when they were matched for strength.

But right now, it mattered. Because Carlotta was different from other women. Because he didn't want to do something wrong in front of Luca.

What she'd said about him seeing pictures…it weighed on him. His father hadn't been an example for him. His father had been the iron fist, in charge of his kingdom, but even more, ruler of his own household.

Rodriguez had started life desperate to stay in line. He had ended up doing just the opposite. Creating scandal for the sake of it.

But now Luca would see that. As would the child he and Carlotta would eventually have. The heir. It was all a lot heavier than the thoughts he was used to dwelling on.

And it kept him from kissing her.

"Sleep well?" he asked, unable to keep the intimate note from his tone.

"Uh, yeah," she said, looking sideways at Luca.

"I had a bad dream," Luca said, applying the question about sleep to himself, clearly.

Rodriguez hesitated, never quite sure how to talk to him. "You did?"

"Yes. It was about lions."

"Lions?"

"Why…" He looked at Carlotta, who seemed fine letting him handle it. "Why lions?"

"They bite," Luca returned, deadly serious.

"I don't think you have anything to worry about, as far as lions go," he said.

"I did in my dream," Luca said, his expression completely serious.

"Dreams aren't real, Luca," Carlotta said, her tone full of warmth.

Rodriguez liked that she talked to Luca. That she never got angry with him for saying what was on his mind. But it made him remember. Dinners that lasted for hours where he was expected to sit and be the heir. Being the heir meant being an object, a collector's item of interest his father might show dignitaries. Somewhere between his collection of pistols and his prize Andalusians.

He remembered being maybe Luca's age, sitting here, too afraid to move or speak. Sitting in a dining chair at this same table, wearing a tie that felt like it was choking him. Knowing that if he moved or spoke he would be punished severely. Which meant his options were to sit and try to listen. Never fall asleep. He'd done that once and the resulting punishment had been enough to make sure he'd never done it again.

The idea of someone treating Luca that way, of someone making him stand without moving for hours, smacking his shins if he dared try anything…it made his blood burn.

"You don't have to be afraid, Luca," he said, his voice hoarse. "Of lions," he finished, not sure why he'd spoken the words out loud. "There are no lions in Santa Christobel. None anywhere near here, except at the zoo. We can…go to the zoo if you like. And you can see some lions. They'll be behind fences though."

Luca eyed him skeptically, his expression so like Carlotta's it was uncanny. "They won't be able to get out?"

"No," he said, slowly realizing that, whatever he'd had planned today, he was going to the zoo instead.

"Then that sounds good. Are you coming, Mama?"

Carlotta's lips curved into a half-smile and she flicked him a glance. "Of course."

A trip to the zoo with Rodriguez wasn't an average trip to the zoo. It involved having overnight bags packed, and a quick ride on his private jet from Santa Christobel to Barcelona.

Luca was captivated by the zoo from the moment they walked in, and he didn't seem to notice the covert security detail that created a people-free bubble around them while they traversed the paths that wound through the park.

Every section of the park had been landscaped with plants native to the environment of the animals, the enclosures made as minimal as possible, everything man-made blending into the background, as much as possible.

"This is lovely, Rodriguez. Did you come here as a boy?"

she asked, watching Luca's eyes go round with delight as they came to an exhibit with two tawny owls.

"Like Sherbie and Sherbet!" he said, running up to the front of their Plexiglas enclosure.

"Yes, darling," she said, laughing at his enthusiasm.

"I've never been to the zoo before," Rodriguez said, his eyes trained on the owls.

"Never? How is that…?"

He shrugged. "We didn't do things like this when I was a boy. And when I was older…I was more interested in women than owls."

"I see." She watched the back of Luca's head, seeing the sun shine on his glossy, dark hair. She suddenly wanted to pull him to her. To hold him close.

She looked at the man standing next to her. She wanted to hold him too. He should have been taken to the zoo.

"Well, we're here now," she said, moving closer to him, but not touching him.

"There's a woman here too. A beautiful one. So clearly I didn't know what I was talking about," he said, offering her one of his lady-slaying grins. It was the first concession he'd made to any kind of attraction all day. It also rang a bit false.

Not because she doubted his attraction, not possible after last night, but because the easy flirty thing wasn't as easy and flirty today as it was sometimes. Or maybe it really never was that easy and she just knew him better now.

"I like those owls!" Luca said, turning and treating them both to a big smile.

Rodriguez let out a short laugh at that and it made a warm spot start in Carlotta's heart and spread outward. That wasn't a sexual feeling either. It was decidedly fuzzy, and directed at Rodriguez. That wasn't good.

She cleared her throat. "Ready to go see something else, Luca?"

Luca frowned. "The lions, I guess."

"You guess?" she asked.

He took a deep breath, his small shoulders rising dramatically. "I'm ready." He looked up at Rodriguez and stuck out his hand.

Rodriguez looked down at the small, outstretched hand and he felt something akin to panic well up in him. He swallowed hard, and looked into earnest green eyes, then up into Carlotta's matching green eyes. And he couldn't hurt either of them by denying Luca's nonverbal request.

He reached out and wrapped his hand around Luca's tiny fingers. He felt small. Fragile. And it reminded him, so vividly, what it was like to be that size. So powerless. And yet, for the first time, it also made him understand what it was to truly want to protect someone.

"Do you have the map, Carlotta?" he asked, his throat tight.

"Yes. For lions, we keep going straight."

"All right then." He tightened his grip on Luca's hand and walked down the cobblestone trail, Luca's legs having to take two steps to his one. He slowed down to try and match the boy's pace and Carlotta moved next to Luca, taking his other hand in hers.

It was a scene of domesticity he'd never quite imagined being a part of. Not as a child, not as…whatever he was to Luca. A stepfather, or at least future stepfather. Strange to think of himself that way. Strange to have Luca cling to him as though Rodriguez was going to offer him protection.

He looked over Luca's head at Carlotta. She could have made Luca the sort of child who didn't trust people. She had ample reason to. But it was clear that Luca simply accepted that anyone his mother deemed all right was trustworthy.

Already, Luca accepted that he was safe with him and that

was… It was humbling in a way he had not anticipated. And still created that bit of panic in him.

"There they are," he said, pointing to the enclosure. There were four lions lounging by the tall fence, and he felt Luca shrink by his side, his little body tense. "We can go if you like," he said. "We don't have to stay." Because more than anything, he didn't want to lose Luca's trust.

When he thought of what his own father would have done in this situation, it made his entire body want to recoil. "I'll look at them," Luca said, his grip tightening on Rodriguez's hand. He stood stiff next to Rodriguez, his eyes fixed on the lions.

"They aren't bad, Luca. See?" he said.

The large golden creatures were lethargic in the midday heat, stretched out by the fence, ears twitching. They didn't seem to notice, or care, that they were being watched.

Gradually, Luca relaxed, but he never released his hold on Rodriguez. "We can go now," Luca said.

Rodriguez laughed and looked at Carlotta. "I'm sure that's fine."

The smile Carlotta gave him was something new too. There was trust there. A different kind than the kind she'd shown him last night. Something that seemed even bigger.

"Lead the way, Luca," Carlotta said, still holding her son's hand.

Luca didn't release his hold on Rodriguez, so he continued on with them, letting Luca cling to him like he was a lifeline, and wondering what the little boy would think if he knew what kind of man Rodriguez really was.

"He's completely exhausted," Carlotta said, closing the door to the bedroom she'd installed Luca in. He had been placed, strategically, on the opposite end of the penthouse to this room, and the room Carlotta had installed herself in.

Angelina's room was next to Luca's, and she was ready to take care of him during the night. He hoped that would entice Carlotta to come to his bed. And stay in it all night.

Angelina had spent the day in Barcelona and had returned late, arms full of shopping bags, ready to stay at the penthouse with Luca, so he could take Carlotta out for the evening.

"I'm not surprised he's tired. I can't even guess how much ground we covered today."

"We kept having to run back and see the lions," she said, a smile curving her full lips. He hadn't touched her all day, hadn't thought he should with Luca there. Now he was aching with the need to pull her into his arms.

To feel her soft, naked body against his.

She'd made him wait two weeks after the explosive kiss in the hall to finally satisfy his desire for her. He'd never waited for a woman before. They'd been interchangeable. Carlotta was not. Carlotta felt necessary.

And after having her once, he only needed her more.

Rodriguez forced a laugh through his constricted throat. "Here's hoping we don't have a nightmare relapse as a result."

"I doubt it. He'll be sleeping too soundly. I love the penthouse, by the way," she said, indicating the glossy, wide-open space around them.

"Thank you. I haven't had a chance to come here in a while. But I moved to Barcelona when I was seventeen. Not here. This is new."

"Gorgeous," she said, walking over to one of the large picture windows and looking out at the city below, lit up and in motion.

"Would you like to go out?" he asked.

"What else haven't you done, Rodriguez?"

He crossed from where he was standing and took her

hand in his, leaning in and pressing a soft kiss to her lips. "I haven't done that yet today. It's a shame."

She let out a long breath. "It really is a shame. I'm glad you've rectified it."

"Me too."

"What else haven't you done? No zoo. Anything else?"

She was so sincere, so sweet. He could sense a caring behind her question that he wasn't certain he'd ever experienced before. It made him uncomfortable. To have her caring for him. Feeling for him.

He moved near her, touching her face, trying to shift the focus back to the physical. "What about you, Carlotta Santina? What haven't you done?"

Her green eyes glittered in the dim light, nothing shy or restrained in her expression. "There are quite a few things I've never done. I've never just wandered around a city. Never just done something for the pure enjoyment of it. Without a real goal beyond simply living."

"I haven't either. Maybe we could share a first?"

"I like that idea very much."

The night air was warm and heavy, the streets of the city teeming with activity. Nightlife in the city was amazing, and Rodriguez had more than taken advantage of his share of it in the past. But this was different. Innocent in a way, and yet, nothing with Carlotta could truly be innocent. Not when his thoughts drifted to the sex every time he looked at her gorgeous curves.

He'd walked through Las Ramblas during the day, but he'd never lingered on the street at night. He was too busy hitting clubs and picking up women back in his college days to do anything as mundane as visiting an open-air market, or enjoying watching street performers.

Nothing about it seemed mundane tonight. Not with

Carlotta, wide-eyed and grinning at his side. They blended in here, not royal, not anything but one of the crowd of hundreds milling around in the wide-open boulevard.

Music from the surrounding restaurants and clubs bled out onto the street, mixing, but not blending, adding to the chaotic atmosphere.

"This is amazing," Carlotta said. "A definite first for me."

"Me too."

She leaned into him, her hand slipping easily into his, her cheek pressed against his shoulder. He leaned down and kissed the top of her head, the action natural, casual in a way he'd never been with a woman before. But he found he liked it. Liked it a lot.

"Oh, Rodriguez, let's go look at the dancer!"

She tugged on his hand and led him through the crowd toward the sound of a guitar rising above the thumping techno music echoing from the clubs.

There was a woman, standing in a clear spot on the cobblestones, a man to her left playing the guitar. She was dancing, high heels stomping hard on the ground, her red dress flaring up to the top of her thighs.

"She's beautiful," Carlotta said, a wistful note in her voice.

"Not more beautiful than you are." It was the truth, and it was usually what a woman wanted to hear when she said something like that.

"No she's…it's different. She's so…free. Everything is so…open and out there. Her passion for life."

"I have tasted your passion, Carlotta." He leaned in and kissed her temple. "You are like living fire in my arms. You don't have to hide anything from me."

She looked at him, her eyes bright. "I can't. You take my control from me."

"It's mutual."

"I'm glad."

"Passion is beautiful," he said, looking at the dancer again. "Your passion is beautiful." He turned his attention back to Carlotta. "It is a shame you were ever made to feel differently."

She smiled at him and he felt it down deep, like a punch in the gut. "I'm learning to see things a bit differently."

Dios. Her smile. He felt strange now. Lighter and heavier at the same time. He wasn't sure how she accomplished things like that. "Do you want dinner?"

"Dinner would be lovely."

He ordered them both beer and tapas and set the baskets on an outdoor table. They were surrounded by street performers dressed as trees, every so often a tree would bend in a different direction. It made everything seem surreal. Not quite of the world he knew. It fit nicely with the things Carlotta was making him feel. "Very good," she said, taking a bite of salted cod.

"What do you think of your first real out-on-the-town experience?"

"Amazing. And what did you think of your first trip to the zoo?"

"I enjoyed it. Even more because of how Luca seemed to get so much out of everything. Especially the lions."

"He's had nightmares about them on and off, don't ask me why, because I'm not really sure. I don't think I ever could have talked him into seeing them in person."

"You think I did?"

"He's different around you. He seems...confident. It's cute."

"I was trying to think what my father might have done if I was afraid of lions," Rodriguez said, not sure why he'd spoken the words out loud. He cleared his throat. "He wouldn't have thrown me in the cage, obviously, since I'm the heir. But...he believed in making me a man."

Carlotta frowned, her well-groomed brows pulled together. "He wouldn't have scared you...."

"Sure he would have. If he thought it would make me into the kind of man who could lead Santa Christobel as he sees fit. As it is, I'm sure he will be disappointed. Well, no, he won't. Because he won't be alive to see it," he said, trying to keep his tone light. Dismissive.

Carlotta studied his face, her heart feeling too large for her chest. After last night she couldn't deny feeling nothing for him. It wasn't just the sex, it was everything. The fact that he'd listened. The fact that she'd even wanted to tell him.

Then today, with Luca. She was right, Luca did scare him, even if she didn't fully understand why. But the way he was with him, the way he tried, that touched her. He might be a natural charmer with women, but he wasn't with children.

Even so, that panic, the way he talked about his father, it all made her feel slightly sick. She didn't really want to ask more. And yet she felt like she had to. Because...she'd told him everything. She wanted to know who he was.

"You seem to know about everything fun in Barcelona. Tell me about it," she said, deciding it was probably a neutral enough topic.

"About what?"

"You. Your penthouse. Why you moved here when you were seventeen."

"Teenagers always want to get away, right?"

"I didn't. I was really good. Until I turned twenty-three. But Natalia was more like that."

"She's your twin?"

"Yes. But we aren't really alike at all. We aren't really very close anymore either. I blamed her for a while but, to be honest, I think I did my share of distancing. I mean, I talk to everyone, but when you're hiding something how close can you really be? I feel like I've been guarding my secret and licking my wounds for the past six years. Hard to maintain meaningful relationships when you're that busy…hiding."

"I imagine. I don't maintain any, so it's never been a problem."

"Oh. So, you didn't make a lot of friends here?"

"I did. I went to college here. Had a lot of friends. Lots of girlfriends. I was able to feel normal for a while. I had a lot of fun here."

"I take it you didn't have fun in Santa Christobel."

He frowned. "I don't feel at home there."

"This place reminds me more of you," she said. Barcelona was alive. Casual and fun. It lacked the pomp and circumstance of his home country.

"I don't feel at home here either," he said. "Don't look at me like that."

"Like what?" She took another bite of her fish.

"Like I'm a wounded puppy. I have never been concerned with concepts of home and family. I have nothing to complain about. I had food. I had shelter. Plenty of people don't have that."

"That's not all people need."

"Sure it is. I came to Barcelona for fun. To get away from my father. Common story," he said. He made it sound light. Casual. He was very good at that. But she knew it wasn't. Because it was there again, that horrible bleakness in his eyes.

He was so good at being charming. At bringing everything back to surface. He had charisma and the power to pretend in a way she could never hope to match. But he was pretending.

She looked down at the basket of food in front of her. "My father expected a lot from me. I don't think either of my parents expected anything from Natalia past a certain point. They just sort of rolled their eyes at her antics. And in some ways, that put more on me. I envied her, a lot. I think it may have been when I really started feeling distant from her. My father especially wanted me to be perfect. Like I was the redemption for the pair of us. When I got pregnant…I'd never seen him like that before. He was so…so angry with me. So disappointed. It hurt more than losing what I'd imagined I had with Gabriel."

"This is the part where I share?" he asked, dark eyebrow lifted.

"I thought you might."

"My father didn't know what to do with a child. He was alone with me. He made mistakes."

"That's all?"

"That's all."

"I don't believe you."

"It's not a big deal, Carlotta," he said, his teeth gritted, his hand drawn into a fist. He unfolded it, flexed his fingers out straight. "He felt that I needed to represent the country. I was his heir. His only child. When my mother left, it became very apparent I would be the only son. That made things more…important."

His tone was even, his expression flat. And the ice in his eyes chilled her through to her bones.

"What did he do to you?" she asked, setting her fork down on the table. "What did he do, Rodriguez?"

He kept his focus on his hand, opening and closing it. "I had to learn to sit still. To be silent, unless I was spoken to."

"Well, you know Luca. How can you possibly…?" She stopped short, the words sticking in her throat. "How?"

He swallowed, his Adam's apple moving, his jaw clenched tight. "It took training." His voice was soft, even, but there was something dark in his tone. "My father had Andalusians. Spirited horses. But he managed to break them. He never hesitated to order that the whip be used." He looked up from his hand, dark eyes locked with hers. "Luckily, he didn't manage to break me. But I did learn when to keep still."

"Rodriguez…he didn't…"

"He didn't use the horsewhip on me, *dios*, no. He had a metal rod that he would slap across my shins when I got too restless. It left bruises, but it didn't damage anything." His words, spoken so casually, as though he were reading from a book. Telling the story of someone else's life. He seemed utterly removed from it. Determined to stay that way.

"He didn't damage anything physically," she said quietly.

"Like I said, Carlotta, we all have our issues. I never went hungry. I never slept out in the cold."

Anger flooded her, filled her, for him, for the child he'd been. For the man he was. "You dismiss it like that, but what if someone were doing that to Luca?"

The glint in Rodriguez's eyes turned to ice. "It would be the last thing he ever did." He stood from the table. "We should go. We will be flying back to Santa Christobel early."

"Oh…I…"

He leaned over and picked up her basket, still full of food. "I have lost my appetite."

Carlotta watched Rodriguez close himself off from her, and she felt her heart splinter in her chest, shards of her soul cracking. He walked ahead of her, and she felt like he was taking some of the broken pieces with him. She felt like she'd found a piece of herself, and lost it all at once.

She walked quickly, closing the gap between them. He looked on ahead, not touching her, not acknowledging her. As though he had shut off a switch inside himself. If only she could do the same. She ached, inside and out, for Rodriguez. For what he'd been through. And he was pretending it didn't matter.

But it was what he did. She could see that. See it and un-derstand it in a way. Because she'd lived that way to a certain extent. What was the point of bleeding for everyone to see when no one could staunch the flow? So much easier to keep the pain inside. To nurture it, as she did. Or to pretend it wasn't there, like Rodriguez did.

And both of them had been doing it alone for so long, neither of them seemed to know how to bring another person into the mix without upending their perfect order.

That was why he'd walked away. He was trying to hang on to the facade he'd created.

Now she had to decide if she was going to let him.

CHAPTER NINE

BACK at the penthouse, Rodriguez headed straight for his room, closing the door behind him. He needed to think. Needed to process. Needed to figure out why he'd shared all of that with Carlotta. It didn't matter. It didn't.

"Rodriguez?"

He turned at the sound of Carlotta's soft, sweet voice. She was standing in the doorway, one hand clutching the frame as though she were keeping herself from turning and running. No, he couldn't actually imagine that. Carlotta didn't run.

He finished shrugging his shirt off and let it fall to the floor. "What?" She just stared at him, green eyes filled with sadness. Pity. For him? For the boy he'd been? He didn't want that.

"Don't look at me like that," he said, more roughly than he'd intended.

"Like what?"

"Like you want to put a Band-Aid on it and make it better. I'm not crying over it, Carlotta. Neither should you."

"I'm not crying," she said, her voice breaking on the last word.

He huffed out a laugh. "My father…he was a terrible father. I don't know what I can offer to Luca, but I know I won't be abusive. I understand that what happened to me wasn't right. But I'm not dwelling."

"You don't think it affects you at all?"

He shrugged, even as a slug of pain hit him in the chest. "No. It was all a long time ago. I moved away when I was a teenager, but even before that, my father hadn't raised his hand to me in years."

He ignored how exposed he felt and worked his belt free of the buckle, tugging it off and throwing it down with his shirt. He wasn't going to do a "sharing your feelings and hug" thing, it wasn't in him.

He moved forward, he didn't worry about what had happened in the past. And until Luca had showed up with his mother, he'd hardly given it a thought in years.

"We all carry the past with us," she said quietly.

"And what doesn't kill us makes us stronger." He moved to where she was standing and touched her bare arm, her skin shockingly smooth beneath his hand. "I don't need psychoanalyzing."

"No?"

He shook his head. "I would take a kiss though." He dug deep in himself and searched for that part of him he'd been clinging to for more than ten years. Tried to find the man who flirted, who knew how to keep everything light and superficial.

But Carlotta didn't respond, at least not in the way he was used to. She didn't giggle, or look away coquettishly. She stared at him, her eyes locked with his, serious, intense.

She put her hands on his face, her fingers stroking the back of his neck. When her lips touched his, it wasn't soft, or tentative. She claimed him, her mouth hard on his, her tongue teasing the seam of his lips, demanding entry. A command he couldn't deny.

He met her kiss, met and matched each thrust of her tongue, wrapped his arm around her waist and pulled her into the room, against his body.

He gripped the door with his other hand and closed it firmly before pressing her against it. She arched into him, full, gorgeous breasts pressed tightly against his chest. This wasn't quite the harmless flirtation he'd been looking for.

This was dark. Intense. Something both of them seemed unable to fight. If either of them cared to. At the moment, he certainly didn't.

She moved her hands over his chest, his back, his buttocks, the touch teasing and tormenting him. He rocked against her, right where he knew she wanted him, for her, for him. To ease some of the building, blinding pressure that was threatening to make him come from the pleasure of a simple kiss.

A kiss hadn't excited him so much since he was a teenager. And for some reason, he felt like one now. Felt like he was on the edge of exploding if he didn't have her now. Hot and hard, against the door.

But along with that feeling came the overwhelming need to deny his own pleasure. Something that was even more foreign.

He was a considerate lover, and his partners always left well pleasured, but their satisfaction was never his primary concern. His own was. That was why he engaged in casual affairs. Because they each took responsibility for themselves, for their needs, the things that turned them on, they pursued their own pleasures, using the other person as an aid to that.

He did it. The women he slept with did the same.

But it wasn't what he wanted now. He wanted to give her pleasure. He wanted to watch her face. He could remember how she'd looked last night when they were together, how she looked when she was completely lost in pleasure.

Just the thought made his erection pulse.

He gritted his teeth and pulled away from her, his body protesting. "It'll be over too fast if we keep going like this."

"I'm fine with fast," she said, her hands on his chest. "I

never have been before. It's never been like this. With you…
all it takes is a look and I'm so close."

"Me too," he said. Not something he'd normally admit.
But it was pointless to deny it when his entire body was
trembling with need that was poised on the brink of becoming satisfaction. But it wouldn't be true satisfaction. Not the
kind he needed, not the kind he craved. The kind that would
only come from bringing her with him.

She pushed the strap of her summer dress down, pulling
one arm through, then the other, so the dress was simply
hanging from her curves. So easy to tug it down, to reveal
her amazing body to his gaze.

He clenched his hands into fists and kept them glued to
his sides. Determined to watch. To let her control the pace.
For now.

She let the dress fall, her curves covered only by a whisper-
thin, lacy bra and panty set. The kind that seemed designed
to frame and accentuate a woman's body, rather than con-
ceal anything.

"I didn't think…after what happened tonight…I didn't
think you'd want this. Want me," she said.

"Oh, I want you," he said, swallowing hard. He extended
his hand, tensed his muscles to try and disguise the trembling
there, and touched the lace edge of her bra, trailing his finger along the line where fine fabric met silken flesh. "Make
no mistake, I want you."

That same sort of heaviness hung in the air, the same
kind he'd felt last night. But rather than turning from it, he
let it drive him. Feeding the hunger that was growing inside
of him until it was a yawning chasm of need that he wasn't
certain he could ever satisfy.

He lowered his head, tracing the path his finger had just
followed with the tip of his tongue. Carlotta shuddered beneath his touch and he felt her deep, intense response reso-

nate within him. Her pleasure becoming his own. Her desire filling him, making his body tight and hard with lust.

"Your body is so amazing. So perfect."

She laughed, a tight, strained sound. "It doesn't look like it used to. Childbirth does that to you."

He lowered himself onto his knees and pressed a kiss to her stomach. It wasn't perfectly tight and flat, it was soft, slightly rounded. So feminine and sexy. "Like I said, it is perfection."

She put her hand on his bicep, fingers moving over the ridges of muscle. "You aren't so bad yourself." She laughed. "Understatement. In fact, I think I'd like to see some more." She put her finger beneath his chin and pushed up. He stood, the pressure not enough to force his movements in any way, but he responded as though it did. "Take off your clothes," she said, her eyes locked on his.

"Are you always like this?"

She shook her head. "Never. But you make me feel different."

She made him feel different too. But he was damned if he'd admit. Not when he could hardly understand it, or even put words to it.

"I like it," he said. Instead of the other things he could have said. Because he did like it. And it was the simplest truth he had.

"Good."

He shrugged his pants and underwear down and stood in front of her. He'd never thought that much about being naked in front of a woman, but he'd felt exposed since their conversation at dinner. And now, he felt like she was looking inside him. As if she could truly see him.

She moved to him, her fingers sliding over his abs and down to his rock-hard erection. He put his hand over hers, halting her movements. "Carlotta, I'm too close," he gritted.

"I'm okay with that," she said, squeezing him.

She leaned in and kissed his neck, her tongue hot and slick against his skin. Everything felt heightened, his blood running hot and fast just beneath the surface of his skin.

"I'm not. I need…"

She continued down, her hand caressing him, her lips and tongue on his chest, his stomach. Then she braced her hands on his thighs, holding him tight as she flicked the tip of her tongue against the head of his arousal.

He sifted his fingers through her hair with the intent of pulling her back, but he couldn't. He could only hold on to her, keep his knees from buckling as she took the length of him into her mouth.

His muscles shook beneath her sensual assault, her hand working in time with her mouth. Fire built in him, low and liquid, spreading through him, bringing him to the brink. Then she would pause, squeeze him hard, and it would ebb, keep it at bay. Somehow she knew just when to pause, knew how to give him just enough to time. Knew how to bring him to the edge without letting him go over.

It was torture. Beautiful, decadent torture. And he couldn't remember ever being so turned on in his life.

Carlotta moaned, deep and low, the sound moving through his body, adding to the sensation. He tightened his grip on her hair and earned another throaty sound from Carlotta.

"Enough," he said tightly.

She raised her head, a satisfied smile curving her lips. She stood, wrapping her arms around his neck, looking him in the eye. He took the chance to unhook her bra and slide her panties down her legs, reveling in the feeling of soft, bare skin against his.

She moved to the bed, stretching out before him across the dark comforter, her smile wicked. A temptation. His pulse was pounding, in time with her name, repeating over and over in his mind. Carlotta. He was so very aware that it was her he wanted, not simply sex and satisfaction, but Carlotta.

His stomach rebelled at the thought. She couldn't be allowed to be that important. He couldn't think straight, and his chest felt full. All of the emotions he'd been battling since she walked into his life felt too close to the surface. Too raw. This was everything he feared, everything he'd spent his life learning to deny.

He looked at her face, her beautiful face. He felt as though someone had reached inside him and twisted his guts. He had to stop it. Had to build the wall back up.

"Turn over," he said, his voice rough.

For one moment her confidence faltered.

"Trust me, Carlotta."

"I do," she said.

Her admission made him feel like a knife had just been pushed into his chest. He ignored it, tried to breathe around the sharp, searing pain. Tried to embrace the deep, dark nothing he knew still lived in him.

She turned over onto her stomach, and for a moment, he felt like he could breathe again. The emotional knot in his chest loosened. He needed to distance himself, but at the same time, he needed to be inside her more than he needed air.

He joined her on the bed, his legs on either side of hers. He traced the line of her back with his fingertips, pressed a kiss to her shoulder blade, while his hand skimmed over her curves, palming her soft buttocks.

She moaned and he moved his hand around so that he was touching her stomach, then lower still so that he could caress the bundle of nerves at the apex of her thighs. "Up on your knees," he said.

She complied, her bottom coming into contact with the hard ridge of his arousal. He bit back a curse as he continued to stroke her, pushing one finger into her slick folds as he reached over to the side table with his other, pulling a condom out of the drawer.

"Ready?" he asked.

"Yes." She breathed the word.

He brought the head of his shaft against the slick entrance to her body and entered her slowly, not wanting to cause her any discomfort, not even for a moment.

"Yes," she said, a sound of satisfaction this time, and he began to thrust in and out of her body.

He held her hip with one hand, while the other was moving over her in time with his strokes. He could hear nothing, think of nothing, beyond the amazing, white-hot blaze of pleasure that was coursing through his body.

"Rodriguez." Every syllable of his name was filled with the evidence of her satisfaction as her internal muscles pulsed around him.

And then he was pushed back into reality, no cocoon of denial to shield him. This was Carlotta. And it was more than sexual pleasure coursing through his veins.

"Carlotta." He gave in to the blinding urge to say her name, to acknowledge the depth of the desire that seemed to be driving him. And when he did that, he gave his body permission to release, his orgasm overtaking him, tearing away every last shred of control that he'd wrapped himself in.

He clung to her as he rode the wave, froze as he emptied himself, his muscles shaking in the aftermath, his heart pounding so hard he was certain she could hear it. He took a few steadying breaths.

"I'll be right back," he said, glad for the need to go and dispose of the condom. Glad for the excuse to gain some distance.

But even when he closed the door to the bathroom he could still feel her. On his skin. Beneath it. He felt tangled in her.

Sex had never done this to him. He'd always held himself back from it, engaging his body but never anything more.

Tonight, he had nearly drowned in the experience. The emotion overtaking the physical, fusing with it, creating a force he could not deny or control.

He had always prided himself on being a man in control, from the time he'd been a boy and control meant the difference between flying under the radar and enduring a beating.

And Carlotta had stripped him of it. Effortlessly, it seemed. And he had not been able to rebuild it. He had been left defenseless. Open and bleeding, raw. Exposed. Vulnerable.

He had vowed he would never be vulnerable again. That no one would ever hold power over him. Have the power to cause him pain.

He discarded the condom and turned on the shower, stepping beneath the cold spray, not waiting for it to heat.

He couldn't lose his control. He could not allow it. He hit his fist against the tile wall, welcoming the bite of pain. Anything to bring him back down, to erase the buzz of arousal that was still coursing through him.

Anything to remind him of who he was, and all that he could never hope to have.

CHAPTER TEN

I'M GOING to have a busy week when we get back home. Rodriguez had said it, and he'd meant it.

After they returned to Santa Christobel, Rodriguez became the man he'd promised to be from the beginning. A man leading a separate life from her.

In the past week he hadn't even come to her at night.

And no matter how much she'd hoped to stay detached, she just wasn't.

Maybe if Carlotta had any clue what she wanted she'd be able to talk to Rodriguez and get everything sorted out. But it all came back down to the fact that she wasn't supposed to care that he was being kept busy with affairs of state.

She blew out a breath and took her cell phone out of her purse, toying with the idea of calling Sophia. It had been too long since she'd talked to her sister. Mostly because it was so much easier to send a text and feign happiness.

And then there was Natalia. Natalia who, at this point, was more like a stranger than a twin these days.

Now she felt even more alone. Great, nice train of thought.

She had Luca, she was comfortable. She was home with him. She shouldn't care that her sisters were in different countries and Rodriguez was barely speaking to her. Of course, she did care. But she didn't know what to do about that.

She scrolled through a litany of her favorite swear words,

in English and Italian, while she watched Luca hopping over a ball in the middle of the expansive lawn from her position on the terrace.

"Watch me!" he shouted as he launched himself over the bright red rubber ball.

"Be careful, Luca," she said. It was almost reflexive to say that, whenever he said, "Watch me."

"I am!"

"Yeah, okay," she said, rolling her eyes, thankful he couldn't see her perform the childish action. She was supposed to be the mom. But she wasn't perfect, even though she tried to be.

She thought of Natalia again, of all the confusing emotion wrapped up in that relationship. Another area of her life she'd been imperfect in. She'd so envied the bright light her sister possessed that she managed to just laugh off the stuff the tabloids wrote about her. That she seemed to have permission, even if it was grudging, to be who she wanted to be. To be who she was instead of trying to force herself into a mold she would never, ever fit into.

But that wasn't Natalia's fault. Carlotta realized that for the first time. Natalia wasn't doing it to her, to hurt her in any way. She was simply living. And Carlotta's own issues were a big part of what kept them so distant from each other.

She scrolled through the numbers on her phone, her fingers trembling. Maybe she should call her. Maybe it was time.

Her phone vibrated in her hand. She looked down and saw Natalia's name on the screen and her heart banged against her chest. It made sense now, why Natalia's name had been so persistent in her mind. She was thinking of her too. But if her sister was calling, the news had to be bad. Something catastrophic, because Natalia never called.

She answered quickly. "Natalia?"

"*Ciao*, Lotta."

No one had called her Lotta in years. No one had been close enough to her to use a nickname. It made her throat feel tight, achy.

"Natalia, what's wrong?"

"Nothing," her sister said, far too quickly. "Congratulations on your engagement."

Carlotta looked down at the ring on her left hand. Oh, yes, she was engaged. But if not for the memory of those two glorious nights in Rodriguez's bed she wouldn't believe it.

But Natalia hadn't called to congratulate her, and her sister's skirting of the issue was getting on her already frayed nerves. She closed her eyes and worked to cultivate a calm tone. "Natalia. Something is wrong, I can tell by your voice. What is it?"

Even after years of distance, Natalia's tone was easy to read. They were twins, and regardless of the fact that they were as opposite as two people could be, she had always felt deeply the things Natalia had felt. Had always sensed when something wasn't right. That also accounted for the restlessness she'd felt a few moments earlier.

"I…" Natalia hesitated. "I just wanted to talk to you. And see how you were doing."

Carlotta didn't believe that for a moment. Her sister was many things, a lot of them good, but after going so long without contact from her, she couldn't really believe she'd suddenly decided she cared about what was happening with her.

I'm falling for the wrong guy again. And I know better. He's probably screwing actresses and models even as we speak, maybe even at the same time, and I'm sitting here feeling like I'm missing half of myself.

"I'm fine," she said, because the truth wasn't going to cut it here. Not when she hated the truth so much.

"Are you really? I mean…this marriage…"

"I'm only doing what we all must do," Carlotta said, her

words not her own. They were her father's words. And right now, she hated them. "I'm more worried about you, Natalia, we haven't spoken—"

"In years, I know," her twin said, her tone defensive.

"Not years." But close.

"We haven't had a real conversation in years."

That insight, coming from Natalia, shocked Carlotta a bit. She was right. They hadn't. She hadn't really had a meaningful conversation with anyone but Rodriguez since she'd gotten pregnant with Luca. She'd just sort of closed off. Her sister had noticed. And it had hurt her, she could hear that in her voice.

That cut deep. That her own issues had affected Natalia that way. That she had let her resentments come between them.

"I just wanted to say," Natalia said, her voice unsteady, "I'm sorry for not being there when you had Luca. And after I…" She paused and Carlotta waited, wondering if she should speak, wondering if she could. "I was afraid."

"I know you were, Natalia," Carlotta said, keeping her voice neutral.

"And angry," Natalia continued. "About a lot of things. About how you were treated and how it would change things. I felt like you were moving on to a whole new life without me."

For some reason, Carlotta laughed, even though she felt no humor. Only a bone-deep sadness. "I was, I suppose."

"But I was selfish. I know that."

Carlotta let the words wash over her, felt them loosen the hold on some of the anger that was wrapped around her heart. Anger she hadn't realized was still so prominent, because it had become such a part of her.

"It was a long time ago," she said, more to herself than to Natalia.

"Still, I just…wanted to be honest."

Carlotta swallowed hard, trying to grasp what her sister had said. Trying to make it matter. Trying to let go of the hurt and anger, and hold on to it at the same time.

Not possible, Carlotta. Let it go, or hang on. There's no halfway.

Coming from Natalia, this was big. Huge. And if there was one thing Carlotta knew, it was that everyone deserved forgiveness. Because everyone would need it at some point in time. She had. She'd made mistakes. She hadn't been perfect, and while it had been easy to blame her twin for the erosion of their relationship, the truth was, Carlotta had shut down.

"What's going on, to provoke all this honesty?" she asked finally.

"Nothing," Natalia said. Too quickly. "I've met someone," she amended. "Someone who's challenged me. Someone who's changed me."

That sounded familiar. More than. Enough to make her feel an uncomfortable stab of emotion in her heart. She'd met someone too. And she felt changed. In every way a different woman than the one who'd first arrived in Santa Christobel.

Because of Rodriguez.

"Changed? Are you engaged as well, Natalia?"

"No," she said.

"Natalia," Carlotta tried again, hoping to extract more from her. "Who is this person?" Man, woman, rent boy? But she didn't want to press, or be flippant. This was important. Somehow, this conversation was essential. And it wasn't the subject matter, so much as the fact that they were having one at all.

"Just someone," she said, her tone so sad that Carlotta felt an echo of the pain in her own heart. "No one important."

"Oh."

She hung up with her sister, feeling…everything. Pain

for whatever Natalia was going through, but overwhelming happiness too, because of the moment of connection. Also, fear. A lot of fear.

Because she was afraid she and Natalia were going through something far too similar at the moment. She was afraid her feelings for Rodriguez were crossing into the kind of territory she needed to stay out of.

She'd been there, done that, made the papers. Falling in love with the wrong man, making an idiot of herself for him. She didn't intend to do it with her own husband.

What if he really was out sleeping with other women? He'd promised fidelity, but what did that really mean? At least she knew that if Rodriguez promised something, he would mean it. At the time. She also knew a man like him was bound to be a little bit fickle.

He'd said it himself. Sex was cheap.

To him it was. But it was costing her. Bits and pieces of her heart and soul. It probably wasn't even the sex. She hadn't been with him since the night they'd spent together in Barcelona.

It felt like it had been longer. And less time too. She still ached for his touch, and she still felt branded by it. He did the strangest things to her.

"I jumped it!" Luca shouted.

"Yay, Luca!" she returned.

"Good job, Luca."

She whirled around and saw Rodriguez standing in the doorway, and her heart immediately jumped into her throat. He was gorgeous, even when she was kind of mad at him. Even when she was confused about her feelings. She was not confused about the gorgeousness.

He ran his hand over his thick, dark hair, his smile wide and thoroughly sexy. Thoroughly angering too.

"Thanks," Luca said, running up to the terrace, Rodriguez

drawing him like a moth to the flame. "Did you have a good day?" Luca asked, his manners on show for once.

Rodriguez's smile turned tight. "I did. You?"

"I jumped over that ball."

"A success then," he said.

"I'm surprised to see you here before dark," Carlotta said, knowing she sounded a little shrewish, and not really caring.

"We have a thing tonight."

"We?" she asked, her voice tight.

"Yes. We. I do not intend to take another woman as my date."

"Some notice would be nice," she practically hissed. "This is becoming a habit with you. I need time to get ready." Oh, she sounded like a nagging wife already and the wedding wasn't taking place for months.

"Three hours should be sufficient."

"I think Angelina had planned on taking the afternoon off. She went out."

"I talked to Angelina."

Annoyance coursed through her. "You talked to Angelina… and you didn't talk to me?"

"Is Angelina going to bring movies?" Luca asked.

"I don't know, Luca," Carlotta said. "What is this thing we're going to?"

"A charity event in the city."

"Can I go?" Luca asked.

Rodriguez looked down at Luca. "You wouldn't like it. You'd have to wear a tie, and you couldn't jump over anything."

Luca made a face. "Then I don't want to go."

"Neither do I," Rodriguez said.

"And we're going because…?" Carlotta asked.

"Because it's a good cause. And apparently my father

goes every year. I didn't find out until this afternoon and I came straight home."

"Oh," she said, feeling a bit subdued by that piece of information. "How is your father?" she asked.

"Not well. But not any worse."

"Well…good…I guess."

He shrugged, his emotions as unreadable as ever.

"Rodriguez, will you watch a movie with me?" Luca asked, his green eyes round and earnest.

Rodriguez hesitated for a moment. "Sure, Luca. We can watch something while your mama gets ready."

Luca smiled and grabbed Rodriguez's hand. And then Carlotta really couldn't feel angry at him, because even though he was still tense with Luca, he was trying. That meant everything to her. If he hadn't been able to treat Luca well…there was no way she could have stayed. No way she could agree to marry him.

"I'll see you in a bit," she said, watching as Luca led Rodriguez inside.

And she fell a little harder for him right then.

Rodriguez didn't know when he'd relaxed, but he had. Gradually his muscles had stopped feeling tense. He'd stopped worrying so much about doing the wrong thing.

And then, at some point, Luca had fallen asleep, his head resting against Rodriguez's shoulder. Now, Rodriguez's arm was asleep and Luca's warmth had crossed over into too hot. But he didn't want to move, for fear of waking the little boy.

He also didn't want to analyze exactly what Luca's trust of him made him feel. Or how badly it would hurt when he lost it.

Because he would.

It was part of his life. No one ever maintained a connection with him. At some point he'd just accepted it was something in him, and he'd made it work for him.

But the thought of losing Luca's trust…

At least he wouldn't lose Carlotta's. He seriously doubted he'd ever had it.

"How was the movie?"

He turned his head and saw Carlotta, her dark hair pulled back, large gold earrings highlighting her perfectly made-up features. She was wearing an ethereal white dress with a bold, black geometric pattern on the bodice, so at odds with the sheer, delicate fabric. But the pattern drew the eye to her figure, to her perfect, heavenly curves.

"He slept through most of it," Rodriguez said, forcing the words through his suddenly dry throat.

"I hope he sleeps through the night. It's too late for a nap." She smiled, the look on her face so sweet, so full of love. A look reserved for her son.

He envied it right then. So much that it was physical. Not just because he wished she would look at him with such emotion, but because he wished someone in his life could have. His mother, his father. Someone, anyone.

Holding Luca against him, it was hard to imagine how anyone could strike a child. How someone could abandon a child. He hadn't even been able to move Luca to allow the blood flow to return to his arm, much less leave him in the room by himself. The thought of walking out of his life forever, and leaving him with someone who would treat him horribly…

Not even he could do that, and he'd always considered himself emotionally broken.

"Angelina is here. She's ready to take him."

"Can I carry him to his room?" he asked, a question he hadn't known he was going to ask until he had.

This time, she did smile at him. "Of course."

He scooped Luca up and stood from the couch, crossing the intimate living area, a room that had been designed for family movie viewings and games nights. One that had gone unused by his family.

It was a short walk to Luca's room, and the little boy didn't even stir when Rodriguez laid him in bed and tucked the covers around his still form.

Carlotta leaned in and kissed Luca's forehead before they left the room.

"Sorry about earlier," she said.

"Sorry I wasn't able to tell you sooner." *Sorry I've been gone all week. Sorry I've been unable to face you.*

He didn't say the last part out loud.

"I understand. Things happen. I was…on edge already." They walked down the stairs and greeted Angelina, who was on her way up, then headed out of the palace. Rodriguez's convertible was parked in front, idling, ready for them. He opened Carlotta's door for her, the subtle hint of perfume and a scent that was uniquely her assaulted him, causing a surge of lust to hit him in the gut.

"Why were you on edge?" he said, as he started the car and maneuvered the vehicle out of the courtyard and through the first gate.

"I talked to Natalia."

"Your twin?"

"Yes. It was…good. I think…" She cleared her throat. "I think we might be on the way to fixing things. And even though she denied it, I think she's met someone special. Natalia needs someone special. I'm happy for her."

"You sound thrilled."

She looked at him, her expression baleful. "It's a lot for one afternoon."

"And Luca jumped over the red ball."

That got a laugh from her. "Yes, he did. Thank goodness

for Luca. He makes everything so much… He brings perspective."

"Yes," Rodriguez said. "He does."

"You seemed more comfortable with him tonight."

Carlotta looked at Rodriguez, trying to gauge his reaction. It was impossible, as always. "I'm figuring this all out. I'm not sure what, or who, I'm supposed to be to him yet. Not sure what he'll want from me."

Carlotta had given it a lot of thought too. "I… He'll always have a lot of friends, Rodriguez. And I have brothers, so he'll have uncles. The one thing he'll never have is a father." She swallowed. "Unless you're willing to step into that role."

Rodriguez tightened his hold on the steering wheel, his knuckles turning white as he turned it sharply, driving expertly along the winding country road that bordered the beach.

"I thought…I thought I would be able to keep distant, but he doesn't allow that, does he?"

"No."

"No child will," he said, almost heavily.

"Is that a problem?"

"I was under the impression a wife and children wouldn't alter my life. It didn't seem to alter my father's all that much."

Carlotta looked at her hands. "You're not the same man as your father, Rodriguez. You must realize that."

"I do," he said, his voice rusty.

"Then it shouldn't surprise you that you can't ignore us quite as easily as your father was able to ignore you and your mother."

"He ignored me until my mother left. Then I became…a target of some kind. The way you look at Luca…I've never understood how she could leave me with him. And now, seeing you with him…she did not love me like that."

"Not every person is meant to be a parent."

"No," he said. "I suppose that's true."

"I'm sorry," she said. And she was, truly, deeply, the pain of his childhood running through her bones, making her ache for him. "You should have been given better. And I know you say it doesn't matter. But it does. They owed you more than they gave you."

"Perhaps. Perhaps not."

She didn't understand the cryptic statement and she didn't have time to ask before he turned the radio on, effectively ending the conversation.

She wished he wouldn't close down on her. She wanted him, all of him. She'd given herself to him, not just her body, but her secrets. Everything in her.

He had her heart. She didn't want to admit it. Not to herself, and definitely not to him, but there wasn't much point in denying it. She was in love with Rodriguez. Not the man he pretended to be, the man he showed the world, but the man he was inside.

The man she sensed beneath that light, flirtatious facade. The man who had listened to her darkest secrets without even a hint of judgment. The man who had made love to her with such passion and fire she thought it would consume her.

The man who took her son to the zoo. Who held him while he slept.

The man he didn't want her to see. The man he didn't seem to want to be.

They drove on in silence, and Carlotta kept her eyes glued to the lights of the city, drawing closer as they drove down the beach highway.

The charity event was being held in Santa Christobel's famous gardens. An expansive, outdoor area with flowers and plants from most of the world's tropical locales.

Rodriguez pulled the car up to the front of the walled garden, and gave his keys to the valet. He came around to her side, ever the charming gentleman, and helped her from the vehicle. She shivered when his hand touched her bare arm. He hadn't touched her in a week. She missed his touch.

Missed his kiss. Missed him most of all.

She ignored the vast well of longing that opened up in her and followed him into the event. The air inside the walls of the garden was thick and perfumed. The expansive lawn area lit up by white paper lanterns.

People were standing around, laughing, talking. Drinking. It was a light event, and money was flowing out of wealthy pockets and into the charity, which was nice to see.

Except she wasn't able to feel as happy about it as she should. Because she was still turning over their conversation in her mind. Trying to dissect it, to find the meaning.

They owed you more than they gave you.

Perhaps not.

Did he really think he hadn't deserved more than a mother who abandoned him and a father who beat him? How was that even possible?

Rodriguez, at their first meeting at least, had seemed arrogant. Full of himself. The kind of man who thought women falling at his feet, or into his bed, was his due. Not the kind of man who would think he deserved the treatment his parents had shown him.

Yet in those moments when she'd glimpsed the haunting emptiness in his eyes, she'd known there was more to him than that. More than that thin facade he wrapped around himself like a cloak.

"Drink?" he asked, pulling two glasses of champagne from a passing waiter's tray without waiting for her answer.

She took it from him. "I thought we agreed that the refreshments at things like this were…"

"Awful?"

"That."

"Alcohol is still alcohol. It makes everything more fun, right?" he asked, his tone clipped.

"I don't know if that's a healthy attitude," she said, sensing a recklessness in him that shocked her. Bothered her a bit.

"Maybe not. But then, I'm not really renowned for healthy attitudes, am I?"

Whatever was on his mind was prevented from escaping by the people who came to talk to them. Everyone wanted a piece of the Crown Prince. The man who would soon be their king. And, of course, she was a fascination as well, since she was wearing his ring.

Carlotta could sense Rodriguez's growing annoyance and she tried to maintain her civility, tried to be friendly to the guests since he didn't seem to be in the mood to play nice.

"What's wrong with you?" she hissed when one well-wisher departed.

"I'm not in the mood for all of this." He turned his dark gaze to her. "I want to be alone with you."

"You've had all week to be alone with me. You avoided me."

He trailed his finger along the line of her jaw. "A mistake, I think."

"Do you?" she asked, her voice flat.

"Carlotta." He leaned in and his cell phone rang. "*Un momento. Hola….Sì….*How long does he have?…Why did no one tell me?" He paused for a moment. "We'll be there in a moment." He snapped the phone shut, his gaze not meeting hers. "We have to go. It's my father. He's… We have to go."

CHAPTER ELEVEN

THE king was in a private wing of the hospital, but it was still very much a hospital. White, pastel and sterile. Carlotta hadn't been in many hospitals.

She hadn't been back to one since Luca was born. She was thankful for it.

The environment was unsettling, the smell of antiseptic stinging her nose. Even more unsettling was the dark emotion rolling off Rodriguez.

When they arrived at his father's room, the priest was there, standing by to administer last rites. Carlotta's stomach clenched tight. This was very likely it, and she knew that Rodriguez wasn't ready. How could he be ready?

Her own father was a tyrant in many ways, and yet, she still couldn't fathom the thought of losing him.

"I will go in alone," he said, his voice hard.

Carlotta stayed outside the room, leaning against the wall, her hands clasped tightly in front of her, her heart pounding hard in her chest, tears threatening to fall. Her throat burned with the effort of keeping them back.

She watched the hands on the clock turn. Watched the priest go in, and come back out. Felt her heart sinking lower.

She finally moved to a chair, felt her eyes growing heavy.

* * *

"It's done, Carlotta." Rodriguez's thick voice shook her from the sleep she hadn't realized she'd fallen into.

"What? No," she said, her heart aching.

"He's gone." Rodriguez's face was set, his expression immovable, flat as though it had been carved from stone.

"Rodriguez, I'm…"

"Let's go," he said.

She stood from the chair, trying to shake off the dizziness that came from being jerked out of such a deep sleep.

She followed him out of the hospital and into the cold night air. She felt her body start to shake. "I don't… What do we do now? What does this mean?"

"We'll hold a press conference. First thing in the morning. And I am king." He walked to where he had parked his car, at the front of the hospital. He had not used a parking space, and no one had corrected him.

He jerked the driver's side door open, then froze. "And my father is gone."

She rounded the car and threw her arms around him, not caring if it was what he wanted or not. He needed it, even if he would never admit it.

"I'm sorry," she whispered, her voice breaking.

One of his arms came around her, his hand resting on her back. She felt his sharp intake of breath against her chest.

"I'm sorry," she said again, holding him to her. Just holding him.

The chill night wind blew in from the sea, cold and wet, salty. It blended with the tears on her cheeks. She squeezed his hand. "Do you want to walk for a while?"

"Yes," he said.

He kept hold of her hand, and they left the car, the door standing open. Everything seemed deserted this late. The hospital was out of the city by a couple of minutes, nestled in the hills, by the ocean. She and Rodriguez walked through the lot, to where it ended and a path began, through the grass and down to the sand. Neither of them spoke until they were standing at the edge of the ocean, the waves lapping near their feet.

"My father is gone," he said again. "And there is no chance of…fixing what passed between us. No chance at reconciliation. No chance for him to…apologize. He never would have, but the possibility was there. And it's gone now. That was all I will ever have with my father. A childhood filled with pain and fear, and then years of stony silence when I avoided him as much as I possibly could."

He sucked in a sharp breath. "I do not know what to feel. If I should feel anything at all."

"There's no right or wrong answer," she said. "Just…whatever you feel. That's what you're supposed to feel."

He didn't speak. He lowered himself to the sand and sat. Carlotta sat with him, not caring that she was getting sand on her dress. Not caring about anything but being next to him. Comforting him.

Rodriguez tried to breathe past the tightness in his chest. He wasn't certain he could. Everything with his father was final now, and with that realization came both relief and a grief that went down into his bones. Made them hurt.

"I have…simplified things," he said slowly, not sure why he was sharing with her, but certain he could no longer hold it in. "I have dealt with my father on my terms, when I could. Separating myself from who I was, who he was, when I was a child. But it was never simple. I thought I could bury it. Make it so that it didn't matter so I could deal with him at functions, in interviews. But so much of me hated him, Carlotta. For what he did to me. For making my mother leave."

His voice broke and he felt weak, humiliating emotion overpowering him, felt moisture in his eyes he couldn't blame on the ocean spray. "Because she couldn't live with a monster and I know, I understand, that she never could have taken his heir from him. But it was easier to be mad at her because she was gone. I didn't have to try to exist with her."

Carlotta put her hand on the back of his neck, her touch strengthening him.

"When she left…he took my toys. Because I was bad, he said. My mother left because I was bad, and a bad boy didn't deserve toys." He'd never told anyone any of this. He'd made himself believe it was stupid. Unimportant. At least he'd tried to force himself to believe it. "And after that, a while after, he hit me for the first time. For fidgeting in church. We're supposed to set an example, you see, and I wasn't being an example. I was Luca's age then. Barely five. That's why I learned to shut it all down. And I never have figured out how to feel…normal again."

She leaned her head against him, her face in the crook of his neck. He felt the dampness of her tears on his skin.

"I'm supposed to be sad," he said. "That he's gone. But all I'm really sad about is that he'll never be my father. Not really. It's finished now. My mother…for all I know she's gone too. I can't ever have it back, and I think part of me believed that I would."

She put her arms around him then and he realized he'd never shared his sadness with anyone before. Had never been held while he cried, or while he felt like crying. Not for as long as he could remember.

He'd never had anyone to listen to him.

He'd invited countless women into his bed, but not into him. He'd never shown anyone who he was. And now she knew. She knew how broken he was. That his own mother had left him, that his father had beaten him.

That his parents had never loved him. His own parents.

A violent pain stabbed at his heart. His own parents hadn't loved him. What must be wrong with him? No wonder he'd ignored feeling for so many years. Damn his father for making him feel again. And Carlotta too.

He pulled away from her, standing, his breath coming hard and fast, his entire body heavy, on fire, as though it were filled with hot lead. Burning him. Weighing him down.

"Rodriguez…"

"No," he said sharply. "You can't make this better. We're not going to have a…a phone call reconciliation like you were able to do with your sister. It's not fixable. It's done."

He turned and walked off the beach. Cursing and kicking his shoes off when they filled with sand, walking the rest of the way to the car in his bare feet, the rocks biting into his flesh, his shoes abandoned.

He got into the car and slammed the door. He waited until Carlotta slid in beside him. He started the engine and pulled out of the hospital lot, his entire body tight, on the verge of breaking.

Neither of them spoke on the ride back to the palace. He wished she would. He wanted to draw strength from her and he hated himself for it. Hated the dependence.

Hated that, somehow, he'd let his emotions start functioning again. And they were eating him alive now.

He didn't care that when he pulled into the palace courtyard he sprayed gravel on the lawn by turning too sharply. He didn't care that the servants stared at him, openmouthed, when he walked through the halls, without shoes.

He went into his room and closed the door firmly behind him. Never looking back. Hardly seeing anything.

He wanted Carlotta. For all he knew she was still sitting down in the car. He wanted her with a ferocity that denied everything he believed about himself.

But tonight, everything he'd tried to make himself was coming unraveled.

No, not just tonight. From the first moment he'd seen

Carlotta. Everything, the carefully laid plans, the vague concept of a wife he hardly noticed, one who didn't interfere… it had all started to erode. And right now, he needed her so badly he couldn't regret it.

He tore open the door to his room and stalked down the hall, taking his shirt off and letting it fall to the marble floor as he did. He pushed open the door to Carlotta's room without knocking.

She whirled around, her eyes wide. She was wearing a cotton nightgown. One she'd probably just put on. He wanted it off.

"I need you," he said, the admission torn from him.

She nodded slowly and moved across the room and into his arms, kissing him with just the right amount of pressure. Somehow she knew what he needed. She always knew.

Her fingers skated over the skin on his back, teasing him, tantalizing him, getting him hot. Pushing away the conflicting knot of emotions with a fire of need that started to burn in his gut and spread through him, cleansing him. Making things seem clearer. Simpler.

She kissed his neck, his collarbone, hands moving to his bare chest, skimming his nipples.

He looked down at her lovely face, stoic with concentration. The burning in his stomach intensified.

"Do you want me?" he asked.

"Yes," she said, her eyes meeting his.

"Not, do you want to fix me? Do you want me?"

"Of course I do."

He held her away from his body, the desperation in him real, overtaking everything else. "I don't want pity sex, dammit. I want you. I want you to want *me*. Like I want you. Not because you're supposed to be my wife, or because you feel sorry me."

"From the moment I met you, I wanted you. You steal my

control, Rodriguez. Wholly and completely," she said, her voice steady. "And I want you now, just like I have every time. Not because anyone's forcing me. As much as you need me right now, I need you just as much. If you told me I could walk away from this, from us, our marriage, right now, I wouldn't. I'm in this with you. For life. I promised it, and I will keep that promise," she vowed.

"Make me forget." He buried his face in her hair, breathing in heavily.

"Don't forget who you're with."

"I want your face to be the only thing I can remember. Your touch. Your face. You, Carlotta, nothing else," he said, lowering his head, pressing a kiss to her cleavage. "Please."

She stepped back and tugged the nightgown over her head, consigning it to the floor while he did the same with the rest of his clothes.

He got into bed with her, sliding beneath the covers, the sheets soft on his skin, her bare body even softer.

He ran his hands over her curves, inhaled her scent, so unique, so Carlotta. "I want you, Carlotta Santina," he said. "Only you."

"I want you, Rodriguez Anguiano." She pressed a kiss to his lips, her tongue sliding along the seam of his mouth.

He put his hand beneath her bottom and she parted her thighs, granting him access. He slid into her hot, wet body, pleasure, emotion, crashing over him. He shuddered as she enveloped him, her arms, her legs, trapping him against her.

They moved in rhythm, their breath blending, hearts pounding in time. She met each of his thrusts, her hands linked with his, fingers laced together.

They reached the peak together, their sounds of pleasure mingling in the quiet room.

And then he held her to him, his breathing fractured, harsh. His heart pounding, the fire in him burning even hotter now than before, edging everything out. Everything but the need for Carlotta, not for sex, that desire was satisfied for now. But for her. To be in her arms. In her bed. Just with her.

Her legs tangled with his, her heavy, satisfied sigh bringing him even more pleasure than his climax had.

For now, at least, things seemed good.

And hopefully, by morning, he could have his walls rebuilt. Could turn off the emotion, the need, the deep, heavy desire for more than a man like him could ever hope to have.

CHAPTER TWELVE

"I'M SORRY."

Carlotta opened her eyes and looked up into Rodriguez's handsome, tormented face. Everything from the night before came flooding back.

"Why?" she asked, rolling to her side, not caring that the sheets had fallen to her waist.

"I was...not myself last night."

"You were in pain," she said. "Your father..."

"It's still no excuse for how I spoke to you."

"Rodriguez, I'm not mad at you for that. I... We hadn't slept together in a week. I get that the timing looked a little bit suspect. But I did want you. I do. I don't regret this part of our relationship at all."

"What about it do you regret?"

"Nothing." She shook her head, biting back the admission that was hovering on the edge of her lips. *I regret that I love you, and you will never love me back.*

"I didn't mean to hurt you. If I did..."

"Rodriguez, I'm not going to break," she said. It was like speaking in code. She wondered if he knew she was talking about feelings, not her body. She wondered if he was talking about feelings.

"That's comforting to know," he said, giving her a look that made her feel hot all the way down to her toes.

"You should get ready," she said.

He nodded once and got out of bed, dragging his pants on and walking out of the door. He had to go back to his room so he could find a suit for the press conference. Get showered and presentable.

Carlotta flung herself backward onto the pillows and threw her arm over her face. "I'm such an idiot." Even still, she smiled.

Her phone vibrated from her purse on the floor and she rummaged around until she found it. "Hello?"

"Carlotta, is that you?"

Carlotta sat up again. "Mother? Is everything all right?"

"Yes. No. I don't know if you heard the news about Anna?"

Her brother's ex-intended, the woman he had ditched for his new fiancée, Allegra. "What about Anna?"

"She's pregnant."

Carlotta's mouth dropped open. "No! She is? What is Alex going to do? Is he still going to marry Allegra or is he…?"

"It's not Alessandro's baby," Zoe said crisply.

"Oh." That truly shocked Carlotta since Anna was about as demure and predictable as they came. Not that that was a bad thing, truly. Carlotta had spent a long time wishing she'd stayed as buttoned up and predictable as sweet Anna. "So…who is…?"

"Leo. Leo Jackson."

Carlotta snorted a laugh in spite of herself. "Those Jacksons." Alex's fiancée's brother had now hooked up with Alex's ex-fiancée. It was like a soap opera. And for the first time, she wasn't the star. And yet, at the moment she didn't really care.

"Well, I hope she's very happy with him."

"How can you say that?" Her mother sniffed. "Now we have no hope! If Alessandro is going to come to his senses—

and he must—we needed all the help we could get. But now Anna is…"

"Mother, he doesn't love Anna."

"What does love have to do with anything?"

Carlotta blew out a breath. Her mother, who had never shared a room with her husband, who would never dream of putting her own needs before duty, didn't really shock her with the statement. And a month ago, Carlotta would have agreed. She'd agreed to marry Rodriguez without love after all.

But now, now she knew differently.

"Love has everything to do with it. Everything to do with life."

"You sound strange. Chipper."

"I am. I'm in love." The admission freed her, made her feel light.

"Please tell me it's with Prince Rodriguez or I really will be apoplectic."

"It is, Mama," she said, using the name she hadn't called her mother by in years. "He's wonderful. And I hope Alex and Allegra, and Anna and Leo, are as happy with each other as I am with him. Tell Anna congratulations if you see her."

"I will," her mother said, clearly still not happy, but mollified. "Give Luca a kiss for me."

Carlotta's heart suddenly felt too large for her chest. "I will. Promise."

She was tempted to tell her mother about Rodriguez's father. But she didn't really want to add to the burden.

"*Ciao.*"

"*Ciao*, Mama," she said, hanging up the phone.

Carlotta laughed into the empty room. Her mother had called her. About someone else's scandal. She ranked as a confidante again.

And she didn't care. She was glad to speak to her mother,

so happy not to feel the icy reserve anymore. To hear warmth, as much as her mother was capable of.

But she didn't care whether her mother approved of her. Whether her father approved of her. It didn't matter. She was happy. Content. Luca was taken care of. She had balance in her life. She wasn't hiding, wasn't pretending to be someone she just couldn't be. She wasn't forgetting she was a woman, she was being both mother and wife. Well, eventual wife.

And it was *her* life. No one else's.

She didn't know why it had taken so long to figure that out. Why half of the guilt and baggage she carried around with her had to do with other people. The way they saw her. Whether or not *they* were happy with how she was living. For some reason, she'd bought into the idea that she some-how didn't deserve love. That she couldn't have it.

But she did. She could.

She rolled out of bed and went to her closet, hunting for what to wear. It was strange, the kind of freedom being in love with Rodriguez brought.

Her supposed love for Gabriel had felt oppressive, secret and shameful even before she'd found out about his wife. But her love for Rodriguez had come spilling out of her. She hadn't wanted to hide it.

And he needed love. Even if he didn't think he could ever give it back, he needed to feel some.

She couldn't grieve his father. Not knowing what he'd done to Rodriguez. Not knowing how he'd hurt him. How he'd taken a little boy's world and filled it with fear and pain. She couldn't erase the past, but she could help make a better future. For all of them.

That started with supporting him while he gave the hard-est speech he would ever have to give.

* * *

Carlotta sat in the front row at the press conference, her heart in her throat, as she waited for Rodriguez to come and stand before them. Before her and the army of press who had assembled themselves at Santa Christobel's palace for the second time that week.

She wished she had some way to relieve the nervous tension in her body, but she didn't want to fidget like a child in a room full of reporters with cameras.

When Rodriguez strode in, she felt everyone in the room draw breath. She did too. He was wearing a black suit, less unruly than normal, but nowhere near respectable.

He moved to the front of the room and held up a hand to silence the chatter. She couldn't take her eyes off him. Off his bearing, the authority he brought with him. Sometime in the past weeks, he'd changed.

Or maybe he hadn't changed. Maybe he was simply free to show the man beneath the layers of protection he had wrapped himself in.

"Thank you all for coming," he said. Then he looked at her, met her gaze. And he didn't look away. "I know it has been in the news already, but I can confirm that my father, King Carlos Anguiano, passed away last night. It is the end of an era for Santa Christobel, and yet I hope we can look to the future. I pledge to rule our country with honor, with integrity and with all the strength I possess."

A murmur of agreement and a sweeping click of camera shutters went through the room.

"And while this is a sad day," Rodriguez continued, "I hope the sadness can be tempered by happy news. I recently learned that I have a son. An heir."

The wave of shocked noise that went through the crowd was short and sharp, and she realized she had gasped too. He didn't mean... Had he fathered a child out of wedlock? Had he just found out? Her heart pounded so fast she was afraid it was going to drain the blood from her head. Afraid she might pass out cold.

Rodriguez waited for everyone to quiet again and she clasped her hands together, squeezing them tight, trying hard to keep her vision from tunneling.

"Luca Santina is my son, with Princess Carlotta Santina, my fiancée, who I know you've already met. He is heir to the throne of Santa Christobel. And he is now to be called Prince Luca Santina Anguiano. He has my name. My protection."

It was hard to breathe. And it was hot. So hot in this tiny, blasted room. The roar of the press was deafening and she could feel them pressing in closer. Nearer to Rodriguez. To her. She couldn't force her thoughts into order.

Finally, a woman in the back was able to make herself heard over the din. "He is...your son?"

"Yes," Rodriguez said, his voice clipped. "I am Luca's father. I think that's fairly clear based on my previous statements. Are there any other questions?"

The room exploded with noise and Carlotta could only sit and listen to it all happening around her.

"How long have you known?"

"When did your affair with the princess begin?"

"Why didn't you claim him years ago?"

A reporter rushed over to her where she was sitting. "Princess, how did you bring yourself to forgive Prince Rodriguez for leaving you pregnant and alone?"

"I...I didn't need to..."

The man pressed. "Or were you simply not certain if he was the father, or if it was another man?"

She felt her cheeks get hot, her entire body shivering from the inside out. Anger, fear and the intense desire to hide from the intensity of the scrutiny. She hated this. More than almost anything else, she hated being at the center of the frenzy.

A reporter on her other side grabbed her arm, turning her

to face him. "Does this mean the only Santina bastard is no longer a bastard?"

There was no air. There was just a teeming throng of suit jackets crushing in on her. Elbows in her face as all the reporters jockeyed for position, as they tried to be the first one to ask the questions, to come up with the most lurid, insulting, vile comments imaginable.

She was pinned in her chair, bodies in front of her and behind her, pressing in. She just wanted to cover her head and hide until they went away, but she couldn't move even that much.

"Everyone move back," she said. The roar of questions was deafening, a sound wall that defeated her.

"Move back." Rodriguez's voice cut through the noise and the reporters began to move away as he physically pushed them away from her.

His dark eyes were on fire with intensity as he grabbed one man, the first one to put his hands on her, and pulled him back forcibly. The other man started to move back in but Rodriguez took hold of him again, his upper lip curled into a snarl. "I said move back, or you may not ever move again."

This time the reporter didn't challenge him. The entire crowd seemed to shrink beneath Rodriguez's rage, moving away from her. She could breathe again.

"You have all forgotten that Princess Carlotta Santina is royalty. She is my future wife, your future queen. You will all hand in your press badges as you leave. What happens with them later, whether or not you will see them returned, will be decided at my convenience. For now, all you need to know is that Luca is my son. Carlotta is my fiancée. There is no salacious story beneath that. You will give them both the respect they are due."

He was lying. For her. For Luca. He was doing so much more than giving Luca his name. He was claiming him in the most unbreakable, unquestionable way. Taking the birth-right from his future biological children and bestowing it onto her son.

Rodriguez walked to where she was sitting and extended his hand. She grasped it and he pulled her to a standing position. She held on to him like a lifeline as they walked out of the press room, her breathing shaky, labored.

She didn't speak, and neither did he, until they were closeted in his office.

Then her entire body started shaking. "I hate this. *Dio*, but I hate this."

Rodriguez stood in front of her, looking at a loss. "What happened was out of line. Beyond the pale. I have half a mind to have some of those men arrested. If I'd had any idea…"

"It's always like that though, isn't it? Maybe not so physical. Maybe not even in person. But the questions and the accusations."

"It's over now, I have declared Luca to be my son. He is my heir. You have no name written in the place designated for a father on his birth certificate, do you?" She shook her head. "Write in mine."

"He's…not your biological son," Carlotta said softly.

"No. But what does that matter, Carlotta? I will protect Luca, I swear it. If anyone ever harmed him…I would end them. And yet my father…my flesh and blood, thought nothing of harming me, keeping me in fear of him. What does blood matter?"

She thought of her own family. She loved them. And she believed they loved her. But it wasn't unconditional. She'd tested the bonds of it, and found they could be broken, and while they had been fixable, they had not healed back the same as they'd been before. He was right. Blood meant nothing.

"It doesn't," she said. She sat in the chair that was positioned by his desk. She felt cold. "I can't stop shaking. I don't know why. It was like this when I was pregnant with Luca. The horrible questions. Constant photos. Headlines. They followed me everywhere. Nothing was mine anymore, not even my own image. They distorted it to make a story. To make money."

Rodriguez looked at Carlotta, at her pale features, her lips chalky white, her eyes dull. He wanted to touch her, to offer her comfort. Something. But he didn't know how. Didn't know what to do, not when he was the one who'd caused her pain.

He shouldn't have had her attend the press conference. He should have anticipated the firestorm. But his decision about Luca had been made suddenly, just before he was preparing to speak.

It had hit him right then, what he had to do. To truly make Luca a part of him. A part of the family. To protect him from rumors, from labels. There would still be rumors, but he had the kind of reputation that would make it easy for his people to believe that he'd fathered a child he hadn't known about.

"I don't know if I can do this," she whispered. "Sometimes I think it was easier when I was in Italy."

Something in his chest broke. Splintered into a million pieces at the soft, sad admission. Still he stood, frozen, unsure of what to do. Unsure if anything he did would ever be enough. If he was the one who was meant to comfort her in this moment.

There was no real way he could ever know. She was here because she'd been manipulated into it. And he hadn't cared. He'd known that she didn't want to marry him, that she was only doing it out of a misguided sense of duty, and he had gone along with it anyway.

Was he truly any better than his father?

She stood, the fatigue etched into her face. "Thank you,

Rodriguez. For what you did. I am grateful. I'm sorry about… this. The emotional stuff. I just hate being in the public eye like that. It's not for me. I guess I have to get used to it though, don't I?"

"You should get some rest."

She needed it, after what those animals had done to her. The image of her, surrounded by the crowd of reporters, the gut-tearing rage he'd felt when that man had grabbed her arm, it threatened to choke him.

"Thank you," she said. She turned and walked out of his office, her shoulders stiff, stress evident in every line of her beautiful body.

He simply stood there, suddenly aware that she was being held prisoner. And that he held the keys to her chains. He was forcing her to stay here. Keeping her with him for what? To make himself happier? No matter the cost to her?

His father had done that. Had tried to hold his mother captive with threats, with power.

But unlike his mother, Carlotta wouldn't leave. She wouldn't abandon her son or her duty to slip out of a situation that made her miserable.

The knowledge cut into his chest like a knife, wounding him, making him bleed. It was a new, strange kind of grief. One that flayed him from the inside out. One that made his body like a stranger's.

Carlotta.

She would stay with him forever, ignore her own comfort, her own desire to do what she felt she had to do. And she would grow to hate him for it.

And he would never be able to bear it.

"I'm not sleepy!" Luca protested, the whine in his tone proving that statement to be a lie.

"Yes, you are," Carlotta said.

"Nope," Luca insisted.

"Luca," Rodriguez said, his tone firm. "Don't argue."

Luca's eyes rounded as he looked at Rodriguez. "Okay. I'm sorry."

"I forgive you," Rodriguez said, trying to ignore the crushing weight in his chest.

He'd spent the afternoon thinking of what he must do. What he had to do for Carlotta's happiness. For Luca's.

"Can you carry me?" Luca asked, stretching his arms out to him, the trust in his eyes implicit. Humbling and undeserved.

"Of course," Rodriguez said, lifting him, surprised at the comfort it gave him.

"Rodriguez?"

"What, Luca?" he asked.

"Are you going to be my dad?"

Luca's question cut straight through him. Would he ever be a father to him? Really? Would he be worthy of it? "Yes, Luca," he said. Because he would do all he could. He would be Luca's father, no matter what happened between him and Carlotta. He would see to that.

Luca patted Rodriguez's face. "Good."

Rodriguez's throat felt tight. Too tight. He carried Luca down the hall and put him in his bed, pulling the covers up around him. It was nice, for one moment, to have the kind of domesticity he'd always wondered about. To know it was real.

To know, even as it tore him to pieces, that love was real.

"Can I have Sherbie and Sherbet?"

Rodriguez reached over to Luca's side table and took the stuffed owls from their perch, placing them in Luca's arms. "Anything else?"

"No. Thank you for tucking me in."

"Good night, Luca."

Rodriguez closed the door behind him and walked down

the hall to where Carlotta was standing. He couldn't remember the last time he'd felt fear. He felt it now.

"Can we talk?" he asked.

She nodded. "Of course. After today it's probably a good idea."

He wanted to touch her. He knew he shouldn't. If he touched her, he would be lost. He would kiss her if he laid one finger on her silken skin, and once his lips met hers, he would be on fire, inside and out, with the need to join his body to hers.

And no matter how much he wanted to be with her, no matter how badly he wanted to make love, he wouldn't use that to manipulate her. And he wouldn't use it to put a Band-Aid on a situation that was mortally wounded.

"The announcement today changed things," he said, working at detaching emotion from his voice, working at detaching himself from his body. Trying to find that place that was free of everything but the necessary numbness he needed to get through life. To get through this.

"Did it?"

He worked at forcing the words out, his body unwilling to say them. "We no longer have to get married."

She said nothing for a moment, her expression blank, her body frozen. "We don't?"

"No. I have claimed Luca as my biological son. As my heir. That negates the need for us to have any more children." Saying that was like driving a knife into his own stomach. It was the death of elusive dreams he had let himself have for brief, fleeting moments. But he would do it a thousand times to avoid the pain a forced marriage would cause Carlotta.

"And the marriage…"

"The unity came from children. The benefits to the nations from the solid bond that us sharing a child would bring.

We share that bond. I…I do think of Luca as my son and I didn't name him as my heir lightly."

"But you don't want to get married?"

Carlotta felt like the world had tilted on its axis and she had remained standing where she was, trying to adjust her perspective in a world that didn't look the same anymore.

Rodriguez's words, words that seemed like they were from another lifetime, came back to her.

I prefer not to marry. But I need an heir.

He'd found a way to get his heir without getting the wife. A way to have what he needed without having to take on the extra baggage a wife would supply.

"What do you…what do you want to do with Luca? With… me?"

"He's my heir and he needs to be in Santa Christobel. If you like, you could live in an apartment on the grounds, or remain in the palace. But somewhere you will both be safe. Be kept away from the public eye."

In the palace? Where she'd have to watch Rodriguez with other women? Where she would have to endure knowing, night after night, that he was down the hall giving them what he had given to her? Something she had thought was special. Different.

What a fool she was.

Because this hadn't been a simple affair. She had given all of herself. Everything, with no reservation. She had stripped off every inhibition, every bit of protection. She had shown Rodriguez who she was. He had shown her who she was. Had taught her things about herself she had never imagined might be true.

He had changed her. And now he was just…leaving her. How could he not want their life together? The one they had planned. How could he have given her the picture of the perfect, domestic family life and then take it back from her? How dare he make her dream again? Make her want and desire and need. And how dare he take those new dreams and tear them into pieces, scattering them in the wind.

"So you have what you want now? And that's…it?"

He looked at her, his eyes flat. Frighteningly dark. This was the man she'd glimpsed beneath the cool, playboy exterior, this was him exposed, stripped of the veneer. He was terrifying, beautiful and utterly heartbreaking.

She wanted to touch him, but she was afraid it might break her. To touch him again and have him reject her.

"I will never have what I want. That's the nature of this life, Carlotta. We live, we try and survive the abuse that is hurled at us, and we either crumble beneath it or we become stronger. There's no light at the end of the tunnel. It's just surviving."

She shook her head. "No. I don't believe that. I want more than that." She swallowed hard, taking a step away from him. "And I'll have that some day. Because I'm not afraid to chase it now. To be me. To grab life with both hands. That's one good thing you did for me, Rodriguez. You showed me that I could be who I am. That I'm happier when I'm not trying to hide. Maybe you should try that. The not-hiding thing."

She turned away from him, because if she looked at him, even for one more second, she would crumble completely. And she couldn't do that. She was going to stay strong. For Luca. For herself. For the new her that Rodriguez had helped her become.

"Where will you go, Carlotta?" he asked, his voice rough.

"Tonight? Just my room. Tomorrow…I don't know."

"And you will take Luca?"

Her stomach tightened. Luca, who loved Rodriguez.

"We will be here, in Santa Christobel. I won't hurt Luca like that." She turned to face him again. "I won't allow you to hurt him."

Rodriguez met her eyes. "I won't."

She believed that. Utterly. Completely. But he would hurt her. He had. He had taken her world and destroyed it. Taken every new and wonderful thing she felt she'd discovered about life and twisted it, handed it back to her a mangled mass of nothing.

She turned again and walked from the room, leaving bits of herself behind. Pieces of herself she didn't think she could ever reclaim.

CHAPTER THIRTEEN

CARLOTTA hadn't left the palace. But she had left him in every way that mattered. She wasn't in his bed. She didn't share meals with him. She hardly spoke to him.

He felt like there was a hole torn through him, raw and bleeding. It made it painful to breathe. He couldn't find solace in retreating from emotions because it had bled into every part of him. It was in his bones.

But he had given her a choice, had told her they didn't have to marry, and she had taken it. It was right. But it was killing him slowly.

To have her so close that all he would have to do was walk down the corridor to be in her arms again, and yet so far that he was certain of her rejection, was torment.

He'd imagined he had known enough pain that he would be dead to it now. He'd been wrong. Laughably wrong.

What he wanted to do was get drunk and forget. Find some artificial happiness and pretend, for a few hours, that it was his reality.

It was what he had done all his life.

But it wasn't enough anymore. It would never be enough again. Carlotta had shown him true happiness. And she had revealed the rest of his life as the shallow counterfeit it was.

Because she had torn the walls around his heart down to the ground. She'd made him love. Had shown him the love a father should have for a son with Luca. Had shown him true love between a man and woman.

He loved her. With every piece of ruined soul, he loved her.

And he had pushed her away because he'd had to. Because if he didn't she would have been unhappy. Because if she stayed he would have to tell her. And she might reject him. It hadn't occurred to him to ask her to stay. He had never believed she would.

He curled his hand into a fist and slammed it down on his desk.

He had never believed he deserved love. Never believed he could have it. He had endless confidence in his skills as a ruler, as a lover. But he had learned to despise who he was deep down. Learned to hate the man that no one could love.

But Carlotta had made him feel differently. Seeing her with Luca had changed the way he saw being a parent. Had made him look at it from the side of the adult, rather than the child. Had made him see that anyone who didn't care for Luca was wrong.

That it was the adult and not the child who was at fault.

He stood from his desk, his heart raging in his chest. Maybe he was wrong. Maybe the hope that was surging through him was for nothing.

But he was going to take a chance. If he laid everything down and was left with nothing, not even a shard of pride, it would be worth it.

Pride he could live without. But he didn't want to live without Carlotta.

"Carlotta. Please let me in."

Carlotta sat up in bed, her chest tightening. She hadn't been sleeping. But she'd done what she'd done every night for the past week. Gone to bed at the same time as Luca, lying there, awake and bleeding emotion until sheer exhaustion forced her into a sleep filled with nightmares.

And she'd imagined Rodriguez coming to her. And in her mind she'd been weak. She'd taken him into her arms with no promises of love, or marriage or anything. Because it seemed like having a piece of him would be better than having nothing of him at all. That was when she had to try to remember that she wanted more. More than what though? More than loving a man with every shred of her being? That was a tall order.

"It's open," she said. Because she wanted to see who would win. Weak Carlotta, or Strong Carlotta. She was rooting for her weaker half.

Rodriguez walked in looking disheveled and more handsome than any man had a right to. More than that, looking at him made her feel sated and starving at the same time. She'd been trying not to look at him if they happened to pass each other. And it was pretty easy to avoid someone in a gigantic palace.

He exhaled and crossed the room in two easy strides, sitting on the bed. She wasn't sure who moved first, only that one moment she was determined to be resolute, and the next she was kissing him. Kissing him like she was starving for him, her fingernails digging into his shoulders, tears streaming down her face.

When they parted, he rested his forehead against hers, his breathing labored. "I am a fool, Carlotta."

"I'm listening," she said.

"You don't have to be my wife. I told you that a few days ago. But I shouldn't have left it there. I should have finished with a question."

"What question?"

"Will you marry me? Because you want to. Because I love you. Not because it's your duty, or because you want Luca to have my name. All of that is covered, and marrying me won't give it to you again. But it will make me the happiest man on earth."

She wiped tears from her cheeks with shaking hands. "What did you just say?"

"I asked you to marry me."

"The other part."

"That I love you?"

"Yes. Say it again."

"I love you, Carlotta. I should have told you this before, but I was too afraid. I was numb for so long, and you brought feeling back. Color. Light. I didn't want to admit how much I needed it. You showed me what life really was, and I didn't think I could live if I lost it. If I confessed it and you didn't feel the same. Somehow, I thought if I could just keep it all inside, I wouldn't have to face it. But I can't deny it. I love you, Carlotta Santina. No woman has ever had my heart. But you do. You have my heart, my mind. My body and my soul."

He cupped her face with his hands. "I cannot deny it. I don't want to. You…you have cast the fear from me with your love. There is no room for it now. I am filled. I am complete."

"I love you too," she said. "I love you so much."

He pulled her to him again, holding her in his arms, just holding her. His breathing ragged, his heartbeat steady and hard against her cheek. "You have no idea how badly I needed to hear that. How much I need your love. I do. I need it. I spent my whole life searching for some kind of happiness, for family. I finally have it. You gave it to me."

"And you gave me freedom. I'm not afraid of myself. Of passion. You accept me as who I am. And you've helped me do the same."

"That's love, Carlotta," he said, as though he was suddenly the expert. "Love has no conditions. No bounds. I didn't realize that until I met you. Thank you," he said, his voice rough. "Thank you for finding me. I was buried underneath a facade I hated. You found me."

Tears slid down her face, matching his. "I have loved every piece of you, Rodriguez. The man you showed the world, the father you are to our son, the man you are just for me. And I always will."

Rodriguez didn't bother to fight the emotion that was rushing through him, emotion he had kept shut off for so long. Emotion unlocked by Carlotta. By her love.

"I believe you."

"Good, because I'll always tell you the truth," she said.

"I know."

"I love you. And I want to marry you. Not to atone for anything, but because with you I'm free. With you I finally know who I am."

"That's good, Carlotta," he said, taking her face in his hands, wiping her tears away. "Because you are exactly who I needed."

EPILOGUE

"WE'RE outnumbered." Rodriguez surveyed the lawn, crowded with toys and climbing structures, and children. Four of them, running everywhere.

Luca was chasing the three smaller children and they were shrieking with glee.

"Yes, we are," Carlotta said, a smile lighting up her beautiful face. Seven years on and Rodriguez didn't think he would ever get used to her beauty. He was struck by it every time he looked at her.

Elizabetta, their youngest daughter, ran over to the slide and took two stuffed owls from the end.

"Those owls have seen better days," he said wryly.

"It's true, but they've been well loved by all."

Rodriguez turned to his wife, his heart, his soul. "Have I told you today that I love you?"

Her lips curved up into a smile. "You told me pretty emphatically this morning right after you…"

"I mean, have I told you since we got out of bed?"

"Once at breakfast. Then again during lunch. I think again when you passed me in the hall."

"Then I should tell you again. I love you, Carlotta Anguiano."

"And I love you too, more today than yesterday."

Rodriguez pulled her close, holding her against his chest

as they watched their children play. For a man who had worked so hard, for so long, chasing happiness, it was a wonderful thing to simply rest in it.

* * * * *

THE GIRL NOBODY WANTED

LYNN RAYE HARRIS

For my in-laws, Larry and Joyce Harris. Fifty years together is quite an accomplishment. You are proof that love can last forever. I'm so happy you're a part of my life, and I love you both.

CHAPTER ONE

ANNA CONSTANTINIDES stood at the edge of the gathered crowd and hoped the serene countenance she'd practiced before the mirror for the past week was holding up. Tonight was, without doubt, the most humiliating night of her life. Her fiancé—correction, former fiancé—was marrying another woman.

It would not have been so bad, perhaps, if her fiancé wasn't Prince Alessandro, heir to the Santina throne. She should have been his queen, yet she was currently the jilted bride.

A fact the media took great delight in reporting.

Again and again and *again*. She'd hardly had a peaceful moment since Alex had dumped her so publicly and humiliatingly for another woman. He hadn't even had the courtesy to inform her personally. No, he'd let her find out in the pages of the tabloids. Simply *mortifying*.

The pity she'd had to endure. The knowing looks—even, surprisingly, a hint of censure. As if it were *her* fault somehow. As if she were the one who'd been caught kissing another man while engaged to someone else, as Alex had been photographed with Allegra Jackson.

Anna wanted nothing less than to be at his engagement party tonight, but she'd had no choice. "Anna," her mother had said when she'd refused, "you must. Protocol demands it."

"I don't give a damn about protocol," she'd replied. And she hadn't. Why, when she'd dedicated her life to protocol and duty and been so spectacularly punished for it?

Her mother took her hands. "Sweetheart, do it for me. Queen Zoe is my oldest and dearest friend. I know she would be disappointed if we were not there to support her."

Support *her?* Anna had wanted to laugh, to shout, to rail against the unfairness of life—but she had not. Ultimately, she had done precisely what her mother asked because, for pity's sake, she felt *guilty.*

Anna stiffened her spine as the king began to toast the happy couple. But she lifted her glass of champagne along with everyone else, and prepared to drink to the health and happiness of Alex and Allegra, the woman who'd turned her preordained life upside down.

At least, thank goodness, she could be certain there were no photographers present tonight. They would be waiting outside the palace gates, naturally, but for now she was safe.

And yet she still had to smile, had to pretend she wasn't dying from embarrassment. She would have to endure the stories, the photos, the quotes from anonymous "friends" who claimed she was holding up well, or that she was fragile, or that her heart had shattered into a million pieces.

Anna sipped her champagne on cue. Only an hour more, and she was out of here. Back to the hotel where she would crawl into her bed and pull the covers over her head. The toast ended, and then the ensemble began to play a waltz. Anna slipped her barely touched glass onto a passing waiter's tray and turned toward the doors to the terrace. If she could escape for just a few moments, she could endure the next hour with a great deal more fortitude.

"Anna," a woman called. "I've been looking for you."

Anna gritted her teeth and turned toward Graziana Ricci, the Amanti foreign minister's wife. The woman sashayed toward her, a bright smile pasted on her cosmetically enhanced face. But it wasn't Signora Ricci who captured Anna's attention. It was the man beside her.

An Englishman, she assumed, as there were so many who had descended upon Santina recently.

He was tall, dressed in a bespoke tuxedo like nearly every other man in the room, and quite striking. Handsome, in a boyish way that somehow wasn't boyish at all. No, it was devilish, as if he knew the temptation he offered merely by existing. Eyes the color of roast coffee glittered in a face that had been carved by Michelangelo. Somehow, the look in those eyes dared her to envision him naked atop a pedestal.

Anna shook herself. Perhaps he was a work of art, but he had not been carved by Michelangelo. How silly.

But he could have been. His face was a study in angles sculpted for the sole purpose of making the owner appear sinfully irresistible to the female of the species. Sharply defined cheeks, a blade-straight nose, firm sensual lips and a small cleft at the base of his chin that deepened when he smiled.

And when he turned that smile on her, her heart skipped a beat.

Several beats.

The picture that filled her mind at that moment was decidedly uncharacteristic of her. She had absolutely no desire to kiss this man, no matter what her mind conjured up. It was stress, pure and simple.

As were the skipped beats. *Stress.*

The man smiled and winked, and Anna very deliberately looked away. *Honestly, what was wrong with her?*

"Anna, this is Leo Jackson," Signora Ricci said, and Anna instantly stiffened. The other woman didn't notice as she giggled, hugging his arm to her surgically enhanced body. *Shameless hussy.* "Leo is Allegra's brother."

As if he could be anyone else.

"How nice," Anna said frostily, her heart careening out of control with anger and helpless frustration. Allegra's brother. As if his sister ruining her life weren't enough, she now had to be faced with another Jackson when she quite simply wished them all to hell. Which wasn't very polite or charitable of her, she knew, but it was how she felt right now. "Welcome to Santina, Mr. Jackson. If you will excuse me, I was just on my way to…to an appointment."

It was a lie and her face flamed the instant she said it. Not because she cared that she'd lied, but because Leo Jackson arched one perfect eyebrow as if he knew she wanted to escape him. His lips quirked, and the flame inside her burned hotter.

But was it embarrassment or something else?

Embarrassment, she decided firmly. There could certainly be no other reason for it. If not for his sister, she wouldn't be in this predicament now. She wouldn't be standing here enduring the humiliation of hundreds of eyes surreptitiously turning upon her every time Alex leaned in close to his new fiancée and whispered something in her ear.

"I'm sorry to hear that, Anna," Leo said, using her given name as if he had every right in the world. Arrogant man! But her skin prickled with heat at the way her name sounded when he said it. Soft, sexy, alluring. Not boring Anna, but beautiful, exciting Anna.

"Nevertheless," she said, standing as straight and tall as she could. "It is the case."

What was wrong with her? Why was she being fanciful? She was simply Anna. And that's precisely who she wanted to be. Anna was safe, predictable, quietly elegant. She was not bold or brassy. Nothing like Signora Ricci, thank heavens.

Signora Ricci's mouth turned down in an exaggerated frown. "This will not take but a moment. I had hoped you could show Leo around Amanti tomorrow. He is thinking of building a luxury hotel."

Anna glanced at Leo Jackson. There was something dark and intense behind those eyes, no matter that one corner of his mouth turned up in a mocking grin. A fire began to burn low in her belly. She might be the tourist ambassador to the neighboring island of Amanti, but that didn't mean she had to personally show this man the sights.

It wasn't safe. *He* wasn't safe. She felt it in her bones.

Besides, his sister had stolen her future, and even if that wasn't his fault, she couldn't forget it if she were forced to spend time with him. No, she wanted nothing to do with this man—with *anyone* named Jackson.

"I'm afraid that's not possible, Signora Ricci. I have other things to attend to. I can arrange for someone else—"

The other woman scoffed. "What is more important than Amanti's economy? This would be good for us, yes? And you are the best for the job. What else do you have to do now that you have no wedding to prepare for?"

Anna swallowed her tongue as bitter acid scoured her throat. If she weren't a dignified person, a calm and controlled person, she might just strangle Graziana Ricci where she stood.

But no, Anna Constantinides had more dignity than that. She'd been raised to be serene, to be a perfect queen. She would not break because one woman dared to insult her on a day when she'd already been insulted by her ex-fiancé and the overwhelming media coverage of his new engagement. She was strong. She could handle this.

"If tomorrow doesn't work," Leo interjected, "the next day surely will." He pulled a card from his pocket and held it out. "My personal number. Call me when you are available."

Anna accepted the card because to do otherwise would be rude. His fingers brushed hers, and a tongue of fire sizzled along her nerve endings. She snatched her hand back, certain she'd find her skin blackened where he'd touched her. Graziana Ricci had turned away, distracted by an elderly matron who gesticulated wildly about something.

"I'm not sure when that will be, Mr. Jackson. It might truly be better for someone else to take you."

"And yet you are the tourist ambassador," he said with a hint of steel underlying the polite veneer in his tone. "Unless, of course, you do not like me for some reason?"

Anna swallowed. "I don't know you. How could I possibly dislike you?"

His gaze cut toward the front of the room where Alex and Allegra were currently standing close together and talking in hushed tones. "How indeed?"

Anna thrust her chin out. It was bad enough she had to endure this night, but for this man to know how she felt? It was insupportable. "Tell me about this hotel you propose to build," she said. "How will this help Amanti?"

His gaze slid down her body, heat trailing behind it. *Dangerous,* a voice whispered.

He took his time meeting her eyes again. "Have you not heard of the Leonidas Group?"

She was proud of herself for not showing her surprise. If the Leonidas Group wanted to build a hotel on Amanti, that could be a very good thing. "Of course I have. They own some of the most luxurious hotels in the world and cater to the wealthiest of clients. Do you work for them, Mr. Jackson?"

His laughter was rich, rolling from him in golden tones that vibrated through her. "I own the Leonidas Group, Anna."

Again with her name, and again with the prickle of awareness skimming along her nerve endings. "How fortunate for Amanti," she said, because she could think of nothing else to say. She felt like a fool for missing the *Leo* in *Leonidas,* though it wasn't an immediately obvious connection. But if he owned the Leonidas Group, he must be very wealthy indeed.

He leaned in closer. "Perhaps you will change your mind about tomorrow, then."

Heat coiled tightly inside her. His voice was a delicious rumble in her ear, though she tried not to notice precisely how delicious. She was tired, that was all. He was just a man, and men were fickle. Unpredictable. Dishonorable.

She closed her eyes, her heart thrumming steadily. It was uncharitable to think of Alex that way, and yet she couldn't help it. He'd made a promise, damn him!

"I will have to check my calendar," she said coolly.

His smile made her heart skip a beat. Too, too charming. Perhaps his sister was equally as charming. Perhaps that's how she'd stolen Alex away.

"And yet, when you wake up and see the morning papers, you will no doubt wish yourself far from Santina."

A current of dread slid through her, icy fingers scraping her soul. The papers. They would be filled with news of Alex and Allegra tomorrow—and she would be mentioned side by side with them. The poor jilted bride. The faithful girl who'd been stood up by a prince. Sad little heiress, no longer a queen-in-waiting.

Anna's throat constricted. She absolutely did not want

to be here tomorrow. And he was giving her a way out, though she would have to endure his company. But which was worse? The media frenzy, or Leo Jackson?

If she took him to Amanti, they wouldn't escape the attention entirely, but at least they would be out of Alex and Allegra's proximity. Perhaps the press might not think her so sad and distraught if she were seen going about her duties.

"I've just remembered," she said, proud that she managed to sound so cold and detached. Professional. "My appointment isn't for tomorrow after all. I keep getting my days mixed up. It's for the next day."

"Is that so?" Leo said, his gaze slipping over her once more. There was heat and promise in that voice, and a hint of possession, as well. It infuriated her—and intrigued her.

"If you wish to tour Amanti," she said crisply, already partially regretting the impulse that had her choosing him over tomorrow's papers, "we can leave around nine in the morning."

"Nine?" he mocked. "I doubt I'll have slept off tonight's debaucheries by then."

Anna felt her ears going hot. She refused to picture *any* debauchery. "Nine o'clock, Mr. Jackson. Or not at all."

"You drive a hard bargain, darling," he drawled, as if he weren't in the least bit dangerous to her sense of well-being. "But we'll do it your way."

Before she knew what he was about, he caught her hand and pressed a kiss to the back of it. Her skin tingled as his warm breath washed over her, his beautiful lips skimming so lightly over her flesh. She couldn't suppress the small shudder that racked her body or the ache of sensation that made her crave more of his touch.

Leo Jackson looked up, his gaze sharp. Too sharp. As if he'd seen through to the core of her and knew what she'd been thinking. That devilish grin was back as his coffee-colored eyes glittered with heat. "Tomorrow, darling," he said. "I look forward to it."

Anna pulled her hand away, tried very hard to ignore the pulsing throb in her belly, between her legs. "I'm not your darling, Mr. Jackson."

He winked. "Not yet. But let's see what tomorrow brings, shall we?"

After a restless night, Anna rose early the next morning, and then showered and dressed with care. She was the tourist ambassador to Amanti, not a woman going on a date, so she chose a fashionable skirt and blazer. She paired the gray suit with a red silk camisole—her one nod to color—her pearls, and gray suede pumps. She wrapped her long dark hair in a neat knot and secured it with pins. Then she slipped on mascara and lip gloss before walking over to the cheval glass and studying her reflection from head to toe.

She looked professional, competent. Precisely the way she wanted to appear. She absolutely did not care whether Leo Jackson found her attractive or not.

Liar.

Anna frowned at herself. She wasn't unattractive; she was professional. And she intended to stay that way. If she could control nothing else about these chaotic past few weeks, she could at least control her image. And this was the image she wanted to project. Serenity in the face of turmoil. Grace under fire. A calm port in the storm.

Anna patted her hair one last time before she whirled away from the mirror, found her handbag and cell phone, checked her calendar to make sure she'd taken care of everything and left her room at precisely twenty to nine. Her room was two floors up from Leo Jackson's room, but first she took an elevator down to the dining room and grabbed a quick cup of coffee and a whole-grain muffin before going back up to Leo's floor. At three minutes to nine, she knocked on his door.

Nothing happened. Anna frowned as she listened for movement behind the door. She checked her watch, studied the sweep of the second hand across the mother-of-pearl face. At nine o'clock precisely, she knocked again. "Mr. Jackson?" she said, pressing her face close to the door in order not to wake any of the other late-sleeping guests in nearby rooms. "Are you in there?"

Two minutes later, when she'd knocked yet again— louder this time, because she was getting very annoyed— the door jerked open.

Anna's stomach flipped at the sight of Leo Jackson in all his bad-boy glory. Heavens above, why did this man have to be so compelling? She should feel nothing for him but contempt. Not only had his family wrecked her perfect life, but he was also not the sort of man a proper lady should ever get involved with.

Yet heat bloomed in her cheeks as she thought of his comment last night about debauchery. Because that's precisely what he looked like—as if he'd spent the night in some lucky woman's bed, debauching her thoroughly.

Before she could control herself, Anna thought that *she* wanted to be debauched. Thoroughly. Repeatedly.

If she could have slapped her palms to her cheeks in horror, she would have done so. She most definitely did *not* want to be debauched—and certainly not by this rogue.

"Hello, darling," Leo said casually, his sensual lips twisting in that arrogant grin that had featured so prominently in her thoughts last night while she'd tossed and turned in her bed. And yet, in the moment before he'd spoken, she'd sensed something behind that playboy demeanor, something tightly leashed in and controlled.

A sleek, dangerous beast on a tether.

"Mr. Jackson," she replied coolly, hoping he couldn't see the thrum of her pulse in her throat. "We had an appointment at nine, I believe."

He ran a hand through his dark hair. His eyes gleamed with interest as his gaze slipped over her. He had a day's growth of beard on his face—and she'd never seen anything sexier in her life.

Neither, it seemed, had some other woman. Or, heaven forbid, *women*. Yes, she definitely could see Leo Jackson taking more than one woman home with him at a time.

Oh, dear... The images in her head were definitely not safe for public consumption.

But he stood in the door, looking so dissolute and sexy in his tuxedo from last night she couldn't form a coherent thought as she studied him. The beast was concealed once more, so that she found herself wondering if she'd imagined it. But she had not, she was certain. He was smooth and magnificent—and not quite what he seemed to be at first glance.

His jacket hung open and his shirt was unbuttoned. The tie and studs were gone, probably tucked into a pocket. A bright smudge of pink was smeared across the pristine white of his collar. Lipstick, she realized with a jolt. And not the color Graziana Ricci had been wearing.

She was positive, looking at him, that he'd not spent the night in his own bed. In fact, she was pretty sure he hadn't slept at all. She tried not to think of what he'd been doing instead—or whom he'd been doing it with.

While she had lain awake thinking about this man, he'd forgotten all about her. Clearly, as his lack of readiness and his delay in answering the door indicated. She only hoped her cheeks weren't scarlet. What if he had a woman in there right now?

"I—I can come back later," she blurted. "If you're, um, busy."

"Not at all," he said smoothly, wrapping a hand around her elbow and pulling her into the room. She caught her heel and stumbled to a halt in the small foyer of his suite, her hands automatically bracing against his chest as she nearly lost her balance.

"Sorry about that, darling," he said, his arms enveloping her. His broad hands were on her back, her waist, searing into her like a flaming-hot brand. Her heart skittered. She had an impression of a sleeping lion rearing its head and sniffing the air for prey.

"I don't think you're sorry at all," she bit out, and then stifled a gasp when she realized what she'd said. No matter how she felt about Leo Jackson, it wasn't permissible to be rude. She'd spent a lifetime learning the art of diplomacy, a skill she would have needed as Queen of Santina one day. And she'd just failed miserably, hadn't she?

No wonder Alex had left her. Except, how was Allegra Jackson any better suited to be a queen, considering how scandalously her family had behaved last night?

If appearances were any indication, *this* particular Jackson had behaved very badly indeed.

Leo laughed, the fingers of one hand caressing the furrow of her spine through her clothing. Oh, if he kept doing that... Heat and light flared inside her, slid through her limbs until she wanted to mold herself to him like a second skin. His body was hard against hers, hot. It disconcerted her, and thrilled her. How could she react to this man so soon after Alex had turned her world upside down?

"Since you've landed in my arms, perhaps I'm not sorry," he said.

No man had ever held her so close. Not even Alex. She'd learned to dance with men, to conduct herself with poise and grace, and she'd been in a man's embrace before. But not this kind of embrace. This hot, needy, sensual embrace that was, on the surface, not improper at all.

Except for how it made her feel. Oh, yes, she felt quite improper when Leo Jackson had his arms around her. As if she wanted to feel skin against skin, mouth against mouth. As if she wanted to burn up in his arms and see what it felt like.

Ridiculous, since she didn't even know him. The stress of the past few weeks had obviously affected her brain.

Anna disentangled herself from his embrace and took a step back. She tugged on the bottom of her jacket to straighten it. Then she patted her hair, happy that no stray wisps had escaped the confinement of her knot.

Leo shook his head as he studied her with an expression of bemusement on his face. "Afraid of what you might feel if you let yourself go, darling?"

Fire burst through her, making twin spots rise in her cheeks. "Stop calling me *darling*," she said firmly. "And stop trying to seduce me, Mr. Jackson. It won't work."

She wouldn't *let* it work.

The gleam in his eyes was predatory. Feral. Exciting. *Dangerous.*

"Really? Not feeling the least bit angry about your fiancé and my sister? Not aching to put it all behind you with a few pleasurable hours?"

Anna lifted her chin. He'd seen right through her, hadn't he? "Actually, that sounds quite lovely. But first I'll need to find someone to spend those hours with."

"I'm wounded," he said lightly, though something in his expression made her take a step back.

"I doubt that," she replied crisply. "You'll have moved on to the next woman on your list without a moment's regret, I'm certain. We are all interchangeable to you."

Was that irritation flaring in his dark eyes? Anger?

Or pain? It shocked her enough that she couldn't decide. But then it was gone so quickly she began to wonder if she'd imagined it. Did she want him to have a conscience so it would make this strange attraction to him more bearable?

Probably.

Still, her outburst went against everything she'd ever been taught. She was out of her depth lately, stressed and furious and hurt. She had to govern herself better. "Forget I said that. It was rude."

"And you can't stand being rude, can you, Anna?" His voice caressed her name exactly as she'd imagined it last night, while lying awake in her bed.

"It's not the way I was raised," she said primly. Then she glanced at her watch, because the air felt suddenly thick and hot and she didn't know what else to do. "We're running late, Mr. Jackson. Our boat is at the dock. We were supposed to leave five minutes ago."

"Heaven forbid we are late. But you can cancel the boat. The tour will go much faster if we take my plane."

Anna blinked. "Plane? Amanti is only twenty-five miles away by sea. The boat will have us there in under an hour, and then we can hire a car to take us around the island."

His expression was patient but firm. "I need to see the coast. We'll fly around the island first, and then land and have a tour, yes?"

Anna reached for her pearls, comforting herself with the solid feel of them between her fingers. He was overriding all her plans. It was too much like what had happened to her life lately, and it made her nervous. Uncertain. Damn, how she hated that feeling.

"But I've already arranged things," she said firmly, attempting to regain control of the situation. "There is no need for you to put yourself out, Mr. Jackson."

He reached for her again, put his hands on either side of her shoulders and bent until his gorgeous eyes were on a level with hers. Her heart flipped. "Arrangements can be changed, Anna. And you really need to call me Leo."

She darted her tongue over her lower lip. "I'd prefer to keep this professional, if you don't mind."

"I do mind," he said, his eyes darkening.

Anna tried not to let the warm, spicy scent of him wrap around her senses. But he was too close, and he smelled so good, and her stomach was knotting with tension at his proximity. He confused her. She ached in ways she never had before, and she wanted things she'd once looked upon with quiet acceptance. She'd expected to be intimate with Alex, of course. She hadn't expected to find out she wanted that intimacy with a kind of earthy sensuality that was completely foreign to her nature.

But not with Alex.

With this man. With Leo.

"Keep looking at me that way, and we won't go anywhere," he murmured, his voice a lovely growl in his throat. She imagined him growling against her skin, his body twining intimately with hers, and swallowed hard.

It was shocking to be thinking these thoughts. And so very, *very* titillating.

She might be a virgin, but she wasn't stupid. She was modern enough to have read a few books on sex. She'd even managed to watch a video, the memory of which had her heart hurtling forward. The way the man had put his head between the woman's legs and—

"Anna," Leo groaned. "Stop."

Anna shook herself. What was wrong with her? Baiting a lion in his den? Was she insane?

"Really, I have no idea what you're talking about Mr.— Leo. You have a very dirty mind."

His sharp bark of laughter was not quite what she expected. He let her go abruptly, and her skin tingled through her clothes where he'd so recently touched her. "I think if this tour stands a chance of getting off the ground, I'd better change."

"That would be wise," she said primly.

She stood in the foyer, uncertain whether to follow or stay where she was. In the end, she decided to stay. She could hear him moving around, hear a soft curse as a door opened and shut again. She looked at her reflection in the mirror, blushed anew at her heightened color. Leo Jackson brought out the worst in her.

She was just beginning to worry about how long she'd been standing there when he reappeared. A jolt of surprise went through her at the sight of him. She didn't know what she'd expected, but his casual attire had not quite been it.

He wore a long-sleeved navy shirt, unbuttoned midchest, with a white T-shirt beneath. Half the shirt was tucked into faded, ripped jeans. The other half hung free in a kind of casual slouch that proclaimed this man didn't care about rules.

But the truth was that he looked utterly gorgeous. The height of Bohemian fashion, while she stood there in her prim suit and felt frumpy. Stuffy. Oh, the suit was expensive, but it was staid. Safe and boring. A generation too old for her, perhaps. The stylist had tried to get her to go with a shorter hem, a nipped-in waist, but she'd refused.

She was regretting it at the moment.

"Ready, my love?" he asked, and her heart skipped a beat.

"Only if you stop calling me names," she said, her jaw

aching with the effort it took to be polite as she forced the words out.

He grinned, and her heart melted. Damn it. Damn *him*.

"I can try, sweet Anna."

Somehow, that was even worse.

CHAPTER TWO

IT WAS a glorious morning in Santina. The sun was shining brightly in the sky and the turquoise water of the Mediterranean sparkled like diamonds beneath it. Anna buckled her seat belt and tried to calm the racing of her heart as their plane began to taxi toward the runway.

Leo was flying. She hadn't quite expected that. When he'd said they would take his plane, she'd assumed he had a flight crew. Which he did, but he'd given them the day off to see the sights.

"Don't you need help?" she'd asked.

"It's a small plane," he'd replied. "Certified for one pilot. I left the 737 at home this time."

"It seems like a lot of trouble to go to for a short trip."

He smiled at her, and her heart turned over. "Relax, Anna. They wouldn't let me take off if I wasn't licensed."

She had to admit that he'd done a thorough check of the plane before they'd gone anywhere. He'd spent time looking at the instruments, walking around the craft, going over a checklist. Finally, when he'd deemed everything to be okay, he'd communicated with the tower.

And now they were turning onto the runway, the plane braking only momentarily while Leo said something else to the tower. Someone gave him the go-ahead, and then the plane was shooting down the runway. Anna bit her lip to stifle the laughter that wanted to break free at that very moment.

She loved everything about taking off. The charge down the runway, the plane lifting into the air, the ground falling away and her stomach going with it. She loved the way they soared into the sky with the landscape below getting smaller and smaller. She could see the rocky outcrop on which the palace was built, the faded terra-cotta roofs of the city, the glint of sunlight on glass and metal.

She slumped into her seat, a strange sense of relief pouring over her. She was leaving it all behind. She was free, at least for the next few hours, and her heart felt suddenly light.

She turned to look out Leo's side and caught him glancing at her. Her stomach flipped.

"Happy?" he asked, and she wondered how he knew. She hadn't given it away. She hadn't laughed, or smiled, or reacted at all. She knew because she'd practiced it for so many years. It was essential, as a queen, to be tranquil. To hide your feelings behind a mask of cool efficiency. She was good at it.

Usually.

"I don't, um, feel happy or sad," she said, stumbling in the middle and hoping he hadn't noticed.

"Liar," he shot at her. But he grinned when he said it, and a current of warmth washed over her. "I've an idea, sweet Anna."

She pointedly ignored his use of her name and the epithet he'd attached to it. "What is this idea?"

The hot, intense look he gave her had the power to melt her insides. He looked at her like he owned her, and it made little sparks fly around inside her like a racquetball bouncing off the walls of the court.

"Let's fly to Sicily. We can spend the day there, eating pasta, viewing the volcano—" one eyebrow arched, his voice dropping an octave before he said the next two words "—making love. We'll return to Amanti tonight and tour tomorrow."

Anna felt her face go red even as her heart rate notched up. "Impossible," she said.

"And why is that? Because you don't like me? You don't need to like me, Anna, for what I have in mind."

She needed a fan turned on her body full blast. "I have no feelings about you at all, Mr. Jackson."

"Really? I find that difficult to believe."

"I don't see why you should."

"Because I am a Jackson, perhaps?"

She crossed her arms and gazed out the window. Below, the ocean rolled in all directions. "I could hardly hold you responsible for what your sister has done."

He seemed to hesitate for a moment. "Whatever she has done," he said softly, "she has not done it alone."

Anna's heart burned. "No, you are quite correct. It takes two, as the saying goes."

"Indeed. Just imagine what the two of us could do together in Sicily." His voice was seductive, full of promise.

"We're going to Amanti. Now," she said firmly.

"Are you sure? I'm quite worth the side trip, I assure you."

"Good heavens, you are vain," she said, her heart racing at the thought of doing something so insane, so out of the ordinary. "No. No, no, *no.*"

But a part of her wanted to say yes. She wanted to be the woman she'd never been allowed to be. She wanted to break free of her suits and her pearls and spend one glorious, hot, naked day with a man. She wanted to know what it felt like to let a man like Leo have his wicked way with her.

No, she told herself quite firmly, *she did not.*

But why not? Everything she'd prepared for, everything she'd thought her life was going to be, had disappeared in the blink of an eye. She was a virgin who'd never even kissed a man because she'd been saving herself for Alex Santina. Alex, who'd never kissed her properly. He'd brushed his lips across her cheek, once over her mouth, but the contact had been so light and perfunctory that she had no idea what it truly felt like to kiss a man.

And Leo wanted to take her to Sicily and make love to her. She shivered with excitement. It was preposterous, and she wasn't going to say yes, but the idea was rather thrilling in an illicit way that had her sex tightening in response.

A static voice came over the headset then, and she jumped in surprise at the sudden sound slicing across her thoughts. She couldn't hear what the voice said, but Leo replied. And then he was pulling on the controls and they were climbing higher and faster.

"What?" she said, her heart thudding for a different reason now. "What is it?"

"Nothing," he replied. "Some unexpected turbulence. We're climbing to avoid it."

"Why did you ask me to go to Sicily? You've filed a flight plan. You can't just change it."

Leo flashed her another of those smiles that did things to her insides. "We aren't a commercial aircraft, darling. I can change it if I wish. Haven't you heard I'm eccentric that way?"

"I've heard nothing at all about you," she said with a sniff. It was only partially true. Last night, when she'd gotten back to her room, she'd done an internet search on Leo Jackson.

"Excellent. So you won't have made up your mind about me yet."

"Oh, I'm sure I have."

"Have you now? And what have you decided?"

Anna studied his profile. Leo Jackson was handsome and wealthy, and reputed to be intense in both his business dealings and personal relationships. He was also a serial womanizer who'd spent the past several years living in the United States, dating Hollywood starlets and supermodels and, on one memorable occasion, a gorgeous actress who was at least twenty years his senior. Of all the women he'd been linked with, that was the only one that had ever seemed to be somewhat serious.

There was no indication about what had ended the relationship, but it was definitely over. The actress had recently married someone else and adopted a baby with him.

"I think you can't be trusted," she said softly.

"Ah. What a shame."

"But you don't deny it."

He shook his head. "That depends on how you define *trust*. Will I seduce you in spite of your denials that you're attracted to me? Possibly. Will I lie to you and leave you heartbroken? Never. Because I will tell you up front that it's not wise to have expectations beyond the physical. We can have a good time, but we aren't getting married."

Anna crossed her legs. Had she really thought going to Sicily with him might be thrilling? "Why would you assume that a woman might have expectations about you? Are you truly that fabulous that no one can resist you? Honestly, I've never met anyone so arrogant as you. Not everyone thinks you're irresistible, you know."

"But you do."

Surely her face was bright red. From anger, not embarrassment, she told herself. "I do not. I don't even like you."

He laughed as if she'd admitted something she shouldn't

have. "And here I thought you didn't have any feelings at all about me."

"I'm rapidly changing my mind."

The look he gave her jolted her to her core. Dark, sensual, breathtakingly intense. "We could have fun in Sicily, Anna. Hot, decadent, pleasurable fun."

Her heart was thrumming. "Please stop saying *we*. *We* aren't doing anything together, Mr. Jackson."

He laughed again. "Back to that? Have you ever considered, sweet Anna, that perhaps it's time you let your hair down a bit? Time to let go of that buttoned-up perfection you try so hard to project and have some fun?"

Anna clenched her hands into fists in her lap. He didn't know her, didn't know what he was saying. He was simply guessing, because that's what men like him did. They got beneath your skin and made you desire them, made you think they understood you when in fact they only understood how to lower your defenses. It was a parlor trick, the kind of thing bogus fortune tellers did every day at the carnival.

She might not be experienced, but she wasn't stupid.

"You're grabbing at straws," she said calmly. "I am well aware I'm not perfect. And I like the way I'm dressed."

"It's not a bad way to dress if you're chairing a board meeting," he said. "But it's not your true style."

"I don't think you have the first clue about my style."

"I'm not sure you do, either," he said. "But we could start with naked and go from there."

Heat flared in her core, impossible heat. Her limbs were jelly whenever he mentioned the word *naked*. She was in danger of turning into a slack-jawed nitwit if he kept it up. "Do you ever quit?"

"I do," he said. "But I don't think we've reached that point yet."

Anna groaned. It was uncharacteristic of her, but she couldn't help it. "Why are you torturing me? Why can't we just fly to Amanti, view the coast and go back to Santina?"

Leo looked at her, his expression suddenly very serious. "Do you really want to go back to Santina? Is that where you want to be today?"

She turned to look out the window. The sea spread in all directions, as far as the eye could see. It was hard to believe they could be in the Mediterranean and it could still feel so remote. As if they were the only two people in the world. There were no boats out here, no other planes, nothing but the blue sky, the bright sun and dazzling water.

She was alone with him, and while he frustrated her, he also made her feel things she'd not felt before: attractive, alive, interesting. She wasn't quite ready to give that up yet.

"No," she said softly. And then she turned to face him, her jaw hardening. "No, I don't want to go back."

Leo wasn't sure why, but he wanted her. She was quite possibly the most uptight woman he'd ever met, but for some reason that intrigued him. Like now, when she sat there beside him and tried to look stony. He wasn't sure she realized it, but stony didn't really work when you had wide jade-green eyes that showed every ounce of hurt you were feeling, whether you wanted them to or not.

And Anna was hurting. He'd seen her across the room last night, looking so isolated and alone, and he'd wanted to know who she was. Graziana Ricci had laughed dismissively. "Oh, that's Anna Constantinides. The jilted bride."

The jilted bride. He'd watched her closely then, wondering what she must be feeling as she listened to the toasts to Prince Alessandro and Allegra. She'd looked so cool, so bored, so perfect and untouchable dressed all in icy white—but then her fingers had strayed to the pearl necklace she wore, and he'd noticed they were trembling. When she'd turned toward him, the light from the chandeliers caught her just right and he'd realized she was on the verge of tears.

Shimmering tears she never once let fall.

She'd been a beautiful ice queen in the center of that gathering, the most regal and elegant of them all—and he'd wanted to see if he could melt the ice surrounding her heart. Leo lived for challenges, and Anna Constantinides was a challenge. It wasn't simply that he wanted to seduce her. He wanted to make her laugh, wanted to see her eyes light up with pleasure.

Anyone who'd seen the newspapers, who'd read those ugly headlines and even uglier stories, would know she was suffering. It made him think of another time, another woman, who had also been deeply hurt by what the papers had said about her. His mother had kept the articles from when her affair with Bobby had been splashed through the papers. He'd found them in her personal documents when he was eighteen. She'd been dead for eight years by then.

Until that moment, he'd thought the most devastating thing she'd had in her possession had been the positive paternity test naming Bobby Jackson as his father—a fact Bobby had denied until the test was brought out in court after Leo's mother's death—but the articles had given Leo a whole new level of understanding about what had happened between his parents.

Though Bobby had raised him from the age of ten onward, their relationship could never be termed ordinary. Bobby didn't seem to know how to be a father, either to Leo or his siblings. He tried, but he was more of a dotty uncle than anything.

After Leo found the articles and confronted his father, their relationship had soured. Soon after that, he'd gone to the States to forge his way in business. He'd wanted to prove he didn't need Bobby, or the Jackson name, to succeed. He'd built the Leonidas Group from the ground up, and he'd made more money than Bobby had ever earned, even at the height of his football career.

Since Leo had returned to London recently, he'd been trying damn hard to forge a new relationship with his father. Though it wasn't perfect, they were finally learning to let go of the past and be friends.

Just then, Anna glanced down at her slim gold watch and turned sharply toward him as she realized how long they'd been flying. "Are we lost? Because we should have been there by now."

Leo flexed his fingers on the controls. "We aren't lost, darling. I thought it might be nice to fly for a little while."

He found flying soothing, especially when he wanted to think.

But Anna was used to structure. Her mouth opened. Closed. Opened again. "But why?" she blurted. "There is much to see on Amanti!"

He glanced over at her. Such an uptight woman. He found himself wanting to unpin her hair and see how long it might be. And he definitely wanted to get her out of that bland suit. Grey. Why was the woman wearing grey? The red of her shirt was the only spot of color in her drab outfit. Didn't she know she should be dressed all in red? In vibrant, sassy colors that made the green of her eyes stand out even more than they already did?

She was utterly beautiful, and trying so hard to hide that beauty. He found himself wanting to know why.

"And do you really want to be on Amanti today?" he asked coolly.

Her eyes were wide, her expression haunted. He didn't have to explain what he meant. The newspapers and tabloids couldn't seem to leave the story of Prince Alessandro's surprise engagement alone, especially since he'd picked Allegra Jackson—of those *scandalous* Jacksons—as his bride.

Anna couldn't help but be dragged into the publicity. She was the antithesis of his family, and probably far more suited to being a royal bride by virtue of her lack of scandalous relations.

Which also meant she was the perfect sacrificial lamb for the roasting fires of the papers that dogged the Santinas' every move.

The press loved every minute of her humiliation. Each story that featured Alessandro and Allegra's forbidden love also featured Anna. She endured it with quiet dignity, but Leo wondered how close she was getting to breaking. She was only human after all. It couldn't be easy to see her former fiancé with Allegra.

"I can't hide forever," she said, drawing herself up regally, shuttering her hurt behind her lowered lashes. "The press will have their fun until they tire of the story. If I run away or hide from the world, it will be a thousand times worse."

Her fingers strayed to her neck, caught at her pearls. "No, I have to endure it until it goes away."

Leo swore. He wanted to protect her, and he wanted to shake her at the same time. "It's acceptable to be angry, Anna. And it's acceptable to want to escape."

"I never said I wasn't angry," she snapped before closing her eyes again and saying something in what he assumed was her native Greek. When she trained those green eyes on him again, they were as placid as a secluded lake. She was good. Very good. But he could see the fire she couldn't quite hide in the depths of that gaze. And it pulled at him more than it ought.

"These things pass," she said. "And now we must go to Amanti and begin our tour. The last thing I need is for the press to think I'm off being promiscuous with you."

"Perhaps you need a little promiscuity in your life," he replied, very aware he was being self-serving as he said it. "A little fun that's about you, not about others or what they expect from you."

"You're only saying this because it would suit *your* purposes if I agreed with you. Stop trying to seduce me, Mr. Jackson. It won't work."

It was close to the mark, and inexplicably it made him angry. Except that he wasn't quite sure if it was her or himself he was angry with. He definitely wanted her. She intrigued him. She didn't seem to care who he was or what he offered her—and that made him think of something else, something he'd not let himself consider before. "Were you in love with him?"

Anna spluttered. He loved ruffling her cool, though he hoped the answer was no. For some reason, he needed it to be no.

"That's none of your business! We hardly know each other, Mr. Jackson," she said, her entire body stiff with outrage. Her long fingers gripped the arm of the seat. Her nails were manicured and neat, and there was a pale line on her left ring finger where her engagement ring had once sat. He imagined those elegant fingers playing his body like a fine instrument, and nearly groaned.

Since when was he interested in prim little schoolteachers anyway? Not that Anna was a schoolteacher—she was far too well bred and rich to have an actual job—but she reminded him of one. The kind of teacher who wore buttoned-up suits to work and lacy knickers beneath. Whether she realized it or not, the woman seethed with pent-up sexuality.

Whoever got her to let her hair down and give in to her sensual nature would be one lucky man. He pictured Anna in a bed, her naked body lying against red sheets, those full kissable lips open and eager as he lowered himself onto her and captured her mouth with his own.

Suddenly, flying was getting damned uncomfortable. Leo forced himself to think of something unsexy—like Graziana Ricci's collagen-plumped lips smeared in cherry-red lipstick—and hoped his body would take the hint.

"How can we possibly get to know each other," he said, "if you keep retreating behind that starched formality every time I ask you a question?"

"We don't need to know each other. I'm taking you to Amanti so you can decide whether or not you want to build a hotel there. Beyond that, I'm sure we'll never see each other again. Now, if you will please take us *to* Amanti, we can get on with the tour."

Leo shot her a glance. She was prickly as hell and completely fascinating. "You don't like it when your plans get changed, do you? You're very much a list girl."

Her head whipped around. "A list girl? What, pray tell, is that?"

"You make lists. You like a long list of things to do and then you check them off one by one. There's no room for spontaneity on your lists." He made a checkmark in the air. "Woke up early, check. Ate breakfast, check."

"There's nothing wrong with being organized, Mr. Jackson," she said. He could hear the starch in her voice, the outrage she tried to keep hidden. She was trying to keep him at a distance, and he wouldn't allow it.

"If you call me Mr. Jackson one more time," he growled, "I'll keep flying until we reach Sicily."

"You wouldn't."

Her arms folded over her prim grey suit, her chin thrusting forward in challenge. Clearly, Anna Constantinides didn't know him very well. No matter how successful he'd become, he'd never shaken that raw, edgy side of his personality that liked to push barriers to their limit. No doubt it came from trying to fit into the Jackson household when he'd been young and motherless and uncertain of his place in their lives. He'd pushed and rebelled, certain his father would throw him out, but Bobby had never wavered in his acceptance once he'd stepped up and admitted paternity.

"I would, in fact," Leo replied. "I've got nothing to lose."

Her jaw clenched tight and he felt suddenly wrong for phrasing it that way. She had everything to lose, or so she thought. A trip to Sicily with him would be devastating in Anna's world. Because she was already the focus of attention and she couldn't fathom drawing yet more. Never mind that if she were only to behave as if she didn't care, the media would soon leave her alone. He knew from experience that they liked nothing better than a victim—and Anna was a perfect victim right now.

"I don't want to go to Sicily, Leo. I want to go to Amanti."

"Tell the truth, Anna. You don't want to do that, either. But you've committed to it and so you want to get there without giving the media anything else to speculate about."

She made a frustrated noise. "Yes. This is precisely the truth. If I could run to Sicily or Egypt or Timbuktu and not have to endure another moment of this shame, I would do it. But I can't run, Leo. I have to carry on as always and wait for the scandal to pass."

It was perhaps the most honest thing she'd said yet. But he wanted more. "Tell me this, then. If you could have an affair, no consequences, no one the wiser, would you do so?"

She didn't say anything for the longest time. "I…I…"

But whatever she was about to say was lost as a light on the instrument panel flashed on. A tight knot formed in Leo's stomach as he turned his focus to the plane. He'd checked everything before they'd left Santa Maria, and everything had been fine. He wouldn't have taken off otherwise.

But something had changed in the half hour since.

CHAPTER THREE

THE plane shuddered and Anna's heart leaped. Whatever she'd been about to say was forgotten as she took in Leo's sudden concentration. "What's happening?"

He didn't look at her. "We're losing fuel pressure," he said as he did something with the switches. The plane shuddered again, and the engine made a high-pitched whining noise that sent her heart into her throat.

"What does that mean?" Because she needed to know, precisely, what he was saying to her. It didn't sound good, and she didn't like the sensation of being out of control. Whatever happened, she was in a plane with Leo, high above the Mediterranean, and there was nothing she could do to fix the problem.

But that didn't mean she intended to sit quietly and hope for the best.

"It means there's a problem in the fuel line. We need to land before we run out of gas."

"Land? Where?" She scanned the horizon, saw nothing but water for kilometers. Her stomach churned. "Leo, there's nothing out here."

He checked the GPS, his long fingers flexing against the controls. "We're too far from Amanti," he finally said, concentrating on the screen. "But there's another island a few miles distant."

Another island? She didn't know what it could be, but she began to pray fervently that they would make it there. The plane bucked again, the engine sputtering before smoothing out once more. Anna gripped her seat, her fingers pressing into the leather so hard that they ached.

"Are we going to die?"

"No." His answer was swift, sure, and she took comfort in it. But doubts began to creep in. What if he was wrong? What if he was only trying to keep her calm? She couldn't abide that. She had to know.

"Tell me the truth, Leo," she finally said, unable to stand it a moment longer. "Please."

Leo's dark eyes glinted with determination as he looked over at her. How could her heart flip at the look on his face when this was serious? How could heat blossom between her thighs at a moment like this?

Because she had regrets, that's why. Because she'd saved herself for years for a husband who had cast her aside before they'd ever even wed. Now that she might die, she fervently wished she'd experienced passion, even if it had just been for one night.

Leo stared at her so intently that she could almost forget where they were, what was happening. For a moment, she could almost wish they'd had that day in Sicily.

"If we can find this island, we'll be fine," Leo said shortly.

She wanted to believe him, but she couldn't simply accept it without question. "But what if there's nowhere to land?"

"There's definitely somewhere to land," he said. "Look around you."

There was nothing but blue as far as the eye could see. She gasped as she finally took his meaning. "The sea?"

"Yes. Now put on your life jacket, and grab that orange backpack from where it's stowed behind my seat."

"But, Leo," she said, panic rising inside her as she thought of them marooned at sea. Assuming they survived the impact. *Oh, God.*

"Anna, trust me," he said firmly. "Get the pack. Get your life jacket."

"What about you?"

"Grab mine, too. I can't put it on yet, but I will."

Anna unbuckled her seat belt and found the life jackets. She clipped hers on with shaky fingers, and then grabbed the heavy orange pack he'd told her to get and brought everything back to her seat. Leo was saying something into the headset, but he didn't appear to be getting an answer.

"No," he said when she started to sit down again. "Sit in one of the seats behind me. It'll be safer on impact."

Anna hesitated only a moment before sinking into the seat beside him and buckling her seat belt. "I want to be here with you," she said. "I insist on it."

She didn't expect him to laugh, but he did. A short, sharp bark of laughter that stole into her soul and made her feel good, if only for a moment. "Dragon lady," he said, and her heart skipped again. At a time like this, how did he make her feel as if she were formidable? As if she mattered? How did he cut through the pain and anger and make her feel important again?

"There it is," Leo said, and she squinted into the distance, searching the horizon. A small gray bump rose up from the sea, growing bigger the closer they got. There were many small islands out here, some of which were inhabited and some not. Any hope she'd had this might be one of the inhabited ones faded quickly when she saw the size of the island.

It was long, narrow and rocky, with a green area at one end and a white sandy beach on one side.

"There's nowhere to land," she said.

"I'm taking us down," he replied. "It might be rough."

That was the only warning he gave her as he pointed the nose down and began his descent. Anna's stomach twisted as the plane dropped in the sky. Sweat broke out on her forehead, between her breasts. Her heart went into free fall as the sea grew bigger and bigger with every passing minute.

The engine sputtered and whined, and Leo's hands were white on the controls. But the plane continued to descend in a controlled manner. Anna grasped her pearls in her fingers, twisted hard and then chided herself for doing so. This was no time to break them. They'd been her grandmother's, the only link she had left to the woman she'd most admired. She would not destroy them.

"Leo," she said helplessly as they sank lower in the sky. She reached for him, put her hand on his shoulder, squeezed. She hoped she was imparting strength, courage, but she had the feeling he didn't need any of those things. No, it was she who needed them and Leo who provided them to her.

She could do nothing but sit there and watch powerlessly as the island got bigger. But the sea was bigger still, so big and azure that it filled her vision from all sides. She focused on the island. There were a few trees, she noted, a wooded copse that might provide shelter—and might have fresh water if the rain had a place to collect. Assuming it rained.

If only they survived the plunge into the sea. *First things first, Anna.* She was so used to planning that she couldn't help herself, when in fact there was nothing to plan if they didn't make it out alive.

"Brace for landing," Leo said as he took the plane dangerously close to the island. Anna closed her eyes at the last minute and gripped her seat for dear life. So many feelings went through her at once that she couldn't process them all. Fear, regret, anger, sadness, love, passion...

Anna's head snapped back as the plane shuddered into the water with a bone-jarring splash. It glided along the surface before coming to an abrupt stop that would have jerked her forward in the seat if not for the belt holding her tightly in place. There was a surreal moment of complete silence as the craft pitched and rolled with the waves. Anna's stomach lodged in her throat. How would they ever escape with the motion throwing them around so much? Once the seat belt was off, two steps forward would turn into four steps back.

"There's not much time," Leo said as he unbuckled his seat belt and flung his door open.

"Your jacket," she said, thrusting it toward him with a shaking hand as she unlocked her seat belt with the other. He took it and threw it out the door, then grabbed her and hauled her toward him. She barely had time to register all the sensations that rocked her as she was pressed against his hard body before she dropped into the sea.

The water was shocking, not because it was too cold, but because it was wet when she'd been so dry. The life preserver kept her from going under, but water still splashed over her head, soaking her. Anna spluttered and began to tread water as Leo landed beside her, the orange pack slung over one shoulder.

"Your life jacket," she said. It was floating just out of reach and she made a grab for it.

"I don't need it." His hair was slicked back from his head, his expression grim and determined.

"Leo," she began.

"I'm fine, Anna. Can you swim to the island?"

She turned and looked at the shore only a few meters distant. "Of course," she said crisply, her heart beating like crazy in her chest as she began to process what had happened. They'd crashed. In the Mediterranean. She couldn't quite wrap her mind around it, and yet the plane bobbed in the water nearby. The scent of salt mingling with jet fuel invaded her senses.

"We need to go now," he said. "Before we get soaked in fuel."

Leo began to stroke toward the island. She followed, easily crossing the distance before stumbling to her knees onto the shore beside him. Her hair was still in its rigid knot, but a few wisps had fallen free and snaked around her neck like tentacles. Her makeup was probably streaked and—

Oh, she'd forgotten her purse! She turned and started wading back into the water when strong arms caught her from behind.

"Where are you going?"

"My purse," she said. "My phone, my identification—"

"It's too late," he growled in her ear.

"But it's not." She pointed. The plane was still on top of the water, though the nose had begun to sink. It wouldn't take her a trifle to get out there and back again.

"It's too dangerous, Anna. Even if the plane wasn't sinking, the remaining fuel is leaching from it. Besides, was there anything irreplaceable in your purse?"

She wanted to tell him yes, of course there was. Instead, Anna slumped in his grip. "No, nothing irreplaceable." Just her lip gloss, her hand sanitizer, her headache tablets and her phone with its calendar of all her events.

Events that were sadly lacking lately. Invitations had dried up since Alex had jilted her.

She stifled a hysterical laugh. They'd crashed in the Mediterranean and she was concerned about her calendar? She needed to be thinking about survival, not social engagements.

Leo held her hard against him. She slowly became aware of his heat, of the solidity of his body where it pressed into hers. They were both soaking wet, dripping onto the sand, and she wondered for a moment why the water didn't sizzle and steam.

Anna put her hand on his where it gripped her beneath the life vest. She wanted to smooth her fingers along his skin, wanted to feel the shape of his hand, the ridges of his knuckles, but instead she loosened his grip and stepped away from him. When she turned, he was looking at her with a kind of laser intensity that made her gut clench in reaction.

Liquid heat flooded her body, her bones. Shakily, she undid the clasp on the vest and shrugged it off. She needed something to do, something that didn't involve looking at Leo.

His shirt was plastered to his chest, delineating every ridge and curve of smooth muscle. She hadn't been able to tell from the tuxedo last night, but Leo was in spectacular shape. His father had once been a famous footballer, she recalled, and Leo looked as if he'd spent quite a bit of time on the field himself. He had the leanly muscled form of an athlete.

"We need to find shelter," he said, and a hard knot formed right below her breastbone. They were stranded, alone, with nothing and no one to help them get home again.

"You were able to tell someone what happened, right?" she said. "They'll be looking for us soon."

His expression remained flat. "We were out of radio

range. I activated the emergency beacon on the plane. They'll know approximately where we went down, but it may take some time since they won't be looking for us yet."

She turned back toward the plane. "If I had my mobile phone…"

"Doesn't matter," he said. "There are no cell towers out here. You'd need a satellite phone to make a call."

"So we're stuck."

"For the time being," he replied, hefting the orange pack onto his shoulder again.

"How long will we be here, Leo?"

He shrugged. "I really don't know. Which is why we need to find shelter."

"What about food? Water? How will we survive if we don't have water?"

He gave her a long look. "We have enough water for a couple of days, if we ration it. Everything's in this pack."

Anna blinked. "You have water?"

"It's an emergency survival kit, darling. There's a bit of everything. Dried food, matches, fuel, blankets—enough to survive a few days in the wild."

He turned and started walking toward the other end of the island where she'd seen the copse of trees. Anna scrambled after him. Her feet were bare since she'd lost her shoes in the sea. She felt a momentary pang for the beautiful suede pumps that were no doubt at the bottom of the Med by now, but it was truly the least of her worries.

Part of the going was rocky, but Anna climbed after Leo and never said a word when the rocks sliced into her feet. She fell behind, but she did not call out. Why should she? He couldn't disappear. The island was small and she knew where they were headed. But Leo glanced over his shoulder at one point, stopping when she wasn't right behind him.

He frowned as she approached, his gaze on her feet. "You've lost your shoes."

"They wouldn't have been much use anyway," she said. "They were five-inch platforms."

Her one concession to impracticality.

He closed the distance between them, and then hooked an arm behind her knees and lifted her into his arms before she realized his plan.

"Leo, put me down!"

His face was close to hers. Too close. Oh, heavens. She wanted to tilt her head back, wanted to nuzzle her face into the crook of his neck and breathe in his scent. And then she wanted to lick him.

Heat flashed through her. The hot Mediterranean sun beat down on them from above, but it wasn't the sun that made her skin prickle or her core melt.

"Once we're over the rocks," he said. "I don't want you cutting your feet."

"Too late," she replied.

His coffee-colored eyes were so beautiful as he stared down at her. There was heat in them, and something darker and more intense. Something so elemental it frightened her. "You should have told me sooner."

"You have the pack," she said, dropping her gaze. Her heart hammered in her breast. Why did he affect her so much? He was completely, utterly wrong for her. He was the kind of man she should definitely avoid, and yet he thrilled her in ways she'd never expected.

He's thrilling because he's dangerous, a voice whispered. *Bad boys are always thrilling.*

"You barely weigh more than the pack does," he said. "If it gets too much for me, I'll put one of you down. Honest."

He winked on that last, and began striding toward the trees again. Anna clung to him, ashamed, miserable, grateful and oddly excited. She had to wrap her arms around his neck, had to press her face in close to his. His fingers splayed over her rib cage, dangerously close to her breast, and she held her breath for a long moment.

Would he touch her there? Did she want him to? What would she say if he did?

But they reached a sandy area and he set her down again. She tried not to be disappointed as he strode away. The sand felt good on her feet, warm on top and cool if she dug her toes down. She scrambled after Leo, catching him right as he reached the trees.

It was cooler here, and the ground was flat and somewhat sandy. Leo kept walking until he found a spot he liked, and then he set the pack down and opened it. Anna watched in amazement as he pulled out a variety of items—heavy-duty plastic sheeting with grommets, a knife and rope—before he stood and began to peel the wet shirt from his body.

If she'd thought the navy shirt molded his chest, she'd had no idea what molding meant until he stood there in a wet T-shirt and jeans. But then he yanked the T-shirt off and his chest was bare and tanned. Her gaze dropped, halted in surprise. He had a dragon tattoo low on his abdomen—

Anna gulped. And turned away. Automatically she reached for her pearls, relieved they were still there as her fingers toyed with them.

"Do I make you nervous?" Leo asked from behind her. She could hear the laughter in his voice. Deliberately she turned, dropping her hand away from her neck. *Calm, cool.*

"Of course not," she said.

He winked. "Good. Because I'm afraid the jeans are next, darling. Can't abide wet clothing."

Anna held her breath as his long fingers flicked open

the button of his jeans. She couldn't have looked away if her life depended on it. Tanned fingers slipped between the waistband and his skin, and then he was pushing the jeans down. Her heart kicked up as his hip bones appeared, and then the elastic waist of his underwear. Armani, she thought crazily. It said so on the band.

But she forgot all about it as the jeans slid down his long, strong legs, revealing tanned skin and acres of muscle. Anna couldn't breathe. Her lungs simply wouldn't fill. Had she ever seen a man as beautiful, as strong and lean and muscled, as this one?

Could this day be any more surreal? Just a few minutes ago, they'd been fully clothed strangers. And now they were marooned together and Leo was stripping out of his clothing.

"Keep staring, darling, and the show is bound to get more interesting," Leo said, his voice a growling purr that slid over her nerve endings and made her shudder.

"I've seen naked men before," she said with a sniff. "You can't shock me."

It was only a small lie: the naked man she'd seen had been on a video, not standing before her looking so vibrant and sexy that she physically hurt from looking at him. Leo wasn't wearing any less than a man might wear while swimming, and yet her insides were twisting and squeezing in a way they never had at the sight of a random man in a Speedo at the pool.

"Is that so?" he asked.

"Definitely." But her limbs felt weak.

Leo shook his head, laughing softly. "Come along then, Anna. Get out of your wet things and help me set up this shelter."

Astonishment riveted her to the spot. He wanted her to remove her clothes? She'd not thought of it before, but now it seemed as if her soaked suit clung to her uncomfortably. Her skin felt cool and clammy under the fabric, though Leo's had looked hot and silky when he'd removed his clothing.

Leo strode over to her and began to gently push her jacket from her shoulders. "Come on, Anna, it's all right. You've had a shock. Let's get you out of these wet things. I'll put everything in the sun and it'll be dry again in no time. You can armor yourself behind your buttoned-up clothing quite soon, I promise."

"There's nothing wrong with my clothes," she protested, though she let him tug her jacket down her arms.

"Nothing at all," he agreed.

"Then why did you say it?" She stepped away from him as the jacket fell free and crossed her arms over her breasts. How could she possibly take off her camisole and skirt? How could she stand before him in her bra and panties?

Leo sighed. "Because you're beautiful, Anna. Your clothes should show how beautiful you are, not hide it."

"I'm not hiding anything," she protested, her heart throbbing at the compliment. "My suit is professional, conservative. There's nothing wrong with that."

"No. But I don't think it's really you."

He'd said that to her earlier, and it was no less irritating now. "How can you conceivably think such a thing? We hardly know each other, Mr. Jackson."

She was proud of herself for sounding frosty, though her insides were sizzling hot. Leo was a stunning man and he was standing before her in nothing but a pair of black briefs with a white waistband. He had a dragon tattoo she oddly wanted to press her mouth to. And he'd just told her she was beautiful.

But she knew he didn't mean it—or he did mean it, but the same as he meant it when he'd told whichever woman he'd spent the night with last night that she was beautiful, too. Leo was a playboy, the kind of man who was pretty to look at—and probably amazing to spend the night with—but who had absolutely no intentions beyond a night of pleasure.

He was a glorious, beautiful creature designed for one thing only: to ruin the women he took to his bed. Not ruin in the old-fashioned sense, but ruin in the sense that she couldn't imagine how they ever found another lover to satisfy them once they'd had a taste of him.

Leo snorted. "And when you don't retreat behind clothing, you retreat behind stiff formality. I think we've crossed some sort of barrier that prohibits us from using the terms *mister* and *miss,* don't you?"

"Not at all. Politeness is always acceptable." It was what she'd been taught. Always be gracious, even when you were aching inside. A lady smiled through adversity. A lady didn't let anyone see when she was hurting. A lady never complained.

His snort turned into full-blown laughter. A hot current of mortification blazed through her at the sound. Why did she say such silly things? Why did she open herself up to his amusement? Leo was the kind of man who said and did what he wanted, and damn the consequences. He couldn't understand her world, couldn't understand why she had to behave stoically and graciously in the face of humiliation.

"Politeness?" he said. "I'm almost naked, darling. And if no one arrives in the next few hours to rescue us, we'll be sharing body heat under a blanket tonight. We've moved far beyond polite, don't you think?"

CHAPTER FOUR

ANNA'S heart pounded in her chest. Leo had an edge that both compelled her and frightened her. And when he talked of sharing a blanket—sharing body heat—she began to shiver deep inside.

"If you don't want to be naked when we share that heat, I suggest you take those clothes off and let them dry in the sun."

She didn't want to do so, and yet she knew she had little choice. It was either that or sit in the sun with her clothes on and risk a severe sunburn while she waited for everything to dry. Since her teeth were beginning to chatter, her only option was removal.

Jerkily, her fingers found her zipper and tugged it down. And then she was peeling the skirt from her body, tossing it aside, daring him to say a word as she did so. She almost lost her courage when it came time to remove the camisole, but she told herself it was the same as wearing a bikini—so she peeled the wet camisole upward and shrugged it off.

She looked up then, met Leo's gaze. Realized he hadn't moved since she'd begun to strip. He was staring at her, his dark eyes gleaming hotly. There was something dangerous in his stare, something too intense to fathom. She was perversely happy she'd put on a matching bra and panty set today. They were lacy, pink and not too revealing. *It's a bikini,* she told herself. *A bikini.*

Except that Leo wasn't looking at her like she was wearing a bikini. No, he was looking at her with far more heat and intimacy than if she were dressed in a swimming costume. No man had ever looked at her quite like that before. It was...thrilling. And nerve-racking.

Anna wrapped her arms around her body self-consciously and walked past him to where the pack lay. "Are we building this shelter or not?" she asked crisply, kneeling beside the heavy plastic sheeting. She had to do something, or make an even bigger fool of herself.

She heard him move, and then he reached down and lifted her gently.

"You're cold," he said. And then he pulled her into his embrace, her bare skin coming into heart-stopping contact with his as he pressed her against him, breast to belly to hip.

Her first instinct was to push away, to put as much distance between them as possible, but he was warm and dry and not the least bit clammy. His heat flowed into her, warmed her cold limbs.

But it was more than that, she realized.

It was sexual heat, embarrassment and longing all rolled into one. Her skin prickled at his nearness. Leo chafed his hands along her arms, her back. For him it was practical while for her...

What an amateur she was! What a pitiful, clueless amateur.

Anna turned her head slightly, breathed in the scent of his skin where her head was pressed to his chest. He smelled like salt, but under that he smelled like soap and spice. She wanted to lick him.

Anna closed her eyes. What was with this constant urge to lick him? Was he an ice cream cone? A lollipop?

Need washed through her, made her knees weak. Thankfully Leo was holding her close, or she'd surely sink to the ground. One hand touched her head, rubbed softly—but no, he wasn't rubbing, he was finding the pins of her knot and pulling them free.

Her hair tumbled loose and she gasped. Automatically she reached up with one hand, wanting to smooth it back into place. But it was a bedraggled rope hanging down her back. No amount of smoothing would help at this point.

She tilted her head back to look up at Leo. His eyes danced with mischief. And something else. Something hot and intense that frightened her as much as it intrigued her. He was a hard man, a ruthless man when he wanted something. She could see that in him, behind the smiles and winks, behind the *darlings*. This was a man who conquered, who took everything and left nothing behind. Would he take her if she allowed it? Would there be anything left when he was done?

Anna shivered again, and not from cold this time. "Why did you do that?" she asked.

"Because your hair will dry faster if you take it down."

Oddly, disappointment spiraled inside her. Part of her had hoped he would say he'd done it because he wanted to see her hair, but of course he was being practical. And yet his eyes darkened, his nostrils flaring as he looked down at her.

His gaze dropped to her lips and her heartbeat slowed to a crawl. He was going to kiss her. She wanted him to kiss her, wanted it almost more than she wanted her next breath. She wanted to feel the heat, the sizzle, the storm of this man's kiss.

But not like this. A thread of panic unwound in her

brain. She didn't want her first real kiss to be an after-thought. For him, it was like breathing. For her, it was ev-erything she'd never had.

"No," she said softly as he dipped his head toward hers, her throat aching as she forced the word out.

Leo stopped, straightened. He looked frustrated. Annoyed.

"I've never," she began, trying to explain. "Never…"

She couldn't say it, couldn't admit the shame of never having been kissed. She was twenty-eight years old. She'd been waiting her whole life for a man who had thought less than nothing about rejecting her at the last possible moment. She'd spent years preparing for a wedding that wasn't ever going to happen. Saving herself for a man who didn't want her.

Anger blazed to life like a bonfire. And sadness. She'd missed so much, hadn't she?

"Never what, Anna?"

Her stomach churned. She dropped her head, closed her eyes. "I've never kissed a man before," she said, her voice a husky whisper. Shame clawed into her, singed her with its icy sting. She was a woman who'd never been kissed, who'd never been loved. She was a woman who should have had all those things, and far sooner than now.

Leo went very, very still. She could feel the incred-ible control he exercised, the restraint, the sudden hum of tension in his body as he stood so still and held her close. "Alessandro never…?"

She shook her head, unable to speak the word. It was humiliating. As if the stories in the papers weren't enough to make her want to hide her head in the sand forever, the secret knowledge that she'd never been kissed properly, never desired, was infinitely worse.

Leo's strong fingers cupped her jaw, tilted her head up.

What she saw in his face made her heart squeeze tight. "He was a fool, Anna. Do you understand me? A bloody fool."

And then he pressed his lips to her forehead, gently, sweetly, and she drew in a soft breath laced with tears. A sob hovered in her throat, but she would not let it escape. She barely knew this man, and here she was pressed against him, hot skin to hot skin, her deepest secrets spilling out as if the dam behind which she kept them had suddenly sprung a leak.

Her fingers curled against the hard plane of his chest. He was so warm, so vibrant and alive. She'd never been so close to a man, never felt the things she was feeling right now.

A dagger of need sliced into her. Her sex ached with want. Her nipples were sensitive points against the lace of her bra. Her breasts tingled. She wanted Leo to touch her everywhere. To show her what it meant to make love.

His body was hard against hers. Some parts were harder than others, she realized. His hips pressed into her, his erection unmistakable where it thrust against her belly. A hot, hollow feeling bloomed in her core. If she were an experienced woman, if she'd done this before and knew what she was doing, she'd run her hands over his torso and slide them beneath the waistband of his sexy, sexy underwear.

But she was a virgin, a stupid, insecure virgin, and she was afraid of what she'd never actually done. Afraid of unleashing something she couldn't control, of losing her reason and sanity.

She ached and she wanted and she stood very still while Leo kissed her forehead. And then he took a step back, setting her away from him. His eyes were hotter than she'd ever seen them, and his body...

Oh, heavens, his body was beautiful, his muscles so

tense and perfect, his erection now straining against the confines of the briefs.

"Leo…" She didn't know what to say, what to do. She wanted him to do it for her.

But he turned away. "Let's fix this shelter," he said gruffly.

Leo was out of his depth and he wasn't accustomed to it. His usual relationships were simple affairs involving women who knew what they were getting into when they dated him. He was typically monogamous, but serial. His affairs lasted days or weeks or, in some cases, months.

There was no falling in love, no happily ever afters. He didn't believe in them anyway. He'd grown up in Bobby Jackson's household, where his father's relationships with women were anything but normal. Women were the revolving door of Bobby's life. Leo figured it was possible to love one woman forever, but not for a Jackson male. The closest he'd come to a stable relationship was with Jessica Monroe, and that had ended in disaster when she'd wanted more than he could give.

Marriage and children were not for him, and he wouldn't be like Bobby and attempt to do something he was genetically doomed to fail at. The least he could do was spare his nonexistent children the shame of having a Jackson for a father.

Dear God, Anna. She was innocent and incredibly sexy, though she didn't seem to realize it, and Leo wanted her so badly he was having a tough time keeping his body from reacting. He could *not* have her. He reminded himself forcefully of that fact as he glanced over at her. She was too innocent to engage in a torrid affair—to *know* that it was simply an affair.

If he made love to her, she'd want forever. She'd thought

that's what she was getting from Prince Alessandro, and she'd happily ordered her life with that end in mind. How could she reformat her thinking simply to gratify Leo's baser urges?

She couldn't, and he wouldn't touch her no matter how he ached.

They'd set up the shelter and he'd gone to lay their clothes in the sun to dry. For once, he prayed they'd be dressed again very soon. Not that he didn't appreciate a gorgeous woman in her underwear, but Anna was so innocent that he felt like a jackass for ogling her. For wanting her.

And he definitely, definitely wanted her. He wanted to fill his hands with her lushness, wanted to slip that lacy pink bra from her shoulders and cup his hands around the mounds of her breasts. He wanted to see the tight points of those nipples he'd felt pressing into him, and then he wanted to fill his senses with her. He wanted to skim his mouth along the sweet skin of her belly and slide her panties from her hips before opening her delicate femininity to his gaze and sliding his tongue along the wet seam of her sex.

He wanted to make Anna come, wanted her to scream his name. He wanted to give her everything she'd missed out on, and he wanted to brand her as his when he did so.

But he couldn't do it. It wasn't fair to her. She was vulnerable and hurting and he couldn't take advantage of her. When he'd thought she was simply an uptight woman who'd been jilted by her fiancé, he'd imagined a bit of sexual fun was exactly what she needed to take her mind off her troubles.

He might be bad, but he wasn't so bad as to seduce an innocent virgin who'd never been kissed before. He had a conscience, no matter if it had often been reported otherwise.

"How long do you think it will take them to find us?" Anna asked, cutting into his thoughts.

He looked over at her and almost wished he hadn't as his gut twisted with longing. Her hair was long, brunette, and she'd finger combed it before it had dried into a tousled, thick mane that suited her far more than her sleek chignons did. He wanted to run his hands through that hair, wanted to bury his fingers in it and tilt her head back while he plundered her mouth with his own.

His body responded in spite of himself, the blood pooling in his groin, filling him. *Ah, damn.* What, was he sixteen again? Unable to exercise even a little bit of control?

Except it wasn't a little control where Anna was concerned, it was a lot. Especially when he could see the raw need shimmering in her eyes.

Leo shrugged casually when he felt anything but casual. "I doubt they'll be looking for us for hours yet."

She frowned. "I was afraid you'd say that."

"We'll be fine, darling," he said lightly. "We have food, water, shelter. All the necessities."

She turned her head away, her hair falling over her shoulder and seemingly caressing one gorgeous breast. He was jealous of her hair at that moment. "That's not what worries me."

It took him a moment to figure out what she meant. At first he thought she meant she was worried to be alone with him, but then he realized it was something far more significant in Anna's world. Something far more insidious. It wasn't being alone with him so much as the perception that being alone with him would create.

"Anna, you can't live your life in fear of what the tabloids will say."

She turned back to him then, her jade-green eyes flashing. "What do you know of it? You're a man, a veritable *god* for all your exploits. I've had nothing but humiliation from them. If they know I'm out here, alone, with you—"

Leo resisted the urge to swear, but barely. "Do you plan to live your entire life by the numbers? Do you think that if only you are good enough, they'll leave you alone?"

She gaped at him. Angry. Fearful. "I…I…"

He wanted to punch something. For her. He wanted her to fight back, wanted her to not give a damn—and he knew he couldn't make her do it. That was his style, not hers. Had his mother given a damn? She must have, since she'd saved the articles. And yet she'd survived it, just as he'd survived the attention later, after her death.

"It doesn't work that way, Anna. Whatever sells magazines or papers is what works. You—and Alessandro and Allegra—are the flavor of the moment. You will *always* be the poor little bride who lost her groom on the eve of the wedding. Always. It's up to you to choose how you deal with it."

She swallowed hard. "How?"

How? It seemed absurd that he was being asked to give advice on dealing with the press since he'd never much cared one way or the other what they'd said about him— since growing up anyway—but he could see she was serious. That she believed he had the answer since his family were in fact a tabloid staple. Thanks to his father.

Bobby didn't care what the press said, so long as they said *something.* His greatest fear, Leo thought, was becoming irrelevant. So long as the media were printing stories, Bobby felt he was doing something right. Even when he'd been in the papers for the wrong reasons—affairs, fights, money trouble, refusing to acknowledge his ten-year-old son until the courts shoved a paternity test in his face. Bobby mined it all and emerged from a pile of excrement smelling like roses.

And yet that wouldn't work for Anna. She didn't want or need the attention. She didn't crave it.

Leo drew in a breath. He told her the only thing he knew how to tell her. "By being happy. By living your life. By refusing to adhere to some standard you believe some anonymous *they* want from you. You're Anna Constantinides and you're free to be your own person. Screw the press and screw whatever you thought you were supposed to do with your life. The truth, sweet Anna, is that nothing you thought you were going to be is possible any longer."

Her eyes flashed with pain and fury. "I know that."

Leo clenched his fists at his sides to keep from pulling her to him and wrapping her in his embrace. Why did he feel such a strong urge to protect this woman? He wanted her, but that wasn't anything unusual for him. But to shelter her from pain? That was a completely new bit of territory he'd broken, and he still wasn't quite sure how to deal with it.

It must be because of his mother, because he'd never forgotten how she must have kept those articles year after year. Had she reread them? Or had she stashed them away and never looked at them again? He would never know. But he couldn't stand the idea of Anna brooding over what the press said for years to come.

"Then do what you want, Anna," he told her fiercely, trying to impart strength. "Stop trying to please whomever you think it is you must please. Be the dragon lady I know you can be."

She dropped her gaze, studied her feet. Or so it seemed. "My mother is Queen Zoe's best friend. Did you know that?"

He did not. And it made the whole thing seem uglier somehow. "No."

"They've been planning this wedding since we were

children. Hoping to unite our families. I have always been Alex's bride, even when I was a six-year-old playing with dolls. It was predestined."

The thought made him angry. Not because he was suddenly judgmental of the way royals ordered their lives, but because someone had told a little girl that this was her destiny and none other would do. She'd never been allowed to choose for herself, never been allowed to grow other than to grow into Prince Alessandro's wife. Everything she'd done had been in preparation for that life. He could see that now.

And it had all come to nothing because Alessandro had met Allegra. Leo loved his sister and wished her all the happiness in the world, but at the moment he was more than furious with Alessandro, a man who'd thought nothing of abandoning his bride-to-be. And he was furious with the Santinas and Constantinideses.

"They were wrong to do that to you, Anna." *All* of them, he silently added. "You should have been allowed to choose for yourself."

She blew out a breath as she combed her fingers through her hair. It was an impossibly sexy gesture. He didn't think she realized it. In fact, he knew she didn't. His groin tightened painfully.

"Perhaps. But it's what I was raised to do. Our mothers planned it when we were toddlers. I've never known quite why, except that I believe my mother and Queen Zoe seemed to think it was the perfect way to ensure the purity of the Santina dynasty."

"The purity? Isn't your father Greek?"

"Yes, but my mother is from Santina originally. Though I don't believe that is the sort of purity they had in mind. It is more of a tradition thing. Someone from another country might not...suit the Santina expectations. They are, as you may have noticed, quite conservative in their thinking. Very traditional. For my parents, it was an honor to have me chosen as the future queen."

"And it never occurred to you to object," he stated.

She shrugged. "Why would it? That was no doubt part of the plan. A girl raised to be a bride, a queen, would not question it, would she?" She shook her head. "Changing everything now—doing what I want to do, as you put it— is a bit like being marooned here with you. Not at all what I expected."

"And did you expect to be here in your knickers?" he teased, though he did not feel like laughing. "What a singular experience, sweet Anna. Think what you will be able to tell your grandchildren."

She looked up sharply, and he wanted to bite his tongue off. Now was not the time to mention progeny to the woman who'd thought she would bear the heir to the throne of Santina some day.

"I think," she said very softly, "that I'll simply see how today goes before I start thinking of the future."

Leo leaned back against a tree trunk and watched her. She was so elegant, so graceful, even in her underwear. She *should* have been a queen. She was the right woman to be a queen. Anger buzzed in his veins like an electrical pulse.

She'd accepted her fate so easily, resigned herself to being a king-in-waiting's future bride. And he suddenly wanted to know if it's what she would have chosen for herself.

"Did you love him, Anna?"

Green eyes brimming with emotion gazed at him steadily. The desire hovering beneath the surface of his psyche flared to life again, its heat scorching and painful. Because it would not be fulfilled. Because he couldn't allow it to be fulfilled.

But Anna pulled at him. Her eyes, her skin, her dark, beautiful hair. Her presence. The wounded woman beneath the buttoned-up suits and dainty femininity drew him in a way that continually surprised him.

He didn't want or need anyone. And yet he wanted *her*. He always got what he wanted because he never gave up until he won. But this time was different. This time, he had to walk away instead of conquer.

"You asked me that already," she said softly. But she didn't look away, didn't dissemble in the way she'd done only a few hours ago.

"And you didn't answer," he replied.

She bit her bottom lip and a shot of lust bolted straight to his groin. *He* wanted to bite that lip. She looked so damn demure in her lacy pink underwear and pearls. Had he ever experienced such a crazy situation in his life? Marooned with a virgin on a deserted island. A virgin who had his libido slipping into overdrive and his body humming with suppressed sexual tension.

"I was," she finally said. "Or I thought I was. When you spend your entire life preparing to marry one person, you start to believe you might love him."

It was an answer, and not an answer. He found it strangely frustrating. "What do you feel now that he's marrying my sister? What bothers you more, the fact you've lost him or the fact the media won't let you forget it?"

She seemed to think about it for a moment before answering. "I thought those feelings were all tangled together, but maybe they aren't. Because I don't hate Allegra, and I don't hate that Alex is marrying her. I hate what it's done to me, how I feel knowing I've wasted so much time preparing for something that won't ever happen."

She shot to her feet then and Leo thought she looked like an Amazon. A petite Amazon, but a fiery one nonetheless. She looked as if she could chew nails for breakfast. He wanted to laugh. Anna was fiery, passionate. She locked it away beneath her suits and her pearls but the woman was a warrior in her soul. A dragon lady.

Her eyes flashed fire. And then she swore long and loud in Greek. Leo leaned back and watched it all happen, amazed and aroused by the display of so much passion. Hell, if she weren't a virgin, they'd burn up together. She'd know what she was getting into and he wouldn't feel in the least bit guilty for taking advantage of her passionate nature.

"I am tired of being the last person everyone thinks about," she said. "I'm tired of doing what's expected of me, of trying so hard to be the best at whatever task I'm given. I'm tired of keeping quiet and bearing it all with a serene smile. I'm tired of following a list of rules that have been drummed into me since I was old enough to talk, and I'm tired of—" here she pressed both hands to her chest "—and I'm tired of being a cold, frigid person that no man wants to touch passionately. I want passion, Leo. I want love and heat and sex. I want it all. And I want it *now*."

CHAPTER FIVE

ANNA'S body was on fire. With fury, with lust, with so many feelings that she couldn't contain them all. He was right, damn him. She didn't really love Alex. She'd thought she had, but she was far angrier over the way she was being portrayed in the media than she was over the fact she would never be the Queen of Santina.

And she was angry with her parents, with the Santinas, because she felt like she'd let them all down by failing to capture Alex's heart when it had never been hers to capture. Not that they'd said anything or chastised her for it, but she felt that way nevertheless. She knew what their hopes had been. Their dreams.

And it was all lying in ruins now.

Alex had never given her a reason to think he loved her, never given her anything beyond the courtesy she'd deserved as his fiancée. He'd never led her to believe there would be love between them.

She'd filled in the blanks on her own. She'd taken his quiet acceptance of their arranged marriage as tacit approval of her and of their future together.

She'd been so blind, so dumb. So damn obedient.

She was through being obedient.

She was through doing what everyone expected.

She was *through*.

Leo was still leaning back against the tree trunk, though he looked anything but casual in that moment. He was watching her with interest. Hot, sharp interest. As if she were a dessert he wanted to devour. As if she were a cold drink of water on a hot day. As if she were a lifeline in a stormy sea.

She was none of those things, but she thrilled to that heated look on his handsome face. She had never, ever been looked at like that before. No man had ever made her tingle like this, or made her limbs soften and ache. She was jumpy, itchy, her skin stretched too tight to contain everything she felt. She would burst with it if she didn't do something soon.

But what? She'd told him she wanted heat and sex and passion right now—and she did, but she was also scared of it. Scared to take the leap and crash and burn instead of soar. It was not like her to leap without a solid plan, without a safety net. It went against everything she'd ever thought about herself.

"Anna," Leo said, his voice edgy and taut.

And she knew then, before she'd even made up her mind about what happened next, he was refusing her. Without another word, without anything else passing between them, she *knew* he was rejecting her. Leo didn't want her. Alex didn't want her. She wasn't desirable, in spite of the way Leo had held her earlier, his body hardening against hers. It had been an illusion, a reaction brought about by proximity and not a true craving.

And the way he'd looked at her just now? Clearly, she was no good at reading the meaning behind his expression. She'd been wrong. Wrong, wrong, wrong.

A fresh wave of humiliation washed over her. Was she truly that clueless? Truly that blind?

Tears of frustration, tears of anger, filled her. And she

would rather do anything else than cry in front of this man. She would gut fish for a living before she would let him know how shattered she was by his rejection.

"I can't do this," he said, and the tears pressed hard against her eyes, demanding release. "I can't take advantage of what you offer, no matter how much I might want to."

"Don't," she bit out, her voice sharper than she'd ever allowed it to be. "For goodness' sake, don't lie to me."

His expression grew stormy. "You think I'm lying about this?"

She laughed, the sound harsh and bitter. "Of course you are! I know who you are, Leo! I have eyes! I saw you this morning—you hadn't even been to bed when I knocked on the door, or at least not to your own bed. When you want a woman, you take her, especially if she offers herself to you." She wrapped her arms around her torso and tilted her chin up. Her lip was trembling badly. "I must conclude then that you do not want *me*."

He swore. "Dammit, you are dense," he grated. "I'm trying to be decent—"

"I don't want you to be decent!" she yelled. "I don't want you *thinking* for me or *telling* me what to do. I'm sick of that, sick of everyone thinking they know what I need more than I do!"

"You're acting on impulse," he growled. "And that's not like you. For pity's sake, *think*. I'm not what you want."

"How dare you," she threw at him. "How absolutely dare you? You're the one who has badgered me since the first moment we met about being my own person, about doing my own thing, about being too uptight and buttoned up and...and...rigid."

"Anna..."

"No," she yelled. "No!" It was too much suddenly. She

turned blindly, before the angry tears that hovered on the edge spilled free, and fled toward the sea. It was only a short distance before she was leaping off a small cliff and into the cool blue water. The tiny cuts on her feet burned anew, but she ignored the pain. She'd treated them with antiseptic from Leo's survival kit earlier, and this didn't burn any worse than that had.

She dove down, down, down, testing her lungs, letting them ache before she turned and kicked hard toward the surface. The sun filtered down into the depths, making the water above ripple and sparkle. It was so quiet down here, so peaceful. She could stay down here forever if only it were possible. Down in the depths of the ocean where pain couldn't touch her. Where no one pointed a finger and laughed at her. Where she wasn't pitiful, but isolated from pity.

She kicked again, realizing she'd gone somewhat deeper than she'd first thought she had. The surface wasn't too far, and she wasn't worried about reaching it, but nonetheless a pair of strong arms enclosed around her body and yanked her skyward.

"Are you insane?" Leo demanded when they breeched the surface together. Anna gulped air, the hot burn of it expanding in her lungs. If felt so good to breathe after she'd denied herself for so long. Almost like learning to live when you'd denied yourself the very basics of life— like passion and love and sexual heat.

Anna threw her head back and laughed. This was what it was like to be alive. This…this—rebellion. Yes, by God, *rebellion.* She'd never rebelled in her life, never questioned her fate or her teaching. She'd done everything they asked, been everything they'd told her to be—

And it hadn't been good enough. She'd failed at the one task they'd set for her.

And she didn't care. Dammit, she didn't care! It was liberating not to care.

"Anna!" Leo cried, gripping her shoulders and shaking her hard. They treaded water together, their limbs brushing each other. Each brush was like the stroke of a tiny flame against her skin. His body was hard against hers, his skin hot where the water was cool. He was so very alive, so vibrant, so large and real and *here*.

She wanted to live in the moment for once in her life, wanted to forget about the past, the future, and just *be.*

"Let me go, Leo!" she cried. Because she didn't want to be held against him like this, didn't want the shame of knowing how badly she'd embarrassed herself with him. She'd had enough embarrassment to last her a lifetime. If he let her go, she could float on her back and laugh up at the sun and tell herself she didn't care about anything at all. Not anymore.

"Why did you do that?" Leo demanded. "You could have hurt yourself!"

She slicked her hair back from her face, tilted her chin up defiantly. "Because I *wanted* to. Because I never do what I want. Because I always do what everyone else wants. Now," she said, her jaw tightening. "Let. Me. Go."

Leo's fingers dug into her ribs. It was exciting, thrilling. "Do you have any idea how beautiful you are when you're angry?" he growled.

Her heart skipped a beat. Her stomach clenched tight. "No, don't you dare say that," she lashed out. "You don't want me. You said so."

"I never said that," he grated. "Never. What I don't want is to take advantage of you."

Anna laughed recklessly. "How can you take advantage of me if it's what I want?"

His dark eyes flashed. His hair was slicked to his head,

molding the fine shape of his skull. His face was hard, handsome, perfectly beautiful. How had she ever, ever thought Alex handsome when Leo was in the world?

"You aren't thinking like yourself," he said. "You're reacting to everything that's happened. Taking what you offer wouldn't be fair. Have you forgotten that only this morning you refused me?"

Her cheeks burned. No, she hadn't forgotten—but everything had changed in the space of a few hours. She was tired of being staid, boring Anna. She was ready to be—if only for a little while—exciting Anna who did what she wanted and didn't regret it.

"God, you are arrogant," she breathed. "So certain you know what's right for me. For the world, I'll bet. But you don't, Leo! I will decide what's best for me. From now on, I'll decide. Isn't that what you said? What you told me to do? How can you turn around now and say I'm wrong?"

His expression hardened. His fingers burned into her. His skin was on fire. Her core flooded with heat, her nipples hardening as he brought her closer. They'd drifted toward the rocks, the gray smooth rocks that she'd dived over in her flight. Nearby was a long strip of white sandy beach.

"This is different," he grated.

"Why? Because I'm a virgin? Because you're worried I'll want something from you that you can't give me?"

He looked stunned for a moment, and she knew she'd hit home. It hurt in a way, and it was also liberating. Yes, Leo Jackson, notorious playboy, was afraid that the jilted bride was looking for a replacement husband. How terribly insulting.

It made her feel bold, wild. Reckless in a way she'd never been. She lifted her legs and wrapped them around his torso. His eyes glittered, something very dangerous springing to life in their depths. "You're playing with fire, sweet Anna."

"Maybe I want to get burned." It was the most irresponsible thing she'd ever said, and she felt so free saying it. Defiant.

Leo brought her closer then, his hips flexing against her. Her breath caught, a tiny current of cold fear threatening to douse her in reality. She was indeed playing with fire.

Because he was hard, the ridge of his impressive erection riding against the thin layer of her panties. Anna nearly swallowed her tongue. What was she doing? Was she really so brave? Was she ready for this? Could she abandon herself for a few hours on this island and then go back to Santina—and Amanti—as if nothing had ever happened?

Maybe.

Or maybe not.

But she was determined to find out. They could have died when the plane crashed into the sea. She would have died without knowing passion. That thought more than any other spurred her forward.

"I'm trying to protect you," Leo said, his voice strained and taut. "I'm no good, Anna. I won't offer you forever. You have to know that."

She thought of him this morning in his tux with the pink lipstick on the collar. He was a playboy, a rogue, a man for whom pleasure was a supreme goal. He winked and smiled and charmed, and women fell into his bed.

But maybe that's why he was the right man for this. He knew what he was doing. She was wildly attracted to him. When they were rescued, they would go their separate ways and she could concentrate on building her life anew. With whomever she wanted. However she wanted.

She was free for the first time in her life. Free to make

her own choice. And though it was one of the most frightening things she'd ever done, she was choosing Leo. For now.

"Who said anything about forever? I'm asking you for your body, nothing else."

His expression was tortured, even while the flames in the depths of his eyes leaped higher. "Anna," he said gruffly as she flexed her hips against him. Sensation streaked through her at the contact. Oh, if she just kept flexing her hips and rubbing herself against him...

He gripped her waist in his broad hands, and she realized he'd moved them toward the beach and could stand on the bottom now. "You'll regret it," he said. "Today, you might want me, but tomorrow you'll be sorry you gave yourself away to someone who doesn't deserve it. Save yourself for a man who loves you, Anna."

Anna threw her head back and blasted the air with a few choice words in Greek. "Stop trying to save me from myself," she finally said. "I'm a grown woman and it's past time I did what I wanted to do. I've been saving myself for one particular man for years. And it's caused me nothing but grief!"

Leo closed his eyes and muttered a curse. And then he was moving with her, taking them up the beach until he laid her down in the wet sand and came down on top of her. A sliver of excitement ricocheted through her as his body pressed into hers. She tilted her hips up, her sex aching with need as sweet sensation hummed inside her.

"Heaven help me, I can't say no," he told her. "I'm selfish, Anna, and I want what you're offering me. Remember that later."

"I don't care," she whispered.

Leo's eyes were dark, hot and full of promise. Anna was afraid—of course she was!—but she was also ready to live. To do something wholly for herself without regard to what anyone else thought or believed.

He propped himself on an elbow, one hand coming up to stroke the wet skin between her breasts. Water beaded in the trail he left behind. And then he was cupping her jaw, tilting her head back, his head lowering so slowly she thought she might scream.

"I'm going to kiss you, Anna. The way you should have been kissed long before now."

Her eyes fluttered closed, and then Leo's mouth was on hers, his lips full and warm against her own. Anna's heart beat hard as he kissed her. It was a soft kiss, a lovely kiss. Everything she could have hoped for in her first real kiss.

And yet she knew there was more, knew that a kiss could grow wild and needy, and she wanted that. Wanted Leo to kiss her like he was starved for her. She moved beneath him, and he made a noise in his throat that sounded so sexy she wanted to melt.

"Patience," he said against her mouth.

"No," she breathed.

He laughed, and then his tongue touched the seam of her lips. She opened to him, her arms drifting up to wrap around his neck as his tongue plunged into her mouth and tangled with her own.

He tasted like salt and mint and his mouth was hot compared to the coolness of the water. Kissing Leo was a revelation, an unveiling of worlds she'd known existed but had never experienced for herself.

So *this* was what kissing was about. How could your body ache so much from the fusing of mouths? How could you feel so hot and unsettled simply from that one act? How could you want so much more than you'd ever wanted before? How could you feel as if you *needed* more or you would die?

Leo's hand left her jaw, slid down her neck until his fingers spanned her breast. Her nipples were tight points, and he made that sound she loved when he realized it. His thumb teased across her aroused flesh, sending little spikes of pleasure shooting through her body. If she were that sensitive when he touched her through the fabric, what would happen when he removed her bra?

His arousal pressed against her, creating the most delicious sensation whenever either of them moved. She wanted more of that feeling, more of the sensation of spiraling out of control. She wanted it before she started to think too much, before she started to remind herself of all the reasons she shouldn't do this. She was determined to be brave, to do her own thing, but a lifetime of habits didn't cease with one decision.

The kiss grew hotter, Leo demanding more from her, and she answered him eagerly, drinking his kisses as if they were water in the desert. He peeled her bra away from one breast, and then he was kneading her nipple between his thumb and forefinger while she gasped and arched into the caress.

He broke the kiss and bent to her breast, sucking her tight nipple between his lips. The desire was explosive. Every tug of his mouth created an answering spike of pleasure in her sex.

The surf gently rolled in, covering their lower bodies on every wave, but Anna didn't care if it covered her head so long as Leo never stopped what he was doing. She realized she was clasping him to her, her fingers buried in his lush, dark hair. He peeled the cup from her other breast and sucked that nipple, too, his fingers taking over where his mouth left off on the breast he'd abandoned.

"Leo," she gasped as she tilted her head back in the sand. The sky above was so bright, so blue. The sun was sinking toward the horizon, and dusk wasn't too far away now. No one had come for them—and she was perversely glad.

Abruptly, Leo stood and reached out for her. "Not here," he said.

She took his hand and let him pull her up and lead her toward the shelter. There, he pressed her down onto the survival blanket he'd laid out earlier. The blanket was silver, made of thin thermal sheeting, and Leo paused for a moment, grinning.

"What?" she said, her heart pounding recklessly.

"Gives new meaning to 'served up on a platter.'"

She looked at him quizzically.

"The blanket is silver, like a serving platter. And you are delectable." He came down on top of her, hovering above her body without quite touching her. "And I am a *very* lucky man."

"Leo, please," she said as his mouth dipped to her throat. She wanted more. She wanted more now. Before she let her brain take over and ruin everything.

"All in good time, sweet Anna. But first, I need you to know you can stop this at any time." He gazed down at her, his expression grave, serious, and her heart turned over in her chest. "Just say no, and I'll stop. Got it?"

Anna nodded. She didn't want to say no, and yet she had to acknowledge that she was uncertain enough of herself to possibly do so. Knowing she could was a huge relief.

He bent to kiss her again, his hand burrowing behind her back. A moment later, she felt her bra snap free. For a brief moment she wanted to hug the fabric to her body, to keep herself hidden, but as Leo tugged it up her arms and off, she let go. His remarkable eyes were so dark, so hot, as his gaze slipped over her.

"You are too perfect for words," he said, before he claimed her mouth again.

By slow degrees his kisses grew more heated, more demanding, his tongue sliding against hers in a rhythm that sent pleasure spiking inside her body, inside the aching core of her sex. The fire burned brighter, hotter with every kiss.

She'd never felt like this, never felt this combination of heat and pain that filled her and made her desperate for relief. When would that relief happen? When would he enter her body and take her over the edge?

She craved it. Feared it. Needed it.

But Leo was in no hurry. He worked his way down her body, kissing her skin, licking her the way she'd wanted to lick him, while she squirmed and gasped. Every touch was a revelation. Every stroke of his fingers and tongue on her body only spiraled the need higher until she was ready to beg him.

"Leo," she said urgently.

"Patience, Anna," he said against her skin, the vibration of his voice humming into the deepest recesses of her soul. "I promise you won't regret it."

His mouth trailed over her abdomen, his tongue dipping into her belly button, and then he was sliding her panties from her hips and pushing her legs open for his view. She made a sound of protest, sudden embarrassment scorching her from the inside out. She'd never opened herself to a man, never experienced that moment when his eyes darkened and his jaw hardened—and then his gaze shot to hers, a question in his gorgeous eyes.

"Shall I stop?" he said, and she knew it wasn't an easy thing for him to ask. He sounded tense, edgy. Cautious. And her heart melted.

He looked so beautiful hovering over her, his jaw shadowed with stubble, his dark eyes glittering hot. His erection strained against the fabric of his briefs and she found herself staring at that part of him, wondering how badly this might hurt the first time.

She wouldn't lie to him. "I want to stop," she said softly. His muscles tensed. She knew in that moment he would stand, would walk away and leave her alone if it was what she truly wanted. "But I want to continue even more."

"Oh, Anna," he groaned. And then he bent and kissed her again, his fingers slipping into the slick heat between her legs, his thumb sliding across her clitoris. Sensation crashed through her. She'd done this for herself, of course, but it was different when he was doing it to her. More intense somehow.

His long fingers shaped her sex, caressed every part of it—the plump outer lips, the delicate inner lips, the tiny ridge at the center where all her pleasure was focused. He stroked her again and again, concentrating all his effort on her most sensitive flesh.

Until she came apart with a cry, her body stiffening in his embrace, her legs shaking with the strength of her release.

She moaned, long and loud, and Leo drank her soft moans into his mouth until she stilled.

"Good?"

She closed her eyes, turned her head into her arm and nodded once. Heat flooded her, but was it the heat of her passion or the heat of embarrassment? She didn't know, and she wasn't entirely sure she cared.

Leo toyed with the pearls which still hung around her neck. "It gets better, Anna."

And then he slid down her body and touched his tongue to her sex. "Leo!"

He pushed her legs open, took her with his mouth. She

was shocked, and not shocked. She'd watched that video, watched the woman's face as her lover had done exactly this.

It was bliss. Sheer, heart-stopping bliss. Every nerve ending she had was focusing on that one spot, gathering tighter and tighter until she wasn't certain she could take another moment of this sweet torture.

Leo gave her no quarter. He was relentless, flicking his tongue over her still-sensitive skin, licking and sucking her until the tension built so, so impossibly high—

"Leo!" she cried, shattering beneath him, her body shuddering and shuddering until she lay on the blanket, her limbs melting, her body limp. She thought that if she never moved again, if she died here and now, she would be happy.

Her body was dissolving, floating in a void, and yet she still felt restless and unsatisfied beneath the haze of pleasure. As if she hadn't quite felt everything she could feel yet.

Leo got up and walked away. The glorious heat of him, the flame and passion, was gone. Stunned, she rose up on her elbows, watched him as he stood with his back to her. He didn't move, other than to rake a hand through his hair. Confusion raced through her.

"Leo?"

"We can't go any further," he told her, not turning to look at her. "We can't risk getting you pregnant."

Anna blinked. And then she got to her feet. She was conscious of her nudity, but the sun was sinking low enough that it was darker beneath the trees. And she felt so very, very naughty right now. Confident and beautiful.

Boldly, she went over to stand behind him. She couldn't help but admire his body. He was so very gorgeous, so perfectly made. The muscles in his back bunched and

stretched as he pulled his hand through his hair again.
She wanted to trace every ridge and swell of him, wanted
to spend hours learning his texture.

Leo was so sexy. So male.

So honorable.

Honorable? Not a word she would have associated with
Leo before today.

She put a tentative hand on his strong biceps, felt the
knot of warm muscle tense beneath her fingertips. Felt the
sizzle of current that passed between them. It was odd,
this feeling, and yet she was beginning to get used to it.
She'd never felt that sizzle with Alex, but maybe that's
because she'd always been so rigid around him. So controlled and cool.

She wasn't cool with Leo. Not now anyway.

"It's okay," she said, her heart thudding like mad. "I
started the Pill six months ago."

CHAPTER SIX

LEO turned to look at her. His expression was taut, controlled.

She shrugged self-consciously. "I wanted to know Alex a bit better before we had children. I—I know it was my duty, but I wasn't quite ready yet."

It was a small rebellion, but after all these years of waiting and preparing, she wasn't going to get pregnant in the first month and then let Alex walk out of her life. She'd wanted more time. She'd needed to know him better, needed to know who she was as his wife. She'd felt illicit when she'd gone to her doctor to ask for birth control, but she'd always intended to tell Alex she was taking the Pill when they wed. She hadn't meant it to be a secret—but it no longer mattered, did it?

Leo put his hands on her shoulders, breathed out hard. Those clever hands slid down her forearms, leaving a trail of fire as they went. Simply from a caress.

"You plan everything to the letter, don't you?"

She swallowed. "I am a bit obsessive about the details," she said somewhat lightly. But deep down she cringed, waiting for his censure.

Instead, he laughed, a deep sexy sound that thrilled her. "Anna, you are something else."

She tried to frown. "I'm not sure I want to be something else. I want to be interesting. Desirable. Not something else entirely."

He drew her to him. "Oh, you are definitely interesting and desirable. The other was a compliment. I can't remember the last time—"

He stopped speaking abruptly, and she reached up to slide her palm against his face. She couldn't help it. She wanted to touch him. "Can't remember the last time what?"

He shook his head. "Nothing. It's nothing."

And then he was scooping her up and taking her back to the blanket beneath the shelter, laying her down gently, kissing her again and again. The fires in her body stoked higher with every touch of his lips against hers. Leo was still wearing his briefs, and she arched against him in frustration.

"You should know," he said softly against her earlobe as he nibbled her there. "I am healthy. You have nothing to fear. I am always cautious with my…liaisons."

Liaisons. The word lodged in her brain, refused to fade away. She knew Leo had many lovers, knew she was only a *liaison.* This was temporary. It was here, now, a celebration of survival. They would be rescued eventually, she was certain, and they would go back to their lives.

A pang of something pierced her but she dared not examine it.

"Now, Leo," she said as her eyes filled with ridiculous tears. "Please, now."

Before she changed her mind. Before the fears she'd buried down deep escaped the Pandora's box of her soul. Before boring Anna took over again.

He shrugged out of his briefs, and then she felt him— the hot, hard head of him at her entrance. "Anna," he said, his voice strangled with the control he exercised. "Are you certain?"

She couldn't think. Couldn't speak. Her pulse drummed in her throat, her ears, even the soles of her feet. She was certain, certain...

She pulled his head down to hers and thrust her tongue into his mouth. He moaned softly—and then he moved, thrusting into her body. There was a slight moment of pain before he broke through the barrier, but then he was inside her fully.

Their bodies were joined together more intimately than she'd ever imagined. It was odd to feel a man so deep inside her, to feel the throb of his pulse as he held himself very still and kissed her softly.

"Are you okay?" he asked.

Anna wrapped her legs around his hips, knowing instinctively that's what she was supposed to do. "Yes," she breathed. "Oh, yes."

The pain was nothing compared to the pleasure. Finally, she'd done something for herself—she'd made a decision and done what she felt was right for her, not what anyone else wanted her to do. It was exhilarating. So damn exhilarating.

Leo began to move, slowly at first and then more quickly as she caught his rhythm and rose up to meet him over and over again. Her heart swelled with feelings she didn't want to examine, and her body caught the edge of the wave and began to soar further and faster as Leo made love to her.

She had no idea what to expect, but she hadn't quite expected this. This perfect joining of bodies, this sharp edge of feeling, this physical pleasure beyond anything she'd imagined before. She was molten, glowing, burning hotter and hotter with every stroke of his body into hers.

And then she reached the peak of sensation, caught herself on the edge of the precipice, held herself suspended there for what seemed an eternity of the most exquisite pleasure/pain she'd ever known as her body kindled. She was a flash fire, a firecracker waiting to explode.

And then she did explode, soaring over the edge, free-falling into nothingness as Leo took one stiff nipple into his mouth and suckled hard.

She was aware of Leo following her, of his body pumping into hers harder and faster, of him stiffening and groaning as he spilled inside her.

He swore, hot words that made her sex clench around him. His breathing was hard, but so was hers. He touched his forehead to hers, being very careful not to crush her beneath him.

"That was amazing," he said. "*You* are amazing."

He was still inside her, still hard, and she tilted her hips slightly, wondering if she would feel anything now that it was over. His breath hissed in.

"You want to kill me, don't you?" he said, and she could hear the laugh in his voice.

"Definitely not," she said, feeling more powerful than she ever had before. "I'm not quite finished with you yet."

He did laugh then.

The sun went down and Leo built a small fire near their shelter. They had a lantern for later, but the fire was enough light for now. After he fanned the flames to life, Leo dragged dried food packets out of the survival kit and they had a picnic. They had also gotten dressed again, their clothes having dried in the sun.

Anna was rather disappointed to sit by the fire with Leo and not be looking at his bare chest, but it was cooler at night and the clothes were definitely needed. She hugged her stiffened jacket around her and glanced over at Leo. Firelight caressed the planes of his face, shadowing his cheeks and the cleft in his chin. Sitting here now, like this, she couldn't believe they'd made love only a short while ago.

She was in some ways a different person than she had been this morning. Oh, not fundamentally different. She was still a nitpicky perfectionist and she still had a desire for order and neatness. Anna sighed. She was also still afraid of looking like a fool in the press, and she still wished she could run away until everything blew over and she ceased being the jilted bride.

But at least she could now say she'd experienced passion. And, oh, what passion. The memory of it made heat flare to life deep in her belly. Leo had initiated her into a world she'd never known. He'd turned her inside out and made her into a raw, needy creature who'd craved his touch.

So much so that she'd begged him to make love to her again soon after the first time. This time, however, he'd rolled onto his back and let her take the lead. She'd been shy at first, afraid, but then she'd discovered how powerful it made her feel when she controlled the pace. Leo was so in charge of his emotions, his reactions—but at one point his head fell back and his eyes closed and he swallowed hard. And that was the moment when triumph swelled in her veins, when she felt her feminine power fully.

Leo looked up then, caught her staring at him. Her first instinct was to glance away, pretend she hadn't been looking, but he smiled and her insides melted. It was so easy being with him like this. Being out here with no one watching, with no fear of prying eyes and lying voices.

Did they even know she was missing yet? Was anyone curious? They knew she'd gone with Leo, so what were they thinking?

Anna frowned. She was pretty sure she knew what they were thinking.

And they weren't wrong, were they? Which was beside the point, because she couldn't really afford for the press to get wind of such an idea. If she was humiliated now, what would happen if they decided to report that she'd spent the night alone on an island with a famous playboy overnight?

"Regrets, Anna?" His voice sliced into her thoughts.

She shook her head. "You?"

"One. That we didn't have a bed."

She shrugged. "I don't mind."

He looked so serious. "You deserved a bed. Flowers, candles, dinner and hours of kissing first."

She shivered in delight. What would it have been like to go on a real date with Leo? To be wined and dined and made love to in a soft bed with fluffy covers they could snuggle into afterward. "Is that how you usually go about it?"

He frowned then, and she wished she hadn't said it quite like that. Jealous, possessive. A clingy virgin. *Former* virgin.

"I did try to warn you," he said mildly, and yet she got the impression he wasn't in the least bit relaxed when he said it.

She was *not* jealous. Not at all.

It was simply her competitive side coming out, the part of her that always had to be the best at everything. The part that planned and made charts and notes and calendars and felt triumphant when everything came off exactly as she'd envisioned.

There was no chart for this, no plan that would see her through. This thing with Leo simply *was*.

She waved a hand airily, as if it were a trifle. They both knew it was not.

"Forget I said that."

He blew out a breath, and she got the distinct impression he was disappointed. In her. "I wasn't with a woman last night, Anna. I was working on a business deal. When you found me this morning, I'd never actually gone to bed."

Anna's heart pounded. She imagined him at his computer all night. And then, because she couldn't quite help it, she imagined him with a woman, some svelte gorgeous thing who wrapped herself around him and wouldn't let go. She called it being real with herself, when in fact it hurt more than it should.

She knew all about wrapping herself around Leo. She wanted to do it again. She was greedy where he was concerned. She felt such a sense of urgency, as if she needed to experience everything she could in this one night. Before her real life intruded.

"There was lipstick on your collar," she told him matter-of-factly. "Not that I care, of course."

He frowned as he thought about it. Then his expression cleared. "Ah, that would be from the drunk woman who launched herself at me in the men's room of the hotel last night."

Anna blinked, scandalized. She may have acted with complete and utter abandon today, but she was too much of a lady ever to make a fool of herself in public. At least, not on purpose. "And what were you doing that she followed you into the men's room?"

Leo shook his head and laughed. "Mistaken identity. She was after another fellow, who'd ducked into a stall to hide."

Anna couldn't stifle a giggle. Odd, since she was not ordinarily the giggling sort. "And what happened when she, um, attacked you? Did he come out of hiding?"

"No, the bastard. Fortunately, she passed out before she did too much damage."

"And then what?"

"I carried her to the lobby and informed the staff they would need to see her to her room."

"Oh, my," Anna breathed. "You are quite the white knight."

"I do what I can," he said, that cocky grin of his making her heart twist. For the first time, she thought the grin might actually be genuine and not a part of the armor he wore to hide the darkness within.

"But, Anna," he went on, turning serious. "You don't have to worry about me embarrassing you. When we're back on Santina, we'll do everything properly. I won't see anyone else while we're together."

Her blood beat in her ears. A current of dread uncoiled in her veins. She didn't want to think about Santina, didn't want to think about what would happen when they returned. It was another world, another life, and she didn't want it intruding on her happiness right now. She couldn't think of them there, couldn't imagine him taking her on a date, much less coming home with her for sex.

No, when they got to Santina, it was over. It had to be. Anguish threatened to eat her from the inside out. She wanted to rage that it wasn't fair, that she'd only now allowed herself to be free, but she knew that the fishbowl of her life wouldn't permit her to see Leo once they left the island. She was brave out here where no one could see them. But when she reached home again?

"Let's not talk about that yet," she whispered, gazing into the fire and watching the flames leap and dance. She didn't want to give him up, and yet she had to. For both their sakes. He was Allegra Jackson's brother. What would the media have to say about a romance between the jilted bride and the brother of the new bride? She shuddered to think about it.

It would shame the Santinas. Her parents. And she couldn't do that to them, could she? Not after everything else. They'd counted on her to unite their houses, and she'd failed.

Her parents would be astonished if they could see her now. Horrified. Her mother had often told her when she was a little girl that her impulsiveness would be her downfall if she weren't careful. So she'd always been careful.

Until today.

Leo put a finger under her chin, forced her to look at him. "Why shouldn't we? I want to see you again, Anna. Not just here, not only like this."

She put her hand on his, gloried in the feel of his skin against hers. A current passed between them, left her aching with renewed want. How much longer did they have together?

"I'm not ready to talk about it. I don't want to spoil anything."

He looked perplexed. "Spoil anything? I'm trying to tell you that I want to see you when we get back. How is that spoiling anything? I *want* to see you, Anna, for as long as we enjoy each other. I thought you'd be delighted."

"Leo, please." She turned her head to the side, pressed a kiss into his palm. He smelled like the smoke from the fire, warm and woodsy, and she closed her eyes to breathe him in deep.

His hand snaked behind her head, drew her toward him. He looked angry, but he was planning to kiss her anyway. A little thrill leaped to life in her belly.

His lips touched hers, softly, lightly. She strained toward him, wanting more, but he withheld himself from her.

"We *will* talk about this," he growled.

"Yes," she breathed, her heart aching. "But not tonight. Please. I don't want to talk about anything tonight. I just want to *feel*."

His breath was warm against her skin as his lips skimmed her jaw. "Fine. Tomorrow, then."

"Thank you."

His voice was a purr against the column of her throat, her jaw. "What do you want from me tonight, sweet Anna?"

Anna hesitated only a moment before she put her hand on his groin, shocking herself with the bold maneuver. But he was hard, ready, and she shivered with anticipation. She ran her fingers along the bulge of his erection, enjoyed it when he sucked in his breath. "You have to ask?"

He smiled against her lips. "I like this side of you," he said, though his voice still contained a note of anger. "It's such a contrast to the buttoned-up side. Rather like a naughty librarian."

A thrill washed through her. "And do you like naughty librarians, Mr. Jackson?"

He kissed her until she couldn't think. "I might."

"What do you do with naughty librarians?" she asked breathlessly, leaning toward him.

"Ah, wouldn't you like to know?"

"I would. I most definitely would."

His hand spread across her thigh, slid upward beneath the hem of her skirt while she held her breath in anticipation. "You enjoy playing with fire, don't you, Anna?" His fingers found her, stroked her over the thin lace of her panties. "But what happens when you get too close to the flame?"

"Show me," she said on a moan. "I want you to show me."

He did. Thoroughly, completely, devastatingly.

CHAPTER SEVEN

THEY slept entangled in each other's arms, waking when the morning light streamed through the trees and pierced the veil of sleep. They ate food from the packets again, and then Leo took a signal mirror and went out into the sun to send blinding flashes into the sky at regular intervals.

Afterward, they stripped down and went for a swim. Anna could hardly believe she was skinny-dipping with a man, but Leo made her laugh so much when they were together that it all seemed perfectly normal. Who needed schedules or protocol or social engagements when they had this?

And then they made love in a shadowed cove with the water flowing over them and the sun dappling their naked bodies through the rock. Anna had never felt so free or so happy as she did when she was with Leo. He moved inside her so expertly, so beautifully, taking her to the peak again and again before they collapsed to catch their breath. She fell asleep on the beach with Leo holding her close.

"How long was I asleep?" Anna asked when she woke and looked up into his handsome face. He'd been watching her, and she blushed to think that she'd probably snored or looked decidedly unsexy while she'd been sleeping.

"Not long. Twenty minutes or so."

She stretched and yawned. She felt so decadent, so hedonistic. She wasn't wearing a stitch of clothing, and she didn't care. She'd even taken her treasured pearls off, tucking them away with her clothing beneath the shelter. She felt like another woman, lying on the beach with her lover, her body sated, and slightly sore, from his amazing love-making. Part of her never wanted to go home again.

"Do you think they'll find us today?" she asked. She almost hoped they didn't, and yet a change of clothing and a hot shower would be welcome. A hot shower with Leo.

No, she couldn't think like that.

He traced a finger over her lips. It was a light caress, nonsexual, and yet her core flooded with renewed heat and moisture. What a revelation it was to be a woman with appetites.

"I don't know," he said. "I hope so. But we have to accept the possibility no one has yet raised the alarm."

"I imagine they would have, since we did not return last night."

He simply looked at her with that combination of sultry and naughty he was so very good at. "You're with me, Anna. No one will be surprised we didn't return."

"Ah," she said, realizing what he meant. That he was Leo Jackson, famous Casanova, and she was a woman who most certainly had been unable to resist his fabled charm. A sliver of helpless anger filtered through her.

And yet it was the truth, wasn't it? She had been unable to resist, like countless other women in his life. In spite of the fact he'd said he wanted to see her when they returned to Santina, she was still only temporary in his life. He wanted her until he tired of her. She was merely another in the parade of women who'd graced his bed.

She'd known it, but it was the one thing she could not be in the real world. The reason this had to end here, on the island, and not later.

"Perhaps now is a good time to talk about what happens when we get back," he said, as if he sensed her turmoil. His dark gaze was so serious and intent as he hovered over her on one elbow.

Anna swallowed, a pang of uneasiness twisting in her stomach. "There's nothing to talk about."

"Nothing at all?" he pressed.

She sighed. "Oh, Leo, you know it won't work."

"Why not? You're a single woman, I'm a single man. Who says we can't see each other?"

She pushed herself upright, turned to look at him. "I can't, Leo. There are...expectations."

He was beginning to look angry. She could see the heat flare to life in his gaze, but it wasn't the kind of heat she liked. It was dark, piercing, scouring her senses. "Expectations? Meaning, I suppose, that I am not quite good enough for those lofty expectations?"

"That's not what I said." The sun had moved higher in the sky now, and the light that had dappled them before was now a strong shaft of sunlight creeping into their cove. Leo's body was golden, hard and lean and perfect. The dragon on his abdomen was fierce, snorting flames that fanned across his hip bone and groin. She'd wanted to trace the line of the dragon with her tongue, but had not been brave enough to do so.

Now, she reached out and traced it with a finger. His muscles clenched beneath her touch. "Where did you get that?"

He caught her hand. "You keep trying to distract me, Anna."

She peered at him from behind lowered lashes. "Is it working?"

"Hardly. Now tell me why we can't see each other on Santina or Amanti or wherever in hell we choose. You aren't marrying Prince Alessandro now. You can do what you want with your life."

She shivered to think so, and yet she knew she had to be careful. She might have been carefree on this island, but she could not afford to be so when they returned. The press would have a field day with this, if they knew, and she refused to be the target of their humiliation any longer. Leo might not be affected by bad press, but she had to live her life the way she always had or be annihilated by it.

"I need time, Leo. I can't just start dating and having affairs. I can't do that to my parents or to the Santinas. Don't you realize what the coverage would be like if we were to start dating? Especially since we seem to have skipped the date part and gone straight to sleeping together? Are you willing to drop me at my door every night with a chaste kiss?"

His eyes flashed. "You are giving them far more power over you than you should." He swore then, shocking words that sounded so coarse and angry coming from his lips. "Why do you care what the headlines say? Don't you know that the true secret to getting them to leave you alone is to do whatever in the hell you want to do? They want a *victim,* Anna—and you have made yourself into a perfect victim."

His words sliced into her, carved themselves into her soul. It hurt. "My reputation—"

"Your reputation," he ground out, "is ruined. You've spent the night on this island alone with me. Once your precious newspapers figure that out, and they will, the headlines about us will make everything up until now seem like a flattering portrayal. You have to show them you don't give a damn what they think."

Her heart throbbed at the anger in his voice. Not only that, but she feared he was right about her reputation. She just had to hope their disappearance together was kept quiet. "It's easy for you, Leo. No one cares that you've slept with your thousandth woman or broken some poor model's heart. They cheer you, applaud you, think you are clever and handsome and fun. But I was supposed to be a queen. They will not be so forgiving of me."

He got to his feet, his body simmering with tension as he looked down at her. "And why do you think you need anyone's forgiveness? You aren't going to *be* a queen, Anna. It's time you stopped acting like you were."

No one came for them that day. Leo signaled with the mirror at regular intervals, but nothing happened. He was tense, angry, and he wasn't quite sure why. It should be so easy, shouldn't it? A beautiful woman who wanted to have hot sex with him and then go their separate ways without any commitment?

He should be ecstatic. It was, after all, his usual modus operandi. He should be buried in her soft, tight body right now, making her moan and scream his name. He should do it as often as they could both tolerate, right up until the minute their rescue arrived. He should, and yet he couldn't.

He was irritated, and that wasn't quite like him. He should be congratulating himself on a lucky escape, but instead he was brooding because the virgin he'd recently bedded only wanted him for sex. And only while they were marooned together.

Pure irony, wasn't it?

He'd never considered that she wouldn't want to see him once they were rescued. No, he'd actually been worried that in spite of her heated pronouncements otherwise, she *would* want more from him. He knew her kind—wide-eyed, idealistic and inexperienced. A sure recipe for disaster in his book.

She was *supposed* to be the kind of woman who wanted

forever. She was supposed to want children, a house, a normal family life that included walks in the park, trips to family vacation destinations and a barking dog that tracked mud into the house and shook its wet fur all over the furnishings.

She was supposed to want all the things he didn't, and he was supposed to be the one who pulled back.

But it wasn't happening quite that way, and it disconcerted him more than it should.

He had to admit, the more he thought about it, that it was probably for the best if they didn't see each other again. Less messy for them both if they made a clean break here on the island. If they didn't, Allegra would quite possibly be unhappy with him for dating her husband-to-be's former fiancée. Not that he typically allowed his sister to have a say in his personal life, but for once it would touch her directly.

Because, yes, the press would have a field day with the news. Anna wouldn't like that at all. Neither, he suspected, would Allegra.

The sun dropped behind the horizon and the temperature cooled as storm clouds moved in. They'd hardly spoken in hours when Leo offered Anna another food packet and some water. She looked up at him with those wide green eyes and a jolt of electricity hit him in the gut.

Sex. It was all he could think about when he looked at her, all he wanted.

And all she wanted, if the way she looked at him was any indication. Like she was starving for something other than food.

He forced himself to turn away. Lightning flashed across the sky in the distance, turning the clouds pink before winking out again. The weather wasn't threatening, but it would probably rain later. Which was a good thing. They were almost out of water, and he'd be able to collect some in the makeshift reservoir he'd created out of plastic sheeting and rocks.

He sat down and they ate in silence as the surf crashed against the beach nearby. It was peaceful out here in a way. So different from his life in London or Los Angeles. There, he was always on the go, always seeking new business opportunities for the Leonidas Group. He traveled and he dated and he moved on to new challenges on a regular basis. Always looking for the next thrill, the next high. It was what he wanted, what he craved.

Anna glanced over at him. He looked up instinctually, as if they were connected on some level he didn't yet understand, and met her gaze. She dropped her chin, stared at the ground.

And then she fixed him with a look. "What did you want to be when you were a child, Leo?"

He didn't attempt to hide the surprise that must have shown on his face. "Where did this come from?"

She shrugged a pretty shoulder. "I'm tired of the silence. And I want to know," she said, pushing her hair from her face. It was thick hair, long and heavy, and he loved wrapping his hands in it while they made love. When she was on top, her hair flowed around them, curtaining them in their own cocoon. Her green eyes watched him carefully. Coolly, as if she expected rejection and had dared to ask anyway.

He thought about denying her, but strangely he didn't want to. Not yet anyway. "I wanted to be a professional footballer, like my father. His career didn't last long, but the perks did."

"The perks?"

"Women," he said without hesitation, and then felt bad for saying it when she dropped her gaze and swallowed.

He'd done it because he was still angry with her, but he wasn't proud of himself for it.

"So why didn't you?" she asked, pressing on.

He finished the packet of dried food and crumpled the foil. What was the point in being an ass? They barely knew each other. They'd had sex—fabulous sex—but they weren't lovers in the usual sense. And they weren't going to be. She'd made that clear.

And Leo Jackson didn't beg.

He didn't need to. Or want to. When they got back to Santina, there would be no shortage of women who wanted his attention. That was the life he was accustomed to, the life he adored. One woman, no matter how sexy, how desirable, wasn't going to change that.

He leaned back on his elbows. "I decided I could make more money catering to the exclusive tastes of the rich and famous. So I did."

"The Leonidas Group."

He could hear the question in her statement.

"Leonidas is my name," he said. He'd hated his name as a child, never understood why his mother had saddled him with something so unwieldy. He'd thought it was because she'd been an heiress and socialite with pretensions beyond her station in life. It wasn't until he was much older that he'd begun to understand she'd wanted him to be strong and brave and fearless.

"Leonidas was a hero king of Sparta," Anna said. "A very brave man."

Leo knew the story by rote. "He led the Greek forces in the Battle of Thermopylae. And he died defending the cause. I prefer to live to fight another day."

"Very sensible of you."

"What about you, Anna?" he asked, wanting to talk about her instead. He didn't like talking about himself. It took him into territory he didn't wish to explore, at least not tonight. He was, quite simply, a man who knew his limitations and hid them behind a strong will to succeed and a wealth of cocky charm he'd inherited from his father. He had no wish to discuss it with her. Or anyone.

But he did want to know what made her tick, who she was in truth. She'd given him glimpses of it last night, today. When she'd been naked beneath him, naked on top of him, surrounding him. She was a passionate woman beneath the uptight exterior. He hated to see that exterior return, and yet he knew it would when their rescue arrived. It was as natural to her as breathing.

"What did you want to be when you were a child? Or was queen your only choice?"

She shook her head. "Oh, no, definitely not. I thought I wanted to be a veterinarian. But then I realized there would be blood, so that idea went away. After that, I wanted to be a celebrity chef for a while. And of course there was the ballerina dream."

"And the princess dream, I imagine."

She tensed. "Of course there was the princess dream. But that one was supposed to come true." She shrugged, yet he knew how difficult it was for her to let the idea be lowered into the ground. "But that is life, yes?"

"Life is many things," Leo said. "Some of them disappointing, some of them frustrating and some of them blissfully happy."

She looked pensive. "Have you ever been blissfully happy?"

He'd opened himself up for that one. "I suppose that depends on how you define happy. But yes, I'd say I have."

If she asked him to name the times, he wasn't sure he could. All he knew was that he must have been very happy at one time or another. He'd lived a hedonistic life. He'd had fun. How could he not have been happy?

He had it all. He had plenty of money and plenty of women. Who needed more?

Anna sighed, the curtain of her hair falling over her forehead as she dipped her chin toward her chest. "I think I'm still waiting for that."

A sharp sensation bloomed in his gut. "Don't wait for it. Make it happen."

She looked up at him, her eyes wide and gleaming in the light of the fire. "I'm trying," she said. "I…" She hesitated before continuing. "It's not that I don't want to see you when we get home again. But I can't. Not yet."

A shaft of lightning lit up the sky, a crack of thunder following hard on its heels. Electricity sizzled in the air. He could smell the sulfur, could feel the bite of it in his throat. It tasted like anger.

"And how long do you think it will take, Anna? One month? Two? Six? A year?"

She swallowed. "I—I don't know."

"Then perhaps you're right," he said tightly. "Perhaps it's best we say goodbye now."

"I knew you'd say that."

Anger whipped through him. "What did you expect me to say? That I'd be happy to wait until you're no longer scared of the media?"

She swallowed. "That's not fair, Leo."

"Nothing ever is," he replied.

The storm broke around midnight. Water poured down onto the plastic sheeting of their makeshift shelter, waking Anna from a deep sleep. Beside her, Leo lay still, one arm propped behind his head as he stared at the roof above their heads. She felt a pang of longing, but shoved it down deep and tried to ignore it. She and Leo were through. And it was best that way.

They lay together beneath the blanket for warmth, but there was no warmth between them. Not any longer.

The thought made a lump form in her throat, a hard heavy knot she couldn't swallow. Tomorrow, perhaps, they would be rescued. And she might never see him again. He was a man of the world, and she was a woman without purpose. She would soon return to her home on Amanti and lock herself away until she could face the world again.

Without Leo. The thought hurt. Crazy.

"Leo," she said—choked, really—and he turned his head toward her. She couldn't stop herself from reaching out and touching his jaw, running her fingers into the silk of his hair.

He stiffened. She expected him to reject her, to push her away, but after a moment he groaned, as if he, too, were unable to stay strong in the face of this overwhelming need.

He caught her hand and pressed a kiss into her palm. Heat flooded her in great waves, softening her limbs, making the ache sharper. He gathered her to him, pulled her into his heat and hardness.

"I want you, Anna. Dammit, I still want you."

"Yes," she breathed. "Oh, yes."

The rain pounded against the sheeting, dripping off the sides, marooning them in a small dry place that became their island within an island. They didn't speak as they stripped and made love. Instead, they spoke in kisses, in touches, in the long luxurious glide of his body into hers. The storm raged around them, between them. Leo managed to take her angrily and tenderly at the same time, and she answered him in kind, their bodies tangling and battling and straining and melting again and again.

When it was over, they collapsed together and slept the

night away until they awoke to a bright blue sky, a clean ocean breeze…

…and a boat anchored offshore.

CHAPTER EIGHT

PREGNANT.

Anna stared at the test stick in her fingers, her entire body going hot and cold and numb all at once. She was pregnant. With Leo's child. How had it happened? How could it *possibly* have happened?

She blinked and fell back against the bathroom counter. Oh, God.

No. *No, no, no.*

It had been a month since they'd been rescued from the island. A month since she'd last seen him. As soon as they'd reached Santina, he'd left again. It had broken her heart, but it's what she'd wanted. What she'd insisted on.

She'd returned to her home on Amanti and hidden herself away, waiting for the media attention to die down.

And it had. There'd been a little bit of a stir over their plane crash and subsequent rescue by Santina's coast guard—but then nothing. Alex and Allegra, and their various siblings, had proven far more interesting to the collective conscious lately, thank goodness.

Leo had gone his merry way, she'd gone hers, and the press had turned their attention to the more flamboyant members of the Jackson family—and even some of the Santinas—and the fallout from the clash of families at the engagement party.

But now…*this*. Oh, God, *this*.

She'd missed Leo. She'd missed his touch, his laugh, his arrogant and cocky grin. She'd missed the feel of his body sliding into hers, the exquisite pleasure he'd given her for two days on that island. She'd missed swimming with him naked, and she'd missed lying beneath a makeshift shelter and making love during a raging storm.

She'd missed everything about being with Leo. But she'd pushed him away, shoved him from her life without so much as a backward glance. It was her fault he was gone.

She looked at the test again, hoping that she'd read it wrong, that the answer had changed somehow. It had not. And she had to tell Leo. He had a right to know. She considered, for one brief moment, terminating the pregnancy.

But she didn't want to. Already, though it frightened her, she loved the idea of a child that was part her and part Leo. How could she not? She'd felt so adrift recently, but now she felt as if she had a renewed purpose, a reason to be the best person she could be. She would stop feeling sorry for herself and she would teach this baby everything she knew. Her baby would have the freedom to be whatever he or she wanted to be.

From this moment forward, Anna would protect her baby at all costs.

She put the test stick in a drawer. As she was turning away, she caught sight of her reflection in the mirror and stopped short. She looked tired, drawn. Her skin was golden, her eyes bright, but there was a strain in her expression that hadn't been there before. She ran a hand over her cheeks, her forehead. There were circles under her eyes. She'd been so, so tired lately.

Now she knew why she couldn't drag herself out of bed in the morning.

A baby. Leo's baby.

She had to call him. But no, she couldn't just ring him up and deliver news like that over the phone, could she? She had to see him. She had to find out where he was and go to him. She hadn't allowed herself to search for information about him, afraid of what she might find, but now she had no choice.

Anna left the bathroom and went into her huge walk-in closet to retrieve her suitcase. Wherever Leo was, she would find him. And she would tell him personally that he was going to be a father. Her heart leaped at the thought of seeing him again.

But her stomach twisted. She was nervous, stunned. What if he had a girlfriend? What if he didn't want to see her or, worse, didn't care about her news? What then?

Anna tossed a folded sweater set into the suitcase. She couldn't think like that. She simply couldn't. If she did, she'd lose her nerve. And she couldn't lose her nerve. In the not too distant future, she would begin to show. How could she face the media then? How could she shame her parents that way after everything else they'd been through? She would *not* be a laughingstock over this, nor would she allow them to be.

This baby meant too much to her, and she wouldn't allow anyone to make her feel ashamed. But she knew that if she was going to protect her child, she needed Leo.

It only took a matter of hours to make the arrangements, and then she was on her way to London. A check of the newspapers had revealed a photo of Leo just last night in a restaurant with a group of businessmen.

He hadn't been with a woman, and that gave her hope. In fact, when she dared to skim the tabloids from the month since he'd returned to London, she found not one mention of him with another woman. Perhaps he'd missed her just a little bit. Perhaps, she thought crazily, he'd even been waiting for her to call him, to tell him she was ready to see him again. The thought gave her courage.

When her plane touched down at Heathrow, it was raining heavily. Anna stood in the chilly London air and hailed a cab to take her to her hotel. It was no mistake she'd chosen a Leonidas Group property. The Crescent Hotel was located in Mayfair, a stunning Victorian-era building that had been renovated and turned into the kind of luxury hotel Leo was famous for.

The address was exclusive, the rooms exquisite, and her reception had been beyond compare. But all she could think about was the owner of the hotel and what he would say when she told him her news.

She stood at the window and gazed out over the view of Hyde Park long after the porter had delivered her luggage. The park was green, but the sky was gray and leaden. Black cabs crawled through the busy streets along with red double-decker buses and cars of all description. It was insane compared to Amanti, and she felt a pang for home. Amanti was modern and busy, but not as busy as London. This city teemed with people going about their hectic lives. Lives she didn't understand.

She felt very small and very lost as she watched the city slide by on the streets below. But she had no time to be lost. She had to find Leo.

His offices weren't very far, so she donned her raincoat and umbrella and followed her phone's GPS directions until she stood outside the tall glass building that housed the Leonidas Group's London headquarters. It had been a bit of a walk from her hotel, but the exercise felt good.

She'd gotten wet during her walk, regardless of the umbrella, and she felt a bit bedraggled and cold, but she would not turn back now. She stood outside the building, staring at the door and trying to gather the courage that had melted on her walk. People streamed by on the sidewalk, oblivious to her torment. The smoky glass of the Leonidas building looked so imposing suddenly, like a black gaping hole into which she would disappear should she be brave enough to enter.

A car pulled up to the curb as Anna stood there, undecided. A moment later, a uniformed driver emerged with an umbrella. He walked past her to the door of the building and waited only a minute before the door swung open and a man came out.

Anna's heart kicked up. A tall, dark-haired man in an expensive suit exited the building. A man she would know anywhere, even were she blindfolded.

A man who was not alone. A fresh chill stole through Anna, rooting her to the spot. The woman with Leo was small, blonde, and clung to his arm as if she'd never let go. She turned her face up to him, smiled, her even white teeth flashing in the semidarkness that was falling on the city.

A hot slice of something passed through Anna then. She almost turned away, almost slunk into the night and back to the hotel. Except she thought of the baby growing inside her—Leo's baby—and courage blazed into her veins again.

"Leo," she said as he passed by.

He ground to a stop as if he'd run into a brick wall. Turned to her, his dark eyes as hot and intense as she remembered them. The woman with him frowned.

"Anna?"

Anna pushed the umbrella back so that her face was no longer shadowed. She was not as beautiful as the woman at his side, not as polished or…as dry, she thought wryly.

"Yes, it's me."

Leo disentangled himself from his companion and came

over to her. He was as hard and handsome as always, and her heart skipped a beat at his nearness.

He did not, she noticed, look very friendly as he gazed down at her. She drank in his scent, that unique combination of subtle spice and man that was Leo. She even thought she could smell a tinge of the ocean, of the salt spray against his sun-warmed skin. It took her back so forcefully that she nearly crumpled on the sidewalk in front of him.

He reached out to steady her, and she realized that she'd nearly crumpled in truth, not merely in her head.

"Are you well?" he demanded.

She shook her head, unable to answer for fear of blurting it out right there on the dark street.

Leo swore softly. And then he was gathering her against him, one arm firmly around her, barking orders to his driver and the woman who stood so forlornly under the driver's umbrella. The door to the limo opened, and then Anna was ushered inside the warm interior and Leo slid in beside her. The woman also joined them, Anna noted sourly.

The driver's door shut with a thud and the car sat motionless, idling in the night.

"What are you doing here, Anna?" Leo asked. His voice was hard, cold, unlike the man she'd known on the island. The man who, a moment ago, had gathered her close and put her into the car. For a moment she'd been thrown back to another time. To the tenderness and passion that had flared between them.

She shivered, a long ripple that slid down her spine and over her skin on icy little feet.

"I need to talk to you," she said, turning her head to look out at the traffic on the street. She could not look at him, or she would crumble. She would blubber everything, regardless of the woman who sat across from them, radiating disapproval and anger.

And that she could not do.

Leo pressed a button and gave his driver instructions, and then they were moving. The woman sat on the seat opposite, arms folded over her ample breasts, jaw set stubbornly as she glared at Anna. Not a business associate, then.

"It's private," Anna added, just in case Leo expected her to say anything with his girlfriend present.

"I gathered," he said shortly.

"Leo," the woman said—whined, really. "You promised you'd take me dancing tonight."

Anna could sense Leo's irritation, even if she couldn't see the expression on his face. "The plan has changed, Donna," he said crisply.

Oddly enough, Anna felt a burst of sympathy for Donna, who seemed to shrink in on herself with Leo's words. It wasn't her fault after all. Donna didn't say another word as the car moved through the city, finally coming to a halt somewhere residential. The door swung open and Leo turned to Anna. "I'll be right back."

He exited the vehicle, held out his hand for Donna, who took it and scooted out the door. Anna could hear raised voices on the sidewalk. Her skin burned, indignation a hot flush beneath the surface.

Leo had been dating. While she'd shut herself away in Amanti and tried to get over their two days on the island, he'd moved blissfully onward, compelled by the strong sensuality that she knew was as much a part of him as breathing.

Had he done the things to Donna that he'd done to her?

Anger was a cyclone inside her, whirling through her with a force that threatened to split her apart at the seams.

It made no sense, since she'd known what he was—*since she'd pushed him away*—but it was true nonetheless.

Leo returned to the car and the door closed behind him. Anna suddenly felt as if she would burst with the fury she felt. It welled inside her with the force of a nuclear reaction. She'd missed him, missed what they'd had, and he'd been with another woman.

She knew it was her fault, knew she'd pushed him away, and yet she couldn't help what happened next, as if it were a chain reaction that had begun the instant he'd walked out of his building with another woman on his arm.

She slapped him.

His head snapped back, the sound like a thunderclap in the quiet car. And then he was glaring at her. She felt wild, dazed, and she lashed out again, an angry sound escaping her as she did so.

This time he caught her wrist in an iron grip. Anna growled, swung with the other hand. It made no sense, but she couldn't stop. He caught that wrist, too, pinned her hard against the seat. And then he was pushing her back, stretching over top of her, pinning her against the seat with his lean, hard-muscled body.

"Did you think I'd be waiting for you, Anna? Is that why you're angry?"

"Let me go," she said, her voice as cold as she could make it. And yet a part of her thrilled at his touch. Her core softened, her body aching for his possession once more. Liquid heat flooded her sex.

He was so close. Too close. His breath fanned across her cheek. "I'm afraid not, darling. I'd rather like to keep my head attached to my shoulders."

Her breath hissed in as he moved against her, so warm and hard and familiar. Anna closed her eyes as a sob built inside her chest. She couldn't want him, not like this. How could she let herself feel this way? How could she want him inside her again, possessing her, making her his in a way no man ever had before? One month since they'd been together, and he'd forgotten her so easily.

What did you expect? You pushed him away.

Anna bit down on the angry tears that threatened to spill free. She'd done what was necessary, and she'd thought of him almost nonstop since. He clearly hadn't had the same problem.

She started to struggle, her body twisting beneath him. A sob broke free as he deflected the knee she'd aimed at his balls.

"Dammit, what is the matter with you?" he growled.

"You," she choked out. "You're a bastard."

She could feel the leashed violence in him. "I am, in fact," he said coldly. "But I doubt my birth is what you've come to discuss."

She lay against the seat, her body trembling beneath his, his heat soaking into her, warming her. Perversely, she wanted to turn her face into his neck, wanted to nibble the skin there.

She would not.

"What do you want, Anna?" Leo demanded. "Why did you come here?"

It was all wrong. Everything she'd wanted to say, wanted to tell him. This wasn't the way it was supposed to happen. He was supposed to be happy to see her again. He was supposed to want her, and she was supposed to be the strong one, the one who pushed him away. As she'd done on the island. She was supposed to tell him in a dignified tone that she was expecting his child.

He was supposed to be grateful she'd returned to his life.

Grateful?

Heavens above, this man was anything but happy to see her. He would be anything but grateful. How could she tell him?

How could she not?

"Not like this," she said. Whimpered, actually.

His grip on her wrists tightened until she nearly cried out in pain, but he released her and shoved back away from her. Then he was pushing his hand through his hair and cursing softly.

Anna sat up. Straightened her damp trousers. Fiddled with the cuffs of her raincoat. All the while breathing deeply, telling herself she would not cry. She'd survived Alex Santina—she could certainly survive Leo! Alex hadn't meant anything to her, but his betrayal had been far more humiliating.

Leo was the man she'd given herself to, the man she'd bared her soul to—and the man she'd pushed from her life. Could she blame him for being so angry with her, so cold?

"Where are you staying?" he demanded in clipped tones.

"The Crescent," she shot back.

"Ah," he said.

Heat flared to life inside her. "And what is wrong with that?"

"Nothing," he said a moment later. He gave instructions to the driver and the car slipped into traffic again.

They rode in silence for some time, until the feelings knotting in her belly demanded release. "It didn't take you very long, did it?"

His head swung toward her. "I beg your pardon?"

"You know what I mean, Leo. The woman. Donna. Is she the first?"

She could feel him stiffen beside her. "If I recall correctly, you're the one who said a relationship between us was impossible."

Shame roiled inside her. "You know why."

"I know why you believed it to be true. Have you changed your mind, sweet Anna? Is that why you're here?"

Her skin prickled at the name he used. He'd called her that on the island, and while she knew it had first been done in jest, it had come to mean so much more in the two days they'd shared.

It meant nothing now.

How had she let this happen? How had she lost her sense of right and wrong in so brief a time on the island? She'd been weak, and she'd allowed him inside the walls she'd erected. She'd wanted to be close to someone, and he'd offered her that. She'd known better, but she'd been weak.

"No," she breathed, unable to say anything else.

But it was a lie. Because she needed him if she were to have this baby and keep scandal from raining down on her head—their heads—like hellfire. She would endure whatever she had to endure for herself, but for her baby she would fight tooth and nail to provide the happiest, safest environment possible. And she needed Leo to help her do it.

"Then what is there to say?" he demanded. "Surely you have not come all this way to see if I have moved on with my life."

Anna folded her arms over her breasts. Her body was trembling, but whether from anger or cold she wasn't certain. "Which wasn't so very hard to do, was it?"

Yes, it stung, and yes, she knew she had no right to be hurt. It didn't change the way she felt seeing him with another woman, however. She'd felt as if someone had reached inside her and ripped her heart from her body. It stunned her, and worried her.

Leo swore. She didn't blame him. "You can't have it both ways, Anna. You might sit in your cold lonely house and congratulate yourself on avoiding another scandal, but you can't expect others to do the same."

"I don't," she said softly.

They traveled in silence for several minutes, the air as crisp and electrical as if a lightning strike had occurred in the center of the car. Anna's throat hurt from the giant lump that wouldn't let her speak the words she needed to say. Leo didn't make it easy on her, either. He sat with his fingers drumming the armrest, his face turned away from her to look out the window. He was so remote, so distant, and she didn't know how to breach that distance. How to say what she had to say.

She'd had no trouble breaching the distance between them on the island, but they'd been stripped to their barest elements there, incapable of erecting the walls that now separated them from each other. These walls were seemingly insurmountable, and yet she had to find a way.

The car pulled to a halt beneath a bright red awning, and she realized they'd reached the Crescent Hotel. Her heartbeat sped up as the uniformed doorman came down the stairs and reached for the car door.

Leo turned to her, his eyes glittering, his jaw hard. He looked so cold and remote, so untouchable, and her stomach knotted in panic.

"Unless you have something you wish to say, I'll say good-night now."

"So you can return to Donna?" she lashed out.

"You assured me this was the way you wanted it, Anna."

Where had he gone, that man who'd been so fierce and tender on the island? In spite of her wish to be strong, a single tear slid down her cheek.

"Something has changed," she said, pushing the words past her aching throat.

He clenched the fingers of one hand in his lap. She sensed that he had grown very, very still. Waiting for her to continue. Waiting for that moment when she would speak the words that would change everything. Did he know what it was? Did he suspect? Or did he simply think she was crazy?

The door swung open, the sounds from the street suddenly louder. The scent of some kind of food on the wind—an Indian curry, perhaps—skated inside the car, made her press a sudden hand to her mouth.

"Anna?" He still sounded cold and distant compared to the island—and yet his hard veneer seemed to crack just a shade.

It wasn't much, but it was enough to give her the sliver of courage she needed. Her heart thudded, her stomach twisting in fear. She rubbed damp palms along the fine weave of her trench coat.

And then the words fell from her mouth as if they'd been hovering there all along.

"I'm pregnant, Leo."

CHAPTER NINE

HE HADN'T heard her correctly. Surely he hadn't. The world seemed to slow, the sounds from outside the car distorting in his ears like he was on a carnival ride. Leo could only focus on her, on her tired face and huge eyes. Her long hair was twisted up high on her head, as always, and she wore the pearls she'd had on the island. Her white raincoat stood out starkly in the dark interior of the car, contrasted with the black V-neck sweater and trousers she wore.

No color, as usual. Anna didn't like color.

"How?" he asked, his voice colder than he wanted it to be. Shocked.

She looked away. Shrugged. "I don't know. I—I was on the Pill, but of course I didn't have it for the two days we were marooned." Her chin dropped to her chest. "I might have messed up the dosage after we returned."

She fingered her pearls, a nervous gesture he knew all too well.

Leo could only blink. A current of ice flowed through him, freezing him to the spot. A baby. His baby. He had no doubt the baby was his. No doubt.

But he couldn't be a father. He was the last person in the world fit to be a father. What if he was too much like Bobby? What if he didn't know what to do when this tiny being came into the world and needed him?

Panic threaded through the ice, melting his immobility. He exited the car smoothly and held out his hand for her. After a brief hesitation, she slipped her fingers into his palm. Fresh sensation rocked him at the touch of her skin on his.

She didn't say anything as he led her inside the hotel and over to the brass-and-wood lift. "Which room?" he asked as the lift operator waited patiently.

"Five-oh-four," she said quietly.

The lift began to move, its speed belying its age as they reached the fifth floor very quickly. "Here you are, Mr. Jackson," the operator said.

Leo took a bank note from his breast pocket and shoved it into the man's hand, uncaring how much it was for, and escorted Anna down the hall to her room. She fished the key card from her pocket, and then he opened the door and let her pass through before he closed it behind him and took a deep breath.

Pregnant.

A lamp burned in the suite, illuminating the sitting area. The room was furnished with the finest antiques, the best silks, the latest electronics—but Leo could focus on none of those things. All he could see was the woman standing across from him. Her raincoat was still buttoned up, her hands shoved in the pockets. Her eyes said she was tired, worn, wary.

Fury burned through him. She was afraid of him? Of *him?* After all they'd been through together?

"You have confirmed this pregnancy?" he said. It wasn't the first time a woman had claimed to be having his baby, though it was the first time he thought it was true.

Her head snapped up, her chin thrusting forward defiantly. "I only took the test this morning. It was positive."

"You have not been to a doctor?"

She shook her head. "I…I panicked. I had to see you."

"And what is your plan now, Anna? What do you want from me?" He knew he sounded callous and cruel, but he couldn't seem to quite wrap his head around the fact he'd fathered a child. An innocent child who deserved far better than Leo could give. "If you are considering terminating the pregnancy, I won't interfere," he added.

Her jaw dropped, her eyes growing wide. She clutched a hand over her stomach, and he felt like an ass.

"I'm not," she said firmly. "I want this baby."

"Why?" He didn't mean to be cruel, but he had to know. His mother had been a single parent up until her death. He'd often wondered if she would have chosen differently if she'd realized how difficult it would be.

"Because I do. Because I'm not without means, and because I'm not so selfish as to deny this baby a chance at life when I have so much to give."

"It won't be easy," he said. "You have to know that."

She looked determined. Fiery. *Dragon lady.*

"I am well aware."

Leo walked over to the stocked liquor cabinet and poured two fingers of Scotch. He needed something to calm the rat-a-tat-tat of his heart, something to ease the jangle of shock coursing through him. *Pregnant.*

He'd always been so cautious. No doubt it was because of the circumstances of his birth—something he swore he would never do to his own child. Leo hadn't even known, until he was ten years old and motherless, that he actually *had* a father.

He lifted the crystal tumbler. The first sip of liquid scalded his throat, his gut. He welcomed it. Needed it. Craved it.

"I will support you and the child, of course," he said, turning back to her. Because he would not abandon his child. He would do the best he could, though he had no idea just yet what his best was.

"We don't need your support," she shot back, head held high. He knew she was still offended that he'd said he wouldn't stand in the way of a termination. But he'd had no idea what else to say. He didn't know how to be a father. In fact, he didn't know what he felt about anything at this moment. "Money is not the issue."

"No, of course not," he said. Anna came from money, and she had an inheritance of her own—rather like his mother had had. But his mother's money hadn't protected her in the end. She'd still died alone, and she'd left him to the care of a father he'd never known existed until she was gone. What a shock that had been, going from one household to another in a matter of weeks. From one loving parent to the other who was a stranger.

Leo knew in his mind where this conversation was leading, where he had to take it, and yet part of him resisted doing so. He sipped the Scotch as if he were savoring the last moments of his freedom.

"I need something else from you," she said, her accent growing heavier with the emotion she was feeling. "Something other than money."

He thought for one terrifying moment that she would sink to her knees and beg, but of course she didn't. This was Anna.

She lifted her head higher, if that were possible, her eyes gleaming with determination. With fire. A bolt of desire shot through him, reminded him forcefully of why he'd wanted her in the first place.

"And what is that, sweet Anna?" But he already knew what she would say before she said it. Because he knew her. Knew what drove her.

The words fell from her lips exactly as he expected they would. "I need your name."

He didn't speak, and she wondered if he'd heard her. He looked so distant, so detached. And so gorgeously male she wanted to weep. He wore a dark suit, custom fit, of course. He wore no tie, but a deep blue shirt open at the neck. He looked like the ladies' man he was, she thought bitterly. His dark hair was combed back from his face, the ends curling up over his collar in sexy little waves she wanted to touch. His perfect face was serious, troubled. Not at all the carefree playboy he was reputed to be.

He cradled the crystal tumbler in one hand, stared at the contents before turning it up and draining it. "Are you asking me to marry you, sweet Anna?" he said, his voice deceptively mild.

Anna swallowed. "Yes." Because it was the best way, the only way, to protect their child. She'd thought about it a lot on the flight today, and she'd known it was right. "But don't fear I mean to tie you down," she continued. "The marriage will be temporary."

One dark eyebrow arched. "Temporary?"

She could hear the ice in his voice, the disdain, but she hurried on anyway. "It makes the most sense. We marry to give our child a name." She licked her lips. "To prevent any scandal…and—and then we divorce after the baby is born. The perfect solution."

"Of course," he said coolly.

She twisted her fingers together in front of her, realized it made her seem uncertain. She made a deliberate effort to stop. To remove her trench coat calmly and lay it across the back of a leather chair. To sink onto the overstuffed couch and lean back against the cushions. To tilt her head up to watch him with what she hoped was a competent and serene expression on her face.

"I'm glad you see it my way," she said.

He set the tumbler down on the bar, stalked across the room like a caged lion suddenly unleashed. "Did I say that?" His voice was so sharp it could cut glass. Cold. Full of thinly veiled rage.

Anna shivered involuntarily. She was tired, and her heart slammed against her ribs. She hadn't eaten a thing all day. She wanted to curl up and go to sleep for hours, and she wanted to wake up and have Leo by her side. Smiling down at her as he brushed the hair from her face and kissed her. Just like on the island.

"You have an alternative plan?" she asked. She sounded so businesslike when in fact she wasn't businesslike at all. Her insides were clenching tight and a tiny muscle in her throat began to throb.

"You've not really thought this through, have you, Anna?"

"I did," she said. "I considered alternatives. This is the best choice."

"For whom?"

She blinked, momentarily disconcerted by the question. "F-for us. For our child. Would you have him or her born under a cloud of scandal?"

A muscle in his cheek flexed. "I think, darling, you are the only one who cares about that. There are worse ways to begin life."

Anna pressed a hand to her belly self-consciously. A current of anger whipped up like a mini dust storm inside her. "You know why it's important to me!"

Hot tears pressed against her eyes. The insanity had calmed a bit since Alex had jilted her over a month ago now, but she knew she was still an object of interest. If she gave the press something scandalous to report, she'd be back in the headlines in what she'd once heard referred to as a New York minute. Which she took to mean blindingly fast.

Leo was still remote and cool. "I know why it's important to you. I simply don't understand why you care. And I don't think you've thought this completely through, Anna."

She sniffed. "Then tell me what I've forgotten."

He came over and put a hand on the couch on either side of her head, trapping her in the circle of his arms. She would have ducked away, but she wouldn't let him know how much he still affected her. Not after Donna. Let him think she was unmoved by him.

Anna tilted her head back while he bent until his face was only inches from hers. She could see the bulge of muscle in his upper arms, the stretch of expensive fabric across his chest. The blue shirt gaped open, revealing tanned skin that had once pressed so sensually against her own.

"You're here, with me, in one of my hotel rooms. You jumped on a plane, without warning, and flew to London to be with me. You had no prior plans to come, you simply leaped without thinking."

"It wasn't like that," she gasped—and yet she knew very well that it was. From the moment she'd seen the two pink lines on the test, she hadn't been thinking clearly. Coherently. She'd simply known she had to see Leo, had to tell him what they'd created together.

"And yet that's what it looks like. If we marry—and I assume you want it to happen quickly—what do you think your precious media will say then? They will put two and two together, don't you think?"

Anna dropped her gaze from his. "It's possible." And then, because she couldn't help herself, she reached up and cupped his face in both hands, her fingers shaking as she spread them over the blades of his cheekbones. She thought he shuddered at her touch, but she couldn't be sure. She didn't have time to be sure. "But, Leo, it won't matter once we marry. It will be nothing more than speculation, and our baby will be safe."

His gaze dropped to her mouth, his lashes dipping over the hot gleam in those dark eyes. A shot of pure lust hurtled to her core. In spite of being tired, in spite of being pregnant, in spite of the pain and anger of seeing him again, her body wanted his. Ached for his.

It was outrageous—and inevitable, she realized. Hadn't she secretly gloried in the idea she would soon be at his side on the long trip to London?

A healthy dose of self-disgust filled her. Was she truly that weak and susceptible? She let her hands fall away from his face. He pushed upright again, the moment broken in ways she didn't understand. What had there been to break?

And yet, looking at the hard angry glint in his gaze, she knew there had been something after all. Regret sliced deep, but she pushed it away. She had no time to puzzle it out. She needed to convince him to marry her and let the rest sort itself out later.

"I should send you home," he said. "Back to your miserable existence."

"But you won't." She was confident he wouldn't. She didn't know why, but she just knew he would *not* send her away. She could feel it in the way he looked at her, in the recognition that flowed between them. They were in this together, like it or not.

He shook his head slowly. "No, I won't. I'll do something far worse."

Her heart skipped a beat. What could be worse than going home to face the media frenzy alone? But she didn't speak. She simply waited.

"I'll marry you, Anna," Leo said softly. "But not on your terms, darling."

Fear spiked, twisting her stomach. "I—I didn't think I offered terms. I simply said it would be temporary."

His smile managed to both chill her and thrill her at the same time. "Temporary implies this would be a false marriage. A pretend marriage. And I won't pretend, Anna. I'm not going to. So if you want this marriage, then know you'll be sharing my bed and my life for as long as it lasts."

Horror seeped into her bones. "But that—" She stopped, swallowed. This was not at all what she'd imagined. She'd imagined a nice, tidy little arrangement that gave her baby a name and had them acting together toward one purpose. Naively, she'd even thought that after a couple of weeks together, they could live apart the majority of the time. Certainly Leo's schedule as a busy entrepreneur would make that possible.

But this…oh, heavens. "That's blackmail," she said, her throat constricting around the words. "You know I have no choice but to accept whatever conditions you attach."

His gaze glittered. "You always have a choice."

Not if she wanted to protect her baby. "Why are you doing this? Why can't we just be civil about it? I've not asked for much from you. Just that you do the right thing and help me protect our child from the scandal that will surely break if I remain unwed." Her voice had risen until she was practically shouting.

Leo was unmoved. He stared at her coldly. "Are you quite finished?"

"For the moment," she said defiantly. Damn him for making her so emotional! Damn him for standing there and looking so unruffled, so cold, while she was a mess of feelings and insecurities. Nothing touched him.

"Have you ever considered," he said, "that perhaps you

are more worried about yourself than you are about the child? Do you honestly believe that it will matter in five years—or ten or twenty—whether or not you were married when you gave birth? Do you think a child cares more for your marital status than whether or not he has a happy and safe home to grow up in?"

Anna swallowed as a tiny sliver of doubt pricked her. There was something in his voice that cut deep. *Was* she more concerned about herself? Was she too afraid to face the fire alone?

"Leo, I—"

He held up a hand, silencing her. "We will marry, Anna. But on my terms. If you can't live with those terms, you *do* have a choice. If you don't make that choice, then don't blame me for your own cowardice."

By the time Leo made it back to his temporary lodgings—Bobby's Knightsbridge apartment—the shock of what had happened tonight was pressing hard against the confines of his head, making his temples throb. He'd gone from bachelor to expectant father in the space of a breath, and now he was getting married.

Married. The second thing he felt completely unqualified to do, fatherhood being the first. And he'd not started this marriage-to-be off on quite the right footing, had he? But he'd been so bloody angry with her, with her plans and schemes. She was having his child and she still thought of him as an accessory. A temporary inconvenience. A sperm donor she only needed for a short while to stave off scandal.

It infuriated him. And yes, it hurt deep down on a level that surprised him. He knew he wasn't fit to be a father, thanks to his genetic material, but she only assumed it to be true. And only on the barest of evidence.

Leo stepped into the private elevator that awaited him. He wasn't accustomed to not being in control of the situation. *He* was the one who made decisions, who made things happen. He wasn't an accessory, and he damn sure wasn't going to be an ornamental husband simply to please her.

Because the one thing he'd realized tonight when she'd landed so forcefully back into his life was that he still wanted her. One brief touch of her skin against his on the street, the scent of her sweet perfume filling his nostrils, and he'd been harder than stone. She'd managed in two seconds what no woman since he'd left the island had managed at all. If he was going to be married to her, then dammit, he was going to enjoy it.

Leo froze as the elevator doors opened onto the foyer of the apartment.

The television blared from the living area, which meant that Bobby had stopped by again. Bobby often let himself in when Leo wasn't home. Since he'd returned to London, his father had come around a lot, almost as if he'd missed Leo over the years. Their relationship had never been much of a father-son relationship, but one of the things Leo had been determined to do when he returned to London was put his anger at his father behind him.

It wasn't always easy, but it was getting easier with time.

Leo had intended to stay in one of his hotels until he found the right place to buy, but Bobby had insisted he stay in the apartment since Bobby rarely used it anymore. Leo had wanted to refuse, but one look at the hopeful expression on his father's face and he'd been unable to do it.

"He's missed you, Leo," Allegra had said.

"Did he say that?" Leo had practically snapped.

His sister had shook her head. She was the good girl in the family, the sweet one who tried to keep peace between them all. "Not in so many words. But he did. He's talked of nothing else since you said you were coming back again."

Leo sighed. Bobby wasn't a bad man; he was simply an impulsive and irresponsible one.

The last person Leo felt like dealing with tonight was Bobby, but he threw his jacket across a chair and headed into the lounge anyway. Bobby was watching a football game and drinking a beer, shouting when his favorite player made a particularly tricky shot. The ball missed the net and Bobby swore.

"Hey, Leo," he said, looking up when the shadow of Leo's form fell across the room.

Leo shoved both hands into his pockets. "Dad."

"Something wrong, boy?" Bobby asked, muting the television as he gazed up at Leo. Somehow, Leo wasn't surprised his turmoil was showing. He *was* surprised that Bobby asked about it, however.

Yes, he wanted to say. *Help me figure this out. Tell me something useful.*

"Nothing I can't handle," he replied instead. He'd learned long ago not to count on Bobby for advice. Bobby meant well, but he had no clue. Like when he'd stood up at Allegra's engagement party and congratulated her on landing a wealthy prince. That had certainly *not* been his finest moment.

Bobby shrugged. "You always were a smart kid. Got that from your mother. I'm right proud of you, you know."

Leo felt a twinge of hurt at the mention of his mother. Bobby had long ago apologized for the way he'd left Leo's mother to raise him alone, but it still hurt sometimes when Bobby mentioned her. "Yeah. Thanks."

His father looked up again, his forehead creasing. "You want me to go?"

He did—and he didn't. "Not if you don't want to."

Bobby leaned back on the couch and took another sip of beer. "Chantelle's having some damn girls' night thing at home and I didn't want to be around for it. Women can be diabolical when they congregate in packs, let me tell you."

Leo went into the kitchen and grabbed a beer of his own before returning and sitting across from Bobby. The game continued unabated, Bobby cursing and cheering depending on who was down at the time.

Leo drank his beer, feeling sour. Why hadn't he just told Bobby to go? Having his father here was like having a college frat brother staying over. You had something in common, you knew you did, but you couldn't for the life of you see what it was.

"Why did you get married?" Leo asked during a lull in the game.

Bobby hit the mute button and swiveled to look at him like he'd grown another head. "Which time?"

"Any of them," Leo said shortly.

Bobby blew out a breath. "Seemed like the thing to do, I guess."

"Were you ever in love?"

Bobby's face split into a grin. "Every single time, my boy."

Leo felt a pang in his gut. "How is that possible?"

His father shrugged. "It just is. What's this about?"

Leo leaned his head back on the seat, closed his eyes. What did it matter? It would be in the papers before too much longer anyway. "I'm getting married," he said shortly.

"You don't sound happy about it."

"I don't know how to feel."

"Is she pregnant?"

"Yeah."

Bobby made a sucking sound with his teeth. "It's the

right thing to do, then. You'll figure it out." Then he stood and put a hand on Leo's shoulder. "It'll work itself out, son."

"I'm sure it will," Leo said, oddly regretful that his father had nothing else to say. Bobby squeezed, almost as if he wanted to say something else, but then his hand fell away and Leo heard his footsteps retreating across the floor.

A few moments later the elevator doors whisked closed, and Leo knew that Bobby was gone. He took out his mobile phone and stared at the face for a long while before he brought up his contacts. He had to let Allegra know before she read about it in the papers. But he couldn't stand to talk to another person tonight, so instead he typed out a message.

Getting married. To Anna Constantinides. Just wanted you to know. Papers will have a field day.

He lay the phone down for barely a moment when it buzzed again.

Wow! I take it more happened on that island than you let on. Congratulations. I think. J Oh, Leo. Please tell me you're happy.

Leo hesitated only a moment before he typed the answer he knew Allegra needed to hear, whether it was true or not.

Don't worry, A. I'm happy.

CHAPTER TEN

ANNA slept pretty well, considering all the stress of the day before. She awoke late, ordered breakfast in her room and dressed hurriedly in navy trousers and a cream blouse with tiny buttons that went almost to her throat. She left the last few unbuttoned so she could wear her pearls, and brushed her hair into a long, thick ponytail fastened loosely at the base of her neck. It was a departure from the usual updo, but it felt like the thing to do today.

She put the brush down and sighed at her reflection. She should be happy. Leo had said he would marry her. Their baby would be safe from scandal. And yet what he'd said to her last night still ate at her. Did she want to be married for the baby's sake or for her own?

She'd thought she was doing this for the baby, but a tiny part of her nagged that she wasn't. That Leo was right and it was herself she feared for. Was she truly that much of a coward?

She thought of the headlines the day after the photo of Alex kissing Allegra Jackson had first appeared in the paper. She'd been stunned by the report that he'd bought an engagement ring for this woman when it was she who had been wearing the official ring.

And then the reporters had started calling her every hour of the day and night, wanting a quote, wanting to catch her in an unguarded moment. Wanting to humiliate her even more than she already had been. She'd gone into seclusion on Amanti and prayed for the storm to pass. It hadn't, though the attention had lessened somewhat as the press focused more and more on Alex and Allegra's whirlwind romance.

Even her crash with Leo had only garnered a bit of attention, more for the spectacular circumstances of the crash and rescue than because she'd been alone with a notorious playboy. She'd been surprised by that, but she'd taken it for the rare gift it was.

But when she married Leo, when her secret was out, it would all change. She only hoped the storm would pass quickly, and she'd be free to live her life out from under the microscope of the media.

At precisely a quarter to eleven, Leo arrived as promised. Her heart turned over again at the sight of him. He wore a charcoal suit with a maroon shirt unbuttoned at the neck. It was stylish and daring and fit Leo to perfection. She envied him the ability to get away with color and still look so powerful and masculine. He made her seem dull in comparison, but perhaps it was the truth. She was dull.

And she wanted to keep it that way. She'd had enough color in the form of media attention to last her a lifetime. Shame flickered to life inside her.

Have you ever considered that perhaps you are more worried for yourself than you are for the child?

"I've made an appointment with one of the city's top obstetricians," Leo said to her. "We'll need to be going if we're to make it on time."

"Is that necessary?" she asked, gripping the door frame. "I feel perfectly fine. And I'd prefer to find someone on Amanti after we're married."

Leo frowned. "I'm not sure how you envision this wedding happening, Anna, but it won't happen today. And it won't happen on Amanti. We are marrying here. And we're staying here."

"I can't stay in London," she said automatically, her pulse throbbing. "I'm the Tourist Ambassador to Amanti. I have things to do. A home, family—"

"So go back to Amanti," Leo said tightly.

She squeezed her fingers on the door frame until her knuckles were white. "I can't do that."

"Then we have an appointment to keep, don't we?" He turned without waiting for an answer and strode down the hall toward the elevator. Fuming, she grabbed her purse and a light jacket and followed him. They took the elevator down to the ground floor and emerged in the bright sunshine of a clear London day. A minute later they were in his limousine, crawling through traffic like everyone else.

"I didn't come here to stay," she said coolly, though her pulse beat erratically beneath her skin.

Leo swung his head around to look at her. "You expect me to leave my business and move to Amanti because you wish it?"

"No. But surely we can work something out."

"What is it you suggest?" he asked.

Anna shrugged. "I could go back to Amanti after we're married. You could visit from time to time—"

"Out of the question," he said. "Did you not hear a thing I said to you last night?"

Her ears felt hot. "I heard you."

"Then you'll know that we're staying here. For the time being."

"Why?" she burst out. "You don't really want this marriage, or me, so why make it any harder than it needs to be?"

His gaze was so very cool. Unemotional. And yet she

thought she saw a glimmer of heat behind those dark coffee eyes. "How do you know what I want, sweet Anna?"

She dropped her head, stared at the purse she clutched in her lap. "I don't want you to pretend, Leo. I know this isn't easy for you, and I appreciate that you're willing to help me—"

He made a noise that brought her head up. His expression, she noted, was patently furious. "You act as if this were an immaculate conception. I believe it takes two to make a baby."

"I know that," she said quietly.

"Then stop attributing motives to me that are designed to make you feel superior."

His words stung. "That's not it at all," she snapped. "But I have eyes, Leo, and I can sense when someone is unhappy. You'd rather be waking up this morning with the lovely Donna, not taking me to the doctor, so don't *you* pretend you're offended by anything I have to say. You'd rather this baby didn't exist, and you'd rather I was back on Amanti and nothing more than a memory."

He leaned toward her, his jaw set in a hard line. "If you're always this charming, it's no wonder Prince Alessandro found my sister more appealing."

Her skin prickled with heat as a sharp pain daggered into her. "Are you always this cruel?"

"That depends," he said. "Are you always this self-righteous?"

She stared at him for a long moment, locked in battle—but she suddenly felt so defeated, as if life had conspired to knock her down at precisely the moment when she was already at her lowest. Anna put her face in her hands, breathed deeply.

"I'm trying to do the right thing," she said, her voice coming out muffled and weak. Which made her angry.

She wasn't weak, dammit! She was strong, as strong as she needed to be to protect her child.

She dropped her hands, thrust her chin up. She would not cower before him.

"There's the dragon lady," he murmured. "If only you would bring her out to play when the press dares to mock you."

"It's an impossible battle to win," she said with a haughty sniff. "And I'd rather save my energy for other things."

The flame she'd seen in his gaze earlier flared to life again. "Yes, perhaps that's a good idea after all."

Anna felt herself coloring. *Cool. She must be cool.*

She might not be a queen-in-training any longer, but she hadn't spent years learning to be serene and unflappable for nothing. She held her head high, determined to be professional and businesslike. "How soon can we be married?"

Leo chuckled. "Eager, are we?"

Even the roots of her hair felt hot. Anna folded her trembling hands over her purse. "I'm eager to move on with the plan," she said. "Before I start to show."

"It will take at least two weeks, possibly three."

She felt her jaw drop. "Three weeks?"

"I'll do what I can, but two weeks is the minimum time needed. You won't be showing by then."

"We could go to Amanti," she said practically. "The wait time is seven days."

Leo shook his head. "That's hardly worth the trip, Anna. Besides, I can't leave my business at the moment."

"You left your business to go to Santina for the engagement party," she said.

"Yes, and I lost several days, most especially when we crashed on the island. Being out of touch with my board of directors for two days during negotiations for a property in Brazil was a bit, shall we say, chaotic."

She didn't like the delay, but what else could she do? She already knew that once the baby was born, everyone would count backward. What did two—or three—weeks at this point matter?

She turned her head away from him. The limo had ground to a halt near Marble Arch, and happy tourists took photos and gawked at the white structure. They looked so carefree it made her ache. When had she ever been that carefree?

On the island, a voice whispered.

Except it wasn't *quite* true, was it? She'd definitely had cares—would they be rescued, what would the press say and so on—but she'd felt more like a different person there than she ever had before. A person without so many worries. A person who could swim naked with a gorgeous man and make uninhibited love on a secluded beach.

Anna clenched her fingers around her purse strap. She could still see him naked, his golden body so hard and perfect in the Mediterranean sun. Leo was flawlessly made, tall and lean and muscular in all the right places. He'd smiled on the island. Made her laugh. Made her moan and beg and shudder.

It had meant so much to her, she realized. Too much. While he'd returned to London and continued as he'd always done, she'd thought of him endlessly.

Despair flickered around the edges of her soul, but she refused to let it in. So she'd lost one man she'd been promised to and another she'd given herself to. So what? Others had it worse, didn't they?

And she had a baby on the way. There were new, more important worries to contend with.

In spite of the traffic, they arrived at the obstetrician's office located in a quiet Georgian town house on a side street a few minutes before the scheduled appointment.

Leo exited the car first before reaching in for her, glancing up and down the street as he did so.

Anna's heart lodged in her throat as she sat on the edge of the seat with one leg poised over the pavement. "Do you see anyone?"

"No," he said curtly. "But it doesn't hurt to be on guard."

No, it certainly didn't. She didn't know how long it would take the press to discover her whereabouts, but she didn't imagine it would be long considering the way Leo's family always seemed to appear in the tabloids.

She joined him on the street, clutching his arm as she put her heel in a grate and nearly lost her balance. Leo held her hard against him, steadying her with an arm around her body as they came together breast to belly to hip.

It was the first time she'd been so close to him since the island, and she swallowed, her hands pressing against his chest for balance. They stood that way for a long moment, Leo gazing down at her as she stared back at him, her entire body humming with his nearness. His eyes dropped to her mouth.

Anna held her breath, surprised at how desperately she suddenly wanted him to kiss her. His fingers skated along her jaw, and her eyes drifted closed. His mouth claimed hers oh-so-lightly that she almost wondered if he'd meant it to happen.

Her heart beat like a trapped bird, her body straining toward his. She wanted the kiss to be hotter, harder, more intense—and yet it was perfect just like this. So achingly sweet and tender.

He lifted his head, and then set her away from him as he took her hand and led her into the doctor's office.

Eight weeks pregnant. It didn't seem possible, and yet the technician explained that the math had to do with the day

of her last menstrual cycle and not the date of conception. Anna stared at the tiny bean on the screen as tears
filled her eyes. She was really, truly expecting a baby.
Leo's baby. She turned her head to look at him. He sat
beside her, his gaze riveted to the screen. She reached for
him without thought and his fingers closed around hers,
squeezing softly.

For the briefest of moments, she thought it might be
all right. That everything would turn out okay. Together,
they would protect this child. Love this child. But then
the technician turned on the Doppler and the sound of the
baby's heart filled the room. It beat so fast that Anna
thought there must be something wrong.

"The heartbeat is perfectly normal, Mrs. Jackson," the
technician said in response to her cry.

"I'm not—" She stopped, swallowed. She felt so guilty,
as if the technician would know that she wasn't actually
Leo's wife yet.

Leo had filled out the paperwork and she hadn't bothered to check it. She'd answered the questions while he
ticked off boxes. It reminded her, forcefully, that this was
simply an arrangement. They would not be raising their
child together, or at least not in the traditional sense. Leo
didn't love her. A wave of depression washed over her at
the knowledge.

"That is, thank you," she said smoothly. "I'm relieved
to know it."

The remainder of the appointment was routine. The
doctor asked questions, prescribed antinausea medication,
told her when she would need to consider taking a birth-
ing class and informed her when the next visit should be
and what would happen then.

And then she was back in the car with Leo and they
were pulling away from the curb, leaving Dr. Clemens's

office behind. Anna chewed the inside of her lip. There was a pain in her chest, right beneath her breastbone, that wouldn't go away. Not a physical pain, but an emotional one.

What kind of mess had she gotten herself into? What had made her think she could barrel into Leo's life and ask him to marry her for the sake of the baby? What had made her think she could do it and remain untouched? Sitting in that room with him just now, his hand wrapped around hers while they listened to their baby's heart, had been one of the most significant moments of her life. How could she feel this way and not acknowledge that at least some of it was due to him?

"How are you feeling?" Leo asked.

How was she feeling? Lost, confused, alone. Uncertain. But she blinked away the moisture in her eyes and turned to him. "I'm fine."

He smiled for once, a rakish grin that had her heart turning over. Did he have to be charming when she was trying to keep her emotional distance? Why couldn't he keep snarling and frowning?

"It was a bit overwhelming," he admitted, and the breath squeezed in her lungs.

"Definitely." She smiled back, though the corners of it trembled. She hoped he didn't notice. "I have a feeling it's going to stay that way for quite some time yet."

He sighed, his expression troubled. "I think you're right."

She bit her lip, glanced away. It hurt to see him look like that. As if everything in his life had made perfect sense until she arrived in it. "I'm sorry, Leo."

He looked surprised. "For what?"

She took a deep breath, her heart burning. "For every-thing. If I'd been stronger on the island—"

"Stop," he said, his voice suddenly rough and edgy. "I was there, Anna. I know what happened as well as you do. And I was every bit as much involved in the decision process that got us to this point. Stop trying to insinuate it's solely your failure that created this situation."

"I didn't mean…" But she did, didn't she? She meant that he was simply a man, a rogue, acting on adrenaline and hormones and that she was the one who should have been smart enough and moral enough to put a stop to the sexual heat between them before it got out of hand. By inference, she was accusing him of thinking with his penis.

Of not thinking at all.

He was insulted, and rightfully so. Anna toyed with her pearls out of habit. Would she ever know the right things to say to this man? A lifetime of etiquette training, and she still couldn't manage to be diplomatic when it counted most. She was not the cool, serene woman she'd always thought she was. What a joke to think she could have been a queen when she could barely govern her emotions when it counted most.

"You're right," she told him. "I'm sorry for suggesting I was the only one who should have been in control."

"I know you think you're supposed to be in perfect control of yourself every minute of every day, but that's not the way it works, Anna. You're human. You're allowed to make mistakes."

She dropped her gaze. "I know that." And even if she didn't, she was learning that mistakes were not completely avoidable.

"I'm not quite sure you do. You live by your calendar and all that bloody training you did to be Alessandro's wife. You think that rigidly controlling every moment of every day will keep you from faltering."

"No one wants to be made a fool of," she said in defense.

And yet it felt like such a weak defense now. She'd been made a fool of more in the past month than she ever had in her life, and she was still here. Still kicking.

"Of course not. But it's only when you care so much that anyone has the power to do that kind of harm."

"That's easy for you to say," she snapped, feeling pinned in from all sides. How could you *not* care when people said the most awful things about you? Printing lies to sell papers without a care for the truth? *She* knew what they said wasn't true, but not everyone did. And it hurt to see censure or pity in the eyes of those around her.

He had no idea what she'd been through, what she would go through if anyone found out she was pregnant before she was ready for them to do so. Santina and Amanti were far more conservative than the world Leo inhabited.

"When have you ever been the subject of negative attention? When has anyone ever said anything less than glowing about you?" she demanded.

He looked at her so steadily that she felt the need to drop her gaze from his. She wouldn't, however. She would hold steady and be brave, no matter what he was about to say. And she was suddenly certain, whatever it was, that she wasn't going to like it.

Once more, she'd blundered. She knew it in her bones.

"Before I was born, sweet Anna." His smile was smooth, polished. "My father had an affair with my mother while he was still married. He was at the height of his football career then, and quite the cad. When news of her pregnancy hit the papers, his first wife divorced him. He denied he was my father, of course. It was all the rage for weeks. You can look it up online if you're curious."

He sounded distant, detached, but she knew it had to bother him still. The way he spoke so carefully, his voice devoid of emotion. His expression sadly mocking. As if to say, *See, it's not so bad. I survived.*

"But you're a Jackson now," she pressed, because she didn't know what else to say. Her palms were damp, her skin prickling with heat. *Keep digging yourself a hole, Anna.*

"Yes. Another tabloid adventure when I was ten. My mother died in a drunk-driving accident, and I inherited not only her money, but also the DNA test she'd had done to prove paternity. After a stint in court, Bobby finally decided to do the right thing."

Her heart throbbed for the boy he'd been. He'd lost a parent who loved him and had then been forced onto another one who had tried to deny him. How terrible would that have been for him? "That must have been difficult," she managed.

He shrugged as if it were nothing. "It was a long time ago. I've moved beyond it now."

"But that doesn't change the hurt." How could it? How could you ever forget that someone hadn't wanted you? She'd grown up in a household where she was cherished, the beautiful, talented, bright daughter. And yet she hurt because she'd failed her parents, failed the King and Queen of Santina. Because Alex hadn't wanted her.

"You really are a sensitive creature, aren't you?" Leo asked. "You've lived your life in a bubble and you've been terrified to step outside it. But now you have, Anna, and you have a choice. Be brave, face it head-on, or crumple and let them defeat you. They *will* find out about the pregnancy. You can't keep a secret like this in our circles. Are you prepared for it?"

She sucked air into her lungs. Was she? Because she knew he was right. She'd come here knowing all the while it was a secret that wouldn't remain hidden for long.

"That's why I'm here, Leo. I'm trying to prepare for it in the only way I know how."

"Then I hope, when the news breaks, you aren't hurt by it."

"If I am, I'll get over it. I've had a lot of practice recently." She said it to be brave, but inside she quaked.

He took her chin in his fingers, held her steady, their gazes locking. "You are a dragon lady, Anna. The fiercest, strongest, bravest woman I know. You survived a plane crash, two days on a deserted island and more bad press than any one person should have to endure. And you've done it all with grace and dignity. You will survive this, too."

His words pierced her to her soul. No one had ever, *ever* called her fierce or strong or brave. Competent, organized, pretty—yes. But fierce?

"It's my intention," she said softly.

"Excellent."

He tilted her chin up, and then leaned in and kissed her. The touch of his mouth was a pleasurable shock. His lips were hot against hers, his mouth infinitely more demanding than it had been on the street in front of Dr. Clemens's office. Anna melted into the kiss, though she told herself she should be more reserved with him. More careful. The only person who could get hurt in this situation was her.

Leo was nothing if not famous for his exploits with women. What meant the world to her was simply passing time to him.

But, like it or not, she felt something for him. She'd known it for the past month, though she'd denied it to herself over and over. Leo made her feel things that Alex never had. She felt beautiful, alive. Wanted, needed. Perhaps they were false sensations, but they were wonderful while they lasted. While she believed them.

His tongue slid across the seam of her lips and she opened to him, unable to stop the little moan that escaped her when their tongues met. He was the only man she'd ever kissed. And she didn't feel deprived by that fact. No other man could kiss her like this, she was certain. No other man could make her feel hot and achy and itchy and wonderful all at once.

Leo pulled her closer, the warmth of his body sinking into her flesh. He tilted her head back to give him better access, one hand cupping her jaw while the other slid to her waist. The touch of his fingers burned into her, through the fabric of her shirt and jacket.

He was her Kryptonite, weakening her until she couldn't resist.

"I've missed this," he said. "Missed you."

"Leo, I—"

He kissed her again, and she lost whatever she wanted to say. But her mind raced ahead, took her back to last night, when she'd first seen him walking out of the Leonidas Group headquarters building. He hadn't seemed to miss her at all then. He'd been so utterly self-assured when he'd strolled out of that building with a woman on his arm.

She pushed against his chest, lightly but firmly, and he leaned back, gazing at her through heavy-lidded eyes. Sensuality was as natural to him as breathing, she thought. She wanted to pull him back to her, forget her confused thoughts and lose herself in the promise those dark eyes made to her.

But she couldn't. "Last night, you were with Donna. If I hadn't come along…"

He blew out a frustrated breath. And then he looked down his fine nose at her. "You do realize that I am quite capable of going without sex for more than a day or so, right? Perhaps even weeks at a time. Being seen with a woman does not equate to having gone to bed with that woman."

She felt a stab of guilt. Once more, she was accusing him of thinking with his penis. A tiny, jealous—yes, jealous—corner of her insisted it must be true. He was Leo Jackson, lover of women, serial breaker of hearts.

"But you were planning on it."

"Probably," he said unapologetically. "But not for another week or two at least. Perhaps longer."

Anna sniffed, both chastened and irritated at once. "Then I'm sorry I ruined your plans."

Leo smiled, a sharp predatory smile that made a tingle start in her toes and work its way deep into her core.

"I'm not," he said. "I've a new plan I like much, much better."

CHAPTER ELEVEN

THE next few days were a whirlwind of appointments and appearances. Photographers had started to show up whenever Leo and Anna appeared in public together. He'd told her to expect it, but she still cringed every time. Inwardly, of course. Outwardly, she smiled and posed and tried to look ecstatically happy.

The headlines screamed at her each morning: *Jilted Bride of Santina's Crown Prince in Torrid Love Affair with Notorious Playboy; "I Had No Idea Anna Was in Love with Leo Jackson," Shocked Friend Says; Love Blooms Between Marooned Couple—But Were They Really Marooned, Or Was it Planned?; Crown Prince Alessandro Calls Anna— Come Back to Me, He Begs.* And the worst one of all: *How Long Will Lucky Leo Last This Time?*

Anna crumpled the morning tabloids and made a noise of disgust. He looked at her over the cup of coffee he'd poured from the silver service sitting nearby.

"It's ridiculous how they make these things up!"

"Surely you aren't surprised."

She ran a hand over the back of her neck, rubbed absently. "No, of course not. But it infuriates me anyway. You'd think they have nothing better to do."

"You did insist," he said. Yes, she had insisted on seeing the papers. When she'd sent the order to the front desk originally, Leo had come barreling in soon after, grumbling at her that it wasn't a good idea. She would get upset and that couldn't be good for the baby.

When she'd pointed out that she'd be more upset *not* knowing, he'd relented, albeit reluctantly.

Now, Leo got to his feet and came over to where she stood near the window, looking out over Hyde Park. The sun was shining today, and people strolled along the sidewalks and sat on park benches. Pigeons congregated around a man throwing something onto the ground. A red double-decker bus glided by on the street below, the top open and filled with tourists craning their necks and aiming their cameras.

Leo's hands settled on the back of her neck, and then he began to rub. Anna bit her lip to stop the moan that wanted to escape. It felt so good to have his hands on her. She wasn't quite sure if it was soothing in the way he intended it to be or titillating.

"You're tense," he murmured against her ear, and an electrical zap of energy shot down her spine, gathering in her core. Leo hadn't touched her since that kiss in the car, other than perfunctory touches for the cameras. She'd thought then that he'd wanted to make love to her again, that he intended to seduce her into his bed. It had excited her and frightened her at the same time.

But he'd done nothing since, and she'd been humming with frustration. It was better this way, she told herself. Better because this marriage would be temporary. Leo must have decided it, too, because he'd not pursued the issue when surely he must have known how easy it would be to send her over the edge. She was a mass of sensation waiting to happen. A collection of tinder anticipating the match.

"I keep expecting something worse," she said, her skin

tingling wherever he touched. His fingers were sure as he kneaded her shoulders and neck.

"Something worse than Lucky Leo?" She could hear the smile in his voice, but she wasn't nearly as amused as he was.

Finally, something to focus on that would distract her from the sensation of his hands on her skin. "That is a rather disgusting name, considering how you earned it."

"By bedding six lingerie models simultaneously."

"It's not funny, Leo," she said, turning to look up at him.

His smile didn't fade. "Perhaps not. But what you desperately want to know, sweet Anna, is if it's true."

She dropped her gaze from his, a jealous fire flaring to life in her belly. *Jealous?* "You couldn't be more wrong," she said haughtily. "It's a vile exaggeration anyway."

His laugh was soft, deep, pulling at something elemental inside her. "Slightly. There were only four of them."

Anna stepped away from him, certain her cheeks were flaming scarlet by now. Leo with four women. Leo, naked and surrounded by *four* women. She didn't want to imagine it. A hot, sharp dagger of anger pierced through her heart. She wanted to choke someone. Four someones. "I said I didn't want to know."

"I'm only telling you the truth, Anna. Why keep secrets when we're about to be married?"

She wrapped her arms around herself. *Because this isn't real! Because it's a game to you!* The words swelled against the back of her throat, aching to escape, making it hard to breathe for the barest of moments. But she swallowed them back, refusing to let them out. "I don't see any need to confess deep dark secrets. This is an *arrangement,* not a true marriage."

He was still smiling, but she could see the hard glint in his eyes. As if she'd angered him. Or insulted him.

"Yes, of course. How could I have forgotten? You only need me to help you get through this difficulty, and then it's back to Amanti where you can play the proper lady. Though perhaps a slightly tarnished one, since you will have been married to me."

A throb of guilt beat a new tempo in her veins. "That's not fair," she said. "You twist my meaning."

The hard look was still there. "Do I? From the first, you've impressed upon me the importance of your reputation. Your status as the *ex*-bride-to-be of a future king." He tsked. "This must be so embarrassing for you, Anna. You've lain down with a mongrel and come home with fleas."

She flung away from him. He twisted everything she said, made her seem so awful and shallow when she was only trying to be fair to them both. To who they were as people. They didn't know each other well, it was true, but she knew what he was. What he'd always been. He'd never denied it, and now he was angry with her over it?

"You act so wounded! But tell me the truth, Leo—did you really want to be a husband and father? Is that what you see yourself doing? Because if so, why didn't you marry Jessica Monroe?"

He didn't react, and yet she knew the name had affected him. The air had changed between them when she'd uttered the name of the woman he'd been linked with in L.A. Grown heavier, thicker, tenser. She waited for him to speak, both fearing and needing to hear his answer.

When he did, his voice was cool. Detached. Clinical. "Jessica and I came to a mutual decision."

But Anna wasn't letting it go that easily. "And then she married some other man six months later and adopted a baby."

"We had different goals."

"Is that what it's called?" Bitterness churned in her belly. How could he not admit the truth when it was right there for everyone to see? He'd lived his life in front of the tabloids, sleeping with and casting off women with the kind of frequency with which most men changed their shirts. *Leo Jackson* and *family man* were not words ever used together in the same breath.

He'd practically said as much to her on the island.

"My relationship with Jessica Monroe has nothing to do with my relationship with you," he said tightly. She had the distinct impression that he was leashing some deep anger—or hurt?—within him. It gave her pause, but only for a moment. "*We* are getting married, and we have a child on the way."

"I've not forgotten it, I assure you," she said crisply, the blood beating in her temples, her throat. Something was going on between them that she didn't quite understand, and it infuriated her. Bothered her. How could she engage in conversation with him and still not quite know what either of them meant by the words they said? It was like going through a carnival fun house and not knowing what to expect around the next corner. "But I still don't believe it's your first choice of occupation."

He was going out of his mind with desire for her. Leo was still furious at their conversation of that morning, but he'd shaken it off as best he could and had taken her out to look at potential homes. He'd been putting the task on the back burner since he'd been so busy lately, but once Anna had arrived with her proposal of marriage, there was no getting past the fact it was high time to find a place and buy it.

Now, they were touring a two-level exclusive flat in a period building in Knightsbridge. Anna had grilled the estate agent on the amenities and led the way through the five-hundred-square-meter property. The agent had finally retired to the walkway out front to smoke a cigarette and make phone calls while he waited for them to finish.

Anna stood in the center of one of the upper bedrooms, staring at nothing that Leo could see. He took a moment to admire her form. She was, as always, buttoned up tight in a cream sweater set and gray skirt with, surprisingly, platform heels that made her legs so long and sexy. The pearls were a fixture around her neck, of course. She was playing with them, as she always did when she was upset or nervous or simply concentrating on something.

Her long dark hair was loose today, and he ached to thrust his fingers into the heavy mass as he took her body for his pleasure. Anna never wore her hair loose. The effect was about to kill him. He'd never been as achingly aroused as he had been for the past hour, watching her bare legs and round bottom as he followed her through the flat.

There was also, he had to admit, a simmering brew of despair and anger mixed in with the arousal. She was convinced he had nothing to offer in the way of being a husband or father. He wasn't sure he did either, but it was damned depressing to think of her leaving him once the baby was born. He'd been thinking about it all morning, and found himself surprisingly affected by it. He wanted to punch something. He wanted to rage and howl and expend a great deal of energy by doing *something* that required him to push himself to physical extremes.

Base-jumping. Mountain climbing. Extreme hiking across the Sahara.

Barring that, he wanted to lock Anna up and never let her out of his sight.

It was true that he didn't know the first thing about babies. They terrified him. So tiny and delicate and dependent on adults to take care of their needs. What if he was terrible at it? What if letting Anna go back to Amanti to raise their baby was the best choice for all of them?

And yet the thought of Anna and his child leaving him to his previous life of empty sex and meaningless relationships made him feel strangely forlorn. What if Anna met someone else and married him? That man would become his child's father, and Leo would have no business in their lives whatsoever.

Something deep and elemental inside him responded with a resounding, *No!*

"I'm not sure, Leo," Anna finally said, cutting into his thoughts as she turned to him in the empty room. Her voice echoed down from the high ceilings.

"Not sure of what?"

"It's gorgeous, but I'm not sure it's you. I see you in a penthouse somewhere, with sleek modern furnishings and a city view."

A flicker of annoyance slid across his soul. "It's not about me, Anna. It's about us. You will have to live here, too."

She dropped her gaze from his, and a current of anger and misery flared to life inside him, scorching him with the force of a thousand burning suns. And yet, could he blame her for thinking what she did? For thinking he was incapable of being what she wanted and needed him to be?

He'd made a second career out of being the kind of man women didn't say no to. He'd never met a woman he couldn't charm straight out of her knickers, and he'd never hidden that fact. Nor had he hidden the fact he wasn't the settling-down type. He'd never thought he would want to. The idea that he might after all gave him pause.

"Jessica wanted to get married. I didn't."

Anna's head snapped up, her jade-green eyes wide. He didn't know why he'd said it since it confirmed everything she thought about him, but he felt compelled to continue. He loved it when she looked at him, he realized. There was a little kick, right beneath his ribs, every time.

"She had a grown daughter, but she wanted a new baby. The roles in Hollywood were drying up for an actress her age. I believed she was latching on to the idea of marriage and a baby as a new challenge in life. She believed I was wrong. The split was mutual."

"Did you love her?" she asked, and he sensed that it cost her something to ask it.

Leo blew out a breath. The answer would do him no credit, but he wouldn't lie. "No."

She blinked. "No? Just like that, no?"

"If I'd loved her, would I have let her go? Or would I have done everything in my power to make her happy?"

"I see," she said.

He didn't think she saw anything. He and Jessica were similar in personality. Neither of them demanded anything from the other. They'd had a good time together. Love had never entered into the equation, for either one of them.

But then the arguments had begun. Small at first, escalating later as Jessica Monroe, once prized for her face and body, had started to weary of the fight for new roles. He'd never quite understood, as she remained to this day one of the sexiest women he'd ever known. But Hollywood was fickle, and that fickleness had driven Jessica to want more from him than he was willing to give.

Ironic that he now stood here with a woman who was not only pregnant with his child, but that he'd also agreed to marry.

He closed the distance between them suddenly. She took a step back, but he caught her and pulled her to him. He didn't know why he had to hold her, but he did. He needed to feel her soft, warm body against his. Needed to know she was real, that their baby was real. He'd never quite known his place in life, never understood where he fit in in the Jackson family. He was the odd man out, the one who'd come in from the outside and tried to belong. Well, maybe Angel knew that feeling, too, but it was different—her father hadn't denied she was his and refused to have anything to do with her. She wasn't a Jackson by blood. He was, though he wasn't sure it had ever meant anything to him.

Anna put her hands on his chest as he caught her close, her head tilting back. She did not try to escape. In fact, he felt a tremor run through her. That faint vibration that let him know she was not unaffected. That she still wanted him as much as he wanted her.

Oh, she'd been good at pretending she did not—but only when he didn't touch her. When he touched her, he knew. And he wasn't prepared to show her any mercy. Not any longer.

"Do you ever think about it?" he asked. "Those two days on the island when there was nothing but sand and sea and *us?* You and me, naked beneath the hot sun?"

Her eyes were green pools of mystery. And warmth, he realized. Warmth for him. She usually hid it, but she wasn't doing a good job at the moment. It gave him hope, though for what he wasn't quite certain.

"I've thought of it," she admitted, her cheeks flushing as she spoke. Such lovely, lovely color, he mused. "How could I not?"

A low throb of arousal pulsed at the base of his spine. He wanted to take her here, now, in the middle of this room with the estate agent outside and the bright London sunshine streaming through the tall paned windows. "Then why are we merely thinking about it," he murmured, "when we could experience it again? In a bed this time, sweet Anna, with all the romance and tenderness you deserve."

"I—I'm not sure that's a good idea," she said, her gaze dropping to study her fingers where they rested on his shirt.

"How can it be a bad idea? You burn for me, Anna. You want me."

"That doesn't mean it's a good idea."

"Doesn't mean it's a bad idea, either," he told her, dipping his head to skim his lips along her jaw. She tilted her head back, her fingers clutching him. His body was stone. Hot, hard stone.

"Leo…"

"We're marrying, Anna," he said, trying not to make it sound like begging. Was he begging? An interesting thought, really. But he would, at this moment, do anything to get her naked and beneath him again. A singular thought. "Shouldn't we see if this could work between us before we assume it will not?"

Before she could answer, he heard a door open and shut, and he knew the estate agent had returned. Anna took advantage of his distraction to disengage from his embrace. But it wasn't a rejection. That much he knew. She tucked a strand of her hair behind her ear and folded her arms over her body. It wasn't a defensive gesture so much as a protective one.

Triumph surged in his bones. She would be his again. Soon.

Tonight.

CHAPTER TWELVE

A TRIO of boxes arrived within a couple of hours after she'd returned to the hotel. Anna directed the porter to place them on a table. Once she'd given him a tip and he'd gone, she turned her attention to the pretty white boxes tied in red ribbon. A card was on the top of the smallest one.

Wear these tonight. Eight o'clock for dinner.

She opened the smallest one first. A pair of slender designer heels with crystal studs on the straps made her heart kick with excitement. She'd never hidden the fact she loved beautiful shoes. Just because she wore conservative clothes didn't mean she needed to wear ugly shoes. That would be a sin against nature.

Next was a box with an electric-blue lacy thong and a matching strapless bra that made a tendril of heat uncoil in her belly. Leo wanted her to wear these tonight because he hoped to see her in them. She wasn't so dumb as to believe otherwise. Nor was she so certain of her answer that she wasn't going to put them on.

When he'd held her in the flat earlier, she'd wanted nothing more than to lie in a soft bed with him, naked skin against naked skin. She knew what awaited her when she did: heat and passion and physical pleasure so intense it would make her sob with joy. She wanted that again, even while it frightened her.

She wasn't afraid because she feared sex with Leo. She was afraid because she feared the truths she might have to admit to herself once he stripped her of her defenses. She turned to the last box with a little shiver of excitement dancing down her spine.

It contained a sequined dress in chili-pepper red. The dress was strapless, of course, and fitted through the bodice, hips and knees until it suddenly burst free in a gorgeous fantail. It was bold, far bolder than anything she'd ever worn in her life, with its blazing-hot color and sleek fit.

Her heart thrummed as she picked it up and went to stand in front of the mirror with it. Everyone would notice the woman who wore a dress like this. Could she bear the scrutiny right now?

Did it even matter? she asked herself a minute later. The press was already scrutinizing her. Since she'd started to appear in public with Leo, photographers had become a fixture in her life once more.

In the end, she decided to put the dress on. And the underwear. She left her hair long and loose, curling the ends so they fell in soft waves over her shoulder. A check of her reflection in the full-length cheval glass featured a woman she hardly recognized. A bright, sassy woman who walked into a room and owned it.

She'd never felt like she owned a room before. She'd been counting on her status after she'd married Alex to make her feel that way, but the truth was she should have learned the art long before. For herself alone.

A few minutes before eight, Leo arrived. He stood in the doorway with his hot coffee-colored gaze drifting over her and she felt as if an explosion had detonated inside her. He was resplendent in his custom-fit tuxedo. The white of his shirt contrasted sharply with his tanned skin and dark hair, making him seem even more devilish than he was. His sensual lips curved in a smile that whispered of sex and sin, and her heart went into a free fall.

She didn't even realize that she'd pressed her hand to her chest until he frowned.

"Are you feeling well?" he asked suddenly, coming into the room and taking her in his arms. "Is it the baby?"

"I'm fine," she managed. "I just felt light-headed for a moment."

And that was the truth. She'd taken one look at Leo and something inside her had shifted for the tiniest moment, taking her breath along with it.

"We can stay in," he said, looking concerned. "I'll order dinner up—"

"No, I'm fine. Really." She clutched his arm. "I want to go out. I didn't put this dress on for nothing."

He smiled, too, but there was worry in his eyes. "And a lovely dress it is, sweet Anna. You should always wear bold colors. They suit you."

She glanced down at the glaring red fabric. Count on Leo to see what she couldn't see for herself. When she'd looked in the mirror, she'd known he was right about the color. "This is a giant leap for me. I'm not accustomed to calling attention to myself."

"You should be," he said, his voice rough and soft all at once. Was that a kernel of need she heard? The idea thrilled her. "You are stunning, Anna. Marvelously stunning."

She laughed, but the sound was nervous, high. Could he tell? "Thank you for the dress. I would have never picked it."

But Leo had. Because he saw something in her that she was only just learning to see for herself. It warmed her, made her pulse kick again. She was prepared for it this time.

"But do you like it?" he asked softly.

"I do, actually. I feel quite special in it."

Leo's smile had the power to make her heart flutter. "Because you are special, Anna." He took her hand and kissed it. "Never doubt it."

The restaurant he took her to was very exclusive. He was greeted by a fawning maître d' and staff, and then they were shown to a table in an empty dining room. The room was exquisite, with deep mahogany paneling on the walls, a frescoed ceiling and crystal chandeliers. The single table was set with crystal wine and water glasses, heavy silver flatware and a profusion of cream roses in a silver vase at the center.

After they were seated and the maître d' walked away, Anna glanced around the empty room and then back at Leo. He lifted an eyebrow, as if waiting for the question he knew must be coming. She laughed, then pressed her hand to her mouth and tried not to. Nerves, she told herself.

He reached over and took her wrist gently, removing her hand so her laugh sprang free again.

"Leo," she said. "This is crazy! Did you buy the restaurant?"

His smile was genuine. Pleased. "No. But I did buy the night."

She shook her head. It was unreal. Romantic. "We could have eaten with other people."

"Not tonight. I wanted you to myself."

"You've had me to yourself nearly every day."

"Not the same," he replied. "It never lasts long enough. Tonight, however, we'll have as much time as we want."

"There are staff," she pointed out, feeling bubbly inside nevertheless. "They aren't going anywhere, I assume."

"No, and later there will be an orchestra."

She blinked. "An orchestra?"

"We've never danced, Anna. I want to hold you in my arms on a dance floor."

She looked down at the white napkin carefully folded across a charger plate bordered in tiny gold scrollwork. Her heart felt as if it would burst from her chest any minute. She was happy, happier than she'd been since the island, and it worried her. What if it all fell apart tomorrow?

"You might be disappointed," she said softly.

"I doubt that." His voice was strong, sure, as if he'd never doubted anything less in his life.

"What if I step on your toes?" she asked, trying to lighten up the moment. Because, for her, it was too intense. Her skin felt too tight, stretched thin over the weight of emotions boiling inside her.

"Can't happen," he said. "You spent years training to be a queen. Queens don't step on toes. Or, if they do, it's quite deliberate."

She laughed again. "So if I step on you, you will chalk it up to malicious intent?"

"Most definitely."

A bow-tied waiter appeared just then with wine for Leo and a nonalcoholic cocktail for her. They talked about small things once he was gone—the weather, the state of tourism in Amanti as compared to London—and then the food began to appear.

Anna found that she was starving for once, and she ate everything placed in front of her, whether it was a seared *fois gras* on a bed of baby greens, a grilled filet with béarnaise sauce or a truffle-stuffed mushroom. Everything was delicious.

After the meal was cleared away and dessert served, Leo placed a velvet box on the table. Anna put her fork down, her pulse skipping into full throttle.

"What is it?" she asked, unable to make herself reach for the small black box.

"I think you know, Anna."

"It's not necessary," she said, though it hurt to say it. She wanted a ring to be inside—

But she wanted the reasons to be real. Anna's breath shortened. Could that really be true? Did she want this to be real?

She did. Oh, God, she did. She wanted him to be marrying her because he wanted to, not because he had to.

Fickle, fickle Anna. This wasn't what she'd wanted when she'd come to London in the first place. Then, she'd only been thinking of her baby and protecting him or her from scandal. Protecting *them both* from scandal, if she were honest with herself. She'd wanted Leo's help, and she'd wanted to continue to play the martyr, the woman who needed no one or nothing to see her through life.

Now, she was realizing that she wanted so much more it frightened her.

"I think it is necessary." He pushed the box toward her.

She picked it up with trembling fingers and popped the top open. The ring was exquisite. A brilliant cut diamond of at least five carats in a platinum setting, surrounded by another two or three carats of smaller diamonds. The ring sparkled like fire in the candlelight, and she felt a pinprick of guilt and sadness. She'd pushed him into this, and she had no one to blame but herself if it wasn't real.

"Well?" he asked.

"It's beautiful," she said, her voice coming out far more hoarsely than she wanted it to.

Leo stood with a growl and took the ring from the box, which he tossed aside as if it were nothing. Then he put it on her finger and kissed her hand, his warm breath sending tiny fingers of sensation crawling down her spine.

When he tilted her head back and kissed her, she didn't resist. She opened to him, her heart filling with love and despair in equal measure.

Love.

She'd been denying it to herself, but she couldn't do so any longer. Anna's heart throbbed with pain and fear and so much love she wondered how she'd denied it for so long. She loved this man, had probably loved him since the moment on the island when he'd kissed her on the forehead instead of the mouth because he'd realized her first kiss should be special. He'd been so tender with her, so thoughtful and selfless. He'd always put her feelings first, and he'd urged her to be her own person without regard to what others wanted from her.

He hadn't done those things because he loved her, she knew that, but it was what made him the kind of man she could love. The man she *did* love.

Oh, God.

His mouth moved over hers so expertly, so hotly, that she wanted nothing more than to melt into him and forget everything but the two of them. He'd planned a romantic evening, given her a ring, but she reminded herself that he was simply doing what she had asked, playing a role she'd wanted him to play in order to protect the baby.

And she had no one but herself to blame. She was in love with this man, the father of her child, but he did not feel the same, no matter how beautifully he kissed her.

He lifted his head, his eyes glittering with need, and her heart squeezed with all she was feeling. With all she could not say.

"Damn the orchestra," he murmured, pulling her to her feet. "I'm through waiting."

Leo didn't take her back to his place. Not because he didn't want her in his space, but because it was Bobby's flat. And

Bobby had taken plenty of women there, both when he was married and when he wasn't. Hell, Leo suspected he still did, though not when Leo was in town.

To take Anna there would be wrong. Anna was not a bit of fluff. She was the mother of his child. His wife-to-be.

He took her back to the Crescent. The ride was silent, fraught with tension as they sat on opposite sides of the limousine. Leo did it to keep from tearing her dress off and taking her inside a car gliding through the London streets at night. He had no idea why she kept her distance. Perhaps for the same reason.

They rode the lift standing at opposite ends while the lift operator hummed and let passengers on and off. Leo wanted to kick everyone off and speed to the fifth floor, but instead he contented himself with watching Anna. She glanced up at him on occasion, her lovely face flushed. She licked her lips, and a spike of pain shot to his groin. He needed her so badly he was beginning to think he might embarrass himself once he was inside her.

When they arrived on the fifth floor, he swept her into his arms while she sighed and strode purposefully toward her door. He thought of fluffy puppies, of sunny fields of grass, of cows munching contentedly—anything but the woman in his arms. He was too completely aware of her. She was in his blood, his bones, and he wanted her utterly.

But he had to think of other things, or their night of bliss would become a minute or two of hurried coupling.

They reached the door and, with a swipe of the key card, were in.

The instant the door closed, her eager mouth fused to his. Leo groaned as he set her down and backed her against the door they'd just entered.

Her hands were on his tuxedo jacket, shoving it from his shoulders until he let it drop at his feet. Next she went for his belt. He found the zipper of her dress and slid it all the way down, pushing the garment down her lush breasts until he forced her to stop and step out of it before continuing with his trousers.

"Beautiful Anna," he said as he tossed the dress onto a chair. She stood there in the electric-blue underwear and heels he'd picked out for her, and she looked even more amazing than he'd dreamed she would. In spite of her protests, he turned her so he could view her lovely bottom in the thong panties. Her cheeks were bare, the thinnest slice of fabric disappearing between them before emerging again in a thin strap he wanted to tear apart with his teeth.

He dropped to his knees and worshipped that bare bottom with his mouth while she gasped. He'd never seen anything more beautiful than Anna's body. Her skin was golden, soft, and he wanted to touch it forever. Wanted to explore every inch of her while she moaned and sobbed and begged him to take her.

He needed her to beg him, he realized. He needed to know she wanted him as desperately as he wanted her.

"Leo," she gasped as his fingers slid beneath her panties and found the wet, hot center of her. He touched his mouth to the hollow of her back, slid his tongue up her spine and then nibbled her ear while his fingers found her most tender spot and stroked against the hot little ridge of flesh.

"Do you want me, Anna?"

She nodded, her eyes closed, her cheek pressed against the door.

"Tell me," he said.

"I want you. I want you so much."

He increased the pressure of his fingers as she began to moan. She shattered with a sharp cry, and then he was turning her, shoving those panties from her hips while she unsnapped his trousers and slid her hand beneath his underwear to wrap around his length.

She made a noise of approval. And then he was grasping her buttocks in his hands, lifting her against the door as his blood roared in his head. She wrapped her legs around him, knowing where he was going with this.

Another moment and he plunged into her as far as he could go. She took him greedily, her body so wet and ready it made him groan. The feelings washing over him were too much to process, so he shoved them down deep and concentrated on what he did best.

"Leo," she gasped as he slammed into her again and again. "Yes, yes, *yes*..."

He lost his mind. Lost what was left of it anyway. He drove into her as desperately and as precisely as he could manage. Had it ever felt this good? This right? Had he ever, ever wanted it to continue without end? Had he ever cared more for someone else's pleasure than his own? Of course he'd always made sure the women he bedded were happy, but had he *cared*?

When she flew apart, he knew. Her body gripped him hard, squeezed him as he thrust into her.

"Leo," she cried. "Leo!"

He gripped her harder, drove into her until he was spent, until he came in a hot rush that stole his breath. And then he swept her into his arms, took her to the plush queen bed in the adjoining room, and did it all over again.

Morning came too soon. Anna awoke slowly to the smell of coffee and hot food, her entire body feeling more languid and relaxed than it had in a very long time. She was boneless, a mass of satisfied nerve endings and raw emotions.

She turned over in the bed, encountered nothing but pillows and sheets. Leo had clearly gotten out of bed already.

Her heart turned over at the thought of him last night, of all that glorious single-minded male lust focused upon her lucky, *lucky* body.

He'd taken her with such animalistic passion against the door, and again in the bed, giving her no quarter at all, no mercy, as he drove her relentlessly toward shattering climax after shattering climax. But early this morning, in the hour after dawn, he'd made love to her much more tenderly, spinning pleasure up slowly and thoroughly until it crested like a high tide.

She'd loved every moment of it, craved it yet again, though it had only been a few hours. But hadn't that been the way on the island, as well? Warmth flooded her as she remembered.

Simply put, Leo Jackson was a drug she didn't want to quit.

Her drug of choice walked in then, carrying two cups of steaming liquid. He was wearing absolutely nothing, and her pulse skipped wildly, a trapped butterfly in a jar.

"Surely you didn't answer the door like that," she said evenly.

He grinned. "Of course not, darling. There was a towel. I seem to have lost it. No doubt to impress you."

"Lucky me."

He bent and kissed her, then handed her a coffee. "Lucky you indeed," he said. "That's decaf, by the way. With cream and sugar, the way you like it."

She took a sip, her lashes dropping over her eyes. He knew how she liked her coffee. It made her heart clench tight in her chest, but she told herself not to read more into it than it was. It was simply coffee, the way she liked it, and decaf because caffeine was bad for the baby. Nothing more, nothing less. He'd had coffee with her enough over the past few days to know what she wanted.

It was not a declaration of love.

Love.

Her stomach did a slow flip. The feeling was still so new, so raw, and sometimes it snuck up on her and grabbed her by the throat. She wanted to tell him, wanted to spill the words and ease the pain of keeping them locked up tight, but she was scared, too. Scared he wouldn't return the feeling, scared that he would look at her pitifully and say something noncommittal.

She couldn't stand it if he did. Better to be silent and hope he felt the same way than to speak and find out he didn't.

She reached out and touched the tattoo on his abdomen, traced the iridescent scales gently. His muscles clenched in response. It was a beautiful piece of art, seemingly alive in the soft light, but it must have hurt like hell when he'd had it done.

"Careful, or you'll wake the sleeping dragon," he said huskily.

"Oh, I think I can handle a dragon," she replied, arching one eyebrow.

He grinned at her. "Indeed you can. Dragon lady."

"Why did you get this?"

He shrugged as he settled on the bed beside her with his coffee. "A youthful decision, no doubt fueled by alcohol and bravado."

"You can't get a tattoo while drunk, Leo. No reputable studio will do it. And this is too fine not to have been done by a brilliant artist."

"No, I wasn't drunk, more's the pity since it hurt so damn much. But I believe I made a drunken wager that led to the tattoo."

"You could have said no," she pointed out.

"I made a bet, Anna. I could hardly renege."

Her heartbeat accelerated at the thought of him carrying on with something that he'd thought better of simply because he'd given his word. She didn't like to think of the implications to their situation now. Her pulse grew thick in her ears. "Do you always do what you promise, even if it turns out to be a bad idea?"

"I like to think I don't commit to things in the first place that are bad ideas. The tattoo is, as you say, beautiful. I don't regret it at all."

It was inevitable, however, that he must regret *some* things. Would she be one of them? She told herself to stop being fanciful, that tattoos weren't women, but she couldn't quite help it. She wore vulnerability like a second skin this morning. "But you do regret some of them in the end, I imagine."

He set the coffee down on the bedside table. "Who wouldn't? That's life, my darling."

She must have been frowning hard, because he leaned over and took her coffee cup away. Then he kissed her until she clung to him, lips and hands and body. Until desire flared to life inside her, hot little fingers of need caressing her and making her ache for him.

But instead of sliding her beneath him and making love to her again, he swung his long legs off the bed and stood. "Now come, you need to eat something. It's been a while since dinner."

Anna tried to push away the hurt throbbing through her at being rejected, though it wasn't *really* a rejection so much as a postponement. Still, it stung more than it ought when she was feeling so vulnerable.

She threw back the covers, determined to be strong, and reached for her robe. "You are the one who interrupted dessert," she reminded him.

"Did I? And here I thought I gave you a much more satisfying dessert."

Anna laughed as she tied the belt on her robe. "What arrogance," she teased lightly, though dread lay heavy on her heart. "Perhaps I would have preferred the cheesecake."

He stood there before her, one leg thrust indolently out to the side, his magnificent body still naked and rippling with muscle, and swept a hand from his shoulder to his groin as if to showcase the goods. "I am, you must admit, quite worth the interruption."

"I wouldn't dream of denying it," she said.

She left him getting dressed and walked over to the breakfast table. There were eggs, sausage, tomatoes and toast beneath the silver lids. Her folded newspapers lay on the table nearby, and she picked them up, wondering what silly thing the press had managed to say about her and Leo today. It was too much to hope they'd lost interest, of course. The Santina press had nothing else to do. The British tabloids were no better, though at least they filled their pages with plenty of celebrity gossip and WAG tales. Back home, she was front-page news. Here, it was a toss-up.

Not today, however, she discovered when she unfolded the first newssheet. The headline blared at her while her insides churned and a hot little flame began to lick at her.

She read it all the way through and then started again, until the moment Leo snatched the paper from her hand, swearing violently and long.

But it was too late. The words were already imprinted on her brain. How could they not be?

Lucky Leo's Luck Runs Out—The Jilted Bride Is Pregnant!

CHAPTER THIRTEEN

"I'm sorry, Anna," Leo said, his voice throbbing with anger. "I had hoped we would have longer."

She was still trying to process it. "They took a picture. Of us kissing in front of Dr. Clemens's office. How did they know so soon? And why did they wait to use it?"

Leo swore again and raked a hand through his hair. He looked murderously, furiously angry. She, however, felt nothing.

Or, rather, she felt numb. That's what it was. She was perfectly numb.

It wasn't what she'd expected to feel. It wasn't what she'd felt when the pictures of Alex and Allegra had appeared, along with the headline proclaiming her a jilted bride. That had been embarrassing, no doubt. This, however...this was a violation. Of her life, of her baby's life.

Of Leo's life.

He came and gripped her shoulders, thrust his face into hers and forced her to look up at him. "It doesn't matter, Anna. We're getting married in five days. We're just going to have to deal with this sooner rather than later."

All her plans were wrecked. She'd wanted to marry so that by the time she began to show, the question of scandal would be dubious at best. Oh, sure, when the baby was born, anyone could count backward and figure it out.

But it would be months past, and she would be a married woman with a new baby.

It had been perfect. And now it lay in ruins around her like a pile of bricks that only a moment before the wrecking ball hit was a house.

"How did they figure it out so soon?" she repeated.

Leo's lips thinned. "I don't know, but I intend to find out."

She held up her hand, the ring sparkling and dazzling in the bright morning light. Last night, she'd felt so special and hopeful when he'd taken her to dinner in an empty restaurant and given her this ring. It was everything a romantic night out should be, except for the fact it was staged. Staged because the marriage was already planned.

But she hadn't cared, really, once he'd kissed her and brought her back here. He'd smashed every notion she'd had about how this marriage would go. He'd stripped her barriers, stripped her body, and forced his way into her soul. He was a part of her, in more ways than one, and she loved him. She'd actually had *hope* after last night that everything would turn out well. That she'd be happy, and that Leo would be happy with her.

Until she'd read the paper and realized their secret was out. No one would ever believe there was anything between them but an adherence to duty for the child's sake.

Did she care? Did it matter?

It shouldn't matter, but she found that it did. How could they ever be happy together if their marriage began under a dark cloud of suspicion and scandal? How could she ever be sure that Leo didn't resent her for the circumstance of their marriage?

As the next few days passed, the scandal grew. The usual made-up nonsense got twisted in with the truth, and everything got blown out of proportion. She refused to talk to reporters, as did Leo—so they made things up. They found witnesses, paid doormen and waitresses and coat-check girls, to say anything and everything outrageous and untrue.

Leo grew stony and distant. They had not spent the night together since the evening before the story broke. And, much to her dismay, pictures of their lovely evening together appeared in the papers. Taken with a telephoto lens through a window, someone had caught the moment when Leo had kissed her senseless before taking her back to the hotel.

Now, it was all about appearances, about making everyone think they were blissfully happy together when they were anything but. Leo still took her to dinner, to the theater, to corporate events he had to attend. Photographers lined up in droves outside the venues, the flashbulbs snapping and questions popping like automatic gunfire.

Anna said nothing. Leo ushered her through the gauntlet with either a firm hand on her back or gripping her hand in his. He made no comment, though he did once stop abruptly when a reporter asked him what it felt like to be trapped into marriage by a gold-digging foreigner.

Anna had wrapped her arm around his and urged him to keep walking. After a minute in which she'd felt the tension stringing through him like a bow drawn to the breaking point, he'd done as she asked and continued down the walkway.

Her parents called. They were shocked, outraged and so disappointed. And yet, when her mother had begun to berate her for her impulsive nature, her father had hissed out a curse. A moment later, there had been a heavy silence.

"Anna," her father had said into the phone while her mother started to cry in the background. "You are our daughter and we love you. If this man is not what you want, come home. We will take care of you."

She'd squeezed the phone in her hand. "I'm getting married, Papa. It's what I want."

"Ne," he had said solemnly. "Then we are happy."

She'd hung up then, feeling miserable because she'd put them through so much. And even more miserable that her marriage to Leo was now overshadowed by her pregnancy.

Or, to be fair, it had always been overshadowed by her pregnancy. But at least it had been between the two of them and not the whole world.

The evening before the civil ceremony was finally to take place, Leo had a business dinner in a penthouse suite overlooking the Thames. Anna accompanied him at his request, since there would be spouses and partners present.

As they entered the penthouse, all the chatter died and a dozen faces turned to them. The silence was awkward until a man suddenly came forward and shook Leo's hand, welcoming him to the gathering. The ice was broken and people behaved normally again, mingling in small groups and chatting, eventually coming together for a dinner that had Anna seated across the table and several spaces down from Leo.

She felt uncomfortable, isolated, and her eyes strayed to Leo. He laughed easily, talked to the people seated on either side of him. Anna made small talk with the old gentleman on her right. On her left, a woman pointedly ignored her, only engaging in polite small talk when it was absolutely necessary.

Anna felt the stares all night. It wasn't that these people were scandalized. She was pretty sure they weren't, being as wealthy and connected as they were. Some of them had no doubt been victims of the press in the past, as well.

No, it was the way they looked between her and Leo, no

doubt wondering if theirs was a marriage that would last. By now, everyone knew they'd been marooned on an island together. And everyone knew, clearly, they'd had sex.

Anna was pregnant, and Leo was stepping up to do the right thing. But, poor man, did he really want to be married to such an uptight woman as she? She was trying so hard, but she was still the woman she'd always been. She still liked her calendars and reminders and intricate plans. She felt grounded that way, and she wouldn't apologize for it.

But she'd allowed herself to wear color recently, and she'd even gone so far as to show a little bit of skin on her shoulders and arms. Leo had made her feel beautiful, and she'd felt confident enough to grow bolder in her choices. Tonight she'd chosen a pale pink sheath dress with tiny straps and a bolero jacket.

But she still wore her pearls and she still held her spine stiff and straight.

What a joke it had been to think she would have ever made a good queen. She didn't know how to relax, in spite of all her training. She was stiff, formal and uncomfortable when she believed people were scrutinizing her. As they would have done constantly had she married Alex.

She hid a yawn behind her hand and glanced at her watch. A quarter to eleven. Leo disengaged from the conversation he was having and came to her side as if he sensed her discomfort.

"Are you tired?"

"Yes. I want to go back to the hotel and go to bed," she said. *With you,* she silently added.

Leo made their excuses to the host and hostess, and then they were sitting in silence in the big limousine. Anna yawned again. She wanted him to hold his arm out, wanted to snuggle into the circle of his embrace and lay her head against his shoulder.

She wanted the warmth and happiness they'd had for that one night together. But it wasn't going to happen. Leo, it seemed, regretted their night. Whereas she thought of it as one of the best of her life. They'd almost been happy together. For the barest of moments, she'd thought they would make this marriage work.

That he would love her as she loved him.

Instead, he sat stony and cold and she was unable to break the silence between them. Unable to utter the correct words to make everything go back to the way it was when he'd taken her to dinner four nights ago and given her an engagement ring.

"It was a nice party," she said into the silence.

"Did you think so? I thought you were unhappy."

She colored in the dark, though he could not see it. "I wasn't unhappy."

He turned his head, and she could see the flash of his teeth. "You were. You hardly said anything tonight."

"That's not true," she replied. "I talked to those around me. The woman on my left at dinner was quite difficult, actually."

"Probably because we dated once, long ago."

Anna blinked. A sliver of anger uncoiled within her. And hurt. "Well, I should have guessed. Lucky Leo strikes again."

"Anna, I'm sorry."

"For what?" she said, trying to keep her voice light and gay when she felt anything but. Hurt and anger spun together in a vortex inside her, sucking her down with it. "You can't help that you've probably bedded half of London. Half of the *planet,* I should say."

"I'm sorry I didn't warn you when I saw her tonight. I wasn't pleased you were seated beside her, but whenever I looked in your direction, you seemed to be doing fine."

"My training, no doubt. I am a born diplomat." Hardly, but she wasn't admitting that particular failure to him tonight.

"It won't happen again, I assure you."

"How can you do that, Casanova? Are we to flee every dinner engagement where you've slept with someone present? I fear we'll never go anywhere."

He took her hand. She jumped at his touch. Her body began to melt, to need. Hot sparks flared to life in her belly, between her legs. It had been days since he'd touched her more than perfunctorily.

"You're nervous and upset. I understand. But let's just get through tomorrow, shall we? We have plenty of time to figure it out from there."

Get through tomorrow, get through tomorrow...

"Of course," she said, removing her hand from his lest she melt into a puddle of need and beg him to take her to bed and hold her close all night long.

He wanted to *get through tomorrow.* As if it were an ordeal to be endured. A sentence to be served. A penalty.

It hurt.

They reached the red awning of the Crescent and he helped her from the car. She deliberately took a step back when they were on the red carpet leading into the hotel. The flash of a bulb lit up the night, followed by another and another. Leo hurried her into the marble-and-glass lobby dotted with potted palms nearly two stories tall.

Anna disengaged from his embrace once they were out of sight of the photographers.

"Let's say good-night here," she said, needing to put space between them. Needing to think and plan and not *feel* so damn much whenever he was near. She could do this if she could only gain perspective.

He frowned. She thought he would say no, and then

he tipped his head. "Very well. I'll pick you up tomorrow morning at ten."

She waved a hand in the air as if it were a trifle. "There's no need, Leo. The registry bureau is in the opposite direction from your office. I'll meet you there at ten-thirty. It'll preserve the mystery, yes?"

His brows drew down. "The mystery?"

"If this were a church wedding, you wouldn't be allowed to see me in the dress before I walked down the aisle. Let's attempt to follow the form."

His frown didn't dissipate. But he acquiesced. "If that's what you wish. I'll send a car for you."

"Very well," she said.

And then she stepped up to him and pulled his head down to hers. She kissed him with all the pent-up passion she possessed, triumphing in the groan emanating from his throat. His tongue slid into her mouth, tangled with hers, and she almost believed it. Almost believed he needed her as much as she needed him.

But he didn't. Or at least not in the same way. She disengaged from the kiss, straightening her jacket, and bid him good-night.

He watched her get into the lift. The doors slid closed and she turned into the corner, pressing her fist to her mouth and willing herself not to cry.

It was all wrong. Once more, it was all wrong.

She wasn't coming. Leo stood in the hallway outside the registry office where they were to be married and processed the information he'd just been given. Anna had not shown up, according to the driver he'd sent over for her. A call to her mobile netted him nothing. Another call to the front desk, and he learned that she'd checked out more than two hours ago.

Rage was the first emotion that coursed through him, scouring his insides like sulfuric acid, eating away at him until he wanted to explode into action. But what sort of action? Punching something would do no good, no matter how exhilarating it might feel.

Despair was the second emotion to pummel him. Somehow, that was harder to deal with. She'd left him. Anna Constantinides, his beautiful uptight Greek with her pearls and her veneer of cool competence that he knew hid a passionate, fiery nature. Anna was molten, no matter how hard she tried not to be. All the buttoned-up clothing in the world couldn't hide that sizzling beauty of hers, no matter what she believed.

He stood in that hallway with people passing around him, going on with their lives and jobs, and he felt suddenly bereft. Empty. As if she'd taken the light with her when she'd gone. He didn't understand it. Why had she left? Why, when this marriage had been so important to her in the first place?

He'd always known she was doing it for reasons that had nothing to do with him. The knowledge that she could dismiss him so easily in her calculations had pricked his pride, but had he given her any reason to do otherwise? His greatest fear was being a horrible father. His second greatest was disappointing Anna.

Twice, she'd pushed him from her life. The first time, he'd been angry and disappointed. This time, he felt as if someone had punched him in the gut. Repeatedly.

He knew what he had to do, the only course of action that made sense.

He had to go after her. He had to stop her before she left. It was the only thing that would halt the agony inside him.

And say what to her, Leo?

His mind cast around for the right words. He had to tell

her that he *could* be a better person, that he *wanted* to be a father and a husband, and that he wanted her to give him that chance. That with her by his side, he knew he could do anything. He wasn't doomed to be his own father, wasn't doomed to a life of poor choices and empty relationships if he didn't choose to be.

Leo shot down the hallway, down two flights of stairs, and burst into the gloom of a rainy day. He didn't have time to wait for his driver to come around, so he hailed a cab. The trip to Heathrow took forever but he was finally there, finally bursting through the doors and sprinting for the British Airways counter to buy a ticket to Amanti. It was the only way to get through security to see her.

He strode straight to the VIP line and breezed through to the counter agent.

"I'm sorry, sir," the agent said when he told the man what he wanted. "But that flight is already on the taxiway."

"Then stop it."

"I'm afraid we can't do that, sir."

Leo wanted to haul the agent over the counter by his collar and demand he stop the plane, but he knew that was the surest way to spend a few days cooling off in a jail cell. Instead, he slammed a fist against the counter and went back out into the rain, hands thrust in his pockets, stomach churning with rage and pain. Eventually, he hailed a cab and had it take him back to Knightsbridge.

She'd left him. She'd bloody well left him standing at the metaphorical altar and run away at the last damn minute. Because she knew he didn't belong in her life. His relationships with women had always been about the physical, never the emotional. He was damaged when it came to knowing how to share the parts of him that went deeper than the surface.

But he'd tried. With her, he'd tried. And it hadn't been

good enough, had it? She'd seen through to the damaged parts of his soul and said, *No way.*

Leo didn't even bother drying off when he entered his father's apartment. He poured a glass of Scotch and slumped on the couch, raindrops sliding down his face and plopping onto his damp clothing.

Bobby found him that way hours later, still sitting, still staring at nothing. His clothes had dried, but they were now stiff and uncomfortable. He didn't care.

"What happened to you, boy?" his father demanded, coming over and taking the empty glass away.

Leo looked up, blinked. His eyes felt gritty, tired. "Got what I deserved," he said. "About time, too."

"What the hell are you talking about?"

"Anna. She left me."

Bobby thrust his lower lip out. "Mmm, I see." He perched on the edge of the table closest to Leo. "You love her?"

He'd been thinking about that for hours now. "Yeah, I think I do."

"Think? Or know?"

Leo rubbed a hand over his eyes, his forehead. "How do you ever know?" He knew he was asking the wrong man, not only because Bobby seemed to have an open-door policy on who he loved and how often, but also because Bobby had never yet offered him any advice of substance. But the lonely little boy inside him still wanted it to happen. Wanted his father to step up and be a father for once, not just another partner in crime.

Bobby blew out a breath and rubbed his hands on his knees. "You know because when she's gone it hurts deep down—" he put a fist to his torso, right below his rib cage "—right here. It hurts and it won't go away. No amount of alcohol can kill it. No amount of sex with other women can kill it. Nothing but time, if she won't take you back. And even then, it continues to burn."

Leo blinked. "Who did you feel that way about?" He was too surprised by what Bobby had just said not to ask the question.

Bobby leaned back, hands still on his legs. "Ah, well that's my secret to bear, isn't it? Suffice it to say I screwed up. But you can fix this, Leo. Go after her, tell her how you feel."

As if it were that easy. He'd tried that. It hadn't worked. Anna had left him without a word. She'd never given him the chance, and he was angry about it. Angry that he'd stood there in the airport and felt as if his world was crumbling from beneath his feet and there was nothing he could do about it.

"What if she doesn't care?"

That was the moment when Bobby said the most profound thing Leo would ever hear him say, even if they both lived another hundred years. "If she didn't care, I doubt she'd have left. Women don't run when they aren't scared of something. If all she wanted was your money or your name, she'd have said those vows faster than lightning. Trust me."

Bobby got up then and clamped a hand on Leo's shoulder. "I love you, Leo. I know I haven't always done right by you, but I love you. You'll be a terrific father, not because you had a great example to follow—and we both know you didn't—but because it's who you are inside. There's nothing you do that you don't excel at."

Leo felt tears pricking at the corners of his eyes. "Why haven't you said this before?"

It was…extraordinary. And just strange enough that he almost thought he must be dreaming.

Bobby shrugged. "Because I wasn't sure you'd welcome it. You're so damned independent—get that from your mother—and so competent that I feel a bit out of sorts with you."

"Out of sorts?"

"Hard to admit your kids know more than you do. If I opened my mouth and removed all doubt, would you ever respect me?" Bobby shook his head. "No, just seemed easier to spend time with you and hope you knew how proud you make me. I can't change the past, but I can let you know I'm here now. I've made mistakes, Leo, but I do love you."

Shame jabbed at Leo's conscience then. "When the story broke in the papers, I wondered for a moment if it was you who'd told them. Not on purpose, but inadvertently."

He knew better now, but his father had been the first flash of a thought. The guilt of it, however briefly it had entered his mind, ate at him, especially after what Bobby had just said.

His father shrugged again. "Of course you did. Who else would be most likely to get drunk and open his mouth?" Then he patted Leo. "I've gotten better about that. It wasn't me, but I don't blame you for thinking it could be."

Bobby started toward the elevator and Leo stood to watch him go. "Dad," he said when the doors opened and his father stepped inside.

Bobby turned, his finger on the button. There was so much Leo wanted to say, so much he wanted to know. This relationship was a work in progress and might always be. But it had just taken a step forward that he'd never expected and there was only one response needed.

"Thanks."

The other man smiled, and then the doors closed and he was gone.

CHAPTER FOURTEEN

"IT SEEMS as if I was wrong about you," a voice said from behind her. "You aren't a dragon lady at all."

Anna whirled, her toes catching in the sand, and nearly fell to her knees. Fortunately, she did not. The early-morning sun was behind him, silhouetting his body in a nimbus of light as he moved down the deserted beach toward her.

But was he a figment of her desperate imagination, or was he real?

"Leo?"

"Expecting someone else?" he said as he came to a stop a few short feet away.

Anna shook her head because no words would come out. It *was* him. And she could hardly believe he was here. She'd left London nearly a week ago, and she'd regretted it every moment since. As he'd implied, she'd been a coward. Hot emotion welled in her chest, her throat, aching to spill forth. But she swallowed it down and stood there, watching him as he watched her. Neither of them said a word for long moments.

And then he broke the silence.

"You left without saying goodbye." There was a hard edge to his voice that made her swallow the lump in her throat.

"I know. I'm sorry."

"That's all?"

"What else do you wish me to say?" she asked, her heart throbbing with hurt and love and passion for this man. He was here and she wanted to throw herself into his arms, sob and beg him to give her another chance.

"Why don't you explain why you thought it necessary to run away without at least telling me you no longer wanted to marry me."

Her heart ached so much. "I wanted to tell you," she said. "I started to tell you."

But every time she'd tried to initiate the phone call, dread had gripped her by the throat and refused to let go. She'd finally realized that the only way to release him from his promise was just to go.

"You should have."

She shook her head. "I couldn't. You would have insisted on going through with it anyway, and I didn't want to do that to you."

Leo growled. And then he shoved a hand through his hair and turned to look out at the whitecaps foaming on the surface of the sea as they broke toward shore. "*You* wanted the marriage, Anna. *You* asked me."

"And you always keep your promises, even when you know you'll regret it later!" she cried, suddenly unable to hold it in any longer. He turned toward her and she ducked her head, embarrassed. "I couldn't bear the thought that you would regret me."

He looked stunned. "That's what this is about? The fact I made a bet over a tattoo and went through with it?"

It sounded stupid when he put it that way. Embarrassment flooded her. "Of course it's not about the tattoo. It's about you being the sort of person who honors his promises."

"My God, Anna, you frustrate the hell out of me. You

wanted the marriage to protect the baby. What happened to change your mind? A bloody tattoo story?"

"Of course not," she said, stung. "I realized once the story broke that you were right. I did want the marriage for me, to protect *me*." She dropped her gaze to the sand, studied the tiny whorls made by sand crabs in the night. "I'm ashamed of that."

She heard him move, and then he was gripping her shoulders and forcing her to look up at him. She felt like whimpering at his touch, but she bit the inside of her lip and kept quiet. She knew she was pitiful.

"Don't say that, Anna. You thought you were doing it for the baby. You *were* doing it for the baby. No one should have to endure the kind of stories you've had to over the past few months. You had every right to think of how our child would have been affected."

A tear trickled down her cheek and she dashed it away. "But I had no right to force changes into your life because of my problems with the press."

His grip tightened. "Anna, this baby is *ours*. I want to be there for him."

"Or her," she added automatically.

"Or her." He pulled her into his embrace suddenly, and she closed her eyes and breathed him in. His heart was thrumming hard and steady, and his skin was so hot beneath his clothes. Searing her. Making her want. She curled her fingers into his shirt and just held him. For a few moments, she could allow herself to enjoy this.

"When I told you about the stories surrounding my mother's affair with my father, and the subsequent stories when she died—I was wrong when I said they didn't affect me. Of course they did. I've been living with their impact all of my life. It's made me who I am, Anna."

She tilted her head back to look at him. "Oh, Leo, I'm sorry."

"I'm not," he said. "I like who I am. But I like who I am with you even better."

Her heart skipped a beat. "You're only trying to make me feel better for wanting to force you into marriage."

He sighed. "Don't you realize by now, sweet Anna, there's no forcing me to do anything I don't want to do? I agreed because I wanted this marriage. I still do."

Her knees were suddenly so weak that if he wasn't holding her tight, she'd have sunk to the ground. "I thought I was forcing you into something you didn't want to do. And I walked out without an explanation. How could you still want to marry me?"

"Isn't it obvious?" he said, teeth flashing white in his handsome face. His eyes were so hot and intense as they raked over her face, daring her to believe.

"I—I'm not sure it is."

He shook his head, but his smile never wavered. "I love you, Anna. I love our baby. I like who I am with you, and I want to spend the rest of my life with you. I want to see you grow big with our child, and I want to be there when he—or she—comes into this world. I want to bring you coffee every morning, and I want to make love to you as often as possible. I want to unbutton your high-necked shirts and make you wear colors more frequently. I want you in my life, and I want to marry you so you can't ever run away again."

The tears she'd been holding in sprang free, sliding hotly down her cheeks. She told herself to hold it together, but it was far easier said than done. She put her forehead against his shirt and sobbed while he held her tight.

When she finally managed to compose herself, she lifted her head to find him gazing at her tenderly. "I thought you didn't care," she said, her breath hitching. "I thought you must hate me for making you go through with a marriage you didn't want."

He looked stunned. "What on earth made you think that?"

"You grew so distant after the story broke. All I wanted was for you to hold me, but you wouldn't touch me." She sniffled. "You wouldn't spend the night with me again."

He squeezed her tighter to him. "I thought you were too upset, that you weren't resting. I knew if I were there, you definitely wouldn't rest. Because I couldn't keep my hands off you."

"You seem to have done a good enough job of it." Her voice sounded small, hurt. She dropped her gaze to his chest, to where she was still clutching him tight.

He swore softly. "I couldn't touch you, Anna. Not without wanting to make love to you. It was safer to keep my distance. I wanted you to rest. It was only four nights. We'd have been together on the fifth."

"But I didn't rest," she said, her fingers trembling as she smoothed the fabric of his shirt. "I tossed and turned because I thought everything was ruined between us. I loved you so desperately, and I thought you despised me."

"Look at me," he said, and she raised her gaze to his. His smile made her heart turn over in her chest. Soft, hopeful, full of tenderness. "You love me?"

She blinked, stunned at the question. "I thought it was obvious."

His laugh was broken. "You forget how good you are at the serene thing." He slid his fingers along her cheek, into her hair. And then he breathed a great sigh. "I'm a lucky, lucky man. And I plan to spend a great deal of time taking advantage of my good luck."

He dipped his head, his mouth claiming hers in a scorching kiss that could have melted ten-gauge steel. Warmth blossomed inside her, rolling through her like hot syrup. She was melting with need, with love.

"I need you, Anna. Come home with me. Marry me. Today."

It was everything she'd ever wanted, ever dreamed. Leo and her...and their baby. *Perfection. Bliss. Rightness.*

"Yes," she said. "Definitely, yes."

He groaned and squeezed her tight, as if he would never let go.

"Remind me," he said a few minutes later, between hot kisses to her lips, her throat, her cheeks, "to send Donna a thank-you note."

"Why is that?" she asked when he let her breathe again.

He lifted his head, his dark eyes glittering with heat. "She's the one who set the reporters on us."

A flash of anger rushed through her, but it was gone like a wisp of smoke on the breeze. How could she possibly be angry when she was so happy? "And that's a good thing because...?"

He grinned at her, and warmth filled her. "Because it opened our eyes to the truth."

And that, she realized, as Leo swept her into his arms and carried her back up the beach, was a very fortunate thing. Sex was fabulous. But love was better.

Fabulous sex *and* love? Bliss.

* * * * *

PLAYING THE
ROYAL GAME

CAROL MARINELLI

CHAPTER ONE

SHE was better off without the job, Allegra told herself.

No one should have to put up with that.

Except that walking in the rain along grey London streets, taking the underground to various employment agencies, the anger that her boss could make such a blatant a pass at her and then fire her for not succumbing started to be replaced with something that felt close to fear.

She needed that job.

Needed it.

Her savings had been obliterated by the bottomless pit that was her family's excess spending. At times it felt as if her lowly publishing wage supported half the Jackson family. Yes, she was the boring reliable one, but they didn't mind her dependability when their erratic ways found them in trouble. Just last week she had lent her step-mother, Chantelle, close to five thousand pounds in cash for credit card debts that her father didn't know about. It was laughable to think that she might now have to have her family support her.

It was a miserable day, with no sign that it was spring; instead it was cold and wet, and Allegra dug her hands deeper into her trench coat pockets, her fingers curling around a fifty-pound note she had pulled out of the ATM.

If her boss refused to put her pay in tomorrow it was all she had before being completely broke.

No!

She'd been through worse than this, Allegra decided. As Bobby Jackson's daughter she was all too used to the bailiffs but her father always managed to pick himself up; he never let it get him down. She was not going to sink, but hell, if she did, then she'd sink in style!

Pushing open a bar door, she walked in with her head held high, the heat hitting her as she entered, and Allegra slipped off her coat and hung it, her hair dripping wet and cold down her back. Normally she wouldn't entertain entering some random bar, but still, at least it was warm and she could sit down and finally gather her thoughts.

There had been a confidence to her as she'd stalked out of her office with dignity. With her track record and her job history, a lot of the agencies had called over the years offering her freelance work.

It had been sobering indeed to find out that they were hiring no one, that the financial crisis and changes to the industry meant that there were no causal jobs waiting for her to step into.

None.

Well, a chance for a couple, but they added up to about three hours' work per month.

Per month!

Allegra was about to head to the bar but, glancing around, saw that it was table service so she walked over to a small alcove and took a seat, the plush couch lined with velvet. Despite its rather dingy appearance from the street, inside it was actually very nice and the prices on the menu verified that as fact.

She looked up at the sound of laughter—a group of well-dressed women were sipping on cocktails and Allegra couldn't help but envy their buoyant mood. As her eyes moved away from the jovial women they stilled for a fraction, because there, sitting at a table near them, lost in his own world, was possibly the most beautiful man ever to come into her line of vision. Dark suited, his thick brown hair was raked back to show an immaculate profile, high cheekbones and a very straight nose; his long legs were stretched out and crossed at the ankle. But despite his rather languorous position, as he stared into his glass there was a pensiveness to him, a furrow between his eyebrows that showed he was deep in thought. The furrow deepened as there was another outbreak of laughter from the women's table, and just as he looked up, just as he might have caught her watching, Allegra was terribly grateful for the distraction of the waitress who approached.

'What can I get you?' Allegra was about to order a glass of house wine, or maybe just ask if they could do her a pot of tea and a sandwich, because she really ought to try a couple more job agencies, but hell, a girl could only take so much rejection in one day and she may well be living off tea and sandwiches for a long while yet!

'A bottle of Bollinger please.' It was an extravagant gesture for Allegra, an unusual one as well. She was extremely careful with her pay cheque, saving twenty percent to put towards her first mortgage before it even hit her account, determined never to be like her family—but where had that gotten her?

The waitress didn't bat an eye; instead she asked how many glasses.

'Just the one.'

She was given a little bowl of nuts too!

'Celebrating?' the waitress asked as she poured her drink.

'Sort of,' Allegra admitted, and then, left alone, she

decided that she was. For months she had put up with her boss's thinly veiled leers and skin-crawling comments. It was worth celebrating just to finally be past all that, so she raised her glass to the window, in the general direction of her old work place.

'Cheers!'

As she turned she caught Mr. Gorgeous watching her—not staring, just idly curious—and she couldn't blame him for that. After all, she was raising a glass to the window. She gave him a brief smile and then turned back to her thoughts, took out a pen and the notebook and list of contacts that she always carried and set about making copious lists, determined, *determined*, that by the end of the week she would be back in work.

Halfway down the bottle and she didn't feel quite so brave. If anything, half a bottle of champagne on an empty stomach had her emotions bubbling and she was dangerously close to tears, especially when the waitress came over.

'You didn't sign the register when you came in,' the waitress said, and even before she continued Allegra knew what was coming and inwardly flinched as realization dawned. 'You are a member, aren't you?' She felt a blush spread on her cheeks. Of course it was a private club that she'd entered, not some bar she'd just wandered into, and just as she was about to apologise and fling down her fifty-pound note and flee, a voice that was as pleasing as its owner saved her the embarrassment.

'Why are you hiding there?' A deep warm voice had both Allegra and the waitress turn around and she found herself looking now into the eyes of the pensive stranger—very brown eyes that stayed steady as hers blinked in confusion. He turned and addressed the waitress. 'Sorry, she's my guest. I'll sign her in in a moment.' The waitress opened her mouth to say something—after all, Allegra had been sitting there alone for a good half an hour or so and he had made no effort to join his *guest*—but perhaps he was a favourite customer, or maybe it was just his impressive stance, because, without comment, the waitress left them to it.

'Thanks,' Allegra said as he took a seat in front of her. 'But no thanks. I'll just settle my bill....' She went to go, but as he moved to stop her, his hand reaching across the table, she shot him a look that told him unwelcome contact would be a *very* foolish mistake on his part. Given the day she'd had, Allegra had enough pent-up energy to give this stranger a little piece of her mind.

'As I said, thank you, but no thank you.'

'At least finish your drink,' said the stranger. 'It would be a shame to waste it.'

It would be a crying shame actually.

Maybe she could take it with her, Allegra thought wildly, having visions of herself walking down the street, half-drunk bottle in hand, bemoaning her situation. She found herself smiling at the very thought—not smiling at him, of course, except he interpreted it as such, because he clicked slender fingers in the direction of the bar and summoned another glass. Allegra sat bristling as the waitress poured him a glass of *her* champagne.

'I'm just trying to enjoy a quiet drink alone,' she said pointedly.

'Then sign in,' he suggested.

'Ha, ha!'

'Or,' he offered, 'you can be my guest, which means you sit with me. I wouldn't hear of it otherwise.' She couldn't place his accent. He spoke English terribly well; in fact, his voice was clipped and well schooled, unlike Allegra's rather more London accent, but there was a slight ring to it, Spanish or Italian perhaps. She was determined not to stay long enough to find out.

'Anyway,' he carried on despite her lack of response, 'you don't look as if you are enjoying it. In fact, apart from the small salute to the window you seem as miserable as I am.' She looked at him and saw that the impressive suit he was wearing wasn't just dark, it was black, and so, too, the tie. Not just from the attire, but from the strain on his face, he had clearly come from a funeral. Now he was close, she could smell him—and he smelt nothing like the usual man in a bar. It wasn't just the delicious hint of cologne that was unusual; he actually smelt of clean—there was no other way to describe it. His eyes were clear and bizarrely she felt herself relax just a little, for this was surely not a man who usually pressed attention, and it wasn't as if she had anywhere else that she needed to be.

'Are you usually so invasive?'

He thought about it for a moment. 'No.' He took a sip of drink and seemed to think about it some more. 'Never. I just saw you looking so fed up and then when the waitress came over I thought…'

'That you'd cheer me up?'

'No.' He gave a small shrug. 'I thought we could be miserable together. Don't look, but there are a group of women…' He gestured his head and as instructed she didn't look, but she knew who he meant. She'd heard their flirting laughter, and had easily guessed it was aimed towards him. 'One of them in particular seems determined to join me.'

'I'd have thought you'd have no trouble at all fighting off unwelcome attention.' Unlike me, she didn't add, but then she wasn't particularly used to men vying for her attention—well, not gorgeous ones anyway. But knowing how to deflect unwelcome attention was surely a prerequisite to him stepping out on the street, because wherever he went he surely turned heads.

'Normally, I have no problem.' He didn't say it in arrogance, merely stated the fact. 'Just today.' She looked at his suit. 'I was just trying to have a drink, to think, to have some silence, perhaps the same as you....' And while she'd have chosen to have some peace, she'd settle for silence too.

'Okay.' She gave a begrudging smile. 'I can manage silence.'

He must be someone, because all she had been given was a small bowl of nuts, but now that he'd joined her she was treated to lots of little bowls of goodies. She didn't care if she looked greedy; the rumble in her stomach reminded Allegra that she hadn't eaten since the slice of toast she'd had while dashing to the Underground some seven hours ago.

'I'd better sign you in,' he said. 'I'm surprised you got to a table. They are normally very...' He didn't finish, but the insinuation that she didn't belong had her blushing to her roots.

'Particular!' Allegra finished for him, and again she went to reach for her bag. She did not need his charity and certainly not his insults. Today really wasn't proving to be the best.

'Thorough.' He actually smiled at her indignation, a lovely smile that suited him—the very first smile from him that she had seen—and it changed him, changed those haughty, guarded features in a way she rather liked. It was a small smile, not a wide one, a smile she somehow knew was one that was rarely shared. It had to be rare, she figured, because the effect was completely devastating. It fostered awareness, made even listening somehow terribly difficult, because what had offended just a moment before hardly mattered a jot as he spoke on. She had to remind herself that a few seconds ago she'd been rather disgruntled, had to force herself to not sit there like an idiot and smile back. 'I meant that they are usually very thorough.'

'You're forgiven then.' And despite her best intentions, Allegra realised she was smiling back.

'What's your name?'

'Allegra,' she said. 'Allegra Jackson. Two *l*'s.'

'I'm Aless…' He hesitated, just for a second. 'Alex.'

And she watched as he headed off, breathed a little sigh of relief, because normally when she said her name there was a frown, or a little flare of recognition. Her family managed to hit the newsstands with alarming regularity, and even though she was, in the main, left out of the scandal and gossip they all generated, her rather unusual first name, combined with the surname of Jackson generally led to the inevitable… 'Are you Bobby Jackson's daughter?'

He headed over to the book and signed her in in the guest column. He'd almost given his real name. It wasn't exactly a secret but in general, and especially in London, he went by Alex Santina, businessman extraordinaire, not HRH Crown Prince Alessandro Santina. He guessed the slip-up was because he'd been sitting there thinking about Santina, thinking about the angry discussion he'd recently had with his father. He was tired too, Alex realised, and that was unusual, for fatigue was a rare visitor for him. But lately he'd felt it, and today, standing in that church, it had washed over him and literally drained him. He did not recognise that he was upset; funerals did not upset him and he had attended many. He'd hardly known Charles after all.

He signed Allegra in and then walked back towards her. He'd seen her arrive and could fully understand the waitress's mistake—often the doors opened and before they were questioned as to their membership people would shrink back, realising their mistake. But she, or rather Allegra, after a brief glance around, had taken off her coat and hung it up. There was a quiet confidence to her, an ease in her surroundings that would, Alex knew, have had the waitress assume she was a member.

He took his seat and then changed his mind and stood to take off his jacket, the waitress practically tripping over herself to catch it.

He didn't smile at the waitress, Allegra noticed, nor did he thank her.

Nor did he glance over to the table of women who had fallen rather silent as he peeled off the black garment to reveal a crisp white shirt that set off his olive skin. There were no horrible surprises beneath his jacket, just a toe-curling moment as he tucked his shirt in a little, and Allegra again breathed in the scent of him, wanted another glimpse of that smile. But it had retreated now and he gave her the silence she'd insisted on and just sat and stared beyond her and out of the window, his index finger idly circling the top of the glass. Maybe it was too much champagne, or maybe he knew exactly what he was doing, maybe he had a doctorate in suggestive flirting, because for a bizarre moment she wished she were beneath his finger, wished it was her that he idly stroked.

'Sorry.' He misinterpreted her shifting in discomfort. 'I'm not much company—today has been a harder one than I expected.'

'Was it someone close?' she asked, for it was clear he had been to a funeral.

'Not really.' He thought for a moment. 'He works for me, or rather he did—Charles. We were, in fact, here last week for his retirement.' He glanced around the room clearly remembering.

'I'm sorry.'

'For what?'

'That's just what you say, isn't it,' Allegra responded, wishing he wouldn't make her cheeks burn so, wishing he didn't make her over-think every last word.

'He wasn't a friend,' Alex said, and topped up his champagne. 'Really, I hardly knew him—you don't have to be sorry.'

'Then I'm not!' She blew up her fringe with her breath, gorgeous to look at he may be, but he really was rather hard work. 'I'm not in the least sorry that you've been to a funeral and that you're feeling a bit low. Funerals do that…' she added. 'Even if you hardly know the person.'

'They don't bother me,' Alex said. 'And believe me, I've been to many.' And then he conceded. 'Well, usually they don't get to me.'

She wasn't going to risk saying sorry again.

'So what's your excuse?' He looked up from his glass. 'Or do you regularly sit nursing a bottle of champagne in the afternoon.'

She actually laughed. 'Er, no. I lost my job.' He didn't fill the silence, he didn't offer condolences as anyone else would; he just sat until it was Allegra who spoke on. 'Or rather I just walked out.'

'Can I ask why?'

She hesitated, and then gave a tight shrug. 'My boss, he…' The blush on her cheeks said it all.

'Not in your job description?' Alex said, and she was relieved that he got it. 'There are avenues for you…tribunals.'

'I don't want to go down that route,' Allegra said. 'I don't want…' She didn't finish what she was saying, not quite comfortable to reveal who her family was, so she moved on without elaborating. 'I thought I'd easily get another. It would seem I was wrong. Things really are tough out there.'

'Very tough,' Alex said, and though she had been looking at him, she flicked her eyes away, bit down a smart retort, for what would a man like him know about tough times?

'I'm very conscious of my responsibility,' Alex explained, something she had never really considered. 'If I screw up...' She felt the tension in her jaw seep out just a little. 'I employ a lot of people.' He did what for him was unusual, yet he did not hesitate; he went into his jacket and handed her his card.

'You just found another job.'

She looked at the name—Santina Financiers—and of course she knew who he was then: Alex Santina. His companies seemed to ride the wave of financial crisis with ease. He was all over the business magazines, and... She screwed up her forehead, trying to place him further, for she had read about him elsewhere, but half a bottle of Bollinger on a very empty stomach didn't aide instant recall.

She looked at the card and then back to him, to liquid brown eyes and the smile that was, frankly, dangerous. There was a confidence to him, an air of certainty—and she knew in that moment why he was so completely successful. There was an absence of fear to him; there was no other way she could describe it. 'You don't even know what I do for a living.'

His mind was constantly busy and he tried to hazard a guess. He doubted fashion—he'd seen the sensible tweed trousers that were beneath the table. And it wasn't makeup—she wasn't wearing a scrap. He could see the teeny indent at the bridge of her nose from glasses....

'Schoolteacher perhaps?' Alex mused, and he saw her pale neck lengthen as she threw her head back and laughed. 'Librarian...' She shook her head. 'Let me guess,' he said.

Was it ridiculous that he was vaguely turned on as he tried to fathom her? He looked into eyes that were very green, a rare green that took him to a place he hadn't been in ages, to long horse rides in Santina, right into the hills and the shaded woods, to the moss he would like to lie her down on. No, he wasn't just vaguely turned on; he saw the dilation of her pupils, like a black full moon rising, and maybe he knew what she did, because there was comfort there in her eyes, there was deep knowing too, and he wanted to stay there. 'Those phone lines—' he moved forward just a little '—when people don't know what to do…' He saw her blink, could feel the warmth of her knee as he brushed against it. 'They ring you?'

'No.' She didn't laugh at this suggestion, she hardly dared move, because she could feel his leg and wanted it to stay there, wanted to lean across the table and meet his mouth, but she snapped herself out of it, pulled back in her seat and ended whatever strange place he had just beckoned her to. 'I work in publishing—I'm a copy editor. Was,' she added. She wanted to signal the waitress, wanted a glass of water, hell, she'd take the jug and pour it over herself this second.

'I'm sure I could find you something….'

That really would be out of the frying pan and into the fire, Allegra thought, offering him back his card with a shake of her head. But her hand trembled slightly as it did so, because what a lovely fire it would be to burn in.

'I'll find something.'

'I'm sure you will,' Alex said. 'Keep it. You might change your mind.'

'Do you normally go around hiring your staff in bars?'

'I leave the hiring to others. If you ring that number you would only get as far as my assistant, Belinda. I can tell her to expect—'

'That won't be necessary,' Allegra interrupted. 'I'm just talking, not asking for a solution.'

'It is how my brain works,' Alex admitted. 'Problem—solve it.'

'When sometimes all you have to do is listen.'

She watched as he visibly wrestled with such a suggestion, guessed that this man was not used to sitting idly by in any situation, that he was more than used to coming up with a rapid solution. But as he took another drink and stared out to the bar where he had stood with his colleague last week, perhaps it dawned on him then that not everything came with a solution, and he gave a small nod. 'Charles had many plans for his retirement—he was talking about them last week. I guess it got me thinking.'

Allegra nodded.

'All the things you want to do,' he continued, 'intend to do…cannot do.'

'Cannot?' Allegra asked, because surely a man like Alex could do anything he wanted. He had looks that opened doors, and from his name, from the cut of his hair to the beautifully shod feet, she knew it wasn't his finances that would stop him.

'This time next year…' He was unusually pensive, not that she could know, but now, this afternoon, he felt as if time were running out. 'I'll be married.'

Allegra gave him a very wide-eyed look. 'If you're engaged then you should not be joining women in a bar and sharing a bottle of champagne with them. Shouldn't be…' She halted, not wanting to voice the word, because for a little while there they'd been flirting—not even flirting, far more than that. It had felt as if they had been kissing. She really was going now anyway; *he'd* nearly finished the bottle. And maybe it was an overreaction to leave so hastily, but there was something about him that screamed warning. Not that he was inappropriate, more the wander of her own thoughts, because his mere finger on a glass had had her mind wandering. Something about him told her he'd make it terribly, terribly easy to break very firm rules.

'Don't leave...' As she put down the note his fingers pressed over hers, wrapped them around the bill and held them a fraction. It was first contact and it was blistering; she could feel the heat from his fingers warm not just her own but race, too, to her face. 'I'm not in love...I'm betrothed.'

'There's a difference?' She smarted, though she was curious as to his unusual choice of word. She'd never heard a man, never heard anyone, describe themselves as betrothed. What *was* the difference?

'God, yes.'

Go, her mind told her, just turn around and go! Except his hand was still curled around her fingers and there was sudden torture in the dark eyes that held hers.

'I am Crown Prince Alessandro Santina.' He was too weary to dodge the facts and so rarely wanting of conversation, strangely willing to reveal his truth. 'I have been told I am to return and fulfill my duties.'

She could not have known just how many times she would replay that moment—could never have guessed how often she would look back to the very last time that she could simply have walked away.

She didn't though.

Despite herself, Allegra sat and heard the rest.

CHAPTER TWO

'SHE was chosen for me.'

She knew about arranged marriages, except she was rather surprised to hear that that might be a problem for him. He didn't look like a man who would do anything he didn't want to, and he was hardly a teenager. 'How old are you?' She said it without thinking and then winced at her own rudeness, realising he could guess at her thought process, but he gave a begrudging smile before answering.

'Thirty-three.' He even gave a half-laugh, gave her a glimpse of those beautiful white teeth, then he sighed. 'And yes, completely able to make my own decisions. It is rather more complicated though. It would seem that my party time in London is over.' He gave a shrug. 'That is how my family see it. I have, in fact, been working, extremely hard, but it's time, my parents tell me, to come back, to face duty.' He drained his glass and refilled it. 'To marry.'

'Do you love her?'

'It's not a question of love, more that we are suited. Our parents are close—it was decided long ago.' He tried to explain what he had been thinking about before she had entered the bar. 'I am happy here in London. There are many things I still wish to do with the business.'

'And you can't once you're married.'

'Once married I must assume royal duties—full-time. Produce heirs...' He saw her blink. 'I've offended—'

'Not at all,' Allegra said. 'I've just never heard it referred to as that—"producing heirs." The term's usually "have children."'

'Not when you will one day be king.'

'Oh.' She seemed to be saying that an awful lot, but really, she had no idea what else to say. It was not exactly a world she could envision.

'I am told I cannot put the official engagement off.'

'Can't you just end it?' Allegra asked. 'Just call it off?'

'For what reason?' Alex asked. 'It would shame her if I said I simply did not want to marry her. She does not deserve that.'

'Does it worry you?' How utterly he intrigued her! 'I mean, if you don't love her, are you worried about...?' She wanted him to fill in the word, but of course he did not. 'Well, I do read the magazines. I might not have known you were a prince, but I do know the name, and if I remember rightly, you do have a bit of a reputation. Does it worry you settling down?'

'Fidelity?' He was so direct, so straight to the point, that she could not help but fidget. She scratched her temple and tried to think of a better way of wording it, but settled for a nod instead, to show him that was indeed her question. 'That won't be an issue—as long as I am discreet.' She was far too expressive, because she screwed up her nose.

'You're walking into a marriage knowing you are going to be unfaithful....'

'It's a duty marriage. Anna has been chosen for she will one day make a most suitable queen. It is not about love,' he explained, but her lips were pursed. 'You don't approve?'

'No.' It had been *her* champagne, he'd chosen to join her—she had every right to be honest, every right to give her opinion if he chose to sit here. 'I don't see the point in getting married if that's how you feel.' She was speaking from the heart—Allegra actually had very firm views on this. She adored her parents, but their rather unique interpretations of marriage vows had had her crying herself to sleep so many times growing up that, on this, she would not stay silent.

'Our ways are different. I am not saying that I will...' He never discussed such things, his family never discussed such things, but there were unspoken rules and his betrothed understood them. 'I don't expect you to understand. I am just talking, not asking for a solution.'

He watched as the pout was replaced by a very reluctant smile. 'Touché,' she said, and after a brief hesitation she nodded, perhaps ready to listen without judging now.

'Our family is very much in the spotlight.'

'Believe me, that part I do understand. I know all about families and spotlights,' Allegra grumbled. And she told him—well, a little, but far more than she usually told another person. After all, if he was a prince then he had far more to lose from indiscretions than she. It actually wasn't down to half a bottle of champagne or a handful of nuts and wasabi peas; it was simply the company, sitting in their little alcove, huddled together and putting the world to rights. It was a tiny pause before they headed back out there.

'My family loves the drama. My sister Izzy was on a talent show....' He had not a clue what she meant. 'To find a pop star.'

Alex shook his head; he rarely watched television and if he did it was only to see the news. 'Why would that impact on you?'

'It's not just Izzy. My dad used to play football in the Premiere League,' she explained. 'He's like royalty here—

except…' She hesitated then looked into his eyes, saw his brief nod and knew she could go on. 'It's just one scandal after another. Last year there was an unauthorised biography published about him.' He watched the colour swoosh up her cheeks. 'It was terrible….'

'Inaccurate?'

'Yes,' she attempted then shook her head. 'No—it was pretty much all true, but you know how things can be twisted.'

'Is that why you didn't want to report your boss?'

He was way too perceptive, Allegra thought.

He was also right.

'They've had a field day with the Jacksons recently.' She told him about the scandals, about her mother, Julie, and the affair that her father had had with Lucinda, that he was now married to Chantelle, but still *friendly* with Julie. She talked about Angel, who was Chantelle's daughter, and Izzy, who belonged to both Bobby and Chantelle. Allegra even had to get out a beer mat at one point and draw a little family tree. 'The book made it all sound so grubby.' She looked down at the beer mat, saw that perhaps it was. 'It really hurt my dad—oh, he said it didn't, did his usual "any publicity is good publicity" spiel, but I know it upset him. I'm trying to put it right.'

'How?'

'I want to write an authorised one—I've started it actually. I've got loads of memories, hundreds, if not thousands, of pictures.' He saw the flare of something he recognised in her eyes—that mixture of focus and passion that met him in the mirror each morning, the commitment that meant it was killing him to walk away from his work. 'I want to set the record straight.'

'Well, you've worked in publishing so you've got the right contacts,' Alex said. 'Write it.'

She laughed, as if it were that easy. 'You've no idea how much work—'

'You don't have a job!' He smiled but she shook her head; he simply didn't get it—and why would he? It hurt too much to sit and talk about impossible dreams, so instead she asked about him.

'What about your family tree? I'm sure it's a lot less complicated than mine, a lot less scandal.'

'Actually...' He stopped then, for the most bizarre moment he had been about to tell her, about to speak about something that was completely forbidden, even within palace walls, *especially* within the palace walls—the constant rumour that his sister Sophia was possibly the result of an affair with a British architect. He looked to her green eyes staring out from beneath her heavy fringe and thought how nice it would have been to tell her, to admit as she so readily had, that his family might not be completely perfect.

'It's pretty straightforward,' he said instead.

'Lucky you.' Allegra sighed. 'I'm the boring, reliable one, of course. They won't believe that I've lost my job.' He watched her snap her eyes closed on panic. 'If I don't get a job soon I won't be able to keep up my rent and I'll end up back at Dad's and be sucked back into the vortex.' He did understand that feeling, her eyes told her that he did, for he leant over and his eyes held hers.

'That is how I feel. That is why I don't want to return just yet. I know that the moment I do...'

'I know,' Allegra said, and she spoke some more, except he was only half listening, his mind elsewhere. He looked to the table where he had sat just last week, with a man on the edge of his dreams who now lay cold in the ground, and he looked to the window and he saw the rain. He did not want to be lying there, cold with the rain and a life half lived, dreams undone. He wanted more for his business, wanted a couple more years before he returned to the fold—but how?

'Can't your brother do it?' She pulled him from his introspection and she saw him frown. 'If you don't want to be king…'

'I never said I did not want to be king,' Alex corrected. 'Just that I would like more time.' He frowned at her. 'Matteo and I have had different upbringings. Of course, were anything to happen to me, he would step in, but…' He tried to explain it, for though he never expected her to understand, today he *wanted* her to. 'You said earlier, that is how people feel at funerals…that people get upset…'

'Of course,' Allegra said. 'Everyone does.'

'No.' He shook his head. 'When I was seven my grandmother died. The funeral was massive. At the cemetery…' He did not really know why he was telling her this; he had not thought of this for years, but somehow he had to make her understand. 'Matteo was upset, my mother hushed him, then my father picked him up—I remember because it was one of the pictures in the newspaper. I started to cry,' Alex said. 'Not a lot, but a little. The coffin was going down and I could hear my brother, and…I started to cry and my father gripped my hand and then he gripped it tighter.' He took a breath. 'He was not holding my hand in comfort.'

'I'm not with you?'

'When we got back to the palace, before the guests arrived, my father took me to the study and removed his belt.' Alex wasn't saying it for sympathy; it wasn't a sob story she was being told. It was facts being delivered. 'He said he would not stop till I stopped crying.'

'You were a seven-year-old boy!' She was the one who was appalled—not Alex.

'I was a seven-year-old prince who would one day be king,' Alex explained. 'He had to teach me difficult lessons. A king does not cry, a king does not show emotion....'

'You were a child.'

'Who would one day be king,' Alessandro said again. 'And around and around the argument goes. You can despise him for it, but it was a lesson my father had to teach—which he did. He taught his firstborn son—perhaps he knew it was a tough lesson, for he gave my brother more rein at least till he was older. I have what it takes—I have been raised for this purpose.'

'I'm not surprised you want more time.' Allegra blew up her fringe. 'Before you have to go back to—'

'I could always fall in love.' His voice halted her midsentence. 'Our people know it is not a love match—Anna knows that too. Surely if I met someone and fell in love... there would be scandal, but it would blow over.'

Allegra looked to him. 'Maybe you should try talking to Anna.' She gestured to the table behind them, to the ladies that had been vying for time with him. 'Maybe she's the one...?'

That made him laugh.

'I will not fall in love.' He said it so assuredly. 'I have no time for such things. But if I *said* that I had...'

There was a flag rising, an alarm bell ringing, but they were slow and in the distance because by the time she registered them, she had already spoken on.

'Said that you had what?'

'Fallen madly in love. That love had swept me off my feet, that I had become engaged.' He indulged in a smile at the ridiculousness of the very thought. 'Of course, in a few short weeks I would come to my senses and realise I had made a mistake, that my new fiancée and I are not suited after all, or more likely the people would strongly object. But by then it would be over between Anna and me, and my family would want me here, in London, at least for a year or two, till things had settled down.'

'Well…' Suddenly her throat was dry. 'Good luck looking.' She watched as he went to top up her glass, except the bottle was empty and he summoned the waitress but Allegra shook her head. 'Not for me.' She needed space, because her mind was bordering on the ridiculous. For a moment there she'd thought he was talking about her, that they were plotting together, that this might be real.

She excused herself and fled to the safety of the ladies', told herself to calm down—except when she looked in the mirror her cheeks were flushed and her green eyes glittered in a way they never had before. Her fringe was stuck to her forehead from the rain and she blasted it under the hand dryer, then dabbed on some powder in an attempt to calm her complexion down.

Had he been suggesting that she…? Allegra halted herself there, because it was ridiculous to even entertain such a thought—yet… Who'd have thought when she stepped inside the bar, or when she had walked out of her job, that just a few hours later she'd be sharing a bottle of champagne with the Crown Prince of Santina.

She would have hid in the ladies' for a little while longer, would have straightened out her thoughts before heading back out there, but a couple of the women Alex had been avoiding came in then and didn't shoot her the most friendly of looks.

'I said that I didn't want any more champagne.' The waitress was about to open another bottle when she returned.

'Just leave it there unopened,' Alessandro said to the waitress as Allegra sat down. 'We might have something to celebrate later.'

'Not with me you won't,' Allegra said.

'We could just take it back to my—'

'I think you've very much got the wrong impression of me,' Allegra said primly, so primly she hoped he could not hazard a guess as to her suddenly wild thoughts, because she would love him to pick up that bottle, would love to dive into a taxi and be kissed all the way back to his place, to sit and drink champagne on a sheet rumpled by their lovemaking. God, but she'd had too much to drink and, mixed with this man, she was having trouble attempting rational thought. 'Half a bottle of champagne and I'm well over my limit—and I don't leave bars with men I've barely met.'

'I was joking,' Alex lied, for he *had* been hoping. 'What about my other suggestion? Do you want to be my fiancée?'

'Alex…' Allegra said. 'Why, when I didn't even want to have a drink with you, do you think I'd even entertain—'

'A million pounds.'

She laughed, because these things didn't happen, and he had to be joking. When he pulled out a chequebook, she laughed even more, because it was crazy. Except when he handed it to her, his hand was completely steady and he wasn't laughing.

'You might not have to do anything. I will fly to Santina tomorrow and tell my family and Anna. The people will be outraged. Soon enough I'll be told to reverse my foolish decision, to come back to London till the scandal dies down.'

'So what are you paying me for?'

'I can't just invent someone—you might have to join me in Santina at some point.' He anticipated her reaction, because as she opened her mouth he spoke over her. 'You would have your own suite—a couple cannot be together until they are married. All you would have to do is smile and hang on to my every word.'

'Until?'

'Until the people dictate otherwise.' He gave a shrug. 'It might be days, it might be weeks.' He looked to the cheque and so, too, did Allegra, and she thought about it—hell, she really thought about it. He wasn't asking for her to sleep with him, just to smile and hold his hand. And what she could do with the money... She could get a flat, a job—actually, she could do what she really wanted....

'You could finally write that book.' It was as if he had stepped into her mind. She heard his voice as if he was inside it, but it was madness, it couldn't work.

'We'll make it work,' he answered her unvoiced words. 'Is that a yes?' Alex asked.

She looked back at him, thought not just of the book she could write but a link to this man, this beautiful man who had entered her life, and somehow she simply wasn't quite ready to let go of him. 'I think so.'

They stepped out onto the street, and she was wrong about taxis, for a luxurious car was waiting and it took them just a few streets down.

'Shouldn't you deposit it?' Alex asked.

'Okay.' She grinned and walked into the bank and watched the eyebrow of the cashier rise a good inch. 'Funds won't be available till the cheque is cleared.'

'Ring my bank and get it cleared now,' Alex said, and she looked at the name on the cheque and did as told. There was the strangest feeling in her stomach as the cashier handed her a slip with her bank balance, a sort of great weight she hadn't been aware she'd been carrying suddenly lifted.

'Now, we shop.'

'Shop?'

'A fiancée needs a ring.'

They poured back into his car, laughed all the way along the street.

'Shouldn't I have royal jewels?' God, she was tipsy.

'You should, but…' They were outside a very smart jewelers. 'At least this you will be able to later sell. The acting starts here,' he warned as he pushed a bell and the door opened. She stood there and looked at rings as the jeweler came out, and the acting did start here, because he held her hand as he spoke with jeweler, told them what he had in mind and they were whisked away, to view jewels kept well away from the window.

'What about this?' Alex turned to his fiancée but he had lost her attention, her eyes drawn not to the diamond ring he was holding, but to another that to Allegra was far more exquisite.

'It's heavenly.' She picked it up—a brilliant emerald, so huge that it looked like a dress-up ring, but Alex shook his head.

'Should be a diamond…'

'Oh!' She put it back down, remembered her place, that this was not real; she was merely playing a part. He put his head to her ear in a supposed romantic murmur. 'Diamonds are more valuable.'

'Perhaps.'

And he saw her longing for the ring, saw the moss of Santina in the jewel of her eyes. Perhaps an emerald would be more fitting and he hesitated for just a moment. After all, what did it matter? Soon it would be done, she would be gone, so she might as well have a ring to her liking.

He slid it on her finger.

'We'll size it,' the jeweler said.

'No need,' Alex said. 'It fits perfectly.'

'I'll give it a polish and box it,' the jeweler said, but Alex's hands were still holding hers, and they looked for all the world like a young couple in love, on the edge of their future, and she felt this wash of emotion for all that was not.

'I don't want to take it off,' she admitted.

Allegra was confused and a little embarrassed to face him after he'd paid and they'd stepped outside.

'Well done,' Alex said. 'You almost had even me convinced, though that is not the ring a future queen would choose.'

'It's heavenly.'

'It's yours,' he said. 'Let's get you home.'

She gave his driver her address and of course they couldn't discuss it in the car, so as they pulled up to her little flat and presumably because he was her fiancé, he saw her to her door, or rather the entrance on the street.

'I'd rather you didn't come up…it's messy. I wasn't expecting—'

'I don't care!' He hushed her excuses.

He didn't care and Allegra knew that—not about the mess in the flat, nor the chaos he was creating. Nor, she must remember, did he actually care about her.

'What happens now?'

'You write your book.' Alex smiled. 'I'll fly to Santina in the next few days and break the news. I guess we should swap phone numbers.'

She tapped in his and when she had finished he picked up her hand and looked at the ring now on her finger. 'It's actually very beautiful.' He looked more closely and then still held her hand and looked at her, saw she was suddenly nervous, perhaps regretting what she had done. 'It really is just for a short while. Allegra, thank you.'

And she knew his kiss was coming. It was a kiss goodbye, a kiss to seal the deal, euphoria perhaps. It wasn't just his smile that was dangerous, his kiss was too.

He lowered his head down and his mouth was warm and firm and just so absolutely expert. She breathed in his scent and she felt his lips and knew in a second he would end it. It was just a kiss to seal the deal, Allegra told herself.

He moved his head back, their lips parting, and she watched as he pressed his together, as if tasting her again. He smiled down at her, just a little, a warning smile, for he indulged again, lowered that noble head to hers. And it was a kiss called euphoria, she told herself, for it was not really her he was kissing, but a glimpse of the freedom he craved. And she kissed him back, because he made her weak, because the stroke of his tongue was completely sublime. He put his hand in the small of her back as if to steady her—and thank goodness he did, for if the previous kiss could have been covered by a handshake, then this one moved completely out of bounds.

His tongue was cool and his hand was warm, and when one hand would not do to hold her, when more than gravity was needed to anchor them to earth, he kissed her all the way to the wall. This dance of lips and hands in hair, two locked mouths and the strength of a wall to hold them up as he kissed her more thoroughly than she'd ever even dreamt of.

Heavens but it was thorough, so thorough that for decency's sake it had to end. She looked up into eyes that were wicked, as if absolutely he knew what he'd do with her, all things she would never allow and it was imperative that she correct him.

'What I said before about us not…' She swallowed. 'I meant it. I don't want to give you the wrong impression.' With that kiss, she knew she just had. 'I think I've had too much champagne….'

'You're a strange mix.' His hand was still in her coat; he wanted to lift her jumper, slide his hand to her skin, but Alex was also sensible, very used to women falling in love with him. In a situation such as this one, that would never do. 'You are right,' he said, 'it might confuse things.'

CHAPTER THREE

'ALLEGRA!' She woke to the ringing of the phone and there was no time to gather her thoughts before answering. 'Allegra, it's me, Angel, what on earth's going on?'

'Hold on a moment,' Allegra said. 'Someone else is trying to get through.' She looked at the caller display, saw it was her brother Leo at the same time as she saw the ring on her finger and heard the bell that meant someone was at her door.

Oh, God!

'Angel…' She couldn't explain it to her stepsister right now—yes, they were close and they spoke about so many things, but this was more the sort of situation Angel might find herself in, not the other way around. 'I've got someone at the door. I'll have to call you back.'

Even as she put down the phone it was ringing again, her father this time.

She didn't answer it.

And she tried to ignore her doorbell, just wanted a moment to gather her thoughts. A coffee would be extremely welcome, except whoever it was must be leaning on the bell, because it was ringing incessantly now. Kids meeting up at the underground for school often pressed it for the sake of pressing it, so she hit the display button to see the camera shot…and saw the face of Alex, pale and unshaven. He looked less than happy.

Well, he could have his ring back, Allegra decided—it had been a stupid game that had got out of hand.

'It's open.' She pulled on a dressing gown and turned on the kettle, then went to the front door as she heard him rounding the top of the stairs.

Somehow he looked both beautiful and terrible at the same time—his olive skin seemed tinged grey, his eyes were bloodshot and he was still in yesterday's suit.

'Coffee!' She could hardly stand to look at him she was so embarrassed—so she turned and headed to her small kitchen. 'Before we say anything, I need coffee…and by the looks of things so do you.' Her blasted phone was ringing and unable to face it she turned it off and then spooned instant granules into mugs. 'You can have the ring back.'

'Oh, no, you don't.' There was something in his voice that sounded like a warning, almost as if he were angry, and she turned around. 'You can't just get out of this.' He held up a newspaper. 'I'm assuming you haven't read the papers or turned on the news.' Allegra went cold as she saw the photo. It was of her and Alex—him tenderly holding her hand and examining the ring that now seemed to burn her on her finger.

'At least—' she tried to stay calm, to think of a positive '—at least it wasn't a few moments later,' she said, 'when we kissed.'

'My kissing a woman would hardly be newsworthy,' Alex said, 'but that the Crown Prince of Santina has bought a woman a ring…'

'It was a mistake,' Allegra said. 'We'll say—' her mind raced for possibilities '—that we're friends, that I was simply showing you—'

'I have just spoken with Anna.' Alex chose not to go into detail; the conversation had been supremely difficult and one he did not want to examine just yet, let alone share. When Allegra asked after the other woman, Alex shook his head. 'Somehow I don't think she'd appreciate your concern.'

His words were like a slap, the implications of the one reckless day of her life starting to unravel.

'I have also spoken to my parents.'

'They've heard?'

'They were the ones that alerted me!' Alex said. 'We have aides who monitor the press and the news constantly.' Did she not understand he had been up all night dealing with this? 'I am waiting for the palace to ring—to see how we will respond.' She couldn't think, her head was spinning in so many directions and Alex's presence wasn't exactly calming—not just his tension, not just the impossible situation, but the sight of him in her kitchen, the memory of his kiss. That alone would have kept her thoughts occupied for days on end, but to have to deal with all this too, and now the doorbell was ringing and he followed her as she went to hit the display button.

'It's my dad.' She was actually a bit relieved to see him. 'He'll know what to do, how to handle—'

'I thought you hated scandal,' Alex interrupted.

'We'll just say—'

'I don't think you understand.' Again he interrupted her and there was no trace of the man she had met yesterday; instead she faced not the man but the might of Crown Prince Alessandro Santina. 'There is no question that you don't go through with this.'

'You can't force me.' She gave a nervous laugh. 'We both know that yesterday was a mistake.' She could hear the doorbell ringing. She went to press the intercom but his hand halted her, caught her by the wrist. She shot him the same look she had yesterday, the one that should warn him away, except this morning it did not work.

'You agreed to this, Allegra, the money is sitting in your account.' He looked down at the paper. 'Of course, we could tell the truth…' He gave a dismissive shrug. 'I'm sure they have photos of later.'

'It was just a kiss….'

'An expensive kiss,' Alex said. 'I wonder what the papers would make of it if they found out I bought your services yesterday.'

'You wouldn't.' She could see it now, could see the horrific headlines—she, Allegra, in the spotlight, but for shameful reasons.

'Oh, Allegra,' he said softly but without endearment. 'Absolutely I would. It's far too late to change your mind.' He drew in a long breath, and even if he wasn't prepared to share it, Anna's tearful words seemed to replay in his head. "I guess you can't argue with love." He had been right; it was the only dignified way out for them both, and to have Allegra back out now, to think of shaming Anna even further by releasing a story that implied he had bought his way out of marrying her, was unthinkable.

She could hear her father running up the stairs; he ran everywhere, was fitter than most men half his age. 'What the hell's going on, Allegra…?' Bobby's voice petered out as he realised his daughter had company. She wanted to run over to him, to tell him, to let him sort it out, except it was Alex who walked towards him.

'Mr. Jackson, I apologise that you had to find out this way.'

'It's true then?' She watched a look that could only be described as incredulous sweep over her father's face, could see him actually try to fathom that his serious, rather plain daughter had just got engaged to a prince. Somehow his shock hurt Allegra, that it might be so impossible that she might actually be desired by someone as stunning as Alex.

She felt Alex join her, his arm slip around her waist and when she couldn't speak he did. 'We were going to come and visit you this afternoon,' Alex explained. 'I was going to formally ask for your daughter's hand.' Allegra saw her father's eyes widen, saw Bobby rather taken aback by Alex's formality, but he was saved from responding as Alex's phone rang and he excused himself to take the call.

'Gawd!' Bobby pulled a face. 'He's not your usual—'

'No,' Allegra said. 'In fact, he's not remotely interested in football.' There was a distinct edge to her voice, because all too often she had found that her dates were rather more interested in impressing her father than her. 'Look—' she swallowed '—we were hoping to take things a little more slowly. It's all got a bit out of hand....'

'That's what happens when the press get hold of things.'

'I know it's a shock, Dad,' Allegra said. 'I'm sorry—'

'Sorry!' Bobby laughed. 'Why on earth would you be sorry? He's a bit straight-laced, but...' His voice trailed off as Alex came back to the room.

'I've spoken with the palace, Mr. Jackson.' He took her hand as he addressed her father. 'Given the news is already out, they think we should formally announce it. There will be an engagement party just as soon as it can be arranged.'

'A party...' Allegra felt his hand tighten around hers. *No!* she wanted to shout, and not just to halt things here. Alex had no idea what he was suggesting, no idea what her family could be like.

'A party!' Bobby's face lit up, and Allegra found she was gripping Alex's hand back. She wanted to pause things, to get not just the cat but a hundred kittens back into the bag, because Alex needed to know what he had let loose.

'I can't imagine...' Her voice was a croak and she turned

urgent eyes to Alex. 'Perhaps something smaller, we don't need to do anything grand.'

'Nonsense.' It was Bobby who answered. 'Why wouldn't you want to celebrate, Allegra? I've got loads of contacts, we can find somewhere—'

'In Santina,' Alex interrupted, and she watched her father's jaw tighten just a fraction. 'Of course, we would love to have your blessing…for your family to join us in Santina to celebrate our engagement.'

CHAPTER FOUR

'YOUR family behaved appallingly.'

Alex hissed it out of the side of his mouth as they headed back to their suites.

'Which is exactly what you wanted,' Allegra said. 'Which is exactly why you made sure there was a photographer to capture every disastrous moment. Well, I hope you're pleased.'

'Oh, I can think of many other words to describe how I'm feeling.' Alex was, in fact, conflicted—he had, to his guilty shame, hoped for a little scandal, just to prove to his family and the people of Santina how completely mismatched they were. He couldn't believe how well his parents had taken the news. His mother had burst into tears on his arrival, thrilled that her son had returned home, and his father, though never effusive, had taken him aside and told Alex he was privately relieved that his son was ready to assume more royal duties. He did not admit as such, but reading between the lines Alex wondered as to his father's health. Not for the first time since Alex had arrived in Santina, realisation was dawning that it *was* time to return and fulfill the role he was born to. But it would now be without the polished presence of Anna—a woman who understood the role, understood the people of Santina's ways.

Instead, tomorrow the papers would be filled with the Jacksons' shenanigans, for they had delivered scandal in spades, and of course it would reflect on him. His family must have thought he had gone insane. Matteo had been appalled; his best friend Hassan had outright asked him if he had completely lost his mind.

'They weren't that bad,' she attempted. Yes, her family had been shocking, but they had also been so happy for her, so genuinely delighted, unlike the royal guests, and Alex's friends—who had all sneered and frostily responded to the Jacksons' exuberance.

Guests were still milling around, spilling out from the ballroom and heading, not just for the manicured gardens but, given it was Allegra's family, no doubt to fill the palace's cornered-off rooms. Despite defending them Allegra was mortified by her family's behaviour—from the arrival of the Jacksons on the island, to their loud carry-on at the very formal party, it had exceeded her fears. Now, as the happy couple walked out, as they headed to their separate suites, as the charade neared its conclusion, suddenly Allegra felt like crying. 'Yours were no better.'

Alex actually stopped midstride and turned around. 'What on earth is that supposed to mean? My family were gracious.'

'They did nothing but look down on mine.' She struggled to keep her emotions contained, a hallway, no matter how lavish, was not the best place for this discussion and there was the photographer from *Scandal* magazine still milling around. But right now she didn't care who heard. 'Matteo hauled Izzy away from the microphone, dragged her away from her own sister's party. All she wanted to do was sing....'

'It's a royal engagement, not a drunken karaoke night! We'll talk about this later,' he said, struggling hard not to shout. But really the palace had never seen anything like it! 'For now, just…' He looked down to her strained face and decided against asking her to resume the besotted facade as she looked positively close to exploding. He simply didn't get it—after all, it was her family that had disgraced themselves. From her drunken sister taking the microphone and attempting to sing, to her father's rambling attempt at a speech. Thank goodness he wasn't actually marrying into them. 'Let's get upstairs.…'

She didn't want to go upstairs, didn't want to again be banished to her turret, to the room she'd been pacing since she'd arrived in Santina. She'd hardly seen Alex, or Alessandro as she had been told to call him now. This was practically the first time they'd been alone together and knowing her family was about to be so publicly ridiculed, that tomorrow they would be torn apart in the newspapers and magazines, she was way past acting for the cameras.

'I've never met such a frosty, uptight lot.' Allegra would not be silenced by his stare, would not accept his derisive words, even if they were merited, and it brought the sting of angry, defensive tears to her eyes. 'At least my father wished us well.'

'He was drunk,' Alex pointed out. 'He said—and forgive me if I misquote—but if I remember rightly, he was thrilled that you'd done so well for yourself.'

'At least he tried,' Allegra said.

'Tried?' Alex could not believe what he was hearing. 'He couldn't even make it back to his hotel—he's sleeping it off in a guest room! I've got a driver going over there to pack a night bag for him. And you think he tried?'

'That's my dad,' Allegra attempted, for how could she even begin to explain to this cold, arrogant man the irreverence that made her father so appealing—at least, it did back home. 'At least he didn't just peer down his nose and…' She couldn't finish; if she did she'd make a fool of herself and start crying. The whole night had been wretched. Her whole time on Santina had been wretched—almost the second they had landed he'd turned into one of them. What had happened to the man she had met in London?

'You've changed.' She said it accusingly but it just served to irritate him.

'Of course I have—here I am Crown Prince…'

Didn't she know it!

He was as cold and aloof as his father. Even tonight as she'd been presented to the king, shy, nervous—petrified, in fact—he'd barely passed comment on her transformation. Dressed in a lavish deep red gown, her hair smoothed and gleaming, still she clearly hadn't passed. She'd seen the slight sniff from his father, the disapproving looks from his family, and she could have put up with that, with just a few words of encouragement from Alex. If it had been real, if they had been in love, it would have been unbearable to be made to feel so second rate.

If they had been in love.

'Well—' she caught up as he marched off '—you got what you wanted.'

He wanted the conversation left there; he had something rather difficult to tell Allegra, a rather unexpected turn of events that she wasn't going to take too well and he certainly didn't want to say it here, didn't want to be seen in a corridor rowing—they were, after all, supposed to be in love. But her words confused him, demanded closer inspection, and maybe some of Bobby's inhibitions had rubbed off on him, maybe one night with the Jackson clan and he was starting to act like them, for he momentarily forget his station, forgot that he must always be one step removed from any conversation. Even though he had taken her wrist and started walking, Alessandro found himself stopping again.

'What do you mean by that?'

'You planned it.'

He would not row here, so instead he opened a door, any door, and went to drag her in, but he was greeted by the sight of a couple—well, the arms and legs of a couple—and they were too far gone to even notice they'd been invaded.

'Good God!' He closed the door and stood in the corridor; the palace had been turned into a seedy nightclub. As he turned, expecting to see her look of horror, he was less than amused when she rolled her eyes and gave a wry grin.

'You think that's funny?'

'At least they're enjoying themselves.'

'Doesn't it abhor you?'

'I think it's lovely.' She didn't actually, Allegra just wanted to shock him now, wanted at least some reaction. 'At least they know how to have a good time.'

He refused to be drawn. Instead, as the corridor was empty, he asked for clarification to the statement that had incensed him. 'What do you mean I planned it?' He could not believe what he was hearing. 'I'm making sure the events manager is fired in the morning! No one would plan for this!'

'You made sure there were photographers...' Allegra pointed out.

'To show that we're madly in love.' Sarcastic though his response he stopped himself, actually gave a brief shake of his head, for he was not going to be drawn.

'It was your plan to shame my family...to make sure that tomorrow there'd be no question that I wasn't suitable.'

'Your family took care of that all by themselves,' Alex said, but that knot of guilt tightened. 'Come on.' He took her hand to lead her, but she was not about to be dismissed.

At the end of the hall they would turn off, would separate, him to his royal suite, she to her guest room, and there was just too much to be said to leave things here.

'I want to talk.'

'We will talk.'

'I don't want to leave things till tomorrow.'

'We won't,' Alex said, and then, because he had no choice but to tell her, he did. 'Now that we're officially engaged we'll be sleeping together.'

'We bloody well won't!'

'Not sleeping together…' he said hurriedly, and at least managed to look a little shamefaced. 'I had an argument with my parents. I was trying to point out how archaic things are, how ridiculous it is…' He watched her face, watched her eyes widen, her mouth open to speak; he could feel her tension, like a can of fizzy drink being shaken and shaken and any moment now she would explode, just fizz out her anger all over the corridor. 'I was talking more about the chosen-bride thing,' he tried to placate her. 'This is my parents' attempt to show me they've moved into the twenty-first century. Now that we're officially engaged we can share a bed.'

'No…' Her reaction was instant, there was absolutely no question, but as she spoke he heard a noise behind him, turned and saw the *Scandal* photographer about to come into the corridor, just as Allegra exploded. 'If you even think for one moment that I'm going to share—'

He had no choice—there was but one way to silence her. He pressed his mouth to hers, but she was having none of it, and jerked her head away, her protest about to continue. So he pinned her to the wall, took her face in his hands and just pressed her right in.

And pushing him off with her rigid lips wasn't working. Alex was tall and strong, so she opened her mouth instead to shout, except he kissed her harder; his hands moved faster than hers and captured her wrists as they moved. He wedged her to the wall and she was furious. Yes, he'd paid her, but not for this!

She did not care if there was a photographer—she'd give them a shot! She wasn't Bobby Jackson's daughter for nothing; she could be as rough as she liked, and her knee went to move upwards, ready to take aim.

There was only one thing that saved him—he ceased the kiss before contact, his reflexes like lightning, and he froze her with a single word. 'Don't.'

She looked at him and for the first time since landing on this bastard of an island he actually looked back.

'Don't you dare,' he muttered.

'Well, that got a reaction,' she taunted. 'Worried about the crown jewels?' she goaded, speaking now into his ear. 'I'm surprised they're not protected.' She was aware of the cameras flashing, and somehow she did behave, didn't finish the job off and storm away from him. Instead, because she could, she stood there, because he dared not move. 'Or perhaps they are…' She gave a low laugh, her hand moving as if to check him and he gripped harder on her wrist to stop her. Not just because the camera was trained on them, not just because a Crown Prince could not be seen being groped in the corridor, but because he was rock hard.

He looked to green eyes that were spitting; he looked and he looked again. He heard his own fast breathing, and now he could feel hers, feel her breasts pressing into his chest with each rapid breath, and he was not thinking, he was just up for the challenge. He dropped her wrist because he wanted her hand instead, except she wasn't so brave now, her hand not moving to its target.

'I thought I was going to get a pat down.'

'There's a camera.'

'It doesn't take photos around corners… They can't see that side.'

'You're disgusting,' she said.

'I can be.'

He said no more, not that Allegra would have heard him anyway; her head was spinning, her ears roaring as blood gushed to her head, her face on fire as a butler opened the door to a private wing. She passed several rooms, and then double wooden doors were opened and she stepped into his bedroom. Had she had a moment to ponder, she would have realised it was perhaps the most beautiful room she had ever seen. The ceilings were high and there was intricate wooden paneling and a fragrant fire was lit to ward off the chill of the late-spring evening. The drapes and furnishings were exquisite, but she barely glanced at them. It was the vast bed that terrified her most and she was also acutely, painfully aware of the palace maids waiting. She had hoped the door would close, that she could have angry, private words with Alex, because this was so not a part of the deal, but instead she was led to a dressing room—her dressing room, it would seem—for Alex headed to another.

She stood, horribly awkward as the zipper of her dress was slid down.

'I can manage now, thank you.' She did not need someone to undress her, except the maid didn't leave. Instead, as Allegra slid out of the ball gown, the maid retrieved it and then handed her a small nightdress that certainly was not one Allegra had brought.

'I can manage now, thank you,' she said again.

'Of course,' the maid responded. 'I need the jewels.'

'Sorry?'

'For safekeeping.'

Left alone, her dress and jewels removed, she could hear

Alex undressing, telling his servant his choice of outfit for the luncheon tomorrow, clearly used to stripping off and dropping his clothes at whim, only to have someone pick up for him.

She took off her underwear and slipped on the nightdress, both nervous and furious at the thought of sharing a bed with him. She wanted her own space to curl up into bed and go over the night by herself. And yes, she wanted to recall their kiss, to relive the feel of his lips, the dizzying absolute pleasure of it even if it had just been for the camera. She wanted to recall it alone, needed a little bit of space before she could look him in the eye again, but instead she had to spend the night with him. She could hear him closer now, thanking the valet, telling them he would not be needing them at all tonight.

'Just breakfast at seven,' came his snobbish orders. 'Oh, and the newspapers, of course.'

She heard the door close and then silence, but Allegra stood there.

'Allegra?'

Still she stood there.

'It's just us now.'

Which was why she was nervous to go out there!

He did not need to know of her nerves; instead she'd show him her anger. She walked out of the dressing room, feeling completely awkward in a short lacy nightdress. Why, she hadn't worn a nightdress since she was about four years old, and certainly not one that came midthigh with tiny straps that would surely snap if she dared roll over in the night. She was rather more used to T-shirts or pyjamas for bed.

She was also more accustomed to bed and a book alone than this vast one that had Alex sitting up in it, reading through texts on his phone. Naked, at least from the waist up, he glanced up as she walked in and then went back to reading his texts. 'And I thought communal changing rooms were bad. She expected me to undress in front of her. Don't you know how to take your own clothes off? They took my dress and jewels....' Alex didn't answer. Since their time here he hadn't indulged in small talk and she'd had enough. 'This,' Allegra said in a voice that was more than a little shaky, 'was not—'

'I know that,' he cut in. 'But there's nothing we can do about it now. Don't worry,' he said. 'I'll sleep on the sofa.' Well, he would in a moment, but right now, the sight of her in that skimpy nightdress, the beauty of her as she had stepped out of the dressing room, meant that, for a couple of moments at least, the decent thing to do was stay under cover and read a garbled text from his brother as she nervously chatted on.

Allegra sat on the edge of the bed, indignant still at the maid's implication. 'As if I'm going to flee in the middle of the night with the Santina royal jewels.'

'I wouldn't put it past your father...' He gave a small laugh. 'Or Chantelle. She used to have a market stall, you said. Maybe...?' He had meant it as a joke, something to lighten the tense mood, but glancing up he saw her face screw up, and his apology was immediate. 'I'm sorry, Allegra, that was—'

'A joke—' she looked at him '—that's all my family are to you.'

'No.'

'Yes.' She closed her eyes for a second. 'That speech of Dad's...' How could she explain her father, how inappropriate he was at times, but how lovable and kind he was too? 'He's a nice person, if any your cold-fish family gave him the chance.'

'Cold!' Alex raised his eyebrows, even bristled a little,

perhaps learning that it was fine for him to insult them, but it touched a nerve when others did. 'My mother cried her eyes out when I returned—that's hardly cold.'

She wasn't going to argue about his family, and it was a waste of time and energy to sit here and defend hers.

'Your bedroom is stunning.' She looked around, because it was far, far safer than looking at him, so now she did take in the extravagance of her surroundings, the gorgeous fire crackling in the huge ornate fireplace, and her eyes drifted up to the carved ceilings and huge lights.

'It's not mine—well, clearly it now is.' She jerked her eyes to him, to where he sat on the bed, his chest gleaming, his shoulders wide and strong and chose to look away. 'It's my first night in here—I've inherited it apparently. This is actually the royal wing.' He looked to where she frowned. 'This is where the crowned ruler sleeps—though they've handed it over a little early.'

'This is your parents' room?'

He gave a mirthless laugh. 'Quarter of a century ago. Once they'd had their children they moved to separate wings. This one has been cornered off since then. They used to use it though—my mother didn't want central heating when it was installed, said that it was bad for the complexion, which is why we're bloody freezing.'

'Your parents sleep apart?'

'I shouldn't have mentioned it.'

'For when I go to the press?'

'I don't for a moment think that you shall, but if you could avoid telling your family...'

'How effortlessly you insult them,' Allegra said.

'That wasn't my intention. You're right, my family aren't exactly warm. They get on with the serious job of ruling Santina. There isn't time to be worrying about—'

'Oh, come on, Alessandro...' she was even starting to

use his real name '…surely you make time, surely when
those gorgeous wooden doors close…' She didn't continue; there really was no point, for were she queen, were
Alessandro her king, no matter how hard the day, no matter
the weight of responsibility… It was pointless considering
it, pointless because tomorrow morning the press would
baying for her to leave.

'They have better things to worry about than keeping
the romance alive.' He rolled his eyes at the very thought
and turned his thoughts to the morning when the people's
verdict would come in—undoubtedly demanding he re-
nounce his right to the throne if he insisted on taking such
an unsuitable bride.

And she was most unsuitable, Alessandro reminded
himself.

He had paid her to be her unsuitable self after all.

Even in the finest gown, she had looked all wrong in the
heavy red dress. He had rather preferred her in those shape-
less tweed trousers she had had on when they'd met—not
corseted and quaffed, all her curves hidden and held in.
But now she sat on his bed, her heavy fringe to one side,
her dark curls a little wild now they had been let down, and
without all the jewels at her throat, without the confines of
the dress, her body was so alluring, so feminine beneath
that skimpy gown. She was slender, yet soft; he could see
dimples on her thigh that, were this a true romance, the paparazzi would later persecute her for. Her breasts through
the skimpy nightdress were larger than he'd imagined. And
yes, more than once in these past weeks, to his own annoyance, he'd imagined them—just not to this delicious detail,
for her nipples seemed constrained beneath the lace, as if
attempting a breakout. Just as it had seemed safe to climb
out of the bed, it became terribly unsafe again.

'I thought you were going on the sofa.' She was sick of

this, she was tired too—and the bed was huge, about the size of five of her own, so she peeled back the sheet and climbed in. 'I guess we can just treat it like a school camp. You don't get to choose who you share with.' She looked over to him. 'I suppose you didn't go on school camp.'

He didn't answer, having returned to his texts, and it was Allegra who pulled out her phone and plugged in an earpiece.

'What are you doing?'

'Well, conversation isn't exactly forthcoming, so I might as well go to sleep. I like to listen to music to fall asleep,' Allegra said, because as tired as she was, there wasn't a hope of her falling asleep unaided with Alex in the room. 'Well, not music exactly—' she was a little nervous, for still he was in the bed '—more the sounds of nature.' He gave her an extremely quizzical look, so she elaborated. 'I listen to the sound of the ocean, it relaxes me.' She gave a little laugh. 'At least till the recording stops.'

'You could just open the window,' Alex said. 'Ah, but you're a Londoner.' Because things had calmed down somewhat he climbed out of bed, and even if he was feeling a touch more appropriate, suddenly Allegra wasn't. His black silk pyjama bottoms rested on his hips and accentuated the length of his legs, and though he had looked beautiful tonight, he was beyond that now, his back gleaming, muscles teasing as he walked across the room and flung open the French windows. She was terribly grateful for the blast of cool air that swept the room, for her face was burning—grateful, too, for the roar of the ocean, for it must surely drown out the sound of her heart that was hammering in her chest.

'The real thing is always better,' Alex said.

The real thing was standing before her now, the absolute dream, the man, the life she could only briefly glimpse, but how she wanted it to be real, for she could still taste his kiss, still and forever would remember the bliss of being held by him. And now he stood, utterly relaxed, maybe even a little bored, as she tried to steady herself on the vast bed. All tonight had done was accentuate how utterly different they were, the gulf between their backgrounds, how impossible this match was—and it would be proven tomorrow, had perhaps been proven already, for, as Alex had pointed out, many of *her* guests had been snapping away on their phones. No doubt the scandalous Jacksons were a trending topic on Twitter! They lived in two different worlds, but for tonight at least they met in this room.

He collected a throw rug and tossed a few cushions to one side of the sofa. When his temporary bed was made, he gave her forewarning.

'I've set my alarm for six-forty,' Alex said. 'They come in at seven, so don't get the fright of your life when I climb in. We don't want to disappoint the maids.' He tried to make a joke of it, but how the hell was she supposed to sleep with this glorious specimen of a man in the room? A man who had kissed her, a man her mind wanted to dream of…? How was she supposed to rest knowing that in—she glanced at the clock—just over four hours he would be climbing in beside her? ''Night then.' She leant over to the night light, her finger on the switch as Alex was about to lie back on the sofa.

'Goodnight, Allegra.'

She was leaning over to turn off the light and just as she had silently predicted, but earlier than even her imagination had allowed for, the delicate strap on her nightdress snapped, one heavy breast escaping. Mortified, she did not look up—hoped, just hoped, he wasn't watching. Somehow she turned off the light, mumbled a goodnight and dived under the sheets, listening to the waves, to the

soothing relentless ocean, desperately trying not to think
of the man in the room.

The man in the room who could not sleep either.

His last image before being plunged into darkness was
of a very soft breast, just sort of dropping, just falling,
and he had wanted to hurtle over to the bed, like some
American baseball game, hurtle across the space and capture it in his hand.

How the hell was he supposed to sleep after that?

CHAPTER FIVE

'YOUR Highness…' The butler was appalled, stunned, that as he served the queen her early-morning tea on her al-fresco terrace, just as he did each morning, a jogger was making his way through the queen's private gardens.

'I'll call security now, come inside….'

'It's fine.' The queen was not perturbed; instead she was vaguely amused by the break to her routine, and somewhat confused when she realised who it was jogging their way across the manicured lawn. Shouldn't he be in bed nursing the most appalling hangover?

'It's Mr. Jackson,' Zoe explained to her anxious butler. 'He mustn't have realised that this area is private.'

'I'll tell him now.' The butler went to do that, went to raise his arm to the man, but the queen always remembered her manners and if she recalled rightly, because he had been in no fit state to make it to the hotel, Bobby had become a last-minute guest of the palace and would be treated as such.

'Mr. Jackson,' she called, except he didn't seem to hear her. 'Bobby…' How strange that name felt on her lips, but she called it and he turned and gave her a very cheery wave and she gave a rather more tentative one back, a little taken aback when he jogged his way over.

'Morning, Zoe!' He'd called her Zoe, and he must have

realised his mistake, for quickly he moved to correct it. 'Oh, sorry, I mean…'

'Zoe's fine—' she smiled '—at least when it's just us, but when there are others around…'

'I'll remember that.' He gave her a very nice smile; in fact, she wasn't quite sure, but did Bobby Jackson just wink? Suddenly the queen was acutely aware that she was dressed in her nightdress, albeit with a heavy silk dressing gown on top. Still, he was wearing very little too—shorts and a vest, really—but the queen had far too many manners to even blink.

'Would you like to join me for some tea?'

Bobby didn't hesitate; after all, he was incredibly thirsty! 'I'd love to.'

He glanced over her shoulder, perhaps expecting the king to appear. 'Out walking, is he?'

'I'm not sure,' she answered, and Zoe, unusually, found herself flushing a little—a touch embarrassed that it was perhaps obvious she slept alone. Bobby frowned and then she was suddenly terribly aware of her attire, because the frown and the look he gave her were more akin to disbelief than pity, more a look that Zoe was terribly, terribly unused to. Oh, there was nothing improper—well, not really; his frown seemed to say he had no idea why the king would leave her alone, and it brought a fire to her cheeks and a slight shake to her hand as she sipped her tea while the butler brought over another cup.

'Did you enjoy last night?' Zoe enquired.

'I can't remember it yet,' Bobby answered, and he started to laugh. After a brief moment Zoe found herself laughing too, though it faded when he continued. 'I don't think my speech went down too well. I didn't even get to finish….'

'We're not really used to impromptu speeches.'

'You wait till you come to ours,' Bobby said, and then he glanced up. 'I'm sorry—' he blew out a breath '—it's a bit awkward, isn't it? I mean, you try to get on with the in-laws, but...' He grinned at the thought of Her Majesty in his mock-Tudor home. 'We'll work it out.'

'I'm sure we shall,' the queen said, though privately she doubted the wedding would even happen. She had seen the stars in Allegra's eyes, but whether it was parental instinct or just years living a life void of emotion, something told her that there was more to this engagement than even Bobby knew—maybe Allegra even—for her son was not one to be guided by his heart. There was more going on and she knew it. Still, sipping tea that morning was bizarrely the high point of the party for Zoe—Bobby Jackson was perceptive and funny and really quite charming, and at times surprisingly pensive too.

'Allegra gets on with her stepmother?' The queen had approached the complicated subject of Allegra's rather extended family.

'She does.'

'And you still get on with your first wife?' Zoe's voice was just a little strained; perhaps she was being impolite asking, but it just intrigued her so, that a man could bring his current wife and his ex-wife to a party, and from the way Bobby behaved with Julie, well, she was quite sure they were still lovers.

'Julie's golden.'

'I see.' Zoe frowned. 'And the other boy...' She blushed because she was fishing, but she'd seen him with Anna, and it was such bliss to gossip. It had been so very long since she had. 'Leonard?'

'You mean Leo,' Bobby corrected. 'The one making eyes at your son's ex?'

The queen hardly recognised the sound of her own

laughter. 'A man that takes notice! So…' She had long ago waved away the butler and it was Zoe that poured more tea. 'Leo's from your first marriage?'

'Er, no…' She heard his cup rattle as he replaced it in the saucer. 'His mother's name was Lucinda—she was a lover of mine.'

'Oh.'

'She's passed away,' Bobby explained. 'Leo's been with me ever since. It took me a while to come to terms with it—I mean, I said that he wasn't mine. She never disputed it, so I assumed I was right. It turns out that she did a DNA test. I should have been there for Leo….'

'Aren't you cross that Lucinda never told you?'

'I admired her for it,' Bobby said, and he looked to the queen. 'There's something about a woman who can keep her silence, something rare about such a woman.' And he was a touch awkward then, remembering suddenly the rumors he had read when finding out a little more about Allegra's fiancé. But the memory actually helped, for he wasn't awkward any more. He looked at the queen and thought there might be a teeny flash of tears in her eyes, and he looked again, for she really was a very beautiful woman. But there was such a sadness to her and, queen or not, Bobby knew how to talk to women. 'I regret a lot of things, but I can't regret how my son was raised—she did a wonderful job. I've made my share of mistakes, but I guess we all do.'

'You can't when you're a queen.'

'You're a woman first.'

'Oh, no.' She shook her head, but Bobby didn't leave it.

'Well, you look like a woman to me. Whole lot of trouble, all of you!' He saw her pale smile. 'Anyway, guilt causes more problems and solves none of them. I need to be a parent to him, not try to be his friend. Like I said, we all make mistakes—'

'We do. Indeed,' Zoe broke in, and they shared a small smile.

'Not Allegra though,' Bobby said. 'If that's what's worrying you. From when she was a little girl I used to say to Julie, that girl was born to be a mum! You should see her with her brothers and sisters. She doesn't seek the limelight, our Allegra, doesn't go looking for drama. She's a great girl, more sensible than the lot of us put together—your son's going to be a very happy man. Anyway...' Bobby stood. 'It's been a pleasure to get to know you a little better, Zoe. I'm looking forward to spending more time with you and your family.'

He was rough, he was crass, but he was completely and utterly charming, and Zoe could see why his women forgave him. Absolutely she could see why his country adored him.

She'd never hinted, not to a soul, that she was anything less than perfect, that mistakes might even be made, yet somehow this morning...

She felt liberated.

She liked the Jacksons' energy that was in the palace.

She liked Allegra too.

She looked at the papers and picked up her tea, her hand shaking a little as she read of the people's reaction to the union, the in-depth pieces, the endless photos and the headlines that screamed, and wondered how the young couple would deal with this morning's news.

The queen often meddled, at least where her children were concerned, and leaving her quarters she crossed the palace, heading to the kitchen, meeting a maid at the lifts.

'You know we have several extra guests this morning.' She gave a reason as to why she was there. 'Where are these going?'

'For Prince Alessandro,' the more senior maid informed her. There were two of them to take up the huge trolley, laden with coffees and pastries and the newspapers; the butler would of course take it in. 'He asked for breakfast at seven.'

'Leave Prince Alessandro.'

'He asked to be woken at seven.' The maid was nervous, but used to this, for often the queen interfered.

'Give him an hour.' The queen smiled, because if she was right, then just about now, Alessandro would be crawling into bed—and if she was wrong, oh, well! 'They did not get to bed till late. If there are any repercussions, just say it was on my orders.'

She watched as the maids wheeled the trolley back towards the kitchen and went back to her quarters and sat down, picked up her set of the newspapers and carried on reading.

Alessandro and Allegra surely needed that hour together, before they had to face this.

Allegra did sleep, not much, certainly not enough to prepare for the wretched day ahead and the barrage of press and demands from his family, but she did sleep a little, listening to the ocean, seeing the shadows of the fire dance across the room. Then she heard a few bleeps of his alarm and then nothing, for Alex did not seem to awaken. She wondered if she should tell him, remind him perhaps, for any minute the servant would be in, but she lay there in silence instead, holding her breath when finally he moved. He closed the windows, for the room was freezing, and stared at the bed where she lay on her side.

He was stiff and cold, a throw rug not really up to a

draughty palace in spring, and neither his long frame nor his status were used to roughing it on a sofa.

Still it was not that which had him irritated, more a night spent trying not to picture her breast, and that body, and when he did close his eyes…

He padded across the room in the dawn light, pulled back the sheet and climbed in. The bed was cold and he lay there a moment. He heard her stir a little, knew that she was awake, and he said what had been on his mind all night. 'I'm sorry, Allegra.'

'It's just for a few minutes.'

'I meant for everything. I know how hard these weeks have been. I know it's not a life that you're used to.'

'It would have helped to have seen you a bit more,' Allegra said, 'and I'm not being needy. But—'

'I know you're not. It's the way it is here—I've had a lot of duties to attend to, as well as trying to keep up with things at work.'

'I can't even go out without an escort. What do they think's going to happen?'

'The people might recognise…' He started with the familiar line, the one his father had drummed into him all these years, except he was older now, could see things more clearly. 'The royals used to be more accessible, there was more freedom, but it does not work.'

She turned over to face him. There was a guardedness in his voice and she wanted to know more, to understand better, but he said no more; it was clearly a closed subject.

'I couldn't live like this.'

Alex was silent.

'I couldn't.'

'Most women would be—'

'I'm not most women,' Allegra said.

'No,' he admitted, 'you're not.'

She turned back from him then, wished she hadn't seen his face on the pillow beside her, for it danced now in front of her closed eyes, a vision she would always remember. Because though she could never live like this, there was a part of her that wanted it to be real, that wanted Prince Alessandro who lay beside her to be her real fiancé, a woman who wanted the dream…

…who wanted him.

He looked at the clock and saw it was almost seven and it would look strange, surely, for two newly engaged people to be sleeping so far apart on the bed.

'Sorry about this.' He moved over, not sorry at all; his feet were freezing and he heard her breath catch as they slipped in between her calves. Her side of the bed was so warm, and for appearances' sake, for his own sake, but not for decency's sake, he moved his body in.

He was male, used to waking next to a woman, not used, though, to a night spent frustrated and alone—so many nights recently, in fact. It was hell being back at the palace—especially as a newly engaged man—and the feel of her next to him, the scent of Allegra and the warmth of a woman, well, it was good. 'You're warm.' He wrapped his arm around her.

'You're freezing.' His foot moved against her calf and she didn't halt him. His long arm slid between hers, his hand looking for a place to settle and she did not move away when it found a home just a whisper away from her breast.

'Did you get some work done?' He had, to his credit, always asked about how her book was going. 'Did you ask your brother about his mother, Lucinda?'

'I didn't really get a chance to talk to him. You should do your family history.'

'It is all documented already.'

'The real version though,' Allegra whispered. 'There are surely things only you know, things only your sisters or brother know. Your parents—'

'Just leave it, Allegra.' She hadn't been prying, she'd just been talking, but feeling him tense, Allegra realised she had stepped on a raw nerve. It was none of her business, of course; she was paid to be his fiancée after all. But more and more she wanted to know him, wanted to understand the workings of this remote family, wanted more of his life. Except there was no more talking and she wondered if he had gone to sleep.

There was something about morning, something special about lying there, waiting for the maids, something a little sad, because here, this very morning, it all came to an end.

Today, she would hear in detail just how very unsuitable she was, which was the plan, of course. It just hurt, more than she had expected it to—and she knew she had to hold on to her heart here. But for a moment, at least, it was nice to pretend that it was real, that Crown Prince Alessandro really did love her, that her family's behavior didn't matter to him a jot—that the man lying beside her, whose ring she wore on her finger, did not deem her such an unsuitable bride. It was a dangerous flight of fancy, and as his hand moved to her breast, as his palm caressed what he had been thinking about for hours, she really ought to push him away, except it was nice to suspend, nice to feel something, safe in the knowledge they were acting, that really it could go nowhere. For any minute now the doors would open, any minute now they would be sitting up, sipping coffee, reading papers, and then the maid would be back to dress her.

She tried to the think of the morning ahead, of the rows that would ensue, of the plane flight home and that soon she would be away from the palace, free from the lie, ready to resume her life, except his palm was on her breast, and his thumb was stroking her nipple and it was nicer to just live in the now. His cold feet moved a little, just a little higher and made her catch her breath again, for they really were cold, and he was idly stroking her naked breast with his hand. No doubt it was just sheer habit, no doubt he was already back to sleep, and just idly fondling whatever was available to him this morning,

But goodness, it felt nice.

'Alex.' She moved his hand away; it was relaxed and he did not answer her.

Asleep she decided, suddenly cross, because what was so effortless and natural and inconsequential to him was having the most dizzying effect on her; even the weight of his hand on her stomach, the weight of him so close, had her wishing she had not interrupted him.

And in sleep he must have felt the same, for his hand wandered back to her breast and his body awoke behind her, and he moved just a little more in.

He was not asleep, but more rested now than he had been all night.

He was loving this side to Allegra, the warmth of her body in the bed, the surprising softness of it, for yes, she was slender, but there was a ripe softness to her and a very unspoiled scent, just a natural fragrance he was unused to.

'Alex.' Again her hand went to move his, except instead it captured his. She did not want an accidental encounter; she had more pride than that at least. 'Someone will be in soon.'

'They'll knock.' She knew then that he was awake, but it was easy for him, so natural for him. Just for a moment she let herself glimpse it, that this was their bed, that the lips near her ear, that the hand on her breast, were just where they should be, that this moment was theirs.

'Wouldn't they expect us to be kissing?' Alex asked, for her kisses had always surprised him, kisses that seemed to unbend her, and now, this morning, his body craved her mouth.

Though she lay so still, her mind wrestled, for she wanted him so, wanted his kiss, wanted a little of what she could never really have.

'Perhaps!'

He turned her to face him. His mouth did not claim hers; instead for a moment they just stared and it was as if they were saying farewell. Allegra felt a sting behind her eyes.

'I make a terrible fiancée.'

'You'd be a wonderful fiancée,' Alessandro said. 'If I wasn't a royal.' He brushed her fringe out of her eyes and he kissed her forehead, easily the most tender thing he had done to date. But more than that, he kissed it again, and then he kissed her eyes, kissed the salty damp lashes and tried to explain, without rowing, just how impossible it was. 'Having you here has been like a breath of air.'

'I've hardly seen you,' Allegra said.

'Which is how it would be...' He looked over to her on his pillow. 'You've been wonderful.' He settled for this instead and she knew that this really was goodbye. His mouth moved to where her lips were waiting, and he kissed them thoroughly, one ear on the door. But then the door was forgotten because of how lovely and warm and how deep was this kiss, how nice the feel of his leg wrapping around hers and hooking her in; he kissed her till her body was more awake than it ever had been, kissed her till their lips were so wet and her fingers knotted in the back of his head.

'Someone...' she reminded again, and his head lowered as he took to his mouth the nipple he had dreamt of all night. It tasted as sweet as he had imagined and for Allegra it felt sublime, especially as he moved his mouth away and then blew, and then kissed and teased her nipple again, as he caressed it with lips that were soft now and tender. He took it deep in his mouth again, and she could feel the scratch of his unshaved chin on her tender flesh.

'Someone might....' she attempted.

'But they would knock,' Alex reasoned, and he tasted her some more. His hands moved around her waist and then played with her bottom, lifted up the nightdress, slid it over her hips, and his fingers pressed into bare flesh. He heard her breath in her throat and he sucked harder; he felt her so warm and aroused in his arms and he willed the door not to open for just a few more precious moments, especially as her hands roamed his torso, as he felt wary fingers slowly work their way down.

She knew they would be interrupted, actually hoped it might be Alex who would remind her of that, that he would halt her hands and stop this nonsense. Instead he moaned as her hand slid into black silk pyjamas and freed him.

Please knock, she thought as he left her breast, as he slid her up the bed and faced her in the darkness while she still held him in her hands. She did not know what to do now, so she felt instead, ran her fingers down the delicious length of him, stroked, so gently, from the tip to the silken hairs at the base and back again.

The bed was not moving, really they were doing nothing, Allegra told herself. If the door opened now, they could release and just close their eyes, pretend to be asleep.

'I think we've been forgotten,' Alessandro said, for once delighted by inefficiency. 'They must be busy this morning....' He ran a hand along his fiancée's thigh and kissed her on the mouth. He succumbed to her tentative exploration, only just hearing a noise in the corridor outside. Allegra heard it too, for she released him, rolled over onto her side and closed her eyes, ready to pretend to be asleep, except her heart was hammering, her body in full arousal.

She was more than a little shocked at the turn of events, almost willing the door to open, so she could get on with her paid duty, not succumb to the bliss of him. For how nearly she had, Allegra thought, screwing her eyes closed tighter, surprised by her own inhibitions. They waited, waited for the door to open, except there were no further noises, no one outside now, and in silence they lay still.

'We can't,' she said as a warm hand slid around her waist. 'They'll be here any moment.'

'I know,' Alessandro said, but he did move in just a little closer, his erection nudging between her legs, his hand snaking to the front of her, down her stomach to a place that was warm. His exploration was not as tentative as Allegra's; he moved slowly but deliberately down, and long fingers so easily found the magic button that had her pushing herself backwards just a little to him, had her parting her legs. When his mouth kissed her shoulder he slipped his erection deeper between her thighs, nudged his way like a homing device to her entrance, and she felt her throat tighten.

Alex never lost his head, ever.

Except, as he lay in the bed, in the bed of a king, with Allegra beside him, for a little while he did lose his head. Centuries of history, perhaps, created a loud whisper that drowned out common sense, for he smelt the pine from last night's fire and the creak of the wood that lined the walls. He felt the nightdress bunched around her waist move against his stomach, her bottom pressed to him. She was so damp beneath his fingers, he wouldn't last a moment once inside; Alex acknowledged that rare fact, for normally he could go for ages. But there wasn't a hope this morning, so he gave her more urgent attention instead, his fingers more insistent, and when she came, when he brought her to that place, he would enter and join her.

'We can't...' Her words were contrary, for her body was on fire in his hands.

'They'll knock.' He didn't care if the whole of Santina walked in on them. In that moment he did not care. He could feel the tremble in her, the tension in the thighs that clamped on his erection and on fingers that were still working. He was as close as she was and he wanted to be inside her. He guided himself to her entrance, moved his face over hers and felt the heat from her cheeks as she spun her head around to him and he suckled her tongue in hungry possession.

She could feel the press of him, the nudge of him, and she wanted him inside her, wanted to scream. She had to tell him to stop, except she was gasping as his fingers brought her close now to heaven, and she felt him press at her entrance. She really had to tell him, her voice breathless when it came, her hips arching away from his hand that was pressing her back to him.

'Alex, no...'

He was aware of three things.

In one second, there were three things.

The word *no*, when she was so wet and oiled there surely should only be a plea; the knock on his door that told him their privacy was about to be invaded; anger, too, for the games she was playing, for the kisses that ended, for the glimpse, for the taste...

...for the tease.

CHAPTER SIX

'I ASKED for breakfast at seven.' He sat up in the bed and lifted one knee to hide the obvious as Allegra lay there, eyes closed, wishing she *was* asleep, wishing as clearly as Alex did that the breakfast *had* been on time, that the last hour had not happened. She heard the harshness of his tone, and knew it had nothing to do with the late breakfast.

'I apologise, Prince Alessandro. The queen said—'

'The queen stopped dictating the time I eat my meals many years ago,' Alex snapped.

'Of course, Your Highness.' His butler bowed. 'Will there be anything else?'

'Nothing,' he snapped. 'I am not to be disturbed.'

He hardly waited for the door to be closed, too used to servants, too ready for confrontation, to attempt patience.

'Talk about lousy timing, Allegra.'

'I assume we're not talking about the door?' He wasn't in the mood for even a vague stab of humour. 'Look…'

'Have you any idea how…?' He was having great trouble keeping from shouting. 'It's a bit late sometimes to change your mind.'

'I know that.'

'Some men…'

'I know!' Her voice was shrill, her cheeks on fire. She simply couldn't tell him her truth, that he'd been about to find out she was a virgin, that there had been no *other men*, that though she had wanted him terribly, she had been scared it might hurt. She put her face in her hands for a moment; she understood he was cross, for she was cross with herself too. She was the last person to lead a man on; it was just with Alex it was so very easy to lead and to follow and then to lead some more, to lead and be led until completely lost, to return hungry kisses, to listen to her body and not her mind. No, she couldn't land all that on him, couldn't tell him he was the only man she'd burnt for, the man who would live for ever now in her dreams. Instead she offered a more sensible reason, which was obvious now—except it hadn't been then. In fact, the thought hadn't entered her head at the time, but she said it now as if it had.

'We weren't using protection.'

He closed his eyes for a brief moment and drew in a deep breath.

'It would complicate things rather, a little Prince Alessandro, Junior...' Allegra warmed to her rapidly chosen subject.

'You're not on the pill?'

'No, I'm not on the bloody pill. I'm not seeing anyone, and I'm certainly not going on it just in case...' She looked over to him. 'Have you heard the one about the prince who walks into a bar...?'

'Ha, ha!' He did not approve of her London humour.

'Anyway—' Allegra smarted, far safer up on her high horse '—it's not just for pregnancy.'

'I don't need a lecture on safe sex,' he hissed.

'Actually, Alex, I'd suggest that you do.' How lovely it was up here, she thought, how lovely to have been so embarrassed, but to now be peering down from a higher moral ground. But it was as if he reached out and jerked her down from there, brought her right back to his bed with a flash of his eyes; she could see the concern in them, felt a little guilty that the rapid excuse she had come up with should provoke such a response.

'I apologise…' He swore under his breath in Italian, and raked a hand through his hair. He moved to the side and sat on the edge of the bed, his head in his hands. 'I always, without exception, have been careful. You have nothing to worry about there.'

'It's fine.' She wanted to reach out and touch his shoulder, could see lines where her nails must have dug in, could scarcely believe the wanton woman he had made her, but the touch to his shoulder was a kinder one. 'Alex…'

He turned his head and she saw that he was beautiful—he was a man who could have not just her body but also her heart in an instant, and she could not let him take all the blame.

She felt his skin beneath her fingers and there was arousal still hovering in the room like a rare mist awaiting its beckon to descend. If she pressed her fingers down just the merest fraction harder, she could blink and it would be summoned. 'I don't know how much of me I can give,' she admitted. 'Just to have it handed back…'

He paused before he gave her a nod that said he understood.

'We have to be affectionate in company…' Her voice faltered. 'We have to pretend we're in love, we have to share a bed…and any minute now, when your family have decided I'm too much trouble, or when the people dictate, I'm going to be sent back. There's only so much I can give in the meantime.'

She stretched over him and selected a paper, leant back on her pillows as he did the same. She braced herself for the usual scandal when the Jacksons hit the headlines—

except she sat speechless as she read the headline, holding her breath, worried to turn her head and see his reaction as he selected a newspaper of his own.

Bravo, Allegra!

Alex put the paper down and took another.

Will the People's Princess Give the Prodigal Prince a Reason to Stay?

And the headlines were shocking, utterly and completely shocking—just not in the way he had predicted.

'What does *Bella Sposa* mean?' Allegra asked.

'Beautiful Bride.' He cleared his throat as he skim-read the articles. 'This one says that the people of Santina await the wedding with deep joy. They love you. I can see that. They think you are the answer to the monarchy's problems, the breath of fresh air the people want....' He swallowed. 'I did not even know that the people were so unhappy.'

He read on: 'Apparently a wedding is what Santina needs....' He was visibly appalled at the prospect. He balled the paper in his fist, scrunching it up, and she felt as if he were squeezing her heart, for his reaction told how her appalled he was at the very idea.

'Us!' He looked at Allegra, a woman who talked about *feelings* and what life could be like behind closed palace doors, a woman who straight up had told him she believed in fidelity, a woman who had said, only moments ago, that she could not live like this. She had no idea how it would be! If she thought this was impossible, then how could she even begin to deal with the road ahead if she were groomed to one day be queen?

He cursed again, stood and paced the room—for he had not just put Allegra in an impossible situation, he had failed the people of Santina too. Not necessarily today, but in the future. He glimpsed it then, the palace ricocheting from one scandal to another, from one headline to another, and he could not put them through this.

'This was not how it was supposed to be—can you imagine?'

She found her voice, right there beneath the shame his reaction had triggered, right there behind the sting of tears in her eyes, and she hauled it to the surface.

'No!' She sounded as if she meant it. Hell, she meant it as he flung the paper across the room. 'We agreed to a few days, a couple of weeks—it's already been far longer than that.'

'I will sort it.' Alex wasn't waiting for the butler; he was pulling on clothes and dressing in haste. 'Right now, right this very morning, I will sort out this mess.'

She jumped at the slam of the door and then stared at the papers that were scattered across the bed, looked at the pictures of them. One especially drew her attention: the happy couple arriving in the huge ballroom, Alex looking down at her. She remembered his words of reassurance, the small squeeze to her waist, and something she must have said in response had produced his rare smile—the same smile that had enthralled her the day they had met. And clearly, it had enthralled her last night, her rapt expression was there for all to see, her eyes sparkling as brightly as the huge chandelier that glittered above them. In that moment Allegro knew the real reason she was here, why she had agreed to the charade, why she had found it impossible to walk away.

Why she climbed out of bed to get dressed herself, for now that the initial shock was wearing off, now that the people's verdict was sinking in, she wanted to speak with Alex before he spoke with the king.

She wanted to speak with her fiancé.

* * *

The king considered it a done deal.

'We need to set a wedding date.' He was pacing, distracted, when Alex came into his study. 'I want you to speak with Antonio, to go through our schedules....'

'We're nowhere near ready to be speaking of dates,' Alex said. 'Allegra needs time to get used to things, to really see if this is the life for her.'

'It became her life when you put that ring on her finger,' the king said. 'It became her life when you ended things with Anna. It's not open for discussion any more. I've got enough on my mind without pandering to your fiancée— Prince Rodriguez is arriving tomorrow to meet Sophia.'

'So?'

'Your sister has disappeared and now I cannot get through to Matteo either.' He looked to his son. 'Last I saw him was with that Jackson girl, the one who was singing—'

'Izzy,' Alessandro said.

'The palace is in a shambles. We need to give the press something to distract them. As soon as they hear the wedding date, that is all they will talk about.'

'I am not giving a date just to appease—'

'You are engaged!' The king swung around. 'Under the circumstances you should be grateful the news has been so well received by the people. Now, I think sooner is better.'

'There will be no announcement till I have discussed things with Allegra.'

'Why would you need to discuss things with her?'

Alex gritted his teeth. 'Because it is the twenty-first century.' He gave a grim smile as his mother joined them.

'The people are delighted.' She greeted him warmly. 'You must be thrilled.'

'Allegra's feeling a bit overwhelmed,' Alex attempted. 'I think last night gave her a glimpse into how it might be and she's not sure that's she's suited.'

'Then ensure that she is,' the king snapped. 'Can she lose that accent?' he said. 'Preferably by lunchtime.'

'It's not just her accent,' Alex said. 'You've seen her family. Her father—'

'I had tea with Mr. Jackson this morning.' The queen smiled. 'He's actually rather charming.'

Alex was tired of flogging the 'it's clear she's totally unsuitable for this life' angle. 'It's not just Allegra feeling it—it was a mistake. Last night has shown me that. I'm taking her back to London.'

'Running away again! Shirking your responsibilities!' The king was not about to let this happen.

'Hardly. I run a multibillion—'

'Don't try to impress me with figures. They do not come close to Santina's worth. This is your duty, and you will not shirk it a moment longer.' He was harsh, but he knew his son was needed, knew what a wonderful ruler he would make. And there was an element of truth in the papers—the royal family wasn't as beloved as it had been. The king knew that and he wanted his son to step in and help, but he could never admit that. 'It's too late to change your mind. You wanted the engagement, you chose this path. Now you either make a date for the wedding and live here in Santina with your bride or you leave and go back to London.'

'Fine.' It was actually far easier than Alessandro had thought. They would leave this afternoon; he'd stay in London till things had calmed down. Alex turned, ready to head back to Allegra, to tell her the news—except his father hadn't quite finished yet. He wanted Alessandro here.

'I am not subjecting the people of Santina to two broken engagements from their heir.'

'Meaning?'

'We had two sons for a reason.' Alex glanced to his

mother, saw the humiliation scald her cheeks, for that was how his father spoke at times. He might love his daughters but bitter had been his disappointment that they had not been sons. 'If you end things with your fiancée, I insist you step aside.'

'I will never step aside!' He had certainly not anticipated this outcome. In that bar, with Allegra, he had been certain, absolutely certain, that his father would demand that they part, that if they insisted on going ahead with the marriage, then he would have to step down. He had promised this to Allegra and now he had been outmaneuvered, and he had to go back up there and tell her. But first he would try to dissuade his father. 'How can I marry her?'

'You should have thought of that when you asked her!'

'It was different in London,' Alex said. 'I see now that here she doesn't fit in. I don't love her....'

'Thank goodness for that,' the king said. 'You can keep your mind on the job then.'

'Alessandro,' his mother urgently interrupted, but Alex was not listening.

'Look, I've realised my mistake—she's completely unsuitable.'

'Well, it's too late for that,' the king said. 'The people—'

'You really want that vulgar family to be welcomed into ours? You really think Allegra would make a suitable queen?'

'Alessandro!' his mother said again, but Alex's mind was only on one thing—he had no intention of stepping aside.

'I am supposed to spend the rest of my life with this woman, a woman so ordinary?'

He heard a gasp.

He knew it was her, before he even turned around.

'Allegra...'

'Please don't...' She put her hand up to stop him. 'I think enough has already been said.'

She didn't run from the study; instead she walked in a daze back to the royal wing, and looked at the bed that was crumpled and scattered with newspapers. To think that she had lain there and held on to a glimmer of hope, that she had actually been going to tell Alex not to say anything too hasty!

He'd have laughed in her face had she told him she would consider it.

'Allegra.'

He didn't knock; it was his bedroom after all, his palace, his people....

Her heart.

'What are you doing?'

'What does it look like?' She was flinging her clothes onto the bed. 'I need a suitcase, my passport...'

'You're not going anywhere.'

'Oh, yes, I am.' She'd tried ringing Izzy, Angel, her brother Ben, but no one was picking up, so instead she would sort it herself. 'I'm going to go over to the hotel—'

'Excuse me?'

'I'm going to tell my family.' Absolutely she was. 'My vulgar family.' She was trying not to cry.

'What you heard down there...I was trying to make my father see how hopeless it was. What I said about you and your family—'

'Was said with such conviction,' she finished for him. 'I'm going to speak to them now. I'm going to tell my dad what I should have told him in the first place.'

'Really?' Alex cut in. 'Perhaps tell him he should ring his friend too, give him forewarning.'

'His friend?'

'The one who wrote the unauthorised biography—he's going to be busy over the coming months....'

'Don't try to threaten me.'

'I'm not threatening you, Allegra. I'm telling you how it will be—because if you think this is all just going to disappear when you tell your father the truth...' He paused for a moment to let his words sink in, to let her glimpse how it would be—and it *would* be! 'My father will not allow the people of Santina to be subjected to two broken engagements in the space of a few short weeks. I agree with him. There are things going on right now, repercussions from last night, that need to be dealt with.'

'What repercussions?'

'Don't concern yourself with that now, we have enough to deal with and the best way to do that is to set a wedding date.'

'No, no.' It was more a moan than a shout, horror sinking in. 'You can't expect me to go along with this now, after hearing what you just said. The next thing you know I'll be marrying you just so we don't upset the people.'

'Would that really be such hell?' It was as if she'd been delivered a terminal sentence instead of the chance to one day be queen. Still, rather than overwhelm her with that, he attempted logic. 'Allegra, I accept that their reaction is unexpected—however, people are fickle. They change their minds easily. For now they are happy, today they celebrate. What you do not understand is that one false move, one indiscreet comment, one mistake, and their minds will change like that.' He snapped his fingers in her face. 'Then, it will be a different conversation I'm having with my father. When my father realises just how unsuited we are, there will be no other alternative than to wait it out here, or to end things and return to London.'

'But that's what you want?' Hope finally sparked. 'Surely.'

'If I break our engagement, I will have to step aside and Matteo will be next in line—but that is not going to happen.' He stood and watched as her mind raced through the labyrinth and sought escape, but he blocked every exit. 'I was born to be king, and I will not give it up, no matter what my father says. But now that I am back in Santina I will assume my full duty as Crown Prince. As my fiancée, you will ensure that there will be no repeat of last night, there will be no more embarrassments, no hushed arguments in palace corridors. You will do me proud.'

'Then how—?' She floundered. 'If I'm busy being perfect, how can we expect the people to change their minds, especially if this is the only way you will still get to be king as well as break off our engagement?'

'They will.' He said it with certainty, such certainty, but it did not appease.

She forced her way through an awkward formal lunch, tried to be polite and focus on conversations, but she was too bewildered by the turn of events to pay much attention to the fact that a fair proportion of both her own and Alex's family were missing. If anything she was relieved, for if she saw Angel now it would be impossible not to break down and confess it all.

Her father gave her a warm hug at the end of a very long day. 'I'm so proud of you, Allegra.' He shook the king's hand and for an appalling moment it looked like he might kiss the queen, but Bobby gave her a brief smile instead and thanked her for her hospitality and then looked over to Alex. 'Look after her, or you'll have me to answer to.' It was affectionately said, but not well received.

'Of course I will look after her.' It was rare guilt that

tightened Alex's throat, for unlike Bobby, he knew this father really was kissing his daughter goodbye, was handing her over to him, to his family, to the people. Of course Bobby would see her again, just never like this. For as Allegra insisted on walking out to the limos with them—her high heels noisy on the marble floor, her voice just a little too loud, her stance a touch too familiar as she thanked a servant—Alex almost missed her already, missed the woman who had walked into that bar and forced his attention, missed the woman he had held this morning in bed, before everything had changed.

Somehow he had to explain things to her, but the subject was closed for now. He saw the shimmer of tears in her eyes as the limos departed and then she pleaded a headache and went to bed. The lights were off and her back was turned when Alex came in.

'Allegra?' He was not going to sleep on the sofa and he knew she was awake, for no one lay so rigid in a bed if they were asleep. 'I know you're awake.

'For now we need to set a date,' he continued. It really was not open for discussion and it burnt in her stomach so much that she started to cry. 'I will stall it for as long as possible—my father was talking a couple of months. I will try for Christmas.'

'And hope in the meantime the people change their mind about me—and then you can appease them by dumping me. Oh, darling, you do say the nicest things.' Despite her sarcastic tone, it hurt that he didn't deny it. 'I didn't sign up for this.'

Alex didn't know what to say. He realised that pointing out that he had paid her a million pounds to take part in this charade would not help matters right now. 'You need to be more affectionate. There were comments after lunch today—we are supposed to be madly in love after all.'

He moved towards her, attempted to comfort her the only way he knew how, in the language he best spoke where women were concerned. His arm moved around her body, drawing her to him. He did not fully understand her tears—yes it would be different and yes it must be a shock, but in his world, he was a prize, the one every woman wanted.

'Allegra, even if it is not how you intended, surely it is better this way. You have everything you could possibly want.' He thought of her old life: losing her job, the tiny bedsit, the demands of her family. Here she had no financial concerns and would be shielded from her family's dramas—the palace would see to that. He could feel her skin warm beneath the lace of her nightie.

And she was wrong—Alex had no intention of waiting for the people to change their minds. He had spent today thinking, weighing up the problems and as always coming to rapid solutions. Soon, she would be a more suitable bride. Elocution and grooming lessons would start with haste, and there was another very unexpected advantage to having Allegra as his fiancée: he had never been attracted to Anna—she felt more like a cousin or a sister than his betrothed—but with Allegra… He pulled her a little more towards him, buried his face in her hair and found the subtle tang of citrus. Yes, there was much solace to be had, for their attraction was undoubtedly wild. He thought of her as she had been this morning, of how very close he had been to finding release with her. Soon he would be back there—except, of course, more prepared this time. She really was delicious, and it would be so easy to lose his head.

'Allegra.' She heard the slight plea in his voice and then the feel of his lips on her shoulder, felt his hand snake a little further around. She frowned as he kissed her shoulder deeper. 'Tomorrow you must see the palace doctor.' What a modern prince he was, Alex thought as he broached the subject. 'We must get you on the pill.' She turned to him so rapidly he was almost on top of her.

'Huh?' *Audacity* was such a pale word for him, because he had it in spades. She could feel his erection against her thigh, and then the crush of his mouth before she could speak, before her mind could catch up with what he had just implied.

Her mouth gaped open and he took advantage. She tasted him, fresh on her tongue, his hand moving unbidden to her thighs; she could feel his urgency, and only this morning it would have consumed her. But so much had changed since then. She moved her face to the side. 'Don't you dare!'

'I don't want to play your games.'

'Oh, this is no game, Alex.' She wriggled out from underneath him. 'There's absolutely no need for me to go on the pill. Do you really think that I'd sleep with you after today?' She was stunned.

'Allegra, for God's sake—we're going to be sharing a bed. To say that nothing is going to happen is bordering on preposterous. You know how we are when we kiss, you know how we are....'

'How we *were*,' Allegra answered, 'before you called me ordinary.' It stung, it burned, just as much to say it as it had to hear it. 'For now your family wants me as your bride and you want me to go along with it. They also want me to be more groomed and polished.' She waited till he nodded. 'Well, they can dictate many things about my life, and I've been left with no choice but to comply, given our arrangement. But they will not dictate my sex life! There, at least, I make the rules.'

CHAPTER SEVEN

THERE were many reasons he had enjoyed London, but a significant one had been that Alex did not like to sleep alone. Here in Santina he had been betrothed to Anna, which meant his visits home had been rare and brief.

But now it was worse. He did not sleep alone, but instead shared a bed with a woman he found incredibly attractive, and who turned her back each night. Yet most nights they found themselves entangled; only in sleep did her body reach for him.

It had this morning.

As the sun had risen so, too, had Alex, Allegra's body coiling into him, her breath on his chest. It had taken every ounce of his willpower to detach her, rather than face the alternative of her recoiling in horror as rather too often she did.

It was unsustainable, Alex decided later as he headed poolside for coffee and to speak as requested with the queen, only to find Allegra doing her laps.

It was completely unsustainable that he should go weeks—no, months—without reward.

He was a man after all.

More than that, he was a prince.

Allegra stroked through the water as she did each morning.

The king and queen generally did not surface till later,

and his various siblings were either away or getting on with their duties. This was the best part of her day, gliding through the water, sometimes swimming faster when another wave of anger struck.

She'd remembered her sunblock. She'd been told to wear it even at 8:00 a.m.—her skin should be pale for the wedding. Every part of her had been analyzed and criticised: her laugh was too loud, her fringe too severe, her walk too heavy. Allegra stroked the water faster, touched the side and did a tumble turn, anger surging her away from the pool wall as she recalled the humiliation of her first language lesson.

She'd thought it was to learn Santinan, the stunning dialect that sounded like Italian with a streak of French. She spoke no Italian but had learnt French at school and was surprised that she understood more than she had expected to, was looking forward to the lesson even. Except it had been her own language that was to be improved upon. The shame still burned.

And there was Alex, as cool as anything, in a dark suit.

The sting of chlorine was a relief because as she climbed out of the pool she had a reason to rub her eyes on the towel.

And Alex watched.

He'd watched his fiancée break the silent morning with her splashing. She wasn't a graceful swimmer, he thought as he glanced up from his paper. There was no elegance as she slid through the water, just far too much noise and the occasional splash that landed at his feet—especially as she turned.

'Buongiorno...' He'd greeted his mother and now, having watched her swim, the butler poured more coffee as his mother came over and Allegra climbed out. 'Why did you want to meet?'

'Allegra needs to sort out her wedding dress,' the queen said.

'And you need to tell me that by the pool?'

'It is where Allegra is each morning.' The queen shrugged. 'I thought I would catch you both—you have much work to do and Allegra is busy with her book.

'Allegra!' She smiled over. 'Come and join us for some juice.'

'No, thank you,' Allegra called, looking around for her robe. She was sure she had brought it down. Instead she dried off with a towel while Alex did his best not to watch.

She was nothing like any woman he was used to—most, if they did venture poolside, would be in a bikini and stretched out on a lounger. Instead Allegra looked as if she were wearing a swimming suit from her school years—it was navy blue and should have been unflattering, except it had ridden up at the back. Which should not merit a blink—on the beaches of Santina women walked around in nothing more than a thong. Except, with Allegra, it was almost a forbidden glimpse. There was a prudishness there that enthralled, and he was envious of her fingers as they pulled the Lycra down, for he would have loved his own to oblige in their place.

'Do join us, Allegra!' The queen was insistent. 'The chef has prepared the most delicious juice.' What choice did Allegra have but to go over, especially as the butler was already pouring her a glass? 'It's watermelon, with mint and just a hint of ginger.' The queen awaited her verdict as Allegra took a sip. 'Nice?'

'Yum!' Allegra agreed, and took a longer drink, for it tasted divine, especially after such a long swim. 'God, that's good,' she said, because it really was, but she saw Alex flick his paper and bury his head in it. No doubt she had chosen the wrong word, or perhaps she should be less exuberant in her praise.

She couldn't win, Allegra decided.

'I am going to work.' He stood, dressed in a suit when all he was doing was going to his study, but he spent half the day video conferencing with that blasted Belinda and his executives and clients. She grudgingly admitted to herself that he probably ought to wear a suit, but it irritated her at times.

'So soon?' The queen frowned. 'I wanted to discuss designers for the dress....'

'You know me well enough to know that wedding details do not interest me in the least. Discuss it with Allegra.'

In fact, Alex was not irritated. But he did have other things on his mind. He could see her nipples straining against the fabric of her swimsuit, could see the beads of water on her arm. Of course his mother would have no idea that the sight of his scantily dressed fiancée was proving bothersome. After all, they slept together each night, at least in the eyes of everyone else. He felt like a teenager this morning, could not look her in the eye, could not look at her at all.

He really needed to get to London.

'Have a great day.' Allegra stood. She had been told to be more affectionate but she found it so awkward at times. She dutifully went over and walked with him as far as the French doors where she would say goodbye and then return to the queen. She smiled up to him but he didn't return it and then she remembered the queen was watching so she stood on tiptoe and kissed him on the lips. Again he didn't return it and instead he grabbed her wrist.

'Enough.'

She was damp and her hair had dripped on his suit so he brushed it down with his free hand.

'Sorry to get *water* on your suit.' Allegra huffed. 'I thought I was supposed to be more affectionate.'

'Allegra. I couldn't care less about the water…but there are more appropriate times to be affectionate, and you hardly dressed and dripping wet and tasting of watermelon…' He halted his words, dropped her wrist. 'There are limits.'

Then he strode off and Allegra couldn't help but smile.

The queen smiled too, and walked over to Allegra. 'I might go and have a little rest—it is terribly warm already.'

'I thought you wanted to discuss designers…' Allegra started, then remembered her place. 'Of course, I mean, I hope you have a nice rest.'

She headed up to her suite, and surprisingly Alex was there, but he ignored her when she walked in. Instead he carried on speaking to his phone while Allegra showered and changed into a robe. She would decide what to wear later, heartily sick of the clothes that had been chosen for her, all so formal, so co-ordinated, so thought out.

She wandered into the bedroom where Alex was concluding his call and the butler had brought in her morning tea and also a glass that contained crystals fizzing in water for Alex. It was the only noise in the room when the butler left.

'What's that?'

He did not answer, just downed the drink and then spoke. 'I will be going to London in the next few days.'

'London!' Her eyes lit up. 'I'll come—'

'I am there for business.'

'I won't get in the way. I can see my family, spend some time—'

'You will not be coming,' Alex said. 'I am going for a very discreet business trip. I am trying to arrange a meeting with a sheikh who is considering buying my business—if we both go it will turn into a media circus.' He shook his head. 'You carry on with the wedding plans, writing your book….'

She was so angry. London was her home and he was the one who got to go. Instead of drinking tea and the slivers of fruit that had been delicately arranged, she headed for the wardrobe.

'Have your tea.'

'I don't want tea.' Allegra looked at the lavish array of clothes. 'I want coffee and cake,' she said. 'I want a vanilla latte and I want to choose my own cake from the display.'

'What are you talking about?'

'I'm going out.'

'The fiancée of the heir to the throne does not just "go out."' He was at his most derisive. 'You are not in your bedsit now, you don't just pop down the road to buy some milk and stop off at a cheap café on the way. This is how it is. If you need some fresh air you can walk in the grounds.' He remembered the last time she'd been this angry, when he had pressed her to the wall after the engagement party just to silence her. But that was no longer an option, so instead he headed for the door. 'I'm going to my office.'

CHAPTER EIGHT

WHEN he had gone, she tried ringing Izzy, but got her voice mail, tried Angel too, but the result was the same. She was so worried about Angel. She'd seen her talking to some distant cousin of Alex's at the party, and in true Angel style, she had married him, just like that!

Except far from hearing of her wedded bliss, Allegra kept getting long emails about how Angel was going out of her mind stuck in the countryside in the middle of nowhere. She knew how she felt—she *completely* knew how Angel felt. But unlike her stepsister, who had begged her to keep what she wrote to herself, Allegra had been told in no uncertain terms that she could confide in no one. It wasn't fear of repercussions that kept her silent; it was the burden it would place on any family member if she told them how it really was. In the end she took her tea out onto the balcony and rang her father.

'They're an odd bloody lot,' Bobby said as the conversation turned to the party and the dramas that had played out since then. 'You know that Ben is still on Santina, and he's managed to get Alessandro's sister Natalia to work for him!'

'No!' How could she not know? 'Why doesn't anyone tell me anything?'

'I guess they figure you're busy,' Bobby answered, and

was silent for a moment before going on. 'He's a cold fish that fella of yours.'

Allegra smiled because she'd used the same term. 'Only around his family,' Allegra said, which was almost true, because when Alex was nice… She looked at her ring, remembered the kiss that had come with it and the conversation before.

'Zoe's nice though.'

'*Zoe?*' Allegra frowned. 'You mean the queen? You can't call her Zoe.'

'She said I could,' Bobby said. 'We had a cuppa together. I got lost when I went jogging the morning after your party.' Allegra couldn't help but giggle; it was the first laugh she'd had in ages. 'She was taking tea out on her little balcony,' Bobby said. 'Alone…' It was then that Allegra's eyes opened and she put down the cup she was holding. She had a sudden vision of her future, for already it was happening. 'It's criminal if you ask me,' Bobby said. 'A good-looking woman like that…'

'What do you mean?'

'Well, there was no king in sight. Just her in her little silk nightdress.'

'Dad!' Allegra gave a loud whisper, had an appalling vision of the butler listening in. 'You can't say that.'

'What! I can't talk to my own daughter?'

'You weren't flirting with her….' She was still whispering. 'Dad, tell me you did not flirt.' Oh, God! Alessandro was right, her family *were* shocking.

'I didn't do anything,' Bobby said. 'We had a cup of tea and a little chat—she's a lovely lady.'

'You mustn't speak about this with anyone,' Allegra said. 'Dad…'

'I'm not speaking to *anyone*—I'm talking to you! Anyway, I've got to get on. I've got an interview to go to.'

'An interview?'

'I'll tell you about it when I know more.'

She hated not knowing what was going on, was positive things were being kept from her. She was just so sick of the confines that as the maid returned, so, too, did Allegra's fire.

'Could you have a car arranged?' Allegra asked, and when the maid just blinked, she upped her order. 'In fifteen minutes.'

'A driver?' the maid asked, and Allegra knew better than to completely break with tradition, at least within the palace walls. 'Yes, a driver—I'd like to see a little of the island. Thank you.'

Of course her phone rang a few minutes later with an aide wanting to clarify a few things.

'I don't want a bodyguard. I just want a driver and a discreet car so I can look around Santina.' Which saw her half an hour later sitting behind blacked-out windows in an unmarked royal car, streaking along the beach and up through the winding villages, through the town. She wanted to open the window, to smell the herbs and garlic, to hear the chatter of the Santina people.

'Here will do.' She opened the door at a small set of traffic lights, gave the driver a beaming smile. 'I'll make my own way back.' She ducked out of the car and walked briskly into a shop, straight through it and out the other side, finding herself in a marketplace. She started walking again, picking up her pace, checking over her shoulder and hoping she hadn't gotten the poor driver into too much trouble. Heaven! The air tasted so sweet, and the simple bliss of walking into a café was incredible.

But her anonymity lasted all of about twenty seconds, the owner blinking and double taking as she walked in.

'Benvenuto!' He welcomed her so warmly, told her to

take a seat, but Allegra wanted to see the cake selection for herself and it was bliss to stand and choose. The owner was marvelous; he was thrilled to have such an esteemed guest and did not want crowds ruining it, so he hastily closed his shop, allowing only the present patrons to remain.

She chose the house specialty, a kind of cannoli filled with pecan ice cream and dusted with icing sugar, and had the best vanilla latte she had ever tasted. She sat alone and read a magazine and it was wonderful. Wonderful to hear the chatter around her once people had gotten over the initial shock of her being there.

'Mi dispiace.' A mother dashed over to stop her daughter, who had taken the flowers out of the vase on their table and was now offering them to Allegra. 'I am sorry,' the woman said, 'of course you want privacy.'

'They're lovely…' Allegra took the bunch. *'Grazia.'* She spoke her first public word in Italian.

'We will leave you to enjoy your space,' the woman spoke in faltering English, 'but we are so happy to see you here, to have you amongst us.'

'I'm happy to be here too.'

Allegra really was—those fifty-eight minutes of freedom were the absolute sweetest she had known in weeks, though Allegra knew it could not last. She could only imagine the chaos she must have caused back at the palace when the driver informed them what she had done, so she was actually expecting the huge black car that slid beside her as she walked along the cobbled streets, bags in hand. She even managed a smile as the window opened and a boot-faced Alex issued extremely clear orders.

'Get in.'

'Pardon?' Allegra said sweetly.

'Don't make a scene, Allegra.' He had a smile plastered on his face as he pulled over and parked, and when she did not get in, just carried on walking, he opened the door and stepped out, taking her in his arms. She got a very brief taste of the mouth that she had craved, but it was cold and hard and his voice was stern as he spoke in her ear. 'Get in the car this minute. I'll speak to you when we are back at the palace.'

'I don't want to go back to the palace.' He looked down at her, chin set in defiance, eyes glittering with rage, her anger barely contained, and was reminded of the night of their engagement—the little spitfire he had hushed with his mouth. But that was impossible now—there were people gathering, astonished to see their prince and his fiancée in deep conversation. 'I want to walk—'

'You can't walk here. We can walk back at the palace.'

'I'm sick of being cooped up.'

She was going to storm off; he knew it. Was this what the future held for the royals? Public rows on the street, drama played out wherever it suited? This mistake of his own making stared back at him. She would do it, he knew, would storm off if he insisted she return, and though he would far rather drag her into the car, he sought a rapid solution; the black moons were rising in her eyes but her pupils were dilated for battle rather than in lust this time.

'We will walk.' He had never been challenged like this, had never had anyone defy him so. He could lead an army, yet could not get her back to the car. As they stared, locked in silent battle but still smiling, he saw not just the black but the green in her eyes, and the shimmer of tears like dew in the morning and he knew where to take her. 'We will go to *verde bosco*....'

'Is that a village?' Allegra asked.

'It's not a place—' he actually smiled '—it is a forest, the foothills—it is where I go,' Alex said, and he saw her slight frown. 'When I need to get away. *Verde bosco* is where I go.'

It was the closest he'd come to admitting that at times perhaps he felt it too.

And also the reason she got in the car.

CHAPTER NINE

'WHAT the hell were you thinking?' So angry was he that for a while he said nothing else. The people watched as the couple got into the car, expecting him to turn around and speed back to the palace, sharing smiles instead when his silver car headed for the hills.

They saw it often when Alessandro was here, the low silver vehicle hugging the bends in the road—and they knew, too, that he used to ride there for hours in the rugged woods. It just hadn't happened in a long time—but now their prince was back, sharing the land he loved with his future bride.

'What were you thinking?' he demanded again.

'That I am being ignored, that I'm stuck locked away and that I wanted a few hours—'

'You are engaged to me,' Alessandro roared. 'I told you this morning that you do not just pop out, you do not go walking....' He halted then; it was safer for now to concentrate on the road, which he did, and when he heard her rapid inhale at a couple of sharper bends, he turned briefly and saw she was scared. 'I am not driving in anger,' he explained. 'I know this road well.'

So well.

He had taken it often when he had lived here, heading for the one place on Santina that soothed him. Even as a child and later as an angry teenager, before he could drive, he would ride for the day, just to get to this place. When he could not stand the confines of the palace, when he could not bear to breathe the stifling air, when all he felt was oppression, it was here he would come, to a place he could breathe, could shout if he chose, could think....

He knew how she felt, for he had felt it once too.

He pressed a button and the roof slid away. When it was safe to do so he glanced over again and saw her more relaxed now, eyes closed enjoying the sun and the wind and air that was fresh.

For Allegra the silence from him was golden; she knew he wasn't so angry now, knew that though she slept beside him every night and joined him at dinner, spoke with him each day, really they had not been alone, had not been themselves, since London.

She opened her eyes as the car slowed down; it was cooler and shaded. When they came to a stop, they both got out without a word, and she let Alex lead her to the place he had once come to.

'I do know what it's like.' He was not shouting; he didn't even seem cross. She was so glad for the drive, for the distance from the palace. She could see it still though, there beneath them in the distance, but she was glad for the expanse of land in between.

'Before I could drive, I used to ride here. I used to stand here and swear I would not go back, though of course I had to—but I promised that I would get away, that for a few years I would live in London, live *my* life for a while, before I returned to their ways.' They walked further into the copse, and he showed her where he would tie his horse. They walked further in till they were bathed in green and they sat on the damp moss that her eyes had reminded him of.

'We should have brought a picnic,' Allegra teased.

'I wasn't exactly planning to come here,' Alex said, but it was good to be back, to lie down on the moss and look up to the glimpses of sky that the trees soared to. To not look at her as he told her what he should not, but what she surely deserved to know. 'You know there is uproar with Sophia missing....'

'She's not missing—she's married to your friend Ash, the maharaja,' Allegra said, for when the young princess had heard that her father was about to marry her off, she had fled instead. 'But yes, there's an uproar.' Prince Rodrigruez had arrived to claim his bride, and the king had decided that Sophia's disgraced sister Carlotta would do instead. Allegra could not understand this family—how appearances rather than feelings mattered.

'There is always uproar around Sophia.' He looked up to her. 'You've heard the rumours? That she isn't...'

Allegra nodded; when he was trying to be more open, she wasn't going to play games and pretend she didn't know what he was talking about.

'My father was always strict with me, but when I was young,' he tried to recall, 'there were times we went out. There seemed more freedom then, or maybe the palace seemed bigger. Then Mother had the twins, and though my father doted on them, especially Natalia, he really wanted more sons. I know he was disappointed, and my mother... she changed.' He tried to explain. 'Maybe you would call it depression. I didn't know what it was then. But when I was twelve I knew there was going to be another baby— which should have been good news—after all, my father wanted another son. I heard them rowing—not just a row!' She looked at him. 'He told her she would bring down the monarchy—that her careless ways would cost the people dear...that her indiscretion...' He looked to the sky and could hear their voices now. 'It was not that she had an affair that upset him, he said. He was worried for the people, the damage a pregnancy—'

'No,' Allegra broke in. 'Of course he was upset.'

'You have to understand—'

'I do understand,' Allegra said, 'because I've heard those types of rows too—hundreds of them—and whatever you think of my father, he's not all that different from yours. I love him dearly, but he's a mire of double standards. If it had been my mother who had had an affair—'

'It is different,' Alex cut in. 'Since then, we must be above rumour or reproach.'

'It's hardly working though,' Allegra pointed out. 'The press are going crazy now with the goings-on. Your family are so busy trying to keep secrets that keep bursting out into the open, so busy trying to prove they're not human, when really that's all they are. Your father wasn't upset about the people—he used that as an excuse to lock her in with guilt. You won't keep me locked in, Alex.'

'You can't just wander off.'

'I promise not to come back pregnant!'

'Allegra, I'm serious. There are things that cannot be changed.' He was silent then, and they both lay still for a moment. 'Can you hear it?'

She could, the buzz of a helicopter. It might not even be for them, but then again, it may well be, yet she would not give in. 'They're here because it's such a rarity...' she attempted. 'Because they're so unused to your family doing things in a normal way. We're supposed to be engaged, we're supposed to be unable to keep our hands off each other—we should be making love in the foothills.'

'I would never compromise you like that,' Alex said.

'I know that.' She gave a small laugh. 'Shame...' And then she winced. 'I didn't mean... I wasn't trying to lead—'

'I understand,' Alex said, and he did understand, because spontaneity could not be a part of his life. And it *was* a shame. 'I would not be here if I was engaged to Anna.' She would never have fled the palace; there would have been no near row on the street. He looked over to her.

'You could have been,' Allegra said. 'You choose to live by the old rules.'

'The people knew we were rowing.'

'Of course they did,' Allegra said. 'They're not stupid.'

'It's not fitting.'

'It's a row!' Allegra shrugged. 'Couples have them all the time.'

He could hear the helicopter overhead; he had no doubt it was the paparazzi. 'Would they find us kissing?' he asked.

'I presume so,' she said. 'Had we made up.'

'Have we?'

'We're talking,' Allegra said. 'Surely that's a start. Please help me, Alex—I can't stay locked in the palace. I feel like I'm losing myself....'

'I will try,' Alex said. 'Perhaps there can be compromise.'

'I guess we've made up then.' She wanted a kiss, even if it was for the cameras; she wanted contact, wanted to feel more of him.

And he would never compromise her; she knew that, so much so that she wasn't offended when he rearranged the set, for he did it with her honour in mind. 'Pull down your dress,' he said, for it had ridden up a little. She pulled it down as far as it would go, and it felt wooden, and formal, like two actors on set, even when he spoke of logistics. 'I will move towards you.' Except it was a relief to have contact, to revisit him.

It was a duty kiss, and there was nowhere it could go.

His hand was on her waist and there it would remain; their bodies suitably apart, just their faces met. It was a gentle kiss, a reunion kiss, and all she felt were his lips and all he had were hers.

She heard the hum of the helicopter so his kiss did not deepen, and slowly he pulled back his mouth. He did not want to be prince in that moment, a normal man would be so much easier, for all he wanted was to taste her again, and he chose to.

He brushed his lips against hers and still it was gentle. It was not, though, a kiss for the cameras; it was a kiss that wished they were totally private, a kiss just for them. Both knew it even if they dared not admit it.

She could feel his breath and the increase of hers.

'Alex…' She pulled back, for it almost killed her not to roll into him. She felt his hand tighten on her waist, felt it bunch the fabric in tortured immobility. 'I don't want anything appropriate in the papers.'

'I told you. I would never compromise you. I thought you wanted us to appear normal.'

He loved kissing her—it was an entirely new sensation, and he had never been playful in his life, never.

Not once.

There was a double forbidden here.

'I don't want you accusing me of teasing.'

'I know that.'

'And we can't do anything that might look…'

He knew that too.

'Just kiss,' Alex said. Maybe it tastes so sweet because it is forbidden, he thought, because there is nothing more they could do. Maybe it had simply been too long without a woman; he could not allow himself to entertain that it was solely for her, for more of her, that he lowered his head again.

And a kiss without contact was torture.

A delicious torture as their mouths met again.

Torture to not be able to roam his body, to not accept him, for she knew he was wild to press into her. To not be able to forget about cameras, Santina and the predicament they were in. Yet torture to forget these things, too, as mouths mingled.

She could feel her breath quicken, her mouth open to take him, except he pulled back. She gave a reluctant moan and wanted to take it back, for she was not supposed to be enjoying it so, but then so, too, did he.

It was the most erotic of moments, a seemingly chaste kiss but with bodies that were flaming.

The helicopter buzzed louder, like the nerves between her legs, and they *had* to keep it tasteful, so he lifted his head and showered her face with small kisses. He smiled down at her, and even in his arms, she could not tell of her pleasure, and even in hers he could not admit to the same.

'If you weren't a prince...' Allegra looked up at him, and then she stopped, because she would now be teasing. For tonight they would be alone again, and she could not succumb, could not give that part of herself and still come out of this sane.

'I *am* one,' he said, for he could never forget.

Except were he not a prince, his hand would be between her legs now, she would be writhing on the moss and his face would be over hers, his body too.

But at least he could kiss her.

Her breasts ached for his hands; her body begged for his weight. There was a purr in her mouth that must have dictated her want, for his breathing was ragged and so, too, was hers. But Alex was right, there *were* limits.

'We should go back.'

She pulled her lips away, dared not admit to the heat

in her body, or that if he kissed her further she would surely come.

'Of course.' He was back to being prince, though his thoughts were the same. 'I think they would have got their shot by now.'

It did not sting to hear his cold words; they were actually welcome, for she needed a reality check.

It was a different drive back to the palace. He showed her the landmarks, the little blue flowers that dotted the hills. She showed him the flowers the girl had given her in the café.

'They're what a little girl gave me.' She picked them up from the concourse, but they were fading fast. 'They need water.'

'They are everywhere,' Alex said. 'They are exclusive to Santina, they flower all year. Really, they are a common weed—we have trouble controlling them.'

'I think they're beautiful,' Allegra said and Alex screwed up his nose.

It was a more relaxed couple that arrived back at the palace. It actually didn't feel strange to walk through the palace holding hands.

She felt rumpled and a bit grubby, but she felt the most normal she had in ages, buoyed from fresh air and company, from his kiss, from their talk. It was impossible not to smile.

Until they were immediately summoned to the king's study. He stood stern and visibly angry, but the queen gave a tentative smile. 'Allegra.' The queen was kind. 'We have been so worried—anything could have happened.'

'Nothing did.'

'You might have been recognised.'

'I *was* recognised.' Allegra was trying not to be rude to the queen. 'I walked into a café and do you know what the owner did? He shut the shop—he let all the people who were currently there stay, but he allowed no one else in, and the people were delightful. They were absolutely thrilled and they let me be. Apart from one little girl.' She looked at their uncomprehending faces, and her mind spun in circles—could they not understand how nice and simple it had been, that a little girl had come and given her a bunch of flowers?

She showed the wilting bunch, but the king just huffed. 'Weeds...'

She told them that she had walked into shops, and that she had made their day, and she looked to the queen. 'I am a poor substitute for you, but they were thrilled. I shopped, and if people approached, it was just to say hello.'

The king, unbidden, reached for her bags. 'Tomorrow the papers will be full of the gifts, of the royals' greed....'

'Leave her things,' Alex snapped, but the king ignored his son's orders and opened the bags. 'Have someone go now and pay—'

'I paid,' Allegra said. 'Of course I paid.' And maybe the king was expecting pearls and jewels to spill from the bags that he shook out on the desk, but it was a few postcards and a couple of souvenirs from Santina and a little snow globe with a tiny castle inside.

That they would do that, take her things and just riffle through them, was too much for Allegra. She would say something rude—but she must not. If she opened her mouth now she would be disrespectful to the king. Whatever they thought of her father, he had taught her better than they knew, so instead just a sob of frustration came from her lips as she fled the room.

'Go after her,' the queen said to her son, and then turned to her husband. 'Eduardo, you should not have touched her things.'

But he did not go after; he faced his father.

'You say the people love her, and yet you try to change her!'

'I rule Santina.' The king picked up the book he had been reading, the book that had caused Allegra's family so much shame. 'You lose your head to her and you will make poor decisions—you will turn this family into a circus. Do you want this for your people? She will act accordingly.'

'She just went for a walk, for God's sake!' The queen's voice was rising. 'She just went for a walk…'

'That's how it starts.' The king turned to his wife, to the woman he had once trusted. 'And then she makes friends, and then she makes closer friends and before you know it…' He looked to his wife. 'The rules are in place for a reason. We are not changing our ways to accommodate your fiancée, Alessandro. It is she who must change hers. When I am dead and gone, you can do what you see fit, but while I rule…' He looked to his son, to his eldest, to the strongest and wisest of his children, and he would not allow him to give in as he once had, would not allow him to open up to the hurt he would feel. As his son strode out of the study, the king hurled the truth to his back and watched it stiffen. 'I am still your king.'

It was a cauldron, an impossible one, and soon enough it had to explode.

CHAPTER TEN

'ALLEGRA.' It was the next morning when he crawled into bed, ten minutes before the maids appeared. It was all he could take—twenty minutes simply killed him and last night he had chosen the sofa. Her eyes were still swollen from crying, for despite his words in the woods, last night he had made it clear—there could be no major changes, just the occasional compromise.

'What?' It was a surly response.

'Stop sulking.'

'I'm not,' she said. 'I'm thinking.'

'About...'

'How impossible this is. How I want to go home.' She turned to him. 'You're going to London soon...can't I at least join you?'

She couldn't—yes, he had work to do in London, but he also had plans and certainly he did not want her around to spoil them.

'To see my family...' There was so much going on, and all she got were glimpses. It was as if she were being cut off even from them. 'I hardly hear from them. I want to see them, talk to them....'

Which was the last thing he could risk. She trusted them implicitly, she defended them at every turn, yet more and more they were becoming entwined with his—her sister

Izzy and his brother, Matteo, were holed up somewhere together, and his cousin Rafe McFarland had married her stepsister.

He could not risk her confiding in them, and must, as his father had pointed out, keep her removed from their scandal.

'You have things to do here.'

'I'm dying here,' Allegra said.

'Stop with the dramatics. You keep insisting you are busy with your book.' There was an aggrieved note to his voice, for her book kept her up late each night, her book made sure he was asleep on the damned sofa by the time she came to bed. Still they could not discuss things further, for the door knocked and Alex called for the maid to enter.

'Just coffee?' Allegra frowned when they pretended to wake after the maid had brought in the trolley. 'Where's breakfast?'

'You didn't take too long to adjust to the lifestyle.' Alex smirked. 'My parents have asked that we join them for breakfast—they want to go over wedding plans. You still need to select a designer for your gown.'

'It seems rather a waste,' Allegra said. 'Given we're both hoping I shan't be wearing it—and anyway,' she admitted, 'there's nothing for me to select, they're all the same.' She heard the whine in her voice and halted herself. Had it really come to this, sitting up in bed with the most beautiful view on God's earth, next to the most stunning man, and complaining about designers? Over and over she had to check herself, tell herself she had nothing to complain about—it was just that she missed him. Missed the man she had met in London so very much, missed the glimpse of the dream.

'Why breakfast?' Allegra asked, because it was all so

formal. Why did this family have to arrange a simple conversation?

'Because my father has commitments all day and I am flying out tonight.'

'And I'm stuck here...' There was that whine again, and even she couldn't bear to hear it, so she put down her cup and climbed out of bed, lay in the bath that the maid had run and tried to calm down, tried not to think of the real reason for his regular jaunts to London—as if a man like Alex would sleep alone for long.

Breakfast was excruciating, from the moment she sat down and selected her favourite croissant.

'Actually,' Zoe said as Allegra smeared strawberry jam over it. 'I've had a word with the chefs and they're going be preparing a light selection for you, Allegra.'

'Excuse me?'

'In preparation for the wedding.'

'You think I need to lose weight?' She waited for Zoe to retract from the mild confrontation, but instead the queen just smiled.

'You have put a little on.'

Allegra couldn't believe her ears. She was slim, always had been. Her father was forever telling her she needed to put weight on.

'Leave it,' Alex said, thankfully to the queen and not to Allegra.

'I'm just trying to help. You know the pressure she's going to be under—the people expect perfection. I don't want Allegra feeling awkward on the day. It's hard for her, I realise that—she has sudden twenty-four-hour access to top class chefs.... I'm just suggesting that, before it becomes an issue, she nip things in the bud.'

'Well, don't.' Alex's voice was loaded with warning, as, too, was the look that he shot his mother. His eyes, though, were surprisingly kind when they turned to her. 'Ignore that,' he said. 'Just completely dismiss it—you look wonderful.' His eyes held hers and she wished for the hundredth time that he meant it, that the public facade was real.

'You need to choose a designer for your dress.' Zoe didn't exactly change the subject, but at least she moved away from Allegra's waistline.

'I know... I just...' She hated all the suggestions, hated them because they were all just a slightly different version of the same. She'd been told, too, to grow out her fringe so that she could wear a more traditional hairstyle. 'I've got a couple more to see this week. What about you?' Allegra asked her fiancé, who was clearly bored senseless by the conversation.

'I'll be wearing military uniform.' He looked at her non-comprehending face. 'I did several years' service, and given it is our family the soldiers serve...' He didn't even bother finishing his sentence, just picked up his ringing phone and carried on a brief conversation.

'That's extremely rude, Alessandro.' The king looked up from his newspaper.

'That call was urgent,' Alessandro responded. 'I've been trying to get hold of someone for two weeks. Belinda was just letting me know that he has accepted an invitation to dinner tomorrow night.'

'It could have waited,' barked the king.

'Somehow I don't think His Royal Highness Sheikh Razim Abdullah likes to be kept waiting.' Alex could out snob anyone, Allegra noted, even his own father. 'Given he is considering buying my business, it seemed prudent to tell Belinda to let him know that tomorrow we would be delighted to join him.'

Allegra's eyes shot to his as she heard the 'we,' but perhaps he realised his mistake, for he did not return her gaze. Instead he took great interest in a bowl of raw sugar cubes, selecting one and then another for his coffee.

'How are your parents?' Zoe must have felt the sudden drop in temperature because she moved the conversation on quickly.

'They're fine, thank you.' Allegra could hardly breathe, but she did her best to be polite. 'I spoke with my father yesterday.' She turned and forced a smile at the queen. 'He's looking forward to seeing Alex when he's over—'

'I shall be working,' Alex said.

'He also asked after you, Your Highness.'

'Oh.'

'You mentioned you might be visiting London too....' Allegra tried to recall the conversation she had had with the queen the other night.

'Just a fleeting visit.' Zoe gave a tight smile. 'Formal.'

'You could pop in for a cup of tea!' The king thought this highly amusing and Allegra really couldn't take it much more. She hated the lot of them.

'Excuse me.' She put down her napkin. 'I need to get ready to speak with the next designer.' She looked to Alessandro. 'Could I have a quick word?' She was very close to crying. 'I'd like your opinion on something.'

She waited till they were in the bedroom and well out of earshot to pick up the conversation where she had left off.

'Because heaven help me if I formed an opinion on my own!'

'Allegra.' He was completely bored with her. 'I don't have time for this. What did you want to speak with me about?'

'Why are they so rude? What's so bloody funny about my father inviting them over that your father can be so rude?'

He merely shrugged, and she moved on to the other

thing that was killing her, the other thing she simply had to know. 'You're going out with Belinda tomorrow night.' He had the audacity to roll his eyes. 'And don't even try saying it's business.'

'I told you and I have told my parents and I am sick of saying it—I don't run a market stall, I don't make a living from reality TV shows. I employ over two hundred people and if I don't dispose of my business interests correctly then that is two hundred people who could be out of work. And yes, Belinda will be joining me for dinner, because it is a business dinner, because the sheikh will be bringing his assistant too.'

'So you've never slept with her.' Allegra knew that he had—she knew, just the way a woman did, from seeing how Belinda looked at him, from the little laughs that wafted over on Skype conversations, that she was so much more than just a PA. 'You really expect me to believe—'

'Of course I've slept with her.' He didn't seem to see what the problem was. 'But I haven't since our engagement—I have to keep up the happy little charade.' He did nothing to soothe her, nothing to comfort her. 'Now, if you'll excuse me, I'm going to my office. You carry on talking weddings....'

'Screw you!'

'Oh, but you won't,' Alex said. 'Hell...' he cussed out. 'The one respite we could have during this torture, the one piece of pleasure we could share, and you've bolted your knees together.' He saw her lips tighten and the two dots of colour burning on her cheeks. Then with a sob she fled.

He called to a maid, had her bring him some more crystals and water, but antacids were no longer working. There was a constant burn in his gut, and though he never went after a woman when she stormed off, this time he did, for he was not proud of his words and he wanted to apologise for them.

* * *

She wasn't in their suite, nor back in her little turret, nor did he find her in the kitchen, the place he had found her after their last row. But finally he found her out at the stables, still fizzing with anger, and she was heaving a saddle onto an equally temperamental mare.

'What on earth are you doing?'

She didn't bother to answer.

'She's not suitable for riding....'

'You ride her,' Allegra said.

'I know how!'

He dismissed the worried-looking stable boy with a flick of his wrist.

'He did warn me,' Allegra said, 'so don't bite his head off later.'

'You cannot ride her.'

'I want to,' Allegra said. 'Anyway, I need the exercise apparently.'

She mounted the horse and felt the power beneath her, and even if she didn't feel quite so brave now, she refused to show it.

'Allegra, you are being ridiculous—this could be dangerous.'

'I've had riding lessons,' she called over her shoulder as she trotted across the yard. 'My father—'

'This is not some docile mare from the local pony club that your father had you join, so he could flirt with the mothers....'

He was loathsome, so loathsome she kicked off, and just tried to concentrate on staying on, because this was a huge powerful beast she was riding, and he was right, this wasn't some little pony she had trotted around a ring on. She couldn't see for her tears, couldn't think for her anger, she just wanted speed and space. And she wanted him to come after her, she admitted with a sob; she wanted him to be with her in this, to be the man she had thought he was.

Suddenly she lost her footing in the stirrup; she sailed through the air and collided with the grassy floor. Her landing didn't actually hurt that much, for she was in agony already, but she felt the thud to her head, and goodness it was a relief to cry, to lie on the grass as he ran over, not to have to hide her tears.

'Lie still.' He was incredibly calm. 'Where does it hurt?'

'I don't know.'

'Did you hit your head?' His fingers examined her; there was a large lump forming on her forehead that was worrisome and his fingers worked their way down her body, a slow perusal as he checked for anything obvious. He expected her to wince or call out in pain, but she just lay there crying.

'Nothing seems broken.' She looked up to him and maybe he had had a fright after all, because he was actually sweating. Or maybe that was more from the rapid ride over to collect his casualty. 'You have a nasty lump on your head though.'

'Sorry...' She looked up but there were three of him, all swimming around. She'd been nothing but trouble, she knew that—he was as trapped as she.

'You've nothing to be sorry for.'

Oh, but she did. She turned her head and was sick into the grass, more embarrassed than she had ever been in her life to be seen like this. 'I should have just broken my neck, then you could have been a poor widower.'

'Allegra...'

'Then you wouldn't have had to marry. You could just sleep with everyone and behave as horribly as you like and they'd say, "But poor Alessandro, who can blame him?"'

'Allegra.' He was very, very calm and she knew she was rambling. 'You have a head injury.'

'Thanks to you.' She was cross-eyed trying to look at him. 'You just let me ride off.' It was the most stupid thing to say, but she was past caring, lying on the grass, slurring her words. 'I could have been miles away....'

'Had I chased you she would have just gone faster—she'd have thought it was a race.' She had no idea the fear that had gripped him as she had ridden off, to stand and watch helplessly as she jumped onto the most temperamental mare. He had come to apologise but instead he had had no choice but to stand and watch the inevitable, to see her tumble. 'Your stomach...' He had not checked it, he was not a doctor, but the thought of a hoof kicking her actually made him feel sick. He was vaguely aware of activity behind him and he shouted orders, called for the doctor to meet them back at the palace and then he turned and spoke gently to her. 'Let's get you back home.'

'It doesn't feel like home though.' There was the indignity of being placed on a golf buggy and driven back to the palace and then a very shaky walk up the stairs.

'I'll carry you,' he offered, but for some reason that just upset her even more.

'You can leave me now.'

'Not yet,' Alessandro said. 'The doctor wants to see you.' He shooed out the maid, because he knew that she hated to be fussed over, and then started to pull at her boots as she attempted her buttons.

'I can manage,' Allegra said.

He was not remotely impressed. 'Believe me, I am getting no kicks out of this,' he said, and that eked a smile. 'There's no perverse pleasure in taking your vomit-stained blouse off.' He picked up the lace nightdress and it was clearly too complicated so he went to a drawer and pulled out one of his T-shirts instead. Even though it must have been laundered to the strict palace guidelines, still she was sure that she caught the scent of him as he slid it over her head.

'Bed.' He pulled the sheets back and she climbed in; her brain seemed to be thumping away at her skull as he opened the door and let the old doctor in. He examined her very thoroughly and she could smell his horrible breath as he shone a light in both eyes then spoke in deep tones to Alex. She heard the words *commozione cerebrale* and if she hadn't been lying down she would have fainted, but then Alex looked over and gave her a smile.

'That's "concussion" to you!' He smiled at her melodrama and then thanked the doctor. Left alone he sat on her bed. 'You have to rest for a couple of days—there will be a nurse to come in and check you hourly throughout the day and night.'

'Is it really necessary?'

'Apparently.'

Allegra woke a little later. The flowers the little girl had given her in the café yesterday had been placed in a small vase by the bed and they had perked up with the water, the blue petals like tiny stars. She gazed on them slowly, replaying the day's events, awareness creeping in that Alex was in the room too. She looked over to where he sat in an armchair dozing—just as beautiful as ever. And even though they were planning a wedding, he was still just as unattainable as ever. She could never have his heart—he had told her the day they met that he didn't do love, that it simply wouldn't happen with him, but it was hard to finally accept it. The nurse came in and took her blood pressure and shone the little light in her eyes and then left them alone.

'I'm alive apparently,' she said as his dark eyes peeked open. She was terribly embarrassed, could sort of remember the stupid things that she'd said out on the field to him, tried to remember if she'd declared undying love or anything equally awful.

'I'm sorry if I made a fool of myself.'

'Stop apologising.'

'I can't actually remember what I said.'

'Something about what a merry widower I'd make.'

'You're supposed to be in London.'

'It doesn't matter.'

'What about Sheikh…' She couldn't remember his name.

'He's a family man—he understood completely when he heard you had had an accident. He sends his best wishes for a speedy return to full health.'

'I'm fine.'

'No,' Alex said, 'you're not. It's not just the fall.' He put on a side light and looked over to where she lay and even if her fringe mainly hid them, there was so much trouble in her eyes. 'When I met you that day—'

'Don't.' She closed her eyes, didn't want to hear how she hadn't lived up to expectations, how he could never have guessed the trouble he was taking on. 'I was boring till I met you.' She opened her eyes and saw that he was smiling.

'I doubt that.'

'Honestly!' She blinked. 'I'm the quiet one in my family.'

'It must get pretty noisy around Christmas.'

'It does,' Allegra said, thinking of the wonderful times she'd had with her family, the rows and the singalongs, the parties and the whole drama that was part and parcel of being a Jackson. 'I can't stand to hear your parents being derisive about them, that it's such a joke that my father might invite—'

'There I must defend them.' He came over and sat on the edge of the bed. 'I know they can be unforgivably rude about your family, my father especially, but that reference to dropping in for tea this morning had nothing to do with you, or anything derisive about your family. It was aimed entirely at my mother.' He saw her frown. 'She had tea with your father apparently.'

'She did.' Allegra nodded. 'My father got lost the morning after the party....' Her mouth gaped open. 'He's jealous!'

'Not jealous...' Alex said, and then thought some more. 'Perhaps.'

'It was innocent.'

'Of course,' Alex agreed, and thought some more. 'Maybe you are right about my parents, maybe my father was hurt more than he admitted about her indiscretion.'

'Maybe he should tell her then.'

Alex shook his head. 'That will never happen.' He looked at her fringe and he wanted to see her eyes so he brushed it aside and winced at the large bruise. 'Your hair is too long.'

'I'm to grow out my fringe apparently.' She gave a tight smile. 'They want a more classical look for the wedding.' And then she smiled a bit wider. 'I can't believe your dad's upset by my father and your mum. I wish you knew my dad... I wish I could see him.'

'I'm sorry that you miss them.'

'I hear everything third-hand—Angel's married your cousin.'

Alex smiled. 'It was a very quick wedding.'

'But even so, there's my brother Ben and Natalia, my sister Ella and Hassan. She's pregnant, and—' All she did was hear about things when she wanted to live them. 'I know you don't understand but I miss them, I love them....'

'I know you do,' Alex said, but no, he didn't understand.

He was actually wonderful company; if you had to spend two days in bed with a thumping headache then Alex made a surprisingly good nurse. His complete ease with silence was soothing, and he was so sparse with words—at least she wasn't asked how she was feeling every ten minutes. He just told her she'd live when she moaned about her headache, or looked up from his computer when she staggered to the bathroom.

But late one afternoon, she returned from a bath run by the maid, dressed now in her Santina lace nightdress, and slipped into freshly laundered sheets. She closed her eyes, exhausted from the simple effort and then suddenly opened them again.

'Has Angel rung?'

'I spoke to her this morning,' Alex said. 'And your father too. I've been keeping them updated on your progress.'

'What about Izzy?'

'I have spoken to her too.' He glanced over. 'She's still here in Santina, staying at the palazzo with my brother, Matteo.'

'And she hasn't been to see me...' Allegra reached for her phone, craving the company of her sister, but Alex came over to the bed. 'I told her you were resting.'

'Well, I'm awake now.'

'Allegra.' He took the phone from her hand and put it on the bedside. 'At the moment you are upset... Wouldn't it be hard not to tell the truth to Izzy if you saw her?'

'Izzy would never tell.'

'She would not tell your brother Leo?' He watched as she frowned. 'It would seem that Leo is now seeing Anna, my ex-fiancée. Allegra, do you understand you cannot speak with your family as you once did?' He saw a glare of defiance and chose to quickly change track. 'As I said, I was speaking with Izzy and I'm sure you're not aware, but Matteo organises a charity concert once a year, out at the amphitheatre. One of Izzy's songs has been billed….'

'Izzy's singing?' Allegra's eyes narrowed. She'd heard his family's reaction when Izzy had attempted to sing at the engagement party. She wouldn't put it past them at all to have her up onstage in front of a huge audience, just for the cheap laugh they might get.

'No.' Alex shook his head. 'But her song will be played and she is going to be watching in the wings. I said that we would attend. It will be nice for you to get out. I know you feel cooped up.' He gave her hand a little squeeze. 'Something perhaps to look forward to.'

'I just miss everyone,' Allegra admitted. 'I feel as if I've dropped off the face of the earth and that no one's actually noticed, that no one even cares.'

'Come here.' He stood and she frowned up at him. 'I want to show you something.' He pulled her pashmina from the chair and wrapped it around her shoulders, and then took her elbow and led her, a bit wobbly, out of the room, down a long corridor and then down a flight of stairs to a vast set of French windows. 'Do you still think no one cares?'

She looked out to the entrance of the palace where there were hundreds and hundreds of flowers laid at the palace gates. Some of the bouquets were formal, but there were also hundreds of posies of little blue stars and it was those that meant the most. 'They're for you,' Alex told her. 'The people heard you'd had a fall and they have been bringing them for the past two days. There are bouquets being delivered hourly—they are down in the drawing room, in the dining room—'

'For me?'

'We've never seen anything like it,' Alessandro admitted. 'The papers did not exaggerate or lie—our people really do love you.'

And it helped, it really did help, made the madness of the situation just a touch more bearable, but as she headed back to bed, he gave her a thin smile. 'I am heading to London. I've been putting it off, but now that you're feeling better... It'll just be for a couple of weeks, I'll be back for the concert.'

'Weeks?'

'There is a lot to be done and I cannot put off Razim again.'

So he would be out tomorrow night with Belinda. And she didn't have the excuse of a *commozione cerebrale*. She had no choice but to lie there and hold on to her feelings, but as he stood he gave her shoulder a brotherly squeeze and then left her. She almost heard the sigh of relief as he closed the bedroom door behind him.

Well, what did she expect? Allegra thought as she lay there. Of course he'd be on the first flight out.

The people might love her; it was the prince who seemed to find it impossible to.

CHAPTER ELEVEN

She couldn't go out while he was away—not because of the strict orders from the palace, more because of the egg on her forehead. So she mooched around the palace, trying not to imagine him out with the hard-nailed Belinda. She rang Izzy, but just got her voice mail, and Angel wasn't responding to her emails either. Allegra looked up when the maid knocked on her door.

'Raymondo is here.'

'Raymond!' corrected a loud, rather effeminate voice. She was so bored looking at wedding dresses, especially when she had no intention of even wearing it. She had to really make an effort to look enthusiastic as Raymond walked in and she waited, waited for the entourage behind him, for the swatches of white fabric, but all it was was him, not even a sketch pad.

'They always do that,' he said by way of introduction. 'They think it makes me sound more exotic!' He was from London too, and she nearly fell on his neck at the sound of his familiar accent. 'So, let's get started. What are your thoughts?' he asked. She drew in a breath, ready to give the appropriate answer when Raymond cut it. 'Actually, I've already been briefed. White Santina lace, yawn, yawn...'

Was it wrong that she giggled?

'In at the waist, full skirt, long train...' He rolled his

eyes and perhaps saw the sparkle of tears in hers. 'It's your wedding day, my dear—' he handed her a tissue '—I promise I will make you look beautiful.'

'I know.' Allegra sniffed. 'Sorry, I don't know what's wrong with me.' She tapped her forehead, tried to blame it on the bruise.

'Maybe you're just marrying the Crown Prince of Santina,' Raymond said wisely. 'It must be the most terrible pressure for an ordinary girl.' And he said *ordinary* so nicely, in a completely different way to Alex, but there was that word again, and along with it more tears.

'You know there are two dresses,' Raymond said. 'One as a backup in case my innovative white Santina lace in-at-the-waist dress design is leaked out.'

He did make her smile. 'I don't think they'd want me wearing anything that might remotely surprise.'

'I still have to make an alternative though,' Raymond pointed out. 'It might make the fittings more fun. What if you could have exactly the dress you wanted…?'

She'd never really thought.

'Think about it,' he said. 'What if you could have your perfect dress?'

'I don't know…' There was a germ of an idea, but she brushed it off; she certainly wasn't going to reveal it to him.

'A good designer is as confidential as a doctor, and,' Raymond added, 'I don't write anything down—you simply tell me your dreams and I create them.'

Was it sad that Raymond was the highlight of her days, especially with Alex away? She loved his visits, loved chatting to him, and as her bruise faded, so too did her reserve. She would stand in the bedroom being measured and fitted and then, when his assistant would walk off with tissue paper and plans, she would tell him her dreams, closing her eyes and imagining walking down the aisle to a husband that loved her, in the dress of her dreams.

'It's going to be stunning,' Raymond said. 'And I'm going to be making a start on it tonight—I can't wait. You've got the concert tonight.'

'I do.'

Her heart was fluttering with excitement, energised from Raymond's visit and Alex had rung to say he was on his way home and tonight she would finally see Izzy.

'What are you wearing?' Raymond asked.

She sighed and pulled out a pale linen dress with a fitted light jacket over the top. She wasn't remotely offended when he screwed up his nose. 'I'm wearing heels there, but I'm bringing pumps to change into.'

'It's a rock concert,' Raymond said.

'I know.'

'Come on, you!'

'Where are we going?'

'Shopping, of course.'

'I can't…' She thought of the last time she'd left the building unannounced, but Raymond wasn't remotely perturbed.

'I'll ring ahead to the boutiques. You're out shopping with your designer, what else is a princess-to-be supposed to be doing?'

'Can we stop for coffee?' Allegra asked.

'Absolutely.' Raymond smiled. 'And cake!'

They did, and it was the most wonderful day—spent shopping and laughing and then, laden with bags, they stopped at what was now Allegra's favourite café, though this time the car waited outside.

Again the owner closed up the shop.

'I hope it doesn't affect his trade,' Allegra said after they had placed their orders.

'Rubbish!' Raymond said. 'It will have multiplied it—everyone will want to eat and drink here, knowing this is where the future princess chooses to come.' He gave her a pensive smile and then he told her more about himself, about the boyfriend who had broken his heart and now wanted to get back with him. What a pleasure it was actually to sit and listen, to hear about his problems instead of focusing on hers.

'Maybe he's realised he loves you,' Allegra offered.

'I'm on the verge of being famous!' Raymond said. 'Thanks to designing your gown. Fernando always accused me of being a bit boring, that my designs did not make enough money.' He looked to Allegra. 'Now he's decided that he misses me—I want to believe he loves *me*, not the glamorous new version.'

He spoke to her heart and she understood.

'I want him to love the real me.'

It played in her head, over and over, as she arrived back at the palace.

She changed into clothes that were far, far more expensive than her old life would have permitted, but the style was one she had once worn.

She was dressed and ready and unbelievably nervous as she went downstairs to wait for Alex to get home, before they headed out to the concert.

'Allegra!' The queen gave her a lovely smile. 'Shouldn't you be getting ready? Alessandro's driver just informed us he'll be here in a moment and then it will be straight to the helicopter.'

'I am changed.' Allegra swallowed.

'You're wearing jeans!'

'And boots,' Allegra said. 'Aren't they divine?' They were, the leather as soft as butter; they were so perfect, so wonderful, that she wanted to name them.

'Your father…' A maid handed her the telephone and Allegra grabbed at it like a lifeline. He'd hardly called in weeks, and whenever she did he was invariably out, but it was such a relief to hear his voice.

'How are you?'

'Great!' Allegra said. 'I haven't heard from you. Why are you ringing me on this phone?' She knew Alex had arrived, but it had been ages since she had spoken to her father so she moved to another room to continue the conversation.

'I thought that was what I was supposed to do,' Bobby said. 'Cheaper than a mobile…' He tried to make a joke except Allegra didn't smile. 'Anyway, you'd have lots to be getting on with, I don't want to get in your way.'

'You don't.'

'Have you seen Izzy?'

'I'm seeing her tonight!' She was so looking forward to it, even if she would only get a bit of time with her at the after party, but she couldn't wait to talk to her.

'I just wanted to check something with you, Allegra. I've been offered a job—it's a regular spot, on a sports quiz show. The money's good and it keeps my face out there….'

'Sounds great, Dad.' Allegra grinned. It was the perfect job for her father; he loved the spotlight and attention. 'So what did you want to check?' Occasionally he asked her to look through a contract before he signed it, but she frowned as her father answered.

'Well, will it make things awkward for you?'

'How could it make things awkward?'

'I just….' She could hear her father's discomfort. 'I don't want to do anything that might embarrass you, like I did with the speech.'

'Dad!'

'And I won't talk about you on the television or anything or in the press.'

'I know that.'

'Well, I just want to make sure I'm doing the right thing.' He said goodbye, but somehow it was awkward.

Alex got to the foyer in time to hear his father scolding the maid for giving Allegra the phone.

'It's her father calling,' Alex pointed out.

'And she's about to go out on an official function—he's been told not to ring for a chat.' The king bristled. 'I'm going to have Antonio have another word with him—and you need to speak with her,' the king said. 'Properly this time. She's not to drop everything when one of her blasted family calls—she needs to be away from their influence. Is it any wonder she's going out dressed like a delinquent teenager, with their poor influence?'

Allegra walked in then and Alex saw she looked hardly like a delinquent teenager, just more like the woman he had first met. London had not been as he'd expected, in fact. All too often he had found himself sitting in the bar where they had met, or walking near her small flat, trying to fathom how he could make up for so drastically changing someone's life—for despite trying to deny it, despite perhaps not understanding it, he knew she had been happy then.

'Allegra.' He gave her a kiss as she walked in, but it was a tired kiss, a weary kiss, and for a moment he held her because he was not looking forward to what he had to say—to tell her in no uncertain terms that she needed to remove herself further from her family. He needed to think, needed some time to work out a better solution, except time seemed to be running away. The date for the wedding would be announced tomorrow and sooner than she knew it the day would be here.

Allegra blinked in surprise when she saw him. He was dressed in his suit, just as he so often did, but he must have missed shaving this morning, for he was the most unkempt she had ever seen him—his black hair tousled, looking so drained, so tired—and she almost felt sorry for him, for the last thing it looked like he needed was a rock concert.

'Allegra's wearing jeans,' Zoe said, waiting for some sort of reaction. 'Alessandro, are you going to get changed?' He completely ignored her.

'Come on,' he said to Allegra, 'the chopper's waiting. This thing is timed down to the last second—Matteo has asked that we not be late.'

'Well, at least put on your tie,' Zoe called as he took Allegra's hand.

'It's a rock concert,' he said.

'And you're a prince.'

'Which means I'll be the only idiot wearing a suit.'

As they walked to the helipad, he asked, 'How have you been? Your bruise is gone.'

'I'm much better thanks.' She gave him a smile. 'I feel a bit more myself.'

'You look it.' She wasn't sure if it was a reference to her jeans, but there was no barb in his words; it was as if all the energy had gone out of him.

'Are you okay?'

'I will be,' he said. 'It's just been a tough couple of weeks.'

There was no chance to talk further, the whir of the chopper was already chasing away their words. Instead they sat in silence for the short ride to the amphitheatre, Alex staring out through the glass. She could not fathom his thinking, wondered perhaps if he was missing Belinda, or just his life back in London, if seeing his fiancée at a charity concert was perhaps the last place he wanted to be. All the excitement just oozed out of her.

The helicopter touched down. The rest of the crowd had been there all day, with the Crown Prince and his fiancée arriving to enjoy the evening section. But instead of being amongst them, they were moved to the front, to a box surrounded by bodyguards.

And cameras flashed, not for five minutes, not for ten, but as the sun lowered and the sky darkened, the cameras continued and Allegra felt so exposed, because at any second someone in the crowd was taking her picture. Alex knew too, for every now and then he would smile and move his head to speak to her, but not once did he touch her. Apart from the walk from the helicopter where he had briefly held her hand, there had been no contact.

There was the most romantic song playing, she was sitting in the amphitheatre with her prince, the people surrounding them delighted by their presence, the whole place full of love, and never had Allegra felt lonelier. She had missed Alex so much, had looked forward to this night and ridiculously so, but now that it was here, it just rammed home the lack of love.

'What was that?' Alex leant forward and spoke to one of his aides. 'There's a change in the programme....' Allegra could not care less; she just wanted the night over. She was sick of sitting, smiling and pretending to be having the time of her life, was sick of being with a man who felt so little for her. 'Your sister is singing.'

And she could not smile, for she felt sick, absolutely sick to her stomach, that the Santinas would stoop so low.

'So she can be publicly ridiculed this time!' She wanted to dash over there, to warn Izzy, to tell her that this was the nail in the coffin, that she was being used just to confirm the Jacksons' unsuitability; she cringed for her sister, how they had all been so derisive at the party.

'I had nothing to do with this,' Alex said.

And it was too late to do anything, Allegra realised. It had been too late since the day she met Alex in the bar and she had been naive enough to think that she could handle this.

There was Izzy, stepping nervous and shy onto the stage dressed in her trademark platform shoes, wearing impossibly short shorts. She looked beautiful to Allegra; she *was* beautiful, but she could just guess as to the palace's reaction.

She watched as her sister took to the piano and offered a silent prayer—she knew Izzy could sing, but there had been sound engineers on that awful reality show. Now it was just her, unrehearsed too. Allegra felt sick to her stomach for her sister, except as the piano played, as Izzy started to sing, Allegra's nerves for her sister faded. She realised she was hearing her true voice—away from the engineers and recording studio, away from people trying to make her conform. Tonight she heard the real Izzy for the first time—and yes, a star was born.

Her voice was like liquid heaven; it filled the amphitheatre and silenced the crowd. Even the cameras that had been trained on Allegra and Alessandro stopped. Izzy was centre stage and this truly was her moment, the crowd holding up their glow sticks. Allegra felt goose bumps as she watched her sister, her little sister, grow up in a moment, watched her shine, watched as her eyes glanced for assurance, not to the royal area, not to her big sister, but to the wing. She was singing for someone and it had to be Matteo. Suddenly Allegra wanted to cry, but she dared not, and she wanted to turn, to tell Alessandro that his plan had backfired, but she was too moved, too lost in the song.

Look at me, I'm not who you see...

Deep inside there's someone else, longing to break free...

She just had, Allegra realised. Izzy had broken free, and though the words seemed aimed at Allegra's heart, from Izzy's shy glances to the side of the stage, from the love that blazed in her eyes, she knew that the words were intended for another.

Alex could feel Allegra beside him as he watched the woman they had all scorned prove so many people wrong.

He wanted to take Allegra's hand, wanted to relax and absorb the moment, but he was sitting next to a woman who loathed the palace, who did not want to be queen, who wanted this duty over.

He looked over to her glassy eyes, heard a tiny sniff. How he wanted to comfort her, to be proud with her, but he couldn't give up his right to the throne. He couldn't.

If he walked away it fell to Matteo.

Matteo was tough, completely capable, but... Alex looked to Izzy, heard the pure talent, a talent that would be silenced. Did Allegra not see what might happen here?

'She was amazing!' Allegra turned to him, but his face was rigid. She did not get this man. Did nothing move him? Was he so embalmed in royal blood that a glorious voice in such a magnificent place could leave him still as cold as the marble statues back at the palace?

'I'd like to see Izzy...' Allegra said. 'Can we go back-stage?'

'I rather think your sister is busy,' Alex said. 'Perhaps we should leave them to it.'

She'd had so much pinned on tonight, had ridiculously got her hopes up, but she couldn't keep up appearances any longer. The flash of the cameras flooded the blacked-out car as they drove back to the palace and she felt Alex's eyes on her.

'Can the tears wait till we get back to the palace at least?'

'Oh, let them see them, maybe they'll report that cracks are starting to appear,' Allegra said. 'Anyway, the press can concentrate on Izzy and Matteo now.' She was appalled that she could be jealous of her own sister—not for the attention, nor for her talent, but because it had been so clear she was singing to someone, that love was in her eyes and voice. That's what burnt. Oh, of course she wanted her sister happy. By the morning she would be okay, but right now, she could not feel lonelier, could not believe the situation she had found herself in, would never have agreed to this if she had known what Alex would be like.

'What happened to you?' She did not care if the driver might be listening, just simply did not care about appearances any more. 'What happened to the man I met in London? The man who came over and spoke to me?'

He could see the palace looming in the night sky and it looked like prison. He could hear her thick voice and knew that tears were falling. He had done this to her—he had trapped her as much as he was trapped himself.

'You've changed.' She hurled the accusation again and he turned his head to face her.

'No.'

'You have!'

'No,' he said it again. 'I have returned to who I am.'

She would never understand him.

'Here I am, Crown Prince Alessandro, here I am on duty at all times. Here there is no time for self, for—'

'Because you make it so,' she insisted. 'Because you and your family lock yourself away in the palace or behind dark glass windows. You're so bloody used to acting the part you've forgotten that you're people too. And your people know it,' she added nastily because, hell, she felt nasty. 'The reason they like me is because I'm real, because I'm *ordinary*.' She hurled the word back at him. 'Because I don't pretend to be perfect, because I don't act as if I'm better than them. No wonder your fans—'

'Fans?' He snorted. 'They are our people, not our fans.'

As they arrived at the palace, before the car had even fully stopped, she jumped out, flew up the steps and into the hall but he was just a step behind her. 'I said the wrong word,' Allegra retorted, 'one wrong word and you jump down my throat, belittle me....' And she did not need to explain herself, did not need a moment more of this.

'What's going on?' His mother came out of the lounge, nursing a brandy, as too often she did these days, her only comfort at night. Alex stood still.

'Nothing.'

'It didn't sound like nothing.'

'She's just upset.' Alex was not about to discuss his love life with his mother! 'She'll be fine in the morning.'

'She'll remember her place, you mean?' Alex blinked at the snarl in his mother's voice. 'Why don't you talk to her?'

'She ran off.'

'Go after her then,' Zoe said, but he just stood there. 'What is it with this family? I thought you were happy, Alessandro. I thought when you brought her home that you wanted a marriage that was worth fighting for.' She gave in then—Zoe, too, did not want to discuss her love life with her son. 'I'm sure she'll be just fine!' she said shrilly, and retreated back to the lounge.

Alex stood—looked up at the stairs—and knew that somehow he had to tell her.

'Leave me alone,' Allegra called as he knocked on the bathroom door. She'd picked up the stupid nightgown that

had been laid out on her bed and stormed into the bathroom and even the nightgown enraged her tonight, made
her want to spit she was so angry—there were probably
hundreds of them, Allegra thought as she undressed. It
was probably like a hospital laundry down there, with hundreds of Santina lace nightdresses all whizzing around and
around. She hated the mould she was being poured into—
had there been scissors in the room she'd have chopped
herself a new fringe! She was so angry! As she undressed
she almost fell over as she took off her panties then pulled
on the beastly gown.

Why, why, why did he have to be like this?

What had happened to the man she had met, the man
who had held her, the man who had come so close to making love to her?

Allegra caught sight of herself in the mirror and let out
a low moan, because just the thought of that night and his
hands on her and her body was leaping with desire, her
angry blush burning darker as she recalled the bliss of his
touch. All this, *all this*, she could take if she had Alex at
night, had the man she loved, the man she craved.

'Allegra.'

She swung around.

Shocked, appalled, embarrassed, because he walked in
uninvited. 'What on earth are you doing here?' she hurled.

'We need to talk.'

'I've said everything I'm going to.' She wanted him out
of there, hated that she craved him like she never had another. Even angry, even furious, even loathing, she was so
turned on she could sink to her knees right now, but furious tears shot out instead.

'I'm going tomorrow.'

'You can't.'

'Just watch me,' she snarled. 'I'm sick of Santina—sick

of living with a family who haven't even got the energy
for a decent row, who can sit at the most amazing concert
completely unmoved.' She glared at him. 'You can't even
pretend to love me—you didn't even hold my hand.'

'You don't understand.'

'I don't want to!'

'You have to!' he shouted. 'For tomorrow our wedding
date is to be announced.'

'Well un-announce it!' she hissed.

'It's too late for that—you know it. You will marry
me….'

'No.' She went to brush past him. 'I'm calling my father.'

'That's another thing…' He blocked the doorway, wondered if she might kick him. But he had to be harsh or he
would take her right now in his arms. 'Allegra, you need to
remove yourself further from your family.' This he found
incredibly difficult. 'You are marrying royalty.' His voice
was firm. 'It's not fitting…' He tried to find the words,
tried to state out what a royal bride-to-be should already
know. Had she been born for this, groomed for this, then
it would not need to be said.

'Let me past.' She was furious, completely over this
madness. She kicked and she pushed, but he stood firm,
held her wrists and told her how it would be.

'If Izzy and Matteo continue, you will see plenty of her.'
She knew what he was saying, had known it in her heart,
had kidded herself that the lack of contact with her family
was just because she was so busy with the wedding and all
the things going on in their lives. But in reality she knew
that they were being slowly peeled apart and she knew that
it must be killing her father, that stepping back to do the
supposed right thing must be breaking his heart.

'Let me past.' She was tousled and angry and more

beautiful than he had ever seen her and it would have been so much easier to lie down with her than to stay standing. He could see her breasts rising and falling as she breathed hard in anger, see her erect nipples beneath the lace, her thighs slightly apart in her angry stance and her knickers on the floor. He wanted to kiss his way out of it, to push her from the bathroom to the bed and lose himself in her, to end this row without it ever having to take place. Yet somehow he stood, somehow he had to explain. He let her pass but as she reached for the phone he spoke some more.

'Think before you speak to your father, Allegra—because if it is hell for you, imagine how it might be for Izzy.'

'Izzy?' She swung around, phone in hand.

'From the way your sister was looking to my brother tonight, I think it is no longer just about you.'

She had wanted honesty, wanted to know what went on behind the iron wall that had been around him since they landed here, but now there was dread in her heart, perhaps it already knew, for slowly, like Chinese water torture, the truth was dropping in. 'What does Izzy have to do with us?' She halted then—it felt as if her throat closed over—and he stood and watched as her hellish realisation dawned.

'If I step aside, or if the marriage does not go ahead, Matteo will assume my role. I am quite sure the people of Santina would not be ready for a karaoke queen—though of course she wouldn't be one, there would be no more singing, no more performances....'

'Izzy would never stop.'

'She would have no choice. If the wedding is not announced tomorrow, I will be forced to step aside. It's up to you, Allegra.'

And she tried to picture it, tried to picture Izzy in this role, and as hard as it was for Allegra, it would be hell for Izzy. There was something about Izzy, something fragile, something wild, something precious that would be crushed in a moment by the weight that was landing on Allegra right now. She felt the fight leave her, stabbed at impossible hope.

'Izzy and Matteo might not last....'

'Perhaps not.' Alessandro shrugged. 'But at least it should run its course.' He looked to his fiancée and hated himself for doing this. 'Tomorrow we announce the wedding date. You can, of course, ring your parents first.'

'You won't stop me from seeing them.' She was depleted but still defiant on that point at least.

'Of course you will see them,' Alessandro said. 'It *will* be different though, and more so after the wedding. They can come and see you.' He was most uncomfortable, for though really he couldn't imagine caring if he didn't see his parents for the foreseeable future, he knew that family meant a lot to her.

'It's already different.' She looked to him. 'Have they been spoken to?'

'I would think that the palace would have met with them—would have told them their role in preparing for the wedding.' And then he was honest. 'They spoke with your father, a couple of weeks after the engagement.'

She thought back to that morning on her balcony, to the last *real* conversation she had had with her father, arguing with him about flirting with the queen, and she was hit with a wave of homesickness so violent she thought the boat might topple over.

'What would they have said to him?'

'To pull back, to make sure that all the family does the same. That you were not to be troubled with day-to-day things.'

Like romances and pregnancies and all their gossip. No

wonder she'd felt so out of the loop; her family had been told to keep her out of it for her sake!

'You should have married Anna.' She meant it. 'I wish that you had.'

And he saw her hurt and the mess he had created, his fiancée who was crushed—and the worst part was it had been by his own hand. So his answer was honest, for Allegra's sake:

'I wish I had too.'

CHAPTER TWELVE

She did see her family in the lead up to the wedding, but Alex was right; it wasn't the same.

Izzy was head over heels and naturally assumed Allegra was—she would talk about Matteo for hours, read out songs she'd penned, clump around in her noisy shoes. Because she was Izzy, because she wasn't going to one day be queen, it didn't seem to incense the royals so.

Izzy got to be her wonderful self while Allegra seemed to forget who she was. Two weeks before the wedding Alex had to fly to London to finalise the transfer of his business and would return on the eve of the wedding.

'The eve…!' There had been a row, of course.

Another one.

'There is much business to take care of—when I am back, I will be back for good. We have our honeymoon to look forward to, we are away for a full month,' he pointed out. 'I am just away for two weeks.'

What a difficult two weeks it was, and though she adored spending time with Izzy, it was her fittings with Raymond that got her through—his endless chatter and the smiles he gave her—little shots of confidence that he seemed to inject with every pin he stuck in.

'You've lost more weight.' He was far from impressed. 'Allegra…'

'I'm not trying to.' Allegra stood there and looked at her stick figure and sallow skin and wondered how in a couple of days she was supposed to transform into a radiant bride. She knew she was too thin. Even the queen was offering her croissants these days and she was accepting them too. It was just the nerves and the knot in her stomach and the loneliness that was like an endless furnace on constant high burn. 'Things will calm down after the wedding.' She had to believe that they would, that once they were more alone, once she and Alex were in an apartment, they could form a new normal, that she might find her place in a life she had not chosen.

'Well, let's get this off—it's the last time you'll see it before the big day.'

'Shall I put the other one on?' Allegra asked, but Raymond shook his head. 'You might need to alter it.'

'No need—it's not anywhere near as fitted.' She was curiously disappointed, for she truly loved the other dress. 'Anyway, it's been cleaned and it's hanging.'

'I wanted to see it.'

'You'll see it after the wedding.' Raymond beamed, busying himself with his pins and tapes, trying to hide his blush. For he deliberately hadn't brought it along today; he knew how much better it looked than the other, knew how much more suited it was to Allegra, and he did not want her to know that, did not want her disappointed with her choice of dress on the big day. She had, he knew, enough to contend with already—in truth he was worried about her. 'So,' Raymond asked. 'What have you got planned? Are you off to spend some time with your family?'

'Not till after the rehearsal tomorrow,' Allegra said, trying to pretend it didn't matter. 'Anyway, my dad's got to film his television show and can't get here till the rehearsal.'

'But the rest of them are here,' Raymond said. He was worried about how pale she looked, figured she needed some time with her family. But, in fact, Allegra was petrified to see them in case she ended up breaking down and begging them to just take her home.

'Alex doesn't get in till lunchtime and then I think he's got some royal duties tomorrow night, but I'll be at the hotel, so if I want to see him before the wedding there's only tomorrow afternoon.'

'You'll feel better when you see him,' Raymond soothed. 'You'll remember why you're doing this in the first place,' he said.

She smiled and said she hoped so, but it was the loneliest day of her life when he had gone. She looked out of the window, could see the activity outside the palace, cameras setting up, barriers in place, all getting ready for the day that was fast approaching.

'Allegra.' She answered the phone to Alex. 'How are things?'

'Fine,' she said. 'I've just had my last fitting for my dress. How are things there?'

'I've been busy,' Alex said. 'I am actually looking forward to having a full month off. Is everything sorted?'

'Pretty much,' Allegra said.

'The book?'

'It's almost finished,' Allegra said.

'Really? Well done.' He actually sounded proud. 'Am I allowed to read it?'

'No,' Allegra said. 'I want my father to be the first… Actually…' She stopped herself. 'It doesn't matter.'

'Does it matter or not?' He was always so straight to the point.

'It matters.'

'Well then?'

'I didn't expect to finish so soon, but now that I have I was hoping to give it to Dad at the wedding, to have the book bound—except Santina is not exactly inundated with office shops.'

'You should get it properly bound.'

'It's only a first draft—it isn't even finished.' She couldn't work out the end, didn't want it to be about her wedding, except so much had happened, there were so many changes in her family.

'Email it to me and I will have it bound.'

'You won't read it?'

'Allegra.' He gave a wry laugh. 'I haven't got time to sleep, let alone read.' When Allegra said nothing he concluded the conversation. 'Send it now and I will get Belinda straight on to it. I'll see you tomorrow.'

'Sure.' She hung up the phone, wondered how she could be marrying a man in two days and having such a stilted conversation with him. Maybe he felt the same because almost the moment she hung up, the phone rang again.'

'Alex…?'

'Sorry, only me…' came the lovely sound of Angel. 'We want Allegra!' She heard the cheers in the background. Heard Leo and Ben, Ella and Izzy, all chanting her name. 'Surely you can escape for an extra night.'

'I've got my hair to sort—'

'Allegra…' Izzy came on the phone. She knew better than the rest just how difficult the palace could be at times. 'Just wait there, I'm going to have Matteo send me a car and we're all coming to the palace to get you!'

She fired Alex an email, considered telling him, but chose not to—he would attempt to dissuade her after all. She loved that her siblings had come to rescue her, loved the evening she spent with them, hearing them laugh, catching up on all the news.

Strange that she missed Alex with all this going on.

So much so that the next day, as soon as she awoke, it was Alex she called, even though she knew he would be on his plane.

'He's busy.' It irritated her that Belinda answered Alex's private number.

'Can I speak to him please?'

'He's specifically asked not to be disturbed,' came the snooty response. 'He's having a lie-down.'

And she tried not to think of the bedroom on the private jet that had brought her to here. Tried not to think of Alex and Belinda confined.

It was too hard to.

Especially when tomorrow she would be marrying him.

CHAPTER THIRTEEN

'WHERE is everyone?' Belinda dropped him off and headed straight to the office as Alex walked into a very empty palace on the eve of his wedding.

He'd expected a hive of activity, for Allegra at least to pretend to be pleased to see him, but the welcoming committee consisted of his father at his irritable worst.

'As if anyone would tell me! Your fiancée left yesterday for the hotel to be with her family.'

'I spoke to her yesterday,' Alex said. 'She said she was joining them after the rehearsal.'

'Well, those sisters of hers turned up unannounced, and that ghastly market woman.'

'Chantelle?'

'I really don't need to know her name. Anyway, they've taken her with them.' His son's frown annoyed him. 'You'll see her at the rehearsal.'

Alex knew he'd been cutting it fine, but he'd banked on seeing her, for an hour or two, to check how she was doing. It never entered his head that the cut-off, out-of-control feeling he was experiencing was one he'd subjected his fiancée to these past weeks while in London.

'How is she?'

The king shrugged. 'Permanently premenstrual, I think. She burst into tears the other night because her father can't get here till late this afternoon.' The king let out a smug laugh. 'He's taking part in some celebrity quiz show, in front of a live audience. I think we were supposed to be impressed! Oh—' the king hadn't finished airing his frustrations '—your ex-fiancée is pregnant—baby due in a few months. You certainly backed the wrong horse. We could have had an heir on the way instead of the traveling gypsies descending on Santina.'

'That's all it is to you, isn't it?' Alex looked to his father, actually saw him as if for the very first time. 'You know, I was a little bit worried about my mother's drinking.' He poured himself a rather large one. 'Now I admire her restraint. You'd need to be sedated to listen to you.' But the king wasn't listening.

'Where is she?' the king demanded as the butler served afternoon tea.

And Alex sat there, as an aide spoke about the wedding guests and dignitaries that would be coming. 'You said she was at the hotel.'

'I was talking about your mother. Where is she?' he demanded again. 'We've got the wedding rehearsal this evening, we have guests arriving tonight.'

'She asked for transport,' the butler answered, but was saved from explaining further as the queen arrived home then.

'Where were you?'

'I went into Santina…' She had very pink cheeks. 'I got my hair done, in a salon.' The king just looked at her as if she were speaking a foreign language. 'And Allegra was right, the owner shut up the shop and I had a delightful time with the other women. They were getting their hair done for the wedding too. They're having a street party.' She looked to her king. 'Do you like my hair?'

It was strawberry blonde now rather than grey, but the

king chose not to notice. He didn't want to notice, for he did not like the changes. These trips out were becoming more frequent and he did not like them one bit.

'Have some tea,' he said.

'I'd like a brandy,' she said to a maid. 'And two head-ache tablets please.'

'It's the crowds,' the king said. 'All the noise giving you a headache.'

'It is not the crowds,' she snapped.

'Have some tea.'

'I don't want tea.'

Alex chose not to listen. Instead he frowned as Belinda came into the room with news he really did not want to hear.

'Bobby Jackson's speaking to the press.'

'You had tea with *him*!' the king said as they moved to the television room. Alex stood at the back, watched Bobby standing at Heathrow Airport, a throng of micro-phones pressed to his face and a crowd gathered around.

'His people like him,' the queen said.

'They're not his people,' the king snapped, 'they're fans.'

And Alex closed his eyes, for he did not want to be like his father. He knew he could be at times and he never wanted to be like that again—especially where Allegra was concerned. Bobby Jackson was talking about player selection, and giving his views, but now, of course, the questions were growing more personal. The press were bored with incessant 'no comments' and so they chose a different line.

'Will you be making a speech at your daughter's wed-ding?'

'No comment.' He gave a grim smile and went to walk off.

'Only, you embarrassed her pretty badly at the engagement...'

And Alex watched as Bobby's shoulders stiffened. 'You had a few too many and said how well she'd done for herself.'

And to Bobby's credit he did walk off, but only for two seconds—a proud man, he soon turned around.

'Had I got to finish my speech, I'd have said that Prince Alessandro had done well for himself too. She's a nice girl is Allegra, she's been the lynch pin of this family.' His voice broke just a little. 'They're so lucky to have her. They've done well for themselves too.'

And Alex stood there, and so badly he wanted to see Allegra.

'So vulgar.' The king huffed. 'Off to his harem he goes. I don't know how those women—'

'I'd kill to be Chantelle or Julie.' Just when he least needed it, just when he wanted for the first time to examine his own feelings, there was another crisis to deal with. The queen, his mother, standing with three decades of fury pooling out, as the maid stood there, as the butler did too, as the fireworks went off and the queen exploded. 'At least he gives them half of his attention. I have one man to myself and all I get is ignored. Bobby Jackson is charming, absolutely charming, and yes, rather sexy too. And for all his mistakes, at least he knows how to treat a woman.'

'She'll calm down in moment,' the king said as Zoe marched out of the room. He clicked his fingers to have more tea then changed his mind. 'I might have a brandy.'

And Alex saw the proud old fool and swore he would never be him, and never did he think he would be giving his father marital advice, but then the palace had changed an awful lot since the Jacksons had been allowed in.

There was emotion at every turn, arguments exploding, and Alex realised he would not change it for the world.

'If I were you, Father, I'd ask for two glasses and I'd take the decanter upstairs.'

'She'll be fine in a moment.'

'And maybe,' Alex overrode him, 'you might notice her hair.' He didn't add, Or someone else might. 'And tonight, when the guests have gone and you have retired, I suggest you read this....' He did not feel guilt as he handed over Allegra's work—always efficient Belinda had had two separate copies bound for Allegra to choose from.

'What's this?'

'It's the real story of Bobby Jackson—it shows a man who knows how to forgive. It speaks of love and pride and his devotion to family. How even if others may not approve, he must be doing something right.' He looked to his father. 'After all, look at the children he has raised. But now, I suggest you apologise to your wife—and if you cannot manage that, at least speak with her.'

He watched as after a moment of painful deliberation his father creaked his way out of the chair and nodded to the butler, who handed him the decanter. He looked as if he was walking to the gallows as he climbed up the stairs. Alex never, ever wanted that for Allegra—had never wanted it for Anna either.

That burn in his gut was back. He turned to the butler, then changed his mind; instead he walked into his office and spoke with Belinda.

'I want transport arranged.'

CHAPTER FOURTEEN

'HE SHOULDN'T be much longer.' Belinda clipped off her phone.

'We don't really need Alessandro…' the king said, because he wanted the rehearsal over, was, in fact, rather looking forward to getting back to the palace with his wife! 'He knows his place. Let's just make sure the Jacksons—'

And Allegra bit back a smart retort. She was so sick of the none-too-subtle barbs that the Santinas knew exactly how to do things. Hell, who needed a groom at a wedding rehearsal?

'Where is he?'

Belinda said nothing, but then she had never bothered with Allegra before.

'I'm going to get some air.'

Allegra walked outside, gulping in the cool evening air. She had so badly wanted to see Alex, just for some reassurance. She jumped a little when Belinda walked up beside her.

'They just want to run through the paces one more time. I'll be Alex.'

Allegra could think of nothing worse. 'I'll wait, thanks.'

'The king wants this wrapped up.' Belinda wasn't exactly enamored with Allegra either.

'Then he should call his son.'

'He knows where he is... For goodness' sake, Allegra, do you really need to make a scene? Let's just get on with it.'

'Where is he?'

'Where do you think?'

At that moment a car pulled up—not a royal car, not Alex's car, but a car she did not recognise. She stood in the shadows of the vestry, watching her own heart be served on a plate, watching Alex, the passenger, turn to the driver. There was no mistaking the tenderness in the gesture—watching his hand reach out and cup the driver's face. No mistaking the affection as he leant over and kissed her on the lips and then on her forehead...and they rested their heads there a moment before he pulled away.

'Who?' She hated that it was Belinda she had to ask.

'Anna.' She almost heard the snap of the last string holding her together. 'I thought she was with your brother,' Belinda carried on. 'No doubt he's reassuring her that nothing will change.' She could hear the spite in Belinda's voice.

'Did he reassure you the same?' Allegra couldn't help but ask.

Hateful were the eyes that turned to her. 'Do you think for a moment that a wedding ring will stop him? Look around, Allegra. So you get the prince, you get the dress and the pomp, and the title. Enjoy it, enjoy every minute of it, but it won't keep you warm at night.'

'No,' Allegra attempted. 'That's my husband's job!'

But Belinda just laughed; she just stood there and laughed. 'You!' She laughed even louder. 'You really don't get it, do you? The people might think they like you now, but Alex knows it won't last. Just look at you, Allegra, you're nothing. Your family are nothing to him.

And sooner or later they'll be nothing to the people—just a rather embarrassing thorn.'

Allegra stood there, trying to bite back her fury, trying to remember the Allegra of old who could think of a smart retort, the Allegra who was Bobby Jackson's daughter, who would turn around and just give her a black eye.

'The people won't blame him a bit for the way he carries on.' It was unfortunate that at that moment Chantelle chose to wander out of a side door and go through her handbag, coughing a bit, before lighting up a cigarette. 'Now, Anna…' Belinda gave a slightly wistful sigh. 'Anna has class—well, she did, till she met with Jacksons. With Anna, he'd at least have had to show discretion. You lot will take any crumbs.'

'All right, love.' Bobby came over. 'Where is that man of yours?'

'Here I am.' Alex walked over.

'About time.' The king huffed and joined them, as Alex gave Allegra a brief kiss on the cheek, but it was only for show, that much she knew.

'Where were you?'

He frowned down, for never had he had to explain himself before and he certainly wasn't about to start now. Here was hardly the best place to tell his bride of tomorrow that he had spent some time with his ex-fiancée—and certainly not with her in this fragile state. He could see she was shaking, and he didn't like the other changes either: her fringe was long gone now, tucked behind her ear; he could see her clavicles poking out of her chest. He hated what his family had done—what he had allowed.

'I had things to sort out. Come on.' He took her by the elbow and they took their positions at the altar for the rehearsal. He could feel her jangling with nerves. He should never have left her alone to deal with this. He had thought he was doing her a favour, giving her a break before they were forced into the union she didn't want, but instead he'd exposed her.

'What things?' Allegra asked. He heard the sharp *T* at the end of her 'what' and he wanted her back, he wanted Allegra Jackson back.

'At this point, you will join hands...' the priest said.

'What things?' she asked again.

'It is not your concern.'

'It is when you...' And what was the point—what was the point of challenging him? Was this to be her life? To wait in the shadows, to lie in bed and wonder where he was, that he could be so blatant, so dismissive. She loved Izzy, loved her sister so very much, but she loved herself too.

Had to love herself more. She couldn't do this.

'There will be a hymn...' the priest droned on.

'No.' Her voice was soft, so soft that no one noticed, and she said it again.

'No.' The chatter stopped and she looked to her grim fiancé, smelt a perfume that was not hers in the air between them, and her voice was firm when next it came.

'I can't marry you.'

She fled from the church, poured herself into a car and begged the shocked driver to move on.

'Nerves.' Bobby grinned, instantly moving to put everyone at ease.

'It's nerves,' said the king.

'I'm not sure...' Angel had seen the agony on her sister's face as she had fled from the church and she looked to Izzy. 'Shall I go and talk to her?'

'I will,' Bobby said.

'Maybe it will come better from a woman,' Chantelle offered, because the last thing she wanted was Allegra turning this down. She had her outfit sorted and she liked being related to royalty. 'Julie?'

Except Alex had already left the church.

CHAPTER FIFTEEN

'You couldn't even last till the wedding!' She opened her hotel door and met him with her rage.

'What are you talking about?'

'I saw you kiss her, saw you hold her....'

'Allegra, you're being ridiculous.'

'I don't want to hear your excuses. You're sleeping with your ex!' Her voice was rising. 'What about Leo, what about my brother? How could you!'

'She's pregnant, for God's sake.'

'I know that.' Allegra sobbed; she was hysterical now, weeks and months of pain, all rising up and there was no horse to jump on to flee away. 'How do I know it isn't yours? You're screwing your ex and—'

He'd heard enough. He grabbed her, his only thought to put an end to her tirade. He could feel anger bubbling up within him, his grip tightening on her, his hand raising to slap her silent and it took every ounce of self-control to lower his hand.

She stared, stunned, appalled, and she waited, breathless, for him to apologise, to recant, but he stood there resolute.

'There would be no self-control if anyone spoke that way of you.'

He meant it.

She knew that and it was not the pain of his hand on her arm but the strange honor in his words that brought tears to her eyes.

'Anna and I have never slept together—she kept herself for me. As future queen this was to be her expected gift. Of course things have changed,' he hurriedly added. 'I have had harsh words with my father that you are never to be questioned, that your past is your own....'

She closed her eyes in shame, because even if it felt things moved at a snail's pace, he had ensured changes, had moved impossible mountains, even if she had not known.

'I went to see Anna because I wanted to speak with her and it seemed imperative I do that before the wedding. For so long there had been guilt. I never intended to hurt her with our engagement, never intended that she find out the way she did, through the press. Ours was supposed to be a brief fling, and now she has had to come attend our wedding. I needed to put things right with her. She's happier than she ever has been. She sees it was the best thing that could happen. Anna and I could never have divorced.'

'Unlike us.'

And she could never read him, could spend the rest of her life trying to work him and still not get him, for even as she stood, he surprised her again.

'I don't want a divorce, Allegra.' He said it as if he meant it. 'I am going to do everything that I can to make this marriage work. There was no attraction with Anna—I care for her,' he admitted, 'but...' How could he say it? 'It would have been my parents' marriage all over again—perfunctory sex to produce an heir.'

'You couldn't put *her* through it, yet you will me.'

'There would be nothing perfunctory about us.'

'A loveless marriage, but with good sex?'

'I can think of worse things.'

'What about Belinda?' Her eyes were savage again. 'She said—'

'Never listen to a scorned woman—you know that. Belinda is bitter. I have not slept with her since you and I met. As of tomorrow, she no longer works for me. I have ensured her position in my old company, or a package if she prefers, but—'

'She wants you.'

He nodded.

'She can't have me though. I will be adhering to my vows. It's up to you if you marry me, Allegra. I am not going to beg. I'm certainly not going to grovel. The choice is yours, but when tonight you make your decision, there is one thing you ought to know. I have no intention of staying celibate, and as I have just told you, no intention of sleeping around—which means you and I will sleep together,' Alex said. 'If you marry me tomorrow we will share a bed.'

'And if I don't?'

'Then don't turn up. I love my brother, but I am not living like a monk for his sake. You know that whatever there is not between us, that much there is....'

'You're so sure.'

Tender now were the fingers that moved along her arm, yet she flinched. He roamed a hand down her body and she curled inside. Then he moved a hand to her cheek and she turned it away, but cool were his lips on her flesh and she closed her eyes, berating the bliss his mouth delivered.

'I hate what you do to me.'

'You won't tomorrow,' Alex said. 'If you come to the church, then know that you will be my wife in every sense of the word. It's up to you. Know that I will be a good husband, a wonderful provider, that your family will be taken care of and you will be too.'

'You need to know something too. The people of Santina have been unhappy for a long time.'

'I do not need your opinion on my people.'

'You can dismiss what I say if you want, but you will do me the courtesy of at least listening. The people want me, because I am ordinary, because I cry and I laugh, even in public, because of—not in spite of—my family's mistakes. You marry *me*, or you can find another wife to wear the nightdresses laid out for her, perhaps one with quieter shoes, and she can be as miserable as your mother is.'

'Don't…'

'Don't what?' Allegra said. 'Don't speak of such things? Why not?' Allegra demanded. 'Why can't you have an honest conversation with the woman who tomorrow might be your wife? And know this too—my family will come and visit me in the palace and I shall fly home and visit them. I will be close with my brothers and sisters. If you want to marry me, know who you're committing to.'

'I do,' Alessandro said, and he surprised her with a smile, the smile he gave her on the first day, the smile that always melted her so. And then he did the impossible, at least the impossible for a prince in Santina—he made a joke. 'I'm just getting in practice for tomorrow. I do, Allegra.'

CHAPTER SIXTEEN

'How is she?' Matteo, Ash and Hassan were waiting when he returned to the palace.

'She's okay,' Alex said.

'Bobby asked if you could ring him and let him know,' Matteo said, and Alex nodded. 'He wants to have a word with you.'

'There's no need.' The king huffed. 'He's probably there now—he can see her for himself.'

Alex ignored him. 'I need his number.'

'Don't you have it?' Zoe asked. 'Didn't you ring him first when you went to ask for his daughter's hand? What about when you were in London?'

There were so many things he had done wrong, so many, many things. As Matteo gave him the necessary number Alex moved into the library to talk with his soon-to-be father-in-law in private, closing his eyes in shame as he spoke to him.

'Right,' the king said as Alessandro came out. 'Let's have a drink—we'll have guests arriving shortly.' They did, dignitaries that had to be entertained on the eve of the wedding, essential duty to be taken care of, but Alex halted the procession making their way to the drawing room.

'Actually there's been a change of plan. I'm going out with Bobby tonight.' He saw Matteo smother a smile, saw

CHAPTER SEVENTEEN

SHE awoke surprisingly calm, and smiled at the room service attendant who brought her coffee. She then sat up in
bed and flicked the remote to turn the television on, finding it hard to believe that the chatter and excitement and
the images playing out on the television screen were for
her wedding.

The streets were filling already, the people of Santina
eager to get the best viewpoint of the guests making their
way to the church, and though logic told her that she should
be nervous, sad even, Allegra was not. She refused to be
the martyr bride.

She was marrying the man she loved today.

And that was something to celebrate.

She sat, eyes closed, as her make-up was done and the
final touches were put to her hair, but opened them when
the door knocked. In came her bridesmaids—Angel and
Izzy looking stunning, and two little cousin princesses
from Alex's side.

'Your dad's got the most terrible hangover.' Angel
laughed as she twirled in her bridesmaid's dress. 'I don't
think your groom will be feeling much better. From all
reports it was quite a heavy night.'

'Alex?' Allegra frowned. 'He was at the palace last
night....'

'How little she knows!' Angel rolled her eyes. 'Your fiancé, Matteo and Hassan were out with Bobby and Co.'

'They came here to the hotel?'

'No.' Angel grinned. 'They went into town. Apparently the locals were thrilled, plying the wedding party with sambuca.'

Allegra let out a gurgle of laughter. She was quite sure Angel must have got it wrong somehow; perhaps Alex had dropped in to be polite or they had somehow run into one another. But it was nice to laugh this morning, especially when there was a knock at the door and Raymond came in with his entourage wheeling the much-coveted dress that was covered in layers of sheets.

'You're looking better.' Raymond beamed.

'I feel better,' Allegra admitted.

'Can I see?' Izzy asked.

'No, you cannot!' Raymond scolded. 'I am not risking a single eyelash falling onto this dress. I want everyone out—you can see her when she's dressed.' And he shooed out the bridesmaids and pulled off a sheet and there it was—full skirt, in at the waist and with a very long train. It glimmered and was absolutely beautiful. The thing was, it simply wasn't the one that she loved.

'I'm wearing the other one, Raymond.'

'Oh, Allegra.' His eyes widened. 'The queen…'

'What's she going to do?' Allegra asked. 'Turn me away at the church?' She saw the excited grin on her designer's face. 'He's marrying me, Raymond. The "me" he first met…' And Raymond understood, for he had got back together with Fernando but had decided to end things.

'You're wonderful,' Raymond said.

'So are you!' She gave him a hug and then Raymond danced off.

'It's so much better!' Raymond admitted, pulling off the sheet. 'So, so much more you.'

It was. It was stunning, so beautiful she could hardly breathe. But before she took off her robe, before she slipped it on, she turned to the hairdresser who was pulling out her veil from a large box.

'I know it's terribly short notice,' Allegra said. 'And I know it's not what we planned, but is there any chance you could cut me a fringe?'

It was nice to find her power, wonderful, at the eleventh hour, to find her voice, to see the real Allegra returning as she stood in the most beautiful dress in the world. She looked into the mirror and smiled at the bride she was and the princess she would become.

She would be a wonderful wife; she would be loyal to her husband and she would readily give the love that inside burnt, but she would be her own person too.

Would have coffee with her sisters and nights out too, would not walk away from her family—no matter what.

'Last-minute change!' A boot-faced florist walked in, cursing in rapid Italian as she added some blue-starred flowers to the heavy white rose bouquet. *'Erbacce...'* the florist sneered. Allegra knew from her lessons that that meant 'weeds,' but they were her favourite weeds in the world. And perhaps, even with the meticulous planning, they had forgotten something blue after all!

'Oh, Allegra.' She looked to her father and he took out a hanky and blew his nose. 'You look amazing.' And then, in that moment before they walked to where the cars were waiting, Bobby had to make sure.

'You do want this?'

She nodded, but she couldn't speak. Tears were terribly close, but despite it all, it was what she wanted.

'It's not too late, you know...' Bobby checked.

'I love him, Dad.'

Bobby rolled his eyes and then conceded. 'I know you do. And yep, I thought he was a cold fish, but he went up in my books last night.' So they had been out! Allegra wasn't too sure that she needed the details, but she did smile at the very thought. 'I just want to make sure you're happy. That you know what you're getting into.'

She knew.

'I always moaned to your mum and Chantelle that you and your sisters' weddings would bankrupt me.' It broke her heart how hard it must be for him. 'This should be a dream come true for a parent, hasn't cost me a penny, and what with Izzy and Matteo, Ella and Hassan, Angel and Rafe...' He faltered for a moment. 'Careful what you wish for, huh!'

'You're not giving me away today, Dad.'

He frowned. 'Another thing they're taking away from me?'

'I meant...' Her voice was very firm, very clear, and her eyes shone, not with tears, but with absolute faith in her words. 'I'm always going to be your daughter—I'm not going to let them change that part of me. We'll still see each other, you'll come here and I'm not missing out on Christmas.' She saw an edge of a smile. 'And I mean that. And if Alex doesn't want to join in, if duty means he can't, I'm going to be there. Maybe just for one night, maybe we'll have to do Christmas some years on Boxing Day, but I'm not missing it—and neither will Izzy, I'll make sure of that. You're not giving me away, Dad.'

'No, I'm gaining a cold fish!'

He always made her laugh.

'Let's do it then.'

CHAPTER EIGHTEEN

'You don't have a cigarette?' He saw Matteo frown. 'Joking,' Alex said, but there was this restlessness in him, this gnaw, as they waited for the car that would take him to the church.

'Worried she might not show up?' his brother teased.

'No,' Alex said, for it was not that which worried him. There was this uneasiness that was ever present these days, this churn in his stomach that had him swallow an antacid and wait for the burn to go—it did not.

'What are you doing?' Alex asked, irritated as his brother tapped on his phone.

'Just checking on Izzy,' Matteo said. 'She'll be nervous about singing at your reception tonight.' He glanced up. 'Sorry. I'm supposed to be taking care of the groom. Mind you, you're hardly the type for nerves.'

'Ask Izzy how Allegra is,' Alex said.

'I was joking about her not showing up.' Matteo grinned, but it was not that that concerned Alex as his brother awaited Izzy's response. It was something else, something he could not place.

'Izzy's already said goodbye to Allegra, she says...' Matteo did not continue, instead he grinned at whatever Izzy had said.

'She makes you happy?' Alex asked.

'You know she does.'

'I don't know,' Alex said, and for a second there it felt as if Matteo were the older one, the wiser one, privy to something he had never seen. 'You love her?'

'I do,' Matteo said, not at all shocked by his brother's question, because in this family love did not rule.

'How did you know?'

'Apart from the fact she was the first woman to swim in my fountain?' He gave a ghost of a smile. 'I'd never met anyone like Izzy before. The woman drove me crazy. And yes, it took me a while to realise that "crazy" was actually love.' He looked at his older brother. 'I nearly lost her, Alex. Don't make the same mistake as me.'

'I'm marrying her today,' Alex pointed out.

'I thought we were talking about love,' Matteo said. 'Which in this family is another subject entirely. Come on,' Matteo continued. 'Can't have the groom being late.'

Alex made a phone call, just a quick one, heard the confusion at the other end, but chose not to justify.

'You will see that it is done,' Alex said then clicked off his phone and climbed in the vehicle, stared unseeing out of the car window as they drove to church. He tried not to think of her smile and the feel of her in bed beside him and her raw tears last night. Tried not to think of the life he had trapped her in, a life she did not want, a loveless marriage that served only the people.

The streets were lined with people all waving and cheering, but they did not expect him to wave, nor even smile, for Alessandro so rarely did, but he did look—he looked at the hopeful faces, saw the pictures they held up of Allegra. They were his people, and reluctant or not, a little too soon for his liking perhaps, now he took his role on, and as he did in everything he would perform to perfection.

He and his bride *would* bring fresh ways to Santina.

The wait was interminable, and despite brave words to his brother, he did wonder if she'd change her mind, if at the last minute she would leave him standing. But then he heard the shift in the music, the excited chatter build in the church behind him, and then a shuffle as the congregation rose. He did not turn around; instead he stared ahead and the moment he had dreaded for the whole of his life was here. Except as he heard the congregation hush, the gnaw in his gut that should have tightened seemed to fade, the ache and the void seemed to fill....

He remembered the day he had met her; the loneliness that had twisted him as he'd sat in the club had been replaced by the first honest conversation he had ever had—how an afternoon with her had made the world seem right.

And he closed his eyes for he could not fathom it.

Then he opened them again, and the thought was the same.

At eight minutes past two as she started to walk towards him, Alex fell in love with his bride.

Had loved her all along, Alex realised as he turned around to see her, spent his days trying not to think of her, trying not to admit what he had thought impossible for him.

And he expected pain in her face and for her to be shaking and full of nerves—except she was smiling, a little pale, holding Bobby's arm tightly as she walked towards him, but she was walking with eyes wide open and her head held high.

His mind was playing a trick on him.

Aware of the cameras on him, aware at a wedding like this there could be no surprises, that till the formalities ended late into the night this was duty, he was, as always, supremely composed as he faced her.

And every camera that was trained for a reaction saw

his slow smile, saw him look away and then back again. He continued to stare, a dust of colour on his neck spreading to his ears, for surely every one could see—for, if he squinted a little, if he left her just a little out of focus, it could almost be their engagement night. She could almost be walking towards him in her nightgown, for the lace draped her body, seeped into chiffon on her arms and around midthigh, the chiffon seeming to fade on her legs and arms. It was Santina lace, and a secret smile played on her face as his thoroughly modern bride walked towards him. Allegra was back and his heart twisted with love and pride as she joined him and peered up at him from beneath her fringe.

'Allegra…' He could feel the cameras on him. He wanted to say it here, but the priest was already talking, the first hymn being sung and time was galloping along. It killed that she'd marry him without knowing that he loved her.

It did not kill her to stand there.

She stared at her groom and said her words clearly.

She would love him till death, she said, for it was true, even if sooner they must part.

Then she looked down, not shy but just deep inside herself, because she could not look him in the eyes as he lied—and did he have to say his vows so clearly, did he have to not waver, to sound so convincing? She felt his hand tighten and she looked up, saw those liquid brown eyes and their intensity; he was a fine actor, for she was the only one in the room who knew the truth.

There was no moment to talk, for each one had been meticulously taken care of. There were photos on the steps of the church and one tiny unscheduled moment when Allegra stepped towards the crowd, throwing her bouquet into the people, returning the flowers that they had given her—the little blooms that she'd carried home after her jaunts into the town, the little petals that had brightened so many lonely days.

Then they were whisked away to the palace, formal photos where the Jacksons stood with wide smiles and the Santinas just a touch more reserved, perhaps in nervous anticipation of the party tonight!

The photographer was respectful but this was his moment and he was damned if he didn't get the perfect shot. But the king was distracted, his wife beaming by his side, and then later at the bridal breakfast, utterly and completely radiant, he'd heard her laughing, a laugh that was unfamiliar, a laugh that maybe he'd missed.

It was hell for Alex, standing there, holding her, smiling with her, knowing she was lonely, knowing the truth he had to share.

They were in the horse carriage, heading back to the palace.

'Just rest for a couple of hours,' the aide informed them, because, well, they needed to and everyone knew that the wedding was just a formality. They'd been sharing a bed for ages after all. 'We'll be back to do your hair and make-up at five—you'll make your entrance at six-thirty.'

And finally they were alone.

'You look amazing,' Alex said.

'It's actually incredibly uncomfortable,' Allegra admitted. She smiled at the maid who came in to help her undress, for she would be expected to wear the gown tonight, but for now it would be a relief to take it off.

'We'll manage, thanks.' It was Alex who dismissed the maid and she was suddenly nervous, knew, despite her confidence in her decisions, that she was now his bride and that all the bravado in the world could not tame her shyness.

'Let me help,' Alex insisted as she stood there impossibly shy, far braver in her role of princess than wife.

He was behind her and his fingers undid the tiny buttons.

'Really, there is nothing very romantic about wedding attire.' She gave a brittle smile as she eyed his military uniform. 'Maybe we should call back the maid...' She was blabbering and terribly so.

'We'll manage,' Alex said, which meant rather than drop his braided jacket to the floor he placed it on a chaise longue and then sat on it and took off long boots. Her heart was in her mouth as she slipped her dress off and stepped out of it.

'I need to hang it.' God, the one time she needed the maid... Instead she was dressed in a stupid basque with hands that were shaking so, for she could feel his eyes now roam her body, could hear the undoing of zips and buckles and guessed he was close to naked now. And somehow she had to hang the most talked-about dress in the country.

'Come to bed, Allegra.'

'I can't sleep with you now.' Determined to be honest, determined to be true to herself, she said it without looking at him. Instead she arranged the chiffon so that it would hang nicely this evening. 'I mean, I know that's probably what's expected, and I know that we will, but—'

'Allegra...'

'I'm just nervous enough about tonight, about the speeches, about my family, about so many things, without...' She padded to the ensuite and slipped off her bridal underwear and slipped on a robe, and chatted nervously away. 'I'm just so tired and so wound up and...' She tried to be honest. 'I don't want to be rushed.' She walked back to the room, glad he had turned off the light, glad for the thick drapes that shut out the late-afternoon light, glad for a couple of hours to regroup. 'And no doubt we will later, but it's hard to explain. I mean, it must be a walk in the park for you....'

'A walk in the park?'

His English was excellent, just there were certain things that didn't translate, and she actually smiled as, still dressed in her robe, she climbed into bed beside him. 'No big deal.'

It was a huge deal, except to tell her that would sound pushy. 'When you're ready.'

He heard her sigh of relief.

'Can I just sleep?' She wriggled at the very pleasure of it. 'I didn't sleep much last night.'

'I know.'

He stared up into the darkness and he waited, for the rush of thoughts, for thirst, for the burn in his gut, and instead he breathed in air that smelt of her and all there was was peace.

'I had Matteo ask after you when he texted Izzy this morning.'

'Mmmm.'

'She was already heading for the cars though.'

Allegra closed her eyes. It was such a minor detail in the scheme of things, but rare for Alex to be the one filling silence, talking about nothing. 'I was worried.'

'That I wouldn't show up?'

'No,' Alex said. 'Though I thought you might not.' He turned and looked at her half dozing. 'You seem...' He did not know how to best describe it. 'I thought you would be more...'

'Miserable.' She peeked open an eye. 'No.'

'How come?' Alex asked, because she was a different woman to yesterday.

'I realised I was marrying the man I love.'

He felt the heat from her body, not passion, but a blush, because it was a brave thing indeed to admit, when you knew it was not reciprocated. He lay there with his breath held in his lungs and he frowned because her eyes were closed and she was half asleep.

'What does it feel like?' he asked.

'Painful,' Allegra said. 'But you learn to live with it.' She rolled over, she really would sleep. She'd told him—it would hardly make the news; after all, everyone thought that she did.

'You love me?'

'Why else would I be in your bed, Alex? Believe me, I'm not here for the million pounds, and as much as I love her, I'm not here for Izzy. My freedom's worth a lot more to me.'

'When?' he asked. 'Since when?'

'I'm not sure…' she mused in the darkness. 'Probably when I excused myself to go the ladies'….'

'The first day we met?' he asked, but he was not waiting for an answer from Allegra. Instead he was questioning himself, for it was that day that he had for the first time truly spoken to another. Not even his brother nor his betrothed had heard his darkest thoughts, yet he had shared them easily with Allegra.

'Tell me this pain.'

'I can't.' She was tired, so tired. Her feet ached, her head pulsed with the sound of cheers and bells and she was lying next to the most beautiful man on God's earth. But if sanity was to be her savior, if she didn't want to fall asleep at her own wedding party, then she really needed to sleep.

'Is it like wanting chocolate?'

'Dunno.'

'Then you eat and that is not what you want.'

'Maybe.'

'Where nothing tastes right?'

'A bit.'

'When you think it is sex you want, but you know it's not what you need.'

'Do we have to talk about…?' She didn't want Belinda in the room with them, didn't want to hear about his failed attempts to screw his way out of this.

'When you can't look at another woman,' Alex continued. And maybe she did want to hear after all. 'Because even though that always worked before, now you find that all you want is her?' He continued and her mind was dizzy. 'Where you ask your brother to text because you want to know, not what she is doing, but that she is okay?'

And she opened her eyes to him.

'Where you kick yourself over and over, where you lie awake at night and berate your choice of a single word, because when you said "ordinary—"' he heard her sob, felt her burn in shame and he hated himself for ever saying it '—that you meant she was normal, that this was not the life for her, and you hate yourself for saying it?'

'Why didn't you tell me?'

'I didn't know.' He lay there bemused by his own revelation. 'Never, not for a minute, did I consider I might love my bride.' He turned to her. 'It was not a factor.…'

'Like describing a rainbow to a blind man.' She saw him frown and she smiled. 'It's a saying. Like, how can you describe something you've never seen, something the other has no comprehension of.'

He looked to his past, to his rich, privileged life, and now that love lay next to him, now that love lived inside him, he understood her words. 'For all that my parents said about your family, for all I have said,' he stepped up, 'there is so much love there. And I do,' he said. 'I do love you.'

'When…' It was her turn.

'At about eight minutes past two,' he admitted. 'When I said my vows I meant them.'

And he kissed her because he couldn't not. A kiss that was different to any Alex had ever delivered, for kisses had always been precursors, just not today. He kissed her and he tasted her and he loved her with his mouth. And because he loved her with his mind, because there was for ever ahead of them, because he wanted this to be right, he pulled away.

'Sleep.'

'How can I possibly sleep now?'

'You're tired,' he said

'Not now.'

'Allegra.' It was Alex who wriggled away, because he was impossibly hard with her next to him, wanted her so badly, but was determined and weighted with responsibility, for an hour had passed and they had at best an hour or more. It had been so far from perfect for her, by his hand, by his cruel mouth, that he wanted at least to get this right.

'Rest now,' he said, 'and then tonight…' He could hardly wait, but for her he would. 'I want to do you properly later.' And sometimes his brain moved faster in his native tongue than his mouth allowed for translation, but if it was crass and not quite what he meant, from her peal of laughter he had not offended.

'You're going to *do* me properly, are you?'

'Yes.' He grinned. 'Now rest. Or…' He couldn't wait to tell her. 'I was going to give you this tonight.' He reached over to the bedside table.

'I don't need a gift…' She didn't, especially when he went to the dresser drawer and pulled out a velvet box. She loved him and everything, and was completely, incredulously delighted that he loved her too, but she'd received so many jewels today. Really, the one she loved most and would love the most for ever was the emerald he had bought on the day they had met.

Still, she knew she had nothing to complain about, so she smiled as she took the box and was ready to say a big wow in surprise as she undid the clip, but instead, as she opened the box, she frowned.

'Keys?'

'They are the thing I miss most when I am here. Even the car is brought around, but as soon as I get to London…' She smiled as she looked at the simple silver key ring holding two keys. Yes, Alex was right, she had not used a key in all the time she'd been in Santina. 'I wanted somewhere for you as I know how much you need your family. I wanted you to have somewhere, a place that was yours when you visit, a place they can go if you choose.…' She looked at the man who must have loved her even when he didn't know it because it was the most thoughtful gift in the world. 'A home in London—maybe you can host Christmas one year.' She laughed through her tears, laughed that he knew how important her family was, and she could feel all the love and hope for their future wrapping around her as did his arms. 'There's a car too,' he said. 'I have to arrange for it to be driven each week, so that the battery doesn't go flat.' She loved his constantly working brain, and he loved that she didn't even care what make the car was and they loved that they finally had each other.

'Oh, Alex…' She didn't know what to say. 'I—'

'Don't!' he interrupted. 'I did not expect a gift. I don't want you to be embarrassed.'

'I'm not,' she said, and she wasn't. 'And I do.'

'What.'

'I'm not embarrassed and I do have a gift. A gift I can only give one other.' And she leant over and gave him a kiss, and then whispered into his ear. She moved back so she could watch it sink in as he found out that his modern bride was, in fact, rather old-fashioned after all.

'Tonight,' he said, overcome with the enormity, pale at the thought of how her first time might have been, for that morning in bed he would not have been gentle. 'Tonight, we will take our time....'

But she could not wait now for tonight, because love unleashed her.

Not her love but his.

His love made her brave and she'd waited so very long, and even a few hours' delay was an impossible task.

As he lay and tried to pretend that he was dozing, as he tried to force his breathing to at least sound deep and even, wondered if he should throw in a snore for good measure, he felt the soft roll of her into him, and the hand that swept along his chest and touched him. He tried very hard to keep breathing as her hand crept down.

She felt the flat firm plane of his chest, the flat smooth areola and the tautness of nipples that had never been beneath her fingers, and she toyed there for a moment, because she could.

Because he was hers and for exploring and she was more curious than shy.

He smelt so clean—he always had, this tangy citrus scent that only belonged to him, her private perfumery. She breathed in the scent she would crave for ever, the private scent of cologne and this man, the undressed aroma that teased in her nostrils and demanded a taste and a kiss on his chest.

And he could not pretend to be sleeping, as he held his breath as her hand slid down to his hardness, his moan confirmed what she knew and no, he could not wait.

He rolled on to her, took her mouth with his and kissed her as he never had, nor never would another. His hands roamed her body, the body that had roamed his mind and that led him to the sweet warm place that had been reserved for him, finding her smooth and oiled, tenderly he stroked her, his fingers moving in to gently stretch but Allegra did not want that.

'You,' she said. 'I want you.' And so badly he wanted her, too, that in answer his legs nudged her thighs apart.

'I won't hurt you,' he said. 'I'll be slow.'

'No,' she said. 'Don't hold back.' He was holding her, his face in her hair, her hands on his back, and she didn't want slow and tender; she wanted the passion and pain that came with love. 'We only get this moment once.'

And this moment was theirs and they shared it. He pressed into her and she accepted; he pierced her and he made her a lover and he captured her heart. It hurt and it was delicious, a unique hurt that he made that bonded her to him. And as she grew accustomed to the feel of him inside her, as she shivered with each measured stroke, she felt him try not to hasten, but her body accepted him now, moved with him now and willed him on to abandon.

'Am I hurting you?'

'No.' She wanted every piece of him, wanted him rough and desperate for she was desperate with new sensations and so too was Alex. An emotional virgin; he lost it, too, that afternoon, because he went to a place where he had never been. He shared his heart and told her he loved her as he came; she wanted to stay in bed with him forever, did not want to dress, wanted to stay behind closed doors.

The phone shrilled by the bed—duty calling loudly, for no servant would dare enter on their wedding day.

'Leave it,' Alex said.

'We'll be late for our own wedding party.'

They would be, by the time they had bathed and hair and make-up was redone, Allegra was back in her wedding gown, Alex in his uniform. They were running a full thirty minutes behind schedule!

'Your father will be having a fit.'

'No.' Alex frowned into his phone as he took a message from Matteo. 'It would seem that my parents are running late too.'

And then he told her.

'I read your book.' He smiled and she blushed. 'I gave it to my father to read too.'

'Alex!'

'I admire your father.'

'Thank you,' Allegra said, because it meant an awful lot to hear, and then she laughed. 'Well, it's lovely of you to say that, but I hope you don't admire him for certain things. I want a very different husband....'

'You've got one,' Alex said, and she didn't just believe him, she knew in her heart it was true. 'But I have learnt from him and I hope my father does too. I will be a better father for reading your words, a better husband and a better prince.' He took her arm and asked if she was ready.

'Are you!' Allegra asked. 'The last party...' She still blushed at the memory, as lovely as they were, her family truly could be shocking.

'I'm looking forward to this one,' Alex admitted; in fact, they both were.

It wasn't out with the old; it was a welcome into the new.

He kissed his new bride and he told her.

'I'm looking forward to life with you.'

EPILOGUE

'ONE more!' The photographer was annoyingly insistent, and as she stood for *one more* shot before she headed into the evening party, Allegra actually wanted to see the photo in the morning, for surely she somehow looked different, surely it would be obvious to the world what had just oc-curred—that the happy couple had just fallen in love? That her body still thrummed from his touch.

But the photographer wanted his final formal shot; for tonight, there were no cameras allowed. As the royal new-lyweds entered and the doors closed behind them, there was a feeling of relief. The day had gone brilliantly, the night…well, who knew, but tonight old money and new would mingle.

'You look stunning.' Bobby beamed as she stepped in and accepted a glass of champagne. 'Oh, and I didn't get a chance to say it earlier. Zoe…' He turned to the queen. 'You look amazing. Love the hair!'

Alex said nothing, at least not till they were safely on the dance floor. In public, even on his wedding night, he was still on duty, still the cold fish her father assumed, but as they danced there were words between them, words no one else heard. The love between them was palpable.

Because as Izzy started to sing, as the senior couples started to dance, everyone saw that she laughed as Alex

said something to his bride, something that made her throw
her head back and laugh.

'He is flirting.'

'He's not.' Allegra laughed. 'He's just…Dad.'

'My poor father.' Alex groaned, watching Eduardo hold
his wife just a little tighter.

'He's never been happier.' Allegra smiled and then
rested her head on his shoulder, could hear Izzy's glorious voice filling the room. Even if she had wanted to stay
in bed, she could now happily stay in this moment forever,
dancing with her husband, her family and his together and
love filling the room.

'Soon we do speeches.' He held her a bit tighter. 'You
could give your father the book then.'

'Can you?' Allegra asked. 'As part of your speech?'

'I would be proud to.'

'After that, you throw your bouquet…' He stopped.
'That's right, you don't have one.'

'I'm sorry,' Allegra said. 'It just seemed the right thing
to do.'

'It was the right thing to do,' Alex said. 'The people
deserve to be a part of today.' He gave her a smile, that
smile, the one that would forever win her heart. 'Did you
like the flowers I had added?'

'You!' Allegra said. 'I thought it was because we'd forgotten blue.'

'Blue?' Alex frowned, because he had never heard of
that tradition. 'Always the bride carries white roses, picked
from the Santina palace—it seemed wrong. When I drive
through Santina now, as my plane comes into land, when
I see those flowers dotted everywhere, always it makes
me think of you.'

'Your common weed,' Allegra teased.

'No—I am having it renamed. It will be our national

flower, the Santina Star. I have realised that to us it is ordinary, but to the world it is extraordinary.' He kissed her
cheek; he pulled her in a little closer and she blossomed
inside, her heart unfurling that last little bit as his mouth
found her ear.

'Just as you are to me.'

* * * * *

LET'S TALK

Romance

For exclusive extracts, competitions
and special offers, find us online:

f facebook.com/millsandboon

⬜ @millsandboonuk

🐦 @millsandboon

Or get in touch on 0844 844 1351*

For all the latest titles coming soon, visit
millsandboon.co.uk/nextmonth

Want even more
ROMANCE?

Join our bookclub today!

'Mills & Boon books, the perfect way to escape for an hour or so.'

Miss W. Dyer

'Excellent service, promptly delivered and very good subscription choices.'

Miss A. Pearson

'You get fantastic special offers and the chance to get books before they hit the shops'

Mrs V. Hall